Tales from the End of Time

The Michael Moorcock Collection

The Michael Moorcock Collection is the definitive library of acclaimed author Michael Moorcock's SF & fantasy, including the entirety of his Eternal Champion work. It is prepared and edited by John Davey, the author's long-time bibliographer and editor, and will be published, over the course of two years, in the following print omnibus editions by Gollancz, and as individual eBooks by the SF Gateway (see http://www.sfgateway.com/authors/m/moorcock-michael/ for a complete list of available eBooks).

ELRIC

Elric of Melniboné and Other Stories

Elric: The Fortress of the Pearl

Elric: The Sailor on the Seas of Fate

Elric: The Sleeping Sorceress

Elric: The Revenge of the Rose

Elric: Stormbringer!

Elric: The Moonbeam Roads
comprising –
Daughter of Dreams
Destiny's Brother
Son of the Wolf

CORUM

Corum: The Prince in the Scarlet Robe
comprising –
The Knight of the Swords
The Queen of the Swords
The King of the Swords

Corum: The Prince with the Silver Hand
comprising –
The Bull and the Spear
The Oak and the Ram
The Sword and the Stallion

HAWKMOON

Hawkmoon: The History of the Runestaff
comprising –
The Jewel in the Skull
The Mad God's Amulet
The Sword of the Dawn
The Runestaff

Hawkmoon: Count Brass
comprising –
Count Brass
The Champion of Garathorm
The Quest for Tanelorn

JERRY CORNELIUS

The Cornelius Quartet
comprising –
The Final Programme
A Cure for Cancer
The English Assassin
The Condition of Muzak

Jerry Cornelius: His Lives and His Times (short-fiction collection)

A Cornelius Calendar
comprising –
The Adventures of Una Persson and Catherine Cornelius in the Twentieth Century
The Entropy Tango
The Great Rock 'n' Roll Swindle
The Alchemist's Question
Firing the Cathedral/Modem Times 2.0

Von Bek
comprising –
The War Hound and the World's Pain
The City in the Autumn Stars

The Eternal Champion
comprising –
The Eternal Champion
Phoenix in Obsidian
The Dragon in the Sword

The Dancers at the End of Time
comprising –
An Alien Heat
The Hollow Lands
The End of all Songs

Kane of Old Mars
comprising –
Warriors of Mars
Blades of Mars
Barbarians of Mars

Moorcock's Multiverse
comprising –
The Sundered Worlds
The Winds of Limbo
The Shores of Death

The Nomad of Time
comprising –
The Warlord of the Air
The Land Leviathan
The Steel Tsar

Travelling to Utopia
comprising –
The Wrecks of Time
The Ice Schooner
The Black Corridor

The War Amongst the Angels
comprising –
Blood: A Southern Fantasy
Fabulous Harbours
The War Amongst the Angels

Tales from the End of Time
comprising –
Legends from the End of Time
Constant Fire
Elric at the End of Time

Behold the Man

Gloriana; or, The Unfulfill'd Queen

SHORT FICTION

My Experiences in the Third World War and Other Stories: The Best Short Fiction of Michael Moorcock Volume 1

The Brothel in Rosenstrasse and Other Stories: The Best Short Fiction of Michael Moorcock Volume 2

Breakfast in the Ruins and Other Stories: The Best Short Fiction of Michael Moorcock Volume 3

Being further experiences of the Iron Orchid, the Duke of Queens, Lord Jagged of Canaria, the Everlasting Concubine, My Lady Charlotina, Bishop Castle and other residents at the End of Time.

With illustrations by

JILL RICHES,
JAMES CAWTHORN,
MAL DEAN AND
MICHAEL MOORCOCK

Tales from the End of Time

MICHAEL MOORCOCK

Edited by John Davey

This edition published in Great Britain in 2014 by
Gollancz
An imprint of the Orion Publishing Group
Orion House, 5 Upper St Martin's Lane,
London WC2H 9EA

An Hachette UK Company

7 9 10 8 6

A CIP catalogue record for this book is available from the British Library

ISBN 978 0 575 09261 7

Printed and bound in Great Britain by Clays Ltd, Elcograf S.p.A.

The Orion Publishing Group's policy is to use papers that are natural, renewable and recyclable products and made from wood grown in sustainable forests. The logging and manufacturing processes are expected to conform to the environmental regulations of the country of origin.

www.multiverse.org
www.sfgateway.com
www.gollancz.co.uk
www.orionbooks.co.uk

Introduction to *The Michael Moorcock Collection*

John Clute

HE IS NOW over 70, enough time for most careers to start and end in, enough time to fit in an occasional half-decade or so of silence to mark off the big years. Silence happens. I don't think I know an author who doesn't fear silence like the plague; most of us, if we live long enough, can remember a bad blank year or so, or more. Not Michael Moorcock. Except for some worrying surgery on his toes in recent years, he seems not to have taken time off to breathe the air of peace and panic. There has been no time to spare. The nearly 60 years of his active career seems to have been too short to fit everything in: the teenage comics; the editing jobs; the pulp fiction; the reinvented heroic fantasies; the Eternal Champion; the deep Jerry Cornelius riffs; NEW WORLDS; the 1970s/1980s flow of stories and novels, dozens upon dozens of them in every category of modern fantastika; the tales of the dying Earth and the possessing of Jesus; the exercises in postmodernism that turned the world inside out before most of us had begun to guess we were living on the wrong side of things; the invention (more or less) of steampunk; the alternate histories; the *Mitteleuropean* tales of sexual terror; the deep-city London riffs: the turns and changes and returns and reconfigurations to which he has subjected his oeuvre over the years (he expects this new Collected Edition will fix these transformations in place for good); the late tales where he has been remodelling the intersecting worlds he created in the 1960s in terms of twenty-first-century physics: for starters. If you can't take the heat, I guess, stay out of the multiverse.

His life has been full and complicated, a life he has exposed and hidden (like many other prolific authors) throughout his work. In

Mother London (1988), though, a non-fantastic novel published at what is now something like the midpoint of his career, it may be possible to find the key to all the other selves who made the 100 books. There are three protagonists in the tale, which is set from about 1940 to about 1988 in the suburbs and inner runnels of the vast metropolis of Charles Dickens and Robert Louis Stevenson. The oldest of these protagonists is Joseph Kiss, a flamboyant self-advertising fin-de-siècle figure of substantial girth and a fantasticating relationship to the world: he is Michael Moorcock, seen with genial bite as a kind of G.K. Chesterton without the wearying punch-line paradoxes. The youngest of the three is David Mummery, a haunted introspective half-insane denizen of a secret London of trials and runes and codes and magic: he too is Michael Moorcock, seen through a glass, darkly. And there is Mary Gasalee, a kind of holy-innocent and survivor, blessed with a luminous clarity of insight, so that in all her apparent ignorance of the onrushing secular world she is more deeply wise than other folk: she is also Michael Moorcock, Moorcock when young as viewed from the wry middle years of 1988. When we read the book, we are reading a book of instructions for the assembly of a London writer. The Moorcock we put together from this choice of portraits is amused and bemused at the vision of himself; he is a phenomenon of flamboyance and introspection, a poseur and a solitary, a dreamer and a doer, a multitude and a singleton. But only the three Moorcocks in this book, working together, could have written all the other books.

It all began – as it does for David Mummery in *Mother London* – in South London, in a subtopian stretch of villas called Mitcham, in 1939. In early childhood, he experienced the Blitz, and never forgot the extraordinariness of being a participant – however minute – in the great drama; all around him, as though the world were being dismantled nightly, darkness and blackout would descend, bombs fall, buildings and streets disappear; and in the morning, as though a new universe had taken over from the old one and the world had become portals, the sun would rise on glinting rubble, abandoned tricycles, men and women going about their daily tasks as though nothing had happened, strange shards of ruin poking into altered air. From a very early age, Michael Moorcock's security reposed in a sense that everything might change, in the blinking of an eye, and be *rejourneyed* the next day (or the next book). Though as a writer he has certainly elucidated the fears and alarums of life in Aftermath Britain, it does seem that his very early years were marked by the epiphanies of war, rather than the inflictions of despair and beclouding amnesia most adults necessarily experienced. After the war ended, his parents separated, and the young Moorcock began to attend a pretty wide variety of schools, several of which he seems to have been expelled from, and as soon as he could legally do so he began to work full time, up north in London's heart, which he only left when he moved to Texas (with intervals in Paris) in the early 1990s, from where (to jump briefly up the decades) he continues to cast a Martian eye: as with most exiles, Moorcock's intensest anatomies of his homeland date from after his cunning departure.

But back again to the beginning (just as though we were rimming a multiverse). Starting in the 1950s there was the comics and pulp work for Fleetway Publications; there was the first book (*Caribbean Crisis*, 1962) as by Desmond Reid, co-written with his early friend the artist James Cawthorn (1929–2008); there was marriage, with the writer Hilary Bailey (they divorced in 1978), three children, a heated existence in the Ladbroke Grove / Notting Hill Gate region of London he was later to populate with Jerry Cornelius and his vast family; there was the editing of NEW WORLDS, which began in 1964 and became the heartbeat of the British New Wave two years later as writers like Brian W. Aldiss and J.G. Ballard, reaching their early prime, made it into a tympanum, as young American writers like Thomas M. Disch, John T. Sladek, Norman Spinrad and Pamela Zoline found a home in London for material they could not publish in America, and new British writers like M. John Harrison and Charles Platt began their careers in its pages; but before that there was Elric. With *The Stealer of Souls* (1963) and *Stormbringer* (1965), the multiverse began to flicker into view, and the Eternal Champion (whom Elric parodied and embodied) began properly to ransack the worlds in his fight against a greater Chaos than the great dance could sustain. There was also the first SF novel, *The Sundered Worlds* (1965), but in the 1960s SF was a difficult nut to demolish for Moorcock: he would bide his time.

We come to the heart of the matter. Jerry Cornelius, who first appears in *The Final Programme* (1968) – which assembles and co-ordinates material first published a few years earlier in NEW WORLDS – is a deliberate solarisation of the albino Elric, who was himself a mocking solarisation of Robert E. Howard's Conan, or rather of the mighty-thew-headed Conan created for profit by Howard epigones: Moorcock rarely mocks the true quill. Cornelius, who reaches his first and most telling apotheosis in the four novels comprising *The Cornelius Quartet*, remains his most distinctive and perhaps most original single creation: a wide boy, an agent, a *flaneur*, a bad musician, a shopper, a shapechanger, a trans, a spy in the house of London: a toxic palimpsest on whom and through whom the *zeitgeist* inscribes surreal conjugations of 'message'. Jerry Cornelius gives head to Elric.

The life continued apace. By 1970, with NEW WORLDS on its last legs, multiverse fantasies and experimental novels poured forth; Moorcock and Hilary Bailey began to live separately, though he moved, in fact, only around the corner, where he set up house with Jill Riches, who would become his second wife; there was a second home in Yorkshire, but London remained his central base. *The Condition of Muzak* (1977), which is the fourth Cornelius novel, and *Gloriana; or, The Unfulfill'd Queen* (1978), which transfigures the first Elizabeth into a kinked Astraea, marked perhaps the high point of his career as a writer of fiction whose font lay in genre or its mutations – marked perhaps the furthest bournes he could transgress while remaining within the perimeters of fantasy (though *within* those bournes vast stretches of territory remained and would, continually, be explored). During these years he sometimes wore a leather jacket constructed out of numerous patches of vari-coloured material, and it sometimes seemed perfectly fitting that he bore the semblance, as his jacket flickered and fuzzed from across a room or road, of an illustrated man, a map, a thing of shreds and patches, a student fleshed from dreams. Like the stories he told, he seemed to be more than one thing. To use a term frequently applied (by me at least) to twenty-first-century fiction, he seemed equipoisal: which is to say that, through all his genre-hopping and genre-mixing and genre-transcending and genre-loyal returnings to old pitches, *he was never still*, because 'equipoise' is all about *making stories move*. As with his stories, he cannot be pinned down, because he is not in one place. In person and in his work, it has always been sink or swim: like a shark, or a dancer, or an equilibrist...

The marriage with Jill Riches came to an end. He married Linda Steele in 1983; they remain married. The Colonel Pyat books, *Byzantium Endures* (1981), *The Laughter of Carthage* (1984), *Jerusalem Commands* (1992) and *The Vengeance of Rome* (2006), dominated these years, along with *Mother London*. As these books, which are non-fantastic, are not included in the current *Michael Moorcock Collection*, it might be worth noting here that, in their insistence on the irreducible difficulty of gaining anything like true sight, they represent Moorcock's mature modernist take on what one might call the rag-and-bone shop of the world itself; and that the huge ornate postmodern edifice of his multiverse *loosens* us from that world, gives us room to breathe, to juggle our strategies for living – allows us ultimately to escape from prison (to use a phrase from a writer he does not respect, J.R.R. Tolkien, for whom the twentieth century was a prison train bound for hell). What Moorcock may best be remembered for in the end is the (perhaps unique) interplay between modernism and postmodernism in his work. (But a plethora of discordant understandings makes these terms hard to use; so enough of them.) In the end, one might just say that Moorcock's work as a whole represents an extraordinarily multifarious execution of the fantasist's main task: which is to *get us out of here*.

Recent decades saw a continuation of the multifarious, but with a more intensely applied methodology. The late volumes of the long Elric saga, and the Second Ether sequence of meta-fantasies – *Blood: A Southern Fantasy* (1995), *Fabulous Harbours* (1995) and *The War Amongst the Angels: An Autobiographical Story* (1996) – brood on the real world and the multiverse through the lens of Chaos Theory: the closer you get to the world, the less you describe it. *The Metatemporal Detective* (2007) – a narrative in the Steampunk mode Moorcock had previewed as long ago as *The Warlord of the Air* (1971) and *The Land Leviathan* (1974) – continues the process, sometimes dizzyingly: as though the reader inhabited the eye of a camera increasing its focus on a closely observed reality while its bogey simultaneously wheels it backwards from the desired rapport: an old Kurasawa trick here amplified into a tool of conspectus, fantasy eyed and (once again) rejourneyed, this time through the lens of SF.

We reach the second decade of the twenty-first century, time still to make things new, but also time to sort. There are dozens of titles in *The Michael Moorcock Collection* that have not been listed in this short space, much less trawled for tidbits. The various avatars of the Eternal Champion – Elric, Kane of Old Mars, Hawkmoon, Count Brass, Corum, Von Bek – differ vastly from one another. Hawkmoon is a bit of a berk; Corum is a steely solitary at the End of Time: the joys and doleurs of the interplays amongst them can only be experienced through immersion. And the Dancers at the End of Time books, and the Nomad of the Time Stream books, and the Karl Glogauer books, and all the others. They are here now, a 100 books that make up one book. They have been fixed for reading. It is time to enter the multiverse and see the world.

September 2012

Introduction to *The Michael Moorcock Collection*

Michael Moorcock

By 1964, after I had been editing NEW WORLDS for some months and had published several science fiction and fantasy novels, including *Stormbringer*, I realised that my run as a writer was over. About the only new ideas I'd come up with were miniature computers, the multiverse and black holes, all very crudely realised, in *The Sundered Worlds*. No doubt I would have to return to journalism, writing features and editing. 'My career,' I told my friend J.G. Ballard, 'is finished.' He sympathised and told me he only had a few SF stories left in him, then he, too, wasn't sure what he'd do.

In January 1965, living in Colville Terrace, Notting Hill, then an infamous slum, best known for its race riots, I sat down at the typewriter in our kitchen-cum-bathroom and began a locally based book, designed to be accompanied by music and graphics. *The Final Programme* featured a character based on a young man I'd seen around the area and whom I named after a local greengrocer, Jerry Cornelius, 'Messiah to the Age of Science'. Jerry was as much a technique as a character. Not the 'spy' some critics described him as but an urban adventurer as interested in his psychic environment as the contemporary physical world. My influences were English and French absurdists, American noir novels. My inspiration was William Burroughs with whom I'd recently begun a correspondence. I also borrowed a few SF ideas, though I was adamant that I was not writing in any established genre. I felt I had at last found my own authentic voice.

I had already written a short novel, *The Golden Barge*, set in a nowhere, no-time world very much influenced by Peake and the surrealists, which I had not attempted to publish. An earlier autobiographical novel, *The Hungry Dreamers*, set in Soho, was eaten by rats in a Ladbroke Grove basement. I remained unsatisfied with my style and my technique. *The Final Programme* took nine days to complete (by 20 January, 1965) with my baby daughters sometimes cradled with their bottles while I typed on. This, I should say, is my memory of events; my then wife scoffed at this story when I recounted it. Whatever the truth, the fact is I only believed I might be a serious writer after I had finished that novel, with all its flaws. But Jerry Cornelius, probably my most successful sustained attempt at unconventional fiction, was born then and ever since has remained a useful means of telling complex stories. Associated with the 60s and 70s, he has been equally at home in all the following decades. Through novels and novellas I developed a means of carrying several narratives and viewpoints on what appeared to be a very light (but tight) structure which dispensed with some of the earlier methods of fiction. In the sense that it took for granted the understanding that the novel is among other things an internal dialogue and I did not feel the need to repeat by now commonly understood modernist conventions, this fiction was post-modern.

Not all my fiction looked for new forms for the new century. Like many 'revolutionaries' I looked back as well as forward. As George Meredith looked to the eighteenth century for inspiration for his experiments with narrative, I looked to Meredith, popular Edwardian realists like Pett Ridge and Zangwill and the writers of the *fin de siècle* for methods and inspiration. An almost obsessive interest in the Fabians, several of whom believed in the possibility of benign imperialism, ultimately led to my Bastable books which examined our enduring British notion that an empire could be essentially a force for good. The first was *The Warlord of the Air*.

I also wrote my *Dancers at the End of Time* stories and novels under the influence of Edwardian humourists and absurdists like Jerome or Firbank. Together with more conventional generic books like *The Ice Schooner* or *The Black Corridor*, most of that work was done in the 1960s and 70s when I wrote the Eternal Champion supernatural adventure novels which helped support my own and others' experiments via NEW WORLDS, allowing me also to keep a family while writing books in which action and fantastic invention were paramount. Though I did them quickly, I didn't write them cynically. I have always believed, somewhat puritanically, in giving the audience good value for money. I enjoyed writing them, tried to avoid repetition, and through each new one was able to develop a few more ideas. They also continued to teach me how to express myself through image and metaphor. My Everyman became the Eternal Champion, his dreams and ambitions represented by the multiverse. He could be an ordinary person struggling with familiar problems in a contemporary setting or he could be a swordsman fighting monsters on a far-away world.

Long before I wrote *Gloriana* (in four parts reflecting the seasons) I had learned to think in images and symbols through reading John Bunyan's *Pilgrim's Progress*, Milton and others, understanding early on that the visual could be the most important part of a book and was often in itself a story as, for instance, a famous personality could also, through everything associated with their name, function as narrative. I wanted to find ways of carrying as many stories as possible in one. From the cinema I also learned how to use images as connecting themes. Images, colours, music, and even popular magazine headlines can all add coherence to an apparently random story, underpinning it and giving the reader a sense of internal logic and a satisfactory resolution, dispensing with certain familiar literary conventions.

When the story required it, I also began writing neo-realist fiction exploring the interface of character and environment, especially the city, especially London. In some books I condensed, manipulated and randomised time to achieve what I wanted, but in others the sense of 'real time' as we all generally perceive it was more suitable and could best be achieved by traditional nineteenth-century means. For the Pyat books I first looked back to the great German classic, Grimmelshausen's *Simplicissimus* and other early picaresques. I then examined the roots of a certain kind of moral fiction from Defoe through Thackeray and Meredith then to modern times where the picaresque (or rogue tale) can take the form of a road movie, for instance. While it's probably fair to say that Pyat and *Byzantium Endures* precipitated the end of my second marriage (echoed to a degree in *The Brothel in Rosenstrasse*), the late 70s and the 80s were exhilarating times for me, with *Mother London* being perhaps my own favourite novel of that period. I wanted to write something celebratory.

By the 90s I was again attempting to unite several kinds of fiction in one novel with my Second Ether trilogy. With Mandelbrot, Chaos Theory and String Theory I felt, as I said at the time, as if I were being offered a chart of my own brain. That chart made it easier for me to develop the notion of the multiverse as representing both the internal and the external, as a metaphor and as a means of structuring and rationalising an outrageously inventive and quasi-realistic narrative. The worlds of the multiverse move up and down scales or 'planes' explained in terms of mass, allowing entire universes to exist in the 'same' space. The result of developing this idea was the *War Amongst the Angels* sequence which added absurdist elements also functioning as a kind of mythology and folklore for a world beginning to understand itself in terms of new metaphysics and theoretical physics. As the cosmos becomes denser and almost infinite before our eyes, with black holes and dark matter affecting our own reality, we can explore them and observe them as our ancestors explored our planet and observed the heavens.

At the end of the 90s I'd returned to realism, sometimes with a dash of fantasy, with *King of the City* and the stories collected in *London Bone*. I also wrote a new Elric / Eternal Champion sequence, beginning with *Daughter of Dreams*, which brought the fantasy worlds of Hawkmoon, Bastable and Co. in line with my realistic and autobiographical stories, another attempt to unify all my fiction, and also offer a way in which disparate genres could be reunited, through notions developed from the multiverse and the Eternal Champion, as one giant novel. At the time I was finishing the Pyat sequence which attempted to look at the roots of the Nazi Holocaust in our European, Middle Eastern and American cultures and to ground my strange survival guilt while at the same time examining my own cultural roots in the light of an enduring anti-Semitism.

By the 2000s I was exploring various conventional ways of storytelling in the last parts of *The Metatemporal Detective* and through other homages, comics, parodies and games. I also looked back at my earliest influences. I had reached retirement age and felt like a rest. I wrote a 'prequel' to the Elric series as a graphic novel with Walter Simonson, *The Making of a Sorcerer*, and did a little online editing with FANTASTIC METROPOLIS.

By 2010 I had written a novel featuring Doctor Who, *The Coming of the Terraphiles*, with a nod to P.G. Wodehouse (a boyhood favourite), continued to write short stories and novellas and to work on the beginning of a new sequence combining pure fantasy and straight autobiography called *The Whispering Swarm* while still writing more Cornelius stories trying to unite all the various genres and subgenres into which contemporary fiction has fallen.

Throughout my career critics have announced that I'm 'abandoning' fantasy and concentrating on literary fiction. The truth is, however, that all my life, since I became a professional writer and editor at the age of 16, I've written in whatever mode suits a story best and where necessary created a new form if an old one didn't work for me. Certain ideas are best carried on a Jerry Cornelius story, others work better as realism and others as fantasy or science fiction. Some work best as a combination. I'm sure I'll write whatever I like and will continue to experiment with all the ways there are of telling stories and carrying as many themes as possible. Whether I write about a widow coping with loneliness in her cottage or a massive, universe-size sentient spaceship searching for her children, I'll no doubt die trying to tell them all. I hope you'll find at least some of them to your taste.

One thing a reader can be sure of about these new editions is that they would not have been possible without the tremendous and indispensable help of my old friend and bibliographer John Davey. John has ensured that these Gollancz editions are definitive. I am indebted to John for many things, including his work at Moorcock's Miscellany, my website, but his work on this edition has been outstanding. As well as being an accomplished novelist in his own right John is an astonishingly good editor who has worked with Gollancz and myself to point out every error and flaw in all previous editions, some of them not corrected since their first publication, and has enabled me to correct or revise them. I couldn't have completed this project without him. Together, I think, Gollancz, John Davey and myself have produced what will be the best editions possible and I am very grateful to him, to Malcolm Edwards, Darren Nash and Marcus Gipps for all the considerable hard work they have done to make this edition what it is.

Michael Moorcock

Contents

Pale Roses

To the memory of George Meredith,
who taught me, at least,
a technique.

LEGEND THE FIRST

Short summer-time and then, my heart's desire,
  The winter and the darkness: one by one
The roses fall, the pale roses expire
  Beneath the slow decadence of the sun.

– Ernest Dowson,
Transition

Chapter One
In Which Werther Is Inconsolable

'YOU CAN STILL *amuse* people, Werther, and that's the main thing,' said Mistress Christia, lifting her skirts to reveal her surprise.

It was rare enough for Werther de Goethe to put on an entertainment (though this one was typical – it was called 'Rain') and rare, too, for the Everlasting Concubine to think in individual terms to please her lover of the day.

'Do you like it?' she asked as he peered into her thighs.

Werther's voice in reply was faintly animated. 'Yes.' His pale fingers traced the tattoos, which were primarily on the theme of Death and the Maiden, but corpses also coupled, skeletons entwined in a variety of extravagant carnal embraces – and at the centre, in bone-white, her pubic hair had been fashioned in the outline of an elegant and somehow quintessentially feminine skull. 'You alone know me, Mistress Christia.'

She had heard the phrase so often, from so many, and it always delighted her. 'Cadaverous Werther!'

He bent to kiss the skull's somewhat elongated lips.

His rain rushed through dark air, each drop a different gloomy shade of green, purple or red. And it was actually wet so that when it fell upon the small audience (the Duke of Queens, Bishop Castle, My Lady Charlotina, and one or two recently arrived, absolutely bemused, time-travellers from the remote past) it soaked their clothes and made them shiver as they stood on the shelf of glassy rock overlooking Werther's Romantic Precipice (below, a waterfall foamed through fierce, black rock).

'Nature,' exclaimed Werther. 'The only verity!'

The Duke of Queens sneezed. He looked about him with a

delighted smile, but nobody else had noticed. He coughed to draw their attention, tried to sneeze again, but failed. He looked up into the ghastly sky; fresh waves of black cloud boiled in: there was lightning now, and thunder. The rain became hail. My Lady Charlotina, in a globular dress of pink veined in soft blue, giggled as the little stones fell upon her gilded features with an almost inaudible ringing sound.

But Bishop Castle, in his nodding, crenellated *tête* (from which he derived the latter half of his name and which was twice his own height), turned away, saturnine and bored, plainly noting a comparison between all this and his own entertainment of the previous year, which had also involved rain, but with each drop turning into a perfect manikin as it touched the ground. There was nothing in his temperament to respond to Werther's rather innocent re-creation of a Nature long since departed from a planet which could be wholly remodelled at the whim of any one of its inhabitants.

Mistress Christia, ever quick to notice such responses, eager for her present lover not to lose prestige, cried: 'But there is more, is there not, Werther? A finale?'

'I had thought to leave it a little longer…'

'No! No! Give us your finale now, my dear!'

'Well, Mistress Christia, if it is for you.' He turned one of his power rings, disseminating the sky, the lightning, the thunder, replacing them with pearly clouds, radiated with golden light through which silvery rain still fell.

'And now,' he murmured, 'I give you Tranquillity, and in Tranquillity – Hope…'

A further twist of the ring and a rainbow appeared, bridging the chasm, touching the clouds.

Bishop Castle was impressed by what was an example of elegance rather than spectacle, but he could not resist a minor criticism. 'Is black exactly the shade, do you think? I should have supposed it expressed your Idea, well, perhaps not perfectly…'

'It is perfect for me,' answered Werther a little gracelessly.

'Of course,' said Bishop Castle, regretting his impulse. He drew

his bushy red brows together and made a great show of studying the rainbow. 'It stands out so well against the background.'

Emphatically (causing a brief, ironic glint in the eye of the Duke of Queens) Mistress Christia clapped her hands. 'It is a beautiful rainbow, Werther. I am sure it is much more as they used to look.'

'It takes a particularly original kind of imagination to invent such – simplicity.' The Duke of Queens, well known for a penchant in the direction of vulgarity, fell in with her mood.

'I hope it does more than merely represent.' Satisfied both with his creation and with their responses, Werther could not resist indulging his nature, allowing a tinge of hurt resentment in his tone.

All were tolerant. All responded, even Bishop Castle. There came a chorus of consolation. Mistress Christia reached out and took his thin, white hand, inadvertently touching a power ring.

The rainbow began to topple. It leaned in the sky for a few seconds while Werther watched, his disbelief gradually turning to miserable reconciliation; then, slowly, it fell, shattering against the top of the cliff, showering them with shards of jet.

Mistress Christia's tiny hand fled to the rosebud of her mouth; her round, blue eyes expressed horror already becoming laughter (checked when she noted the look in Werther's dark and tragic orbs). She still gripped his hand; but he slowly withdrew it, kicking moodily at the fragments of the rainbow. The sky was suddenly a clear, soft grey, actually lit, one might have guessed, by the tired rays of the fading star about which the planet continued to circle, and the only clouds were those on Werther's noble brow. He pulled at the peak of his bottle-green cap, he stroked at his long, auburn hair, as if to comfort himself. He sulked.

'Perfect!' praised My Lady Charlotina, refusing to see error.

'You have the knack of making the most of a single symbol, Werther.' The Duke of Queens waved a brocaded arm in the general direction of the now disseminated scene. 'I envy you your talent, my friend.'

'It takes the product of panting lust, of pulsing sperm and eager ovaries, to offer us such brutal originality!' said Bishop Castle, in reference to Werther's birth (he was the product of sexual union, born of a womb, knowing childhood – a rarity, indeed). 'Bravo!'

'Ah,' sighed Werther, 'how cheerfully you refer to my doom: to be such a creature, when all others came into this world as mature, uncomplicated adults!'

'There was also Jherek Carnelian,' said My Lady Charlotina. Her globular dress bounced as she turned to leave.

'At least he was not born malformed,' said Werther.

'It was the work of a moment to re-form you properly, Werther,' the Duke of Queens reminded him. 'The six arms (was it?) removed, two perfectly fine ones replacing them. After all, it was an unusual exercise on the part of your mother. She did very well, considering it was her first attempt.'

'And her last,' said My Lady Charlotina, managing to have her back to Werther by the time the grin escaped. She snapped her fingers for her air car. It floated towards her, a great, yellow rocking horse. Its shadow fell across them all.

'It left a scar,' said Werther, 'nonetheless.'

'It would,' said Mistress Christia, kissing him upon his black velvet shoulder.

'A terrible scar.'

'Indeed!' said the Duke of Queens in vague affirmation, his attention wandering. 'Well, thank you for a lovely afternoon, Werther. Come along, you two!' He signed to the time-travellers, who claimed to be from the 83rd millennium and were dressed in primitive transparent 'exoskin', which was not altogether stable and was inclined to writhe and make it seem that they were covered in hundreds of thin, excited worms. The Duke of Queens had acquired them for his menagerie. Unaware of the difficulties of returning to their own time (temporal travel had, apparently, only just been re-invented in their age), they were inclined to treat the Duke as an eccentric who could be tolerated until it suited them to do otherwise. They smiled condescendingly, winked at each other, and followed him to an air car in the shape of a cube whose sides were golden mirrors decorated with white and purple flowers. It was for the pleasure of enjoying the pleasure they enjoyed, seemingly at his expense, that the Duke of Queens had brought them with him today. Mistress Christia waved at his car as it disappeared rapidly into the sky.

At last they were all gone, save herself and Werther de Goethe. He had seated himself upon a mossy rock, his shoulders hunched, his features downcast, unable to speak to her when she tried to cheer him.

'Oh, Werther,' she cried at last, 'what would make you happy?'

'Happy?' his voice was a hollow echo of her own. 'Happy?' An awkward, dismissive gesture. 'There is no such thing as happiness for such as I!'

'There must be some sort of equivalent, surely?'

'Death, Mistress Christia, is my only consolation!'

'Well, die, my dear! I'll resurrect you in a day or two, and then...'

'Though you love me, Mistress Christia – though you know me best – you do not understand. I seek the inevitable, the irreconcilable, the unalterable, the inescapable! Our ancestors knew it. They knew Death *without* Resurrection; they knew what it was to be Slave to the Elements. Incapable of choosing their own destinies, they had no responsibility for their own actions. They were tossed by tides. They were scattered by storms. They were wiped out by wars, decimated by disease, ravaged by radiation, made homeless by holocausts, lashed by lightnings...'

'You could have lashed yourself a little today, surely?'

'But it would have been *my* decision. We have lost what is Random, we have banished the Arbitrary, Mistress Christia. With our power rings and our gene banks we can, if we desire, change the courses of the planets, populate them with any kind of creature we wish, make our old sun burst with fresh energy or fade completely from the firmament. We control All. Nothing controls us!'

'There are our whims, our fancies. There are our *characters*, my moody love.'

'Even those can be altered at will.'

'Except that it is a rare nature which would wish to change itself. Would you change yours? I, for one, would be disconsolate if, say, you decided to be more like the Duke of Queens or the Iron Orchid.'

'Nonetheless, it is *possible*. It would merely be a matter of decision. Nothing is impossible, Mistress Christia. Now do you realise why I should feel unfulfilled?'

'Not really, dear Werther. You can be anything you wish, after all. I am not, as you know, intelligent – it is not my choice to be – but I wonder if a love of Nature could be, in essence, a grandiose love of oneself – with Nature identified, as it were, with one's ego?' She offered this without criticism.

For a moment he showed surprise and seemed to be considering her observation. 'I suppose it could be. Still, that has little to do with what we were discussing. It's true that I can be anything – or, indeed, anyone – I wish. That is *why* I feel unfulfilled!'

'Aha,' she said.

'Oh, how I pine for the pain of the past! Life has no meaning without misery!'

'A common view, then, I gather. But what sort of suffering would suit you best, dear Werther? Enslavement by Esquimaux?' She hesitated, her knowledge of the past being patchier than most people's. 'The beatings with thorns? The barbed-wire trews? The pits of fire?'

'No, no – that is primitive. Psychic, it would have to be. Involving – um – morality.'

'Isn't that some sort of wall-painting?'

A large tear welled and fell. 'The world is too tolerant. The world is too kind. They all – you most of all – *approve* of me! There is nothing I can do which would not amuse you – even if it offended your taste – because there is no danger, nothing at stake. There are no *crimes*, inflamer of my lust. Oh, if I could only *sin*!'

Her perfect forehead wrinkled in the prettiest of frowns. She repeated his words to herself. Then she shrugged, embracing him.

'Tell me what sin is,' she said.

Chapter Two

In Which Your Auditor Interposes

OUR TIME-TRAVELLERS, ONCE they have visited the future, are only permitted (owing to the properties of time itself) at best brief returns to their present. They can remain for any amount of time in their future, where presumably they can do no real damage to the course of previous events, but to come back at all is difficult for even the most experienced; to make a prolonged stay has been proved impossible. Half an hour with a relative or a loved one, a short account to an auditor, such as myself, of life, say, in the 75th century, a glimpse at an artefact allowed to some interested scientist – these are the best the time-traveller can hope for, once he has made his decision to leap into the mysterious future.

As a consequence our knowledge of the future is sketchy, to say the least: we have no idea of how civilisations will grow up or how they will decline; we do not know why the number of planets in the Solar System seems to vary drastically between, say, half a dozen to almost a hundred; we cannot explain the popularity in a given age of certain fashions striking us as singularly bizarre or perverse. Are beliefs which we consider fallacious or superstitious based on an understanding of reality beyond our comprehension?

The stories we hear are often partial, hastily recounted, poorly observed, perhaps misunderstood by the traveller. We cannot question him closely, for he is soon whisked away from us (time insists upon a certain neatness, to protect her own nature, which is essentially of the practical, ordering sort, and should that nature ever be successfully altered, then we might, in turn, successfully alter the terms of the human condition), and it is almost inevitable that we shall never have another chance of meeting him.

Resultantly, the stories brought to us of the Earth's future assume the character of legends rather than history and tend, therefore, to capture the imagination of artists, for serious scientists need permanent, verifiable evidence with which to work, and precious little of that is permitted them (some refuse to believe in the future, save as an abstraction; some believe firmly that returning time-travellers' accounts are accounts of dreams and hallucinations and that they have not actually travelled in time at all!). It is left to the Romancers, childish fellows like myself, to make something of these tales. While I should be delighted to assure you that everything I have set down in this story is based closely on the truth, I am bound to admit that while the outline comes from an account given me by one of our greatest and most famous temporal adventuresses, Mrs Una Persson, the conversations and many of the descriptions are of my own invention, intended hopefully to add a little colour to what would otherwise be a somewhat spare, a rather dry recounting of an incident in the life of Werther de Goethe.

That Werther will exist, only a few entrenched sceptics can doubt. We have heard of him from many sources, usually quite as reliable as the admirable Mrs Persson, as we have heard of other prominent figures of that age we choose to call 'the End of Time'. If it is this age which fascinates us more than any other, it is probably because it seems to offer a clue to our race's ultimate destiny.

Moralists make much of this period and show us that on the one hand it describes the pointlessness of human existence or, on the other, the whole point. Romancers are attracted to it for less worthy reasons; they find it colourful, they find its inhabitants glamorous, attractive; their imaginations sparked by the paradoxes, the very ambiguities which exasperate our scientists, by the idea of a people possessing limitless power and using it for nothing but their own amusement, like gods at play. It is pleasure enough for the Romancer to describe a story; to colour it a little, to fill in a few details where they are missing, in the hope that by entertaining himself he entertains others.

Of course, the inhabitants at the End of Time are not the creatures of our past legends, not mere representations of our ancestors' hopes and fears, not mere metaphors, like Siegfried or Zeus or Krishna, and this could be why they fascinate us so much. Those of us who have studied this age (as best it can be studied) feel on friendly terms with the Iron Orchid, with the Duke of Queens, with Lord Jagged of Canaria and the rest, and even believe that we can guess something of their inner lives.

Werther de Goethe, suffering from the *knowledge* of his, by the standards of his own time, unusual entrance into the world, doubtless felt himself apart from his fellows, though there was no objective reason why he should feel it. In a society where eccentricity is encouraged, where it is celebrated no matter how extreme its realisation, Werther felt, we must assume, uncomfortable: wishing for peers who would demand some sort of conformity from him. He could not retreat into a repressive past age; it was well known that it was impossible to remain in the past (the phenomenon had a name at the End of Time: it was called the Morphail Effect), and he had an ordinary awareness of the futility of re-creating such an environment for himself – for *he* would have created it; the responsibility would still ultimately be his own. We can only sympathise with the irreconcilable difficulties of leading the life of a gloomy fatalist when one's fate is wholly, decisively, in one's own hands!

Like Jherek Carnelian, whose adventures I have recounted elsewhere, he was particularly liked by his fellows for his vast and often naïve enthusiasm in whatever he did. Like Jherek, it was possible for Werther to fall completely in love – with Nature, with an Idea, with Woman (or Man, for that matter).

It seemed to the Duke of Queens (from whom we have it on the excellent authority of Mrs Persson herself) that those with such a capacity must love themselves enormously and such love is enviable. The Duke, needless to say, spoke without disapproval when he made this observation: 'To shower such largesse upon the Ego! He kneels before his soul in awe – it is a moody king, in constant need of gifts which must always seem rare!' And what is Sensation, our Moralists might argue, but Seeming Rarity? Last year's gifts regilded.

It might be true that young Werther (in years no more than half a millennium) loved himself too much and that his tragedy was his inability to differentiate between the self-gratifying sensation of the moment and what we would call a lasting and deeply felt emotion. We have a fragment of poetry, written, we are assured, by Werther for Mistress Christia:

At these times, I love you most when you are sleeping;
Your dreams internal, unrealised to the world at large:
And do I hear you weeping?

Most certainly a reflection of Werther's views, scarcely a description, from all that we know of her, of Mistress Christia's essential being.

Have we any reason to doubt her own view of herself? Rather, we should doubt Werther's view of everyone, including himself. Possibly this lack of insight was what made him so thoroughly attractive in his own time – *le Grand Naïf*!

And, since we have quoted one, it is fair to quote the other, for happily we have another fragment, from the same source, of Mistress Christia's verse:

To have my body moved by other hands;
Not only those of Man,
But Woman, too!
My Liberty in pawn to those who understand:
That Love, alone, is True.

Surely this displays an irony entirely lacking in Werther's fragment. Affectation is also here, of course, but affectation of Mistress Christia's sort so often hides an equivalently sustained degree of self-knowledge. It is sometimes the case in our own age that the greater the extravagant outer show the greater has been the plunge by the showman into the depths of his private conscience: consequently, the greater the effort to hide the fact, to give the world not what one is, but what it wants. Mistress Christia chose to reflect with consummate artistry the desires of her lover of the day; to fulfil her ambition as subtly as did she, reveals a person of exceptional perspicacity.

I intrude upon the flow of my tale with these various bits of explanation and speculation only, I hope, to offer credibility for what is to follow – to give a hint at a natural reason for Mistress Christia's peculiar actions and poor Werther's extravagant response. Some time has passed since we left our lovers. For the moment they have separated. We return to Werther…

Chapter Three
In Which Werther Finds a Soul Mate

WERTHER DE GOETHE's pile stood on the pinnacle of a black and mile-high crag about which, in the permanent twilight, black vultures swooped and croaked. The rare visitor to Werther's crag could hear the vultures' voices as he approached. 'Nevermore!' and 'Beware the Ides of March!' and 'Picking a Chicken with You' were three of the least cryptic warnings they had been created to caw.

At the top of the tallest of his thin, dark towers, Werther de Goethe sat in his favourite chair of unpolished quartz, in his favourite posture of miserable introspection, wondering why Mistress Christia had decided to pay a call on My Lady Charlotina at Lake Billy the Kid.

'Why should she wish to stay here, after all?' He cast a suffering eye upon the sighing sea below. 'She is a creature of light – she seeks colour, laughter, warmth, no doubt to try to forget some secret sorrow – she needs all the things I cannot give her. Oh, I am a monster of selfishness!' He allowed himself a small sob. But neither the sob nor the preceding outburst produced the usual satisfaction; self-pity eluded him. He felt adrift, lost, like an explorer without chart or compass in an unfamiliar land. Manfully, he tried again:

'Mistress Christia! Mistress Christia! Why do you desert me? Without you I am desolate! My pulsatile nerves will sing at your touch only! And yet it must be my doom for ever to be destroyed by the very things to which I give my fullest loyalty. Ah, it is hard! It is hard!'

He felt a little better and rose from his chair of unpolished quartz, turning his power ring a fraction so that the wind blew harder through the unglazed windows of the tower and whipped at his hair, blew his cloak about, stung his pale, long face. He raised one jackbooted foot to place it on the low sill and stared through the rain and the wind at the sky like a dreadful, spreading bruise overhead, at the turbulent, howling sea below.

He pursed his lips, turning his power ring to darken the scene a little more, to bring up the wind's wail and the ocean's roar. He was turning back to his previous preoccupation when he perceived that something alien tossed upon the distant waves; an artefact not of his own design, it intruded upon his careful conception. He peered hard at the object, but it was too far away for him to identify it. Another might have shrugged it aside, but he was painstaking, even prissy, in his need for artistic perfection. Was this some vulgar addition to his scene made, perhaps, by the Duke of Queens in a misguided effort to please him?

He took his parachute (chosen as the only means by which he could leave his tower) from the wall and strapped it on, stepping through the window and tugging at the rip cord as he fell into space. Down he plummeted and the scarlet balloon soon filled with gas, the nacelle opening up beneath him, so that by the time he was hovering some feet above the sombre waves, he was lying comfortably on his chest, staring over the rim of his parachute at the trespassing image he had seen from his tower. What he saw was something resembling a great shell, a shallow boat of mother-of-pearl, floating on that dark and heaving sea.

In astonishment he now realised that the boat was occupied by a slight figure, clad in filmy white, whose face was pale and terrified. It could only be one of his friends, altering his appearance for some whimsical adventure. But which? Then he caught, through the rain, a better glimpse and he heard himself saying:

'A child? A child? Are you a child?'

She could not hear him; perhaps she could not even see him, having eyes only for the watery walls which threatened to engulf her little boat and carry her down to the land of Davy Jones. How could it be a child? He rubbed his eyes. He must be projecting his hopes – but there, that movement, that whimper! It *was* a child! Without doubt!

He watched, open-mouthed, as she was flung this way and that by the elements – *his* elements. She was powerless: actually powerless! He relished her terror; he envied her her fear. Where had she come from? Save for himself and Jherek Carnelian there had not been a child on the planet for thousands upon thousands of years.

He leaned further out, studying her smooth skin, her lovely rounded limbs. Her eyes were tight shut now as the waves crashed upon her fragile craft; her delicate fingers, unstrong, courageous, clung hard to the side; her white dress was wet, outlining her new-formed breasts; water poured from her long, auburn hair. She panted in delicious impotence.

'It *is* a child!' Werther exclaimed. 'A sweet, frightened child!'

And in his excitement he toppled from his parachute with an astonished yell, and landed with a crash, which winded him, in the sea-shell boat beside the girl. She opened her eyes as he turned his head to apologise. Plainly she had not been aware of his presence overhead. For a moment he could not speak, though his lips moved. But she screamed.

'My dear...' The words were thin and high and they faded into the wind. He struggled to raise himself on his elbows. 'I apologise...'

She screamed again. She crept as far away from him as possible. Still she clung to her flimsy boat's side as the waves played with it: a thoughtless giant with too delicate a toy; inevitably, it must shatter. He waved his hand to indicate his parachute, but it had already been borne away. His cloak was caught by the wind and wrapped itself around his arm; he struggled to free himself and became further entangled; he heard a new scream and then some demoralised whimpering.

'I will save you!' he shouted, by way of reassurance, but his voice was muffled even in his own ears. It was answered by a further pathetic shriek. As the cloak was saturated it became increasingly difficult for him to escape its folds. He lost his temper and was deeper enmeshed. He tore at the thing. He freed his head.

'I am not your enemy, tender one, but your saviour,' he said. It was obvious that she could not hear him. With an impatient gesture he flung off his cloak at last and twisted a power ring. The volume of noise was immediately reduced. Another twist and the waves became calmer. She stared at him in wonder.

'Did you do that?' she asked.

'Of course. It is my scene, you see. But how you came to enter it, I do not know!'

'You are a wizard, then?' she said.

'Not at all. I have no interest in sport.' He clapped his hands and his parachute reappeared, perhaps a trifle reluctantly as if it had enjoyed its brief independence, and drifted down until it was level with the boat. Werther lightened the sky. He could not bring himself, however, to dismiss the rain, but he let a little sun shine through it.

'There,' he said. 'The storm has passed, eh? Did you like your experience?'

'It was horrifying! I was so afraid. I thought I would drown.'

'Yes? And did you like it?'

She was puzzled, unable to answer as he helped her aboard the nacelle and ordered the parachute home.

'You *are* a wizard!' she said. She did not seem disappointed. He did not quiz her as to her meaning. For the moment, if not for always, he was prepared to let her identify him however she wished.

'You are actually a child?' he asked hesitantly. 'I do not mean to be insulting. A time-traveller, perhaps? Or from another planet?'

'Oh, no. I am an orphan. My father and mother are now dead. I was born on Earth some fourteen years ago.' She looked in faint dismay over the side of the craft as they were whisked swiftly upward. '*They* were time-travellers. We made our home in a forgotten menagerie – underground, but it was pleasant. My parents feared recapture, you see. Food still grew in the menagerie. There were books, too, and they taught me to read – and there were other records through which they were able to present me with a reasonable education. I am not illiterate. I know the world. I was taught to fear wizards.'

'Ah,' he crooned, 'the world! But you are not a part of it, just as I am not a part.'

The parachute reached the window and, at his indication, she stepped gingerly from it to the tower. The parachute folded itself and placed itself upon the wall. Werther said: 'You will want food, then? I will create whatever you wish!'

'Fairy food will not fill mortal stomachs, sir,' she told him.

'You are beautiful,' he said. 'Regard me as your mentor, as your new father. I will teach you what this world is really like. Will you oblige me, at least, by trying the food?'

'I will.' She looked about her with a mixture of curiosity and suspicion. 'You lead a spartan life.' She noticed a cabinet. 'Books? You read, then?'

'In transcription,' he admitted. 'I listen. My enthusiasm is for Ivan Turgiditi, who created the Novel of Discomfort and remained its greatest practitioner. In, I believe, the 900th (though they could be spurious, invented, I have heard)...'

'Oh, no, no! I have read Turgiditi.' She blushed. 'In the original. *Wet Socks* – four hours of discomfort, every second brought to life and in less than a thousand pages!'

'My favourite,' he told her, his expression softening still more into besotted wonderment. 'I can scarcely believe – in this age – one such as you! Innocent of device. Uncorrupted! Pure!'

She frowned. 'My parents taught me well, sir. I am not...'

'You cannot know! And dead, you say? Dead! If only I could have witnessed – but no, I am insensitive. Forgive me. I mentioned food.'

'I am not really hungry.'

'Later, then. That I should have so recently mourned such things as lacking in this world. I was blind. I did not look. Tell me everything. Whose was the menagerie?'

'It belonged to one of the lords of this planet. My mother was from a period she called the October Century, but recently recovered from a series of interplanetary wars and fresh and optimistic in its rediscoveries of ancestral technologies. She was chosen to be the first into the future. She was captured upon her arrival and imprisoned by a wizard like yourself.'

'The word means little. But continue.'

'She said that she used the word because it had meaning for her and she had no other short description. My father came from a time known as the Preliminary Structure, where humankind was rare and machines proliferated. He never mentioned the nature of the transgression he made from the social code of his day, but as a result of it he was banished to this world. He, too, was captured for the same menagerie and there he met my mother. They lived originally, of course, in separate cages, where their normal environments were re-created for them. But the owner of the menagerie became bored, I think, and abandoned interest in his collection...'

'I have often remarked that people who cannot look after their collections have no business keeping them,' said Werther. 'Please continue, my dear child.' He reached out and patted her hand.

'One day he went away and they never saw him again. It took them some time to realise that he was not returning. Slowly the more delicate creatures, whose environments required special attention, died.'

'No-one came to resurrect them?'

'No-one. Eventually my mother and father were the only ones left. They made what they could of their existence, too wary to enter the outer world in case they should be recaptured, and, to their astonishment, conceived me. They had heard that people from different historical periods could not produce children.'

'I have heard the same.'

'Well, then, I was a fluke. They were determined to give me as good an upbringing as they could and to prepare me for the dangers of your world.'

'Oh, they were right! For one so innocent, there are many dangers. I will protect you, never fear.'

'You are kind.' She hesitated. 'I was not told by my parents that such as you existed.'

'I am the only one.'

'I see. My parents died in the course of this past year, first my father, then my mother (of a broken heart, I believe). I buried my mother and at first made an attempt to live the life we had always led, but I felt the lack of company and decided to explore the world, for it seemed to me I, too, could grow old and die before I had experienced anything!'

'Grow old,' mouthed Werther rhapsodically, 'and die!'

'I set out a month or so ago and was disappointed to discover the absence of ogres, of malevolent creatures of any sort – and the wonders I witnessed, while a trifle bewildering, did not compare with those I had imagined I would find. I had fully expected to be snatched up for a menagerie by now, but nobody has shown interest, even when they have seen me.'

'Few follow the menagerie fad at present.' He nodded. 'They would not have known you for what you were. Only I could recognise you. Oh, how lucky I am. And how lucky *you* are, my dear, to have met me when you did. You see, I, too, am a child of the womb. I, too, made my own hard way through the uterine gloom to breathe the air, and find the light of this faded, this senile globe. Of all those you could have met, you have met the only one who understands you, who is likely to share your passion, to relish your education. We are soul mates, child!'

He stood up and put a tender arm about her young shoulders.

'You have a new mother, a new father now! His name is Werther!'

Chapter Four

In Which Werther Finds Sin at Last

HER NAME WAS Catherine Lily Marguerite Natasha Dolores Beatrice Machineshop-Seven Flambeau Gratitude (the last two names but one being her father's and her mother's respectively).

Werther de Goethe continued to talk to her for some hours. Indeed, he became quite carried away as he described all the exciting things they would do, how they would live lives of the purest poetry and simplicity from now on, the quiet and tranquil places they would visit, the manner in which her education would be supplemented, and he was glad to note, he thought, her wariness dissipating, her attitude warming to him.

'I will devote myself entirely to your happiness,' he informed her, and then, noticing that she was fast asleep, he smiled tenderly: 'Poor child. I am a worm of thoughtlessness. She is exhausted.'

He rose from his chair of unpolished quartz and strode to where she lay curled upon the iguana-skin rug; stooping, he placed his hands under her warm-smelling, her yielding body, and somewhat awkwardly lifted her. In her sleep she uttered a tiny moan, her cherry lips parted and her newly budded breasts rose and fell rapidly against his chest once or twice until she sank back into a deeper slumber.

He staggered, panting with the effort, to another part of the tower, and then he lowered her with a sigh to the floor. He realised that he had not prepared a proper bedroom for her.

Fingering his chin, he inspected the dank stones, the cold obsidian which had suited his mood so well for so long and now seemed singularly offensive. Then he smiled.

'She must have beauty,' he said, 'and it must be subtle. It must be calm.'

An inspiration, a movement of a power ring, and the walls were covered with thick carpets embroidered with scenes from his own old book of fairy tales. He remembered how he had listened to the book over and over again – his only consolation in the lonely days of his extreme youth.

Here, Man Shelley, a famous harmonican, ventured into Odeon (a version of Hell) in order to be reunited with his favourite three-headed dog, Omnibus. The picture showed him with his harmonica (or 'harp') playing *Blues for a Nightingale* – a famous lost piece. There, Casablanca Bogard, with his single eye in the middle of his forehead, wielded his magic spade, Sam, in his epic fight with that ferocious bird, the Malted Falcon, to save his love, the Acrilan Queen, from the power of Big Sleepy (a dwarf who had turned himself into a giant) and Mutinous Caine, who had been cast out of Hollywood (or paradise) for the killing of his sister, the Blue Angel.

Such scenes were surely the very stuff to stir the romantic, delicate imagination of this lovely child, just as his had been stirred when – he felt the frisson – he had been her age. He glowed. His substance was suffused with delicious compassion for them both as he recalled, also, the torments of his own adolescence.

That she should be suffering as he had suffered filled him with the pleasure all must feel when a fellow spirit is recognised, and at the same time he was touched by her plight, determined that she should not know the anguish of his earliest years. Once, long ago, Werther had courted Jherek Carnelian, admiring him for his fortitude, knowing that locked in Jherek's head were the memories of bewilderment, misery and despair which would echo his own. But Jherek, pampered progeny of that most artificial of all creatures, the Iron Orchid, had been unable to recount any suitable experiences at all, had, whilst cheerfully eager to please Werther, recalled nothing but pleasurable times, had reluctantly admitted, at last, to the possession of the happiest of childhoods. That was when Werther had concluded that Jherek Carnelian had no soul worth speaking of, and he had never altered his opinion (now he secretly doubted Jherek's origins and sometimes believed that Jherek merely pretended to have been a child – merely one more of his boring and superficial affectations).

Next, a bed – a soft, downy bed, spread with sheets of silver silk, with posts of ivory and hangings of precious perspex, antique and yellowed, and on the floor the finely tanned skins of albino hamsters and marmalade cats.

Werther added gorgeous lavs of intricately patterned red and blue ceramic, their bowls filled with living flowers: with whispering toadflax, dragonsnaps, goldilocks and shanghai lilies, with blooming scarlet margravines (his adopted daughter's name-flower, as he knew to his pride), with soda-purple poppies and tea-green roses, with iodine and cerise and crimson hanging johnny, with golden cynthia and sky-blue truelips, calamine and creeping larrikin, until the room was saturated with their intoxicating scents.

Placing a few bunches of hitler's balls in the corners near the ceiling, a toy fish-tank (capable of firing real fish), which he remembered owning as a boy, under the window, a trunk (it could be opened by pressing the navel) filled with clothes near the bed, a full set of bricks and two bats against the wall close to the doorway, he was able, at last, to view the room with some satisfaction.

Obviously, he told himself, she would make certain changes according to her own tastes. That was why he had shown such restraint. He imagined her naïve delight when she wakened in the morning. And he must be sure to produce days and nights of regular duration, because at her age routine was the main thing a child needed. There was nothing like the certainty of a consistently glorious sunrise! This reminded him to make an alteration to a power ring on his left hand, to spread upon the black cushion of the sky crescent moons and stars and starlets in profusion. Bending carefully, he picked up the vibrant youth of her body and lowered her to the bed, drawing the silver sheets up to her vestal chin. Chastely he touched lips to her forehead and crept from the room, fashioning a leafy door behind him, hesitating for a moment, unable to define the mood in which he found himself. A rare smile illumined features set so long in lines of gloom. Returning to his own quarters, he murmured:

'I believe it is Contentment!'

A month swooned by. Werther lavished every moment of his time upon his new charge. He thought of nothing but her youthful satisfactions. He encouraged her in joy, in idealism, in a love of Nature. Gone were his blizzards, his rocky spires, his bleak wastes and his moody forests, to be replaced with gentle landscapes of green hills and merry, tinkling rivers, sunny glades in copses of poplars, rhododendrons, redwoods, laburnum, banyans and good old amiable oaks. When they went on a picnic, large-eyed cows and playful gorillas would come and nibble scraps of food from Catherine Gratitude's palm. And when it was day, the sun always shone and the sky was always blue, and if there were clouds, they were high, hesitant puffs of whiteness and soon gone.

He found her books so that she might read. There was Turgiditi and Uto, Pett Ridge and Zakka, Pyat Sink – all the ancients. Sometimes he asked her to read to him, for the luxury of dispensing with his usual translators. She had been fascinated by a picture of a typewriter she had seen in a record, so he fashioned an air car in the likeness of one, and they travelled the world in it, looking at scenes created by Werther's peers.

'Oh, Werther,' she said one day, 'you are so good to me. Now that I realise the misery which might have been mine (as well as the life I was missing underground), I love you more and more.'

'And I love you more and more,' he replied, his head a-swim. And for a moment he felt a pang of guilt at having forgotten Mistress Christia so easily. He had not seen her since Catherine had come to him, and he guessed that she was sulking somewhere. He prayed that she would not decide to take vengeance on him.

They went to see Jherek Carnelian's famous 'London, 1896', and Werther manfully hid his displeasure at her admiration for his rival's buildings of white marble, gold and sparkling quartz. He showed her his own abandoned tomb, which he privately considered in better taste, but it was plain that it did not give her the same satisfaction.

They saw the Duke of Queens' latest, 'Ladies and Swans', but not for long, for Werther considered it unsuitable. Later they paid a visit to Lord Jagged of Canaria's somewhat abstract 'War and Peace in Two Dimensions', and Werther thought it too stark to please the girl, judging the experiment 'successful'. But Catherine laughed with glee as she touched the living figures, and found that somehow it was true. Lord Jagged had given them length and breadth but not a scrap of width – when they turned aside, they disappeared.

*

It was on one of these expeditions, to Bishop Castle's 'A Million Angry Wrens' (an attempt in the recently revised art of Aesthetic Loudness), that they encountered Lord Mongrove, a particular confidant of Werther's until they had quarrelled over the method of suicide adopted by the natives of Uranus during the period of the Great Sodium Breather. By now, if Werther had not found a new obsession, they would have patched up their differences, and Werther felt a pang of guilt for having forgotten the one person on this planet with whom he had, after all, shared something in common.

In his familiar dark green robes, with his leonine head hunched between his massive shoulders, the giant, apparently disdaining an air carriage, was riding home upon the back of a monstrous snail.

The first thing they saw, from above, was its shining trail over the azure rocks of some abandoned, half-created scene of Argonheart Po's (who believed that nothing was worth making unless it tasted delicious and could be eaten and digested). It was Catherine who saw the snail itself first and exclaimed at the size of the man who occupied the swaying howdah on its back.

'He must be ten feet tall, Werther!'

And Werther, knowing whom she meant, made their typewriter descend, crying:

'Mongrove! My old friend!'

Mongrove, however, was sulking. He had chosen not to forget whatever insult it had been which Werther had levelled at him when they had last met. 'What? Is it Werther? Bringing freshly sharpened dirks for the flesh between my shoulder blades? It is that Cold Betrayer himself, whom I befriended when a bare boy, pretending carelessness, feigning insouciance, as if he cannot remember, with relish, the exact degree of bitterness of the poisoned wine he fed me when we parted. Faster, steed! Bear me away from Treachery! Let me fly from further Insult! No more shall I suffer at the hands of Calumny!' And, with his long, jewelled stick he beat upon the shell of his molluscoid mount. The beast's horns waved agitatedly for a moment, but it did not really seem capable of any greater speed. In good-humoured puzzlement, it turned its slimy head towards its master.

'Forgive me, Mongrove! I take back all I said,' announced Werther, unable to recall a single sour syllable of the exchange. 'Tell me why you are abroad. It is rare for you to leave your doomy dome.'

'I am making my way to the Ball,' said Lord Mongrove, 'which is shortly to be held by My Lady Charlotina. Doubtless I have been invited to act as a butt for their malice and their gossip, but I go in good faith.'

'A Ball? I know nothing of it.'

Mongrove's countenance brightened a trifle. 'You have not been invited? Ah!'

'I wonder... But, no – My Lady Charlotina shows unsuspected sensitivity. She knows that I now have responsibilities – to my little Ward here. To Catherine – to my Kate.'

'The child?'

'Yes, to my child. I am privileged to be her protector. Fate favours me as her new father. This is she. Is she not lovely? Is she not innocent?'

Lord Mongrove raised his great head and looked at the slender girl beside Werther. He shook his huge head as if in pity for her.

'Be careful, my dear,' he said. 'To be befriended by de Goethe is to be embraced by a viper!'

She did not understand Mongrove; questioningly she looked up at Werther. 'What does he mean?'

Werther was shocked. He clapped his hands to her pretty ears.

'Listen no more! I regret the overture. The movement, Lord Mongrove, shall remain unresolved. Farewell, spurner of good intent. I had never guessed before the level of your cynicism. Such an accusation! Goodbye, for ever, most malevolent of mortals, despiser of altruism, hater of love! You shall know me no longer!'

'You have known yourself not at all,' snapped Mongrove spitefully, but it was unlikely that Werther, already speeding skyward, heard the remark.

And thus it was with particular and unusual graciousness that Werther greeted My Lady Charlotina when, a little later, they came upon her.

J.CAWTHORN

She was wearing the russet ears and eyes of a fox, riding her yellow rocking horse through the patch of orange sky left over from her own turbulent 'Death of Neptune'. She waved to them. 'Cock-a-doodle-do!'

'My dear Lady Charlotina. What a pleasure it is to see you. Your beauty continues to rival Nature's mightiest miracles.'

It is with such unwonted effusion that we will greet a person, who has not hitherto aroused our feelings, when we are in a position to compare him against another, closer, acquaintance who has momentarily earned our contempt or anger.

She seemed taken aback, but received the compliment equably enough.

'Dear Werther! And is this that rarity, the girl-child I have heard so much about and whom, in your goodness, you have taken under your wing? I could not believe it! A child! And how lucky she is to find a father in yourself – of all our number the one best suited to look after her.'

It might almost be said that Werther preened himself beneath the golden shower of her benediction, and if he detected no irony in her tone, perhaps it was because he still smarted from Mongrove's dash of vitriol.

'I have been chosen, it seems,' he said modestly, 'to lead this waif through the traps and illusions of our weary world. The burden I shoulder is not light...'

'Valiant Werther!'

'... but it is shouldered willingly. I am devoting my life to her upbringing, to her peace of mind.' He placed a bloodless hand upon her auburn locks, and, winsomely, she took his other one.

'You are tranquil, my dear?' asked My Lady Charlotina kindly, arranging her blue skirts over the saddle of her rocking horse. 'You have no doubts?'

'At first I had,' admitted the sweet child, 'but gradually I learned to trust my new father. Now I would trust him in anything!'

'Ah,' sighed My Lady Charlotina, 'trust!'

'Trust,' said Werther. 'It grows in me, too. You encourage me, charming Charlotina, for a short time ago I believed myself doubted by all.'

'Is it possible? When you are evidently so reconciled – so – happy!'

'And I am happy, also, now that I have Werther,' carolled the commendable Catherine.

'Exquisite!' breathed My Lady Charlotina. 'And you will, of course, both come to my Ball.'

'I am not sure…' began Werther, 'perhaps Catherine is too young…'

But she raised her tawny hands. 'It is your duty to come. To show us all that simple hearts are the happiest.'

'Possibly…'

'You must. The world must have examples, Werther, if it is to follow your Way.'

Werther lowered his eyes shyly. 'I am honoured,' he said. 'We accept.'

'Splendid! Then come soon. Come now, if you like. A few arrangements, and the Ball begins.'

'Thank you,' said Werther, 'but I think it best if we return to my castle for a little while.' He caressed his ward's fine, long tresses. 'For it will be Catherine's first Ball, and she must choose her gown.'

And he beamed down upon his radiant protégée as she clapped her hands in joy.

My Lady Charlotina's Ball must have been at least a mile in circumference, set against the soft tones of a summer twilight, red-gold and transparent so that, as one approached, the guests who had already arrived could be seen standing upon the inner wall, clad in creations extravagant even at the End of Time.

The Ball itself was inclined to roll a little, but those inside it were undisturbed; their footing was firm, thanks to My Lady Charlotina's artistry. The Ball was entered by means of a number of sphincterish openings, placed more or less at random in its outer wall. At the very centre of the Ball, on a floating platform, sat an orchestra comprised of the choicest musicians, out of a myriad of ages and planets, from My Lady's great menagerie (she specialised, currently, in artists).

When Werther de Goethe, a green-gowned Catherine Gratitude

upon his blue velvet arm, arrived, the orchestra was playing some primitive figure of My Lady Charlotina's own composition. It was called, she claimed as she welcomed them, 'On the Theme of Childhood', but doubtless she thought to please them, for Werther believed he had heard it before under a different title.

Many of the guests had already arrived and were standing in small groups chatting to each other. Werther greeted an old friend, Li Pao, of the 27th century, and such a killjoy that he had never been wanted for a menagerie. While he was forever criticising their behaviour, he never missed a party. Next to him stood the Iron Orchid, mother of Jherek Carnelian, who was not present. In contrast to Li Pao's faded blue overalls, she wore rags of red, yellow and mauve, thousands of sparkling bracelets, anklets and necklaces, a headdress of woven peacock's wings, slippers which were moles and whose beady eyes looked up from the floor.

'What do you mean – waste?' she was saying to Li Pao. 'What else could we do with the energy of the universe? If our sun burns out, we create another. Doesn't that make us conservatives? Or is it preservatives?'

'Good evening, Werther,' said Li Pao in some relief. He bowed politely to the girl. 'Good evening, miss.'

'Miss?' said the Iron Orchid. 'What?'

'Gratitude.'

'For whom?'

'This is Catherine Gratitude, my Ward,' said Werther, and the Iron Orchid let forth a peal of luscious laughter.

'The girl-bride, eh?'

'Not at all,' said Werther. 'How is Jherek?'

'Lost, I fear, in time. We have seen nothing of him recently. He still pursues his paramour. Some say you copy him, Werther.'

He knew her bantering tone of old and took the remark in good part. 'His is a mere affectation,' he said. 'Mine is Reality.'

'You were always one to make that distinction, Werther,' she said. 'And I will never understand the difference!'

'I find your concern for Miss Gratitude's upbringing most worthy,' said Li Pao somewhat unctuously. 'If there is any way I can help. My knowledge of twenties' politics, for instance, is considered unmatched – particularly, of course, where the 26th and 27th centuries are concerned...'

'You are kind,' said Werther, unsure how to take an offer which seemed to him overeager and not entirely selfless.

Gaf the Horse in Tears, whose clothes were real flame, flickered towards them, the light from his burning, unstable face almost blinding Werther. Catherine Gratitude shrank from him as he reached out a hand to touch her, but her expression changed as she realised that he was not at all hot – rather, there was something almost chilly about the sensation on her shoulder. Werther did his best to smile. 'Good evening, Gaf.'

'She is a dream!' said Gaf. 'I know it, because only I have such a wonderful imagination. Did I create her, Werther?'

'You jest.'

'Ho, ho! Serious old Werther.' Gaf kissed him, bowed to the child, and moved away, his body erupting in all directions as he laughed the more. 'Literal, literal Werther!'

'He is a boor,' Werther told his charge. 'Ignore him.'

'I thought him sweet,' she said.

'You have much to learn, my dear.'

The music filled the Ball and some of the guests left the floor to dance, hanging in the air around the orchestra, darting streamers of coloured energy in order to weave complex patterns as they moved.

'They are very beautiful,' said Catherine Gratitude. 'May we dance soon, Werther?'

'If you wish. I am not much given to such pastimes as a rule.'

'But tonight?'

He smiled. 'I can refuse you nothing, child.'

She hugged his arm and her girlish laughter filled his heart with warmth.

'Perhaps you should have made yourself a child before, Werther?' suggested the Duke of Queens, drifting away from the dance and leaving a trail of green fire behind him. He was clad all in soft metal which reflected the colours in the Ball and created other colours in turn. 'You are a perfect father. Your métier.'

'It would not have been the same, Duke of Queens.'

'As you say.' His darkly handsome face bore its usual expression of benign amusement. 'I am the Duke of Queens, child. It is an honour.' He bowed, his metal booming.

'Your friends are wonderful,' said Catherine Gratitude. 'Not at all what I expected.'

'Be wary of them,' murmured Werther. 'They have no conscience.'

'Conscience? What is that?'

Werther touched a ring and led her up into the air of the Ball. 'I am your conscience, for the moment, Catherine. You shall learn in time.'

Lord Jagged of Canaria, his face almost hidden by one of his high, quilted collars, floated in their direction.

'Werther, my boy! This must be your daughter. Oh! Sweeter than honey! Softer than petals! I have heard so much – but the praise was not enough! You must have poetry written about you. Music composed for you. Tales must be spun with you as the heroine.' And Lord Jagged made a deep, an elaborate bow, his long sleeves sweeping the air below his feet. Next, he addressed Werther:

'Tell me, Werther, have you seen Mistress Christia? Everyone else is here, but not she.'

'I have looked for the Everlasting Concubine without success,' Werther told him.

'She should arrive soon. In a moment My Lady Charlotina announces the beginning of the masquerade – and Mistress Christia loves the masquerade.'

'I suspect she pines,' said Werther.

'Why so?'

'She loved me, you know.'

'Aha! Perhaps you are right. But I interrupt your dance. Forgive me.'

And Lord Jagged of Canaria floated, stately and beautiful, towards the floor.

'Mistress Christia?' said Catherine. 'Is she your Lost Love?'

'A wonderful woman,' said Werther. 'But my first duty is to you. Regretfully I could not pursue her, as I think she wanted me to do.'

'Have I come between you?'

'Of course not. Of course not. That was infatuation – this is sacred duty.'

And Werther showed her how to dance – how to notice a gap in a pattern which might be filled by the movements from her body. Because it was a special occasion he had given her her very own power ring – only a small one, but she was proud of it, and she gasped so prettily at the colours her train made that Werther's anxieties (that his gift might corrupt her precious innocence) melted entirely away. It was then that he realised with a shock how deeply he had fallen in love with her.

At the realisation, he made an excuse, leaving her to dance with, first, Sweet Orb Mace, feminine tonight, with a latticed face, and then with O'Kala Incarnadine who, with his usual preference for the bodies of beasts, was currently a bear. Although he felt a pang as he watched her stroke O'Kala's ruddy fur, he could not bring himself just then to interfere. His immediate desire was to leave the Ball, but to do that would be to disappoint his ward, to raise questions he would not wish to answer. After a while he began to feel a certain satisfaction from his suffering and remained, miserably, on the floor while Catherine danced on and on.

And then My Lady Charlotina had stopped the orchestra and stood on the platform calling for their attention.

'It is time for the masquerade. You all know the theme, I hope.' She paused, smiling. 'All, save Werther and Catherine. When the music begins again, please reveal your creations of the evening.'

Werther frowned, wondering her reasons for not revealing the theme of the masquerade to him. She was still smiling at him as she drifted towards him and settled beside him on the floor.

'You seem sad, Werther. Why so? I thought you at one with yourself at last. Wait. My surprise will flatter you, I'm sure!'

The music began again. The Ball was filled with laughter – and there was the theme of the masquerade!

Werther cried out in anguish. He dashed upward through the gleeful throng, seeing each face as a mockery, trying to reach the side of his girl-child before she should realise the dreadful truth.

'Catherine! Catherine!'

He flew to her. She was bewildered as he folded her in his arms.

'Oh, they are monsters of insincerity! Oh, they are grotesque in their apeing of all that is simple, all that is pure!' he cried.

He glared about him at the other guests. My Lady Charlotina had chosen 'Childhood' as her general theme. Sweet Orb Mace had changed himself into a gigantic single sperm, his own face still visible at the glistening tail; the Iron Orchid had become a monstrous newborn baby with a red and bawling face which still owed more to Paint than to Nature; the Duke of Queens, true to character, was three-year-old Siamese twins (both the faces were his own, softened); even Lord Mongrove had deigned to become an egg.

'What ith it, Werther?' lisped My Lady Charlotina at his feet, her brown curls bobbing as she waved her lollipop in the general direction of the other guests. 'Doeth it not pleathe you?'

'Ugh! This is agony! A parody of everything I hold most perfect!'

'But, Werther…'

'What is wrong, dear Werther?' begged Catherine. 'It is only a masquerade.'

'Can you not see? It is you – what you and I mean – that they mock. No – it is best that you do not see. Come, Catherine. They are insane; they revile all that is sacred!' And he bore her bodily towards the wall, rushing through the nearest doorway and out into the darkened sky.

He left his typewriter behind, so great was his haste to be gone from that terrible scene. He fled with her willy-nilly through the air, through daylight, through pitchy night. He fled until he came to his own tower, flanked now by green lawns and rolling turf, surrounded by songbirds, swamped in sunshine. And he hated it: landscape, larks and light – all were hateful.

He flew through the window and found his room full of comforts – of cushions and carpets and heady perfume – and with a gesture he removed them. Their particles hung gleaming in the sun's beams for a moment. But the sun, too, was hateful. He blacked it out and night swam into that bare chamber. And all the while, in amazement, Catherine Gratitude looked on, her lips forming the question, but never uttering it. At length, tentatively, she touched his arm.

'Werther?'

His hands flew to his head. He roared in his mindless pain.

'Oh, Werther!'

'Ah! They destroy me! They destroy my ideals!'

He was weeping when he turned to bury his face in her hair.

'Werther!' She kissed his cold cheek. She stroked his shaking back. And she led him from the ruins of his room and down the passage to her own apartment.

'Why should I strive to set up standards,' he sobbed, 'when all about me they seek to pull them down? It would be better to be a villain!'

But he was quiescent; he allowed himself to be seated upon her bed; he felt suddenly drained. He sighed. 'They hate innocence. They would see it gone for ever from this globe.'

She gripped his hand. She stroked it. 'No, Werther. They meant no harm. I saw no harm.'

'They would corrupt you. I must keep you safe.'

Her lips touched his and his body came alive again. Her fingers touched his skin. He gasped.

'I must keep you safe.'

In a dream, he took her in his arms. Her lips parted, their tongues met. Her young breasts pressed against him – and for perhaps the first time in his life Werther understood the meaning of physical joy. His blood began to dance to the rhythm of a sprightlier heart. And why should he not take what they would take in his position? He placed a hand upon a pulsing thigh. If cynicism called the tune, then he would show them he could pace as pretty a measure as any. His kisses became passionate, and passionately were they returned.

'Catherine!'

A motion of a power ring and their clothes were gone, the bed hangings drawn.

And your auditor, not being of that modern school which salaciously seeks to share the secrets of others' passions (secrets familiar, one might add, to the great majority of us), retires from this scene.

But when he woke the next morning and turned on the sun, Werther looked down at the lovely child beside him, her auburn hair spread across the pillows, her little breasts rising and falling in tranquil sleep, and he realised that he had used his reaction to the masquerade to betray his trust. A madness had filled him; he had raised an evil wind and his responsibility had been borne off by it, taking Innocence and Purity, never to return. His lust had lost him everything.

Tears reared in his tormented eyes and ran cold upon his heated cheeks. 'Mongrove was perceptive indeed,' he murmured. 'To be befriended by Werther is to be embraced by a viper. She can never trust me – anyone – again. I have lost my right to offer her protection. I have stolen her childhood.'

And he got up from the bed, from the scene of that most profound of crimes, and he ran from the room and went to sit in his old chair of unpolished quartz, staring listlessly through the window at the paradise he had created outside. It accused him; it reminded him of his high ideals. He was astonished by the consequences of his actions: he had turned his paradise to hell.

A great groan reverberated in his chest. 'Oh, now I know what sin is!' he said. 'And what terrible tribute it exacts from the one who tastes it!'

And he sank almost luxuriously into the deepest gloom he had ever known.

Chapter Five

In Which Werther Finds Redemption of Sorts

HE AVOIDED CATHERINE Gratitude all that day, even when he heard her calling his name, for if the landscape could fill him with such agony, what would he feel under the startled inquisition of her gaze? He erected himself a heavy dungeon door so that she could not get in, and, as he sat contemplating his poisoned paradise, he saw her once, walking on a hill he had made for her. She seemed unchanged, of course, but he knew in his heart how she must be shivering with the chill of lost innocence. That it should have been himself, of all men, who had introduced her so young to the tainted joys of carnal love! Another deep sigh and he buried his fists savagely in his eyes.

'Catherine! Catherine! I am a thief, an assassin, a despoiler of souls. The name of Werther de Goethe becomes a synonym for Treachery!'

It was not until the next morning that he thought himself able to admit her to his room, to submit himself to a judgement which he knew would be worse for not being spoken. Even when she did enter, his shifty eye would not focus on her for long. He looked for some outward sign of her experience, somewhat surprised that he could detect none.

He glared at the floor, knowing his words to be inadequate. 'I am sorry,' he said.

'For leaving the Ball, darling Werther! The epilogue was infinitely sweeter.'

'Don't!' He put his hands to his ears. 'I cannot undo what I have done, my child, but I can try to make amends. Evidently you must not stay here with me. You need suffer nothing further on that score. For myself, I must contemplate an eternity of loneliness. It is the least of the prices I must pay. But Mongrove would be kind to you, I am sure.' He looked at her. It seemed that she had grown older. Her bloom was fading now that it had been touched by the icy fingers of that most sinister, most insinuating of libertines, called Death. 'Oh,' he sobbed, 'how haughty was I in my pride! How I congratulated myself on my high-mindedness. Now I am proved the lowliest of all my kind!'

'I really cannot follow you, Werther dear,' she said. 'Your behaviour is rather odd today, you know. Your words mean very little to me.'

'Of course they mean little,' he said. 'You are unworldly, child. How can you anticipate… ah, ah…' and he hid his face in his hands.

'Werther, please cheer up. I have heard of *le petit mal*, but this seems to be going on for a somewhat longer time. I am still puzzled…'

'I cannot, as yet,' he said, speaking with some difficulty through his palms, 'bring myself to describe in cold words the enormity of the crime I have committed against your spirit – against your childhood. I had known that you would – eventually – wish to experience the joys of true love – but I had hoped to prepare your soul for what was to come – so that when it happened it would be beautiful.'

'But it *was* beautiful, Werther.'

He found himself experiencing a highly inappropriate impatience with her failure to understand her doom.

'It was not the right *kind* of beauty,' he explained.

'There are certain correct kinds for certain times?' she asked. 'You are sad because we have offended some social code?'

'There is no such thing in this world, Catherine – but you, child, could have known a code. Something I never had when I was your age – something I wanted for you. One day you will realise what I mean.' He leaned forward, his voice thrilling, his eye hot and hard, 'And if you do not hate me now, Catherine, oh, you will hate me then. Yes! You will hate me then.'

Her answering laughter was unaffected, unstrained. 'This is silly, Werther. I have rarely had a nicer experience.'

He turned aside, raising his hands as if to ward off blows. 'Your words are darts – each one draws blood in my conscience.' He sank back into his chair.

Still laughing, she began to stroke his limp hand. He drew it away from her. 'Ah, see! I have made you lascivious. I have introduced you to the drug called lust!'

'Well, perhaps to an aspect of it!'

Some change in her tone began to impinge on Werther, though he was still stuck deep in the glue of his guilt. He raised his head, his expression bemused, refusing to believe the import of her words.

'A wonderful aspect,' she said. And she licked his ear.

He shuddered. He frowned. He tried to frame words to ask her a certain question, but he failed.

She licked his cheek and she twined her fingers in his lacklustre hair. 'And one I should love to experience again, most passionate of anachronisms. It was as it must have been in those ancient days – when poets ranged the world, stealing what they needed, taking any fair maiden who pleased them, setting fire to the towns of their publishers, laying waste the books of their rivals: ambushing their readers. I am sure you were just as delighted, Werther. Say that you were!'

'Leave me!' he gasped. 'I can bear no more.'

'If it is what you want.'

'It is.'

With a wave of her little hand, she tripped from the room.

And Werther brooded upon her shocking words, deciding that he could only have misheard her. In her innocence she had seemed to admit an understanding of certain inconceivable things. What he had half-interpreted as a familiarity with the carnal world was doubtless merely a child's romantic conceit. How could she have had previous experience of a night such as that which they had shared?

She had been a virgin. Certainly she had been that.

He wished that he did not then feel an ignoble pang of pique at the possibility of another having also known her. Consequently this was immediately followed by a further wave of guilt for entertaining such thoughts and subsequent emotions. A score of

J·CAWTHORN·74

conflicting glooms warred in his mind, sent tremors through his body.

'Why,' he cried to the sky, 'was I born! I am unworthy of the gift of life. I accused My Lady Charlotina, Lord Jagged and the Duke of Queens of base emotions, cynical motives, yet none is baser or more cynical than mine! Would I turn my anger against my victim, blame her for my misery, attack a little child because she tempted me? That is what my diseased mind would do. Thus do I seek to excuse myself my crimes. Ah, I am vile! I am vile!'

He considered going to visit Mongrove, for he dearly wished to abase himself before his old friend, to tell Mongrove that the giant's contempt had been only too well founded; but he had lost the will to move; a terrible lassitude had fallen upon him. Hating himself, he knew that all must hate him, and while he knew that he had earned every scrap of their hatred, he could not bear to go abroad and run the risk of suffering it.

What would one of his heroes of Romance have done? How would Casablanca Bogard or Eric of Marylebone have exonerated themselves, even supposing they could have committed such an unbelievable deed in the first place?

He knew the answer.

It drummed louder and louder in his ears. It was implacable and grim. But still he hesitated to follow it. Perhaps some other, more original act of retribution would occur to him? He racked his writhing brain. Nothing presented itself as an alternative.

At length he rose from his chair of unpolished quartz. Slowly, his pace measured, he walked towards the window, stripping off his power rings so that they clattered to the flagstones.

He stepped upon the ledge and stood looking down at the rocks a mile below at the base of the tower. Some jolting of a power ring as it fell had caused a wind to spring up and to blow coldly against his naked body. *The Wind of Justice*, he thought.

He ignored his parachute. With one final cry of 'Catherine! Forgive me!' and an unvoiced hope that he would be found long after it proved impossible to resurrect him, he flung himself, unsupported, into space.

Down he fell and death leapt to meet him. The breath fled from his lungs, his head began to pound, his sight grew dim, but the spikes of black rock grew larger until he knew that he had struck them, for his body was a-flame, broken in a hundred places, and his sad, muddled, doom-clouded brain was chaff upon the wailing breeze. Its last coherent thought was: *Let none say Werther did not pay the price in full.* And thus did he end his life with a proud negative.

Chapter Six
In Which Werther Discovers Consolation

'OH, WERTHER, WHAT an adventure!'

It was Catherine Gratitude looking down on him as he opened his eyes. She clapped her hands. Her blue eyes were full of joy.

Lord Jagged stood back with a smile. 'Reborn, magnificent Werther, to sorrow afresh!' he said.

He lay upon a bench of marble in his own tower. Surrounding the bench were My Lady Charlotina, the Duke of Queens, Gaf the Horse in Tears, the Iron Orchid, Li Pao, O'Kala Incarnadine and many others. They all applauded.

'A splendid drama!' said the Duke of Queens.

'Amongst the best I have witnessed,' agreed the Iron Orchid (a fine compliment from her).

Werther found himself warming to them as they poured their praise upon him; but then he remembered Catherine Gratitude and what he had meant himself to be to her, what he had actually become, and although he felt much better for having paid his price, he stretched out his hand to her, saying again, 'Forgive me.'

'Silly Werther! Forgive such a perfect rôle? No, no! If anyone needs forgiving, then it is I.' And Catherine Gratitude touched one of the many power rings now festooning her fingers and returned herself to her original appearance.

'It is you!' He could make no other response as he looked upon the Everlasting Concubine. 'Mistress Christia?'

'Surely you suspected towards the end?' she said. 'Was it not everything you told me you wanted? Was it not a fine "sin", Werther?'

'I suffered...' he began.

'Oh, yes! *How* you suffered! It was unparalleled. It was equal, I am sure, to anything in History. And, Werther, did you not find the "guilt" particularly exquisite?'

'You did it for me?' He was overwhelmed. 'Because it was what I said I wanted most of all?'

'He is still a little dull,' explained Mistress Christia, turning to their friends. 'I believe that is often the case after a resurrection.'

'Often,' intoned Lord Jagged, darting a sympathetic glance at Werther. 'But it will pass, I hope.'

'The ending, though it could be anticipated,' said the Iron Orchid, 'was absolutely right.'

Mistress Christia put her arms around him and kissed him. 'They are saying that your performance rivals Jherek Carnelian's,' she whispered. He squeezed her hand. What a wonderful woman she was, to be sure, to have added to his experience and to have increased his prestige at the same time.

He sat up. He smiled a trifle bashfully. Again they applauded.

'I can see that this was where "Rain" was leading,' said Bishop Castle. 'It gives the whole thing point, I think.'

'The exaggerations were just enough to bring out the essential mood without being too prolonged,' said O'Kala Incarnadine, waving an elegant hoof (he had come as a goat).

'Well, I had not…' began Werther, but Mistress Christia put a hand to his lips.

'You will need a little time to recover,' she said.

Tactfully, one by one, still expressing their most fulsome congratulations, they departed, until only Werther de Goethe and the Everlasting Concubine were left.

'I hope you did not mind the deception, Werther,' she said. 'I had to make amends for ruining your rainbow and I had been wondering for ages how to please you. My Lady Charlotina helped a little, of course, and Lord Jagged – though neither knew too much of what was going on.'

'The real performance was yours,' he said. 'I was merely your foil.'

'Nonsense. I gave you the rough material with which to work. And none could have anticipated the wonderful, consummate use to which you put it!'

Gently, he took her hand. 'It was everything I have ever dreamed of,' he said. 'It is true, Mistress Christia, that you alone know me.'

'You are kind. And now I must leave.'

'Of course.' He looked out through his window. The comforting storm raged again. Familiar lightnings flickered; friendly thunder threatened; from below there came the sound of his old consoler the furious sea flinging itself, as always, at the rocks' black fangs. His sigh was contented. He knew that their liaison was ended; neither had the bad taste to prolong it and thus produce what would be, inevitably, an anticlimax, and yet he felt regret, as evidently did she.

'If death were only permanent,' he said wistfully, 'but it cannot be. I thank you again, granter of my deepest desires.'

'If death,' she said, pausing at the window, 'were permanent, how would we judge our successes and our failures? Sometimes, Werther, I think you ask too much of the world.' She smiled. 'But you are satisfied for the moment, my love?'

'Of course.'

It would have been boorish, he thought, to have claimed anything else.

White Stars

To Angela Carter

LEGEND THE SECOND

Rose of all Roses, Rose of all the World!
You, too, have come where the dim tides are hurled
Upon the wharves of sorrow, and heard ring
The bell that calls us on; the sweet far thing.
Beauty grown sad with its eternity
Made you of us, and of the dim grey sea.
Our long ships loose thought-woven sails and wait,
For God has bid them share an equal fate;
And when at last, defeated in His wars,
They have gone down under the same white stars,
We shall no longer hear the little cry
Of our sad hearts, that may not live nor die.

– W.B. Yeats,
The Rose of Battle

Chapter One

A Brief Word from Your Auditor

IF THESE FRAGMENTS of tales from the End of Time appear to have certain themes in common, then it is the auditor and his informants who must be held responsible for the selection they have made from available information. A fashion for philosophical and sociological rediscovery certainly prevailed during this period but there must have been other incidents which did not reflect the fashion as strongly, and we promise the reader that if we should hear of some such story we shall not hesitate to present it. Yet legends – whether they come to us from past or future – have a habit of appealing to certain ages in certain interpretations, and that factor, too, must be considered, we suppose.

This story, said to involve among others the Iron Orchid, Bishop Castle and Lord Shark, is amended, interpreted, embellished by your auditor, but in its essentials is the same as he heard it from his most familiar source, the temporal excursionist, Mrs Una Persson.

Chapter Two

A Stroll Across the Dark Continent

'WE WERE ALL puzzled by him,' agreed the Duke of Queens as he stepped carefully over an elephant, 'but we put it down to an idiosyncratic sense of humour.' He removed his feathered hat and wiped his brow. The redder plumes clashed horribly with his cerise skin.

'Some of his jokes,' said the Iron Orchid with a glance of distaste at the crocodile clinging by its teeth to her left foot, 'were rather difficult to see. However, he seems at one with himself now. Wouldn't you say?' She shook the reptile loose.

'Oh, yes! But then I'm notorious for my lack of insight.' They strolled away from Southern Africa into the delicate knee-high forests of the Congo. The Iron Orchid smiled with delight at the brightly coloured little birds which flitted about her legs, sometimes clinging to the hem of her parchment skirt before flashing away again. Of all the expressions of the Duke's obsession with the ancient nation called by him 'Afrique', this seemed to her to be the sweetest.

They were discussing Lord Jagged of Canaria (who had vanished at about the same time as the Iron Orchid's son, Jherek). Offering no explanation as to how his friends might have found themselves, albeit for a very short while, in 19th-century London, together with himself, Jherek, some cyclopean aliens and an assortment of natives of the period, Jagged had returned, only to hide himself away underground.

'Well,' said the Duke, dismissing the matter, 'it was rewarding, even if it does suggest, as Brannart Morphail somewhat emphatically pointed out, that time itself is becoming unstable. It must be because of all these other disruptions in the universe we are hearing about.'

'It is very confusing,' said the Iron Orchid with disapproval. 'I do hope the end of the world, when it comes, will be a little better organised.' She turned. 'Duke?' He had disappeared.

With a smile of apology he clambered back to land. 'Lake Tanganyika,' he explained. 'I knew I'd misplaced it.' He used one of his power rings to dissipate the water in his clothing.

'It is the trees,' she said. 'They are too tall.' She was having difficulty in pressing on through the waist-high palms. 'I do believe I've squashed one of your villages, Duke.'

'Please don't concern yourself, lovely Iron Orchid. I've crowded too much in. You know how I respond to a challenge!' He looked vaguely about him, seeking a way through the jungle. 'It is uncomfortably hot.'

'Is not your sun rather close?' she suggested.

'That must be it.' He made an adjustment to a ruby power ring and the miniature sun rose, then moved to the left, sinking again behind a hillock he had called Kilimanjaro, offering them a pleasant twilight.

'That's much better.'

He took her hand and led her towards Kenya, where the trees were sparser. A cloud of tiny flamingoes fluttered around her, like midges, for a moment and then were gone on their way back to their nesting places.

'I do love this part of the evening, don't you?' he said. 'I would have it all the time, were I not afraid it would begin to pall.'

'One must orchestrate,' she murmured, glad that his taste seemed, at long last, to be improving.

'One must moderate.'

'Indeed.' He helped her across the bridge over the Indian Ocean. He looked back on Afrique, his stance melancholy and romantic. 'Farewell Cape City,' he proclaimed, 'farewell Byzantium, Dodge and Limoges; farewell the verdant plains of Chad and the hot springs of Egypt. Farewell!'

The Duke of Queens and the Iron Orchid climbed into his monoplane, parked nearby. Overhead now a bronze and distant sun brightened a hazy, yellow sky; on the horizon were old, worn mountains which, judging by their peculiar brown colouring, might have been an original part of the Earth's topography, for hardly anyone visited this area.

As the Duke pondered the controls, the Iron Orchid put her

head to one side, thinking she had heard something. 'Do you detect,' she asked, 'a sort of clashing sound?'

'I have not yet got the engine started.'

'Over there, I mean.' She pointed. 'Are those people?'

He peered in the direction she indicated. 'Some dust rising, certainly. And, yes, perhaps two figures. Who could it be?'

'Shall we see?'

'If you wish, we can –' He had depressed a button and the rest of his remark was drowned by the noise of his engine. The propeller began to spin and whine and then fell from the nose, bouncing over the barren ground and into the Indian Ocean. He pressed the button again and the engine stopped. 'We can walk there,' he concluded. They descended from the monoplane.

The ground they crossed was parched and cracked like old leather which had not been properly cared for.

'This needs a thorough restoration,' said the Iron Orchid somewhat primly. 'Who usually occupies this territory?'

'You see him,' murmured the Duke of Queens, for now it was possible to recognise one of the figures.

'Aha!' She was not surprised. It had been two or three centuries since she had last seen the man who, with a bright strip of metal clutched in one gauntleted hand, capered back and forth in the dust, while a second individual, also clasping an identical strip, performed similar steps. From time to time they would bring their strips forcefully together, resulting in the clashing sound the Iron Orchid had heard originally.

'Lord Shark the Unknown,' said the Duke of Queens. He called out, 'Greetings to you, my mysterious Lord Shark!'

The man half-turned. The other figure leapt forward and touched his body with his metal strip. Lord Shark gasped and fell to one knee. Through the fishy mask he always wore, his red eyes glared at them.

They came up to him. He did not rise. Instead he presented his gauntleted palm. 'Look!' Crimson liquid glistened.

The Iron Orchid inspected it. 'Is it unusual?'

'It is blood, madam!' Lord Shark rose painfully to his feet. 'My blood.'

'Then you must repair yourself at once.'

'It is against my principles.'

Lord Shark's companion stood some distance away, wiping Lord Shark's blood from his weapon.

'That, I take it, is a sword,' said the Iron Orchid. 'I had always imagined them larger, and more ornate.'

'I know such swords.' Lord Shark the Unknown loosened the long white scarf he wore around his dark grey neck and applied it to the wound in his shoulder. 'They are decadent. These,' he held up his own, 'are finely tempered, perfectly balanced épées. We were duelling,' he explained, 'my automaton and I.'

Looking across at the machine, the Iron Orchid saw that it was a reproduction of Lord Shark himself, complete with fierce shark mask.

'It could kill you, could it not?' she asked. 'Is it programmed to resurrect you, Lord Shark?'

He dismissed her question with a wave of his bloodstained scarf.

'And strange, that you should be killed, as it were, by yourself,' she added.

'When we fight, is it not always with ourselves, madam?'

'I really don't know, sir, for I have never fought and I know no-one who does.'

'That is why I must make automata. You know my name, madam, but I fear you have the advantage of me.'

'It has been so long. I looked quite different when we last met. At Mongrove's Black Ball, you'll recall. I am the Iron Orchid.'

'Ah, yes.' He bowed.

'And I am the Duke of Queens,' said the Duke kindly.

'I know you, Duke of Queens. But you had another name then, did you not?'

'Liam Ty Pam $12·51 Caesar Lloyd George Zatopek Finsbury Ronnie Michelangelo Yurio Iopu 4578 Rew United,' supplied the Duke. 'Would that be it?'

'As I remember, yes.' A sigh escaped the gash which was the shark's mouth. 'So there have been some few small changes in the outside world, in society. But I suppose you still while away your days with petty conceits?'

'Oh, yes!' said the Iron Orchid enthusiastically. 'They have been at their best this season. Have you seen the Duke's "Afrique"? All in miniature. Over there.'

'Is that what it is called? I wondered. I had been growing lichen, but no matter.'

'I spoiled a project of yours?' The Duke was mortified.

Lord Shark shrugged.

'But, my lonely lord, I must make amends.'

The eyes behind the mask became interested for a moment. 'You would fight with me. A duel? Is that what you mean?'

'Well...' the Duke of Queens fingered his chin, 'if that would placate you, certainly. Though I've had no practice at it.'

The light in the eyes dimmed. 'True. It would be no fight at all.'

'But,' said the Duke, 'lend me one of your machines to teach me, and I will return at an agreed hour. What say you?'

'No, no, sir. I took no umbrage. I should not have suggested it. Let us part, for I weary very swiftly of human company.' Lord Shark sheathed his sword and snapped his fingers at his automaton, which copied the gesture. 'Good day to you, Iron Orchid. And to you, Duke of Queens.' He bowed again.

Ignoring the Iron Orchid's restraining hand upon his sleeve, the Duke stepped forward as Lord Shark turned away. 'I insist upon it, sir.'

His dark grey, leathery cloak rustling, the masked recluse faced them again. 'It would certainly fulfil an ambition. But it would have to be done properly, and only when you had thoroughly learned the art. And there would have to be an understanding as to the rules.'

'Anything.' The Duke made an elaborate bow. 'Send me, at your convenience, an instructor.'

'Very well.' Lord Shark the Unknown signed to his automaton and together they began to walk across the plain, towards the brown mountains. 'You will hear from me soon, sir.'

'I thank you, sir.'

They strolled in the direction of the useless monoplane. The Duke seemed very pleased. 'What a wonderful new fashion,' he remarked, 'duelling. And this time, with the exception of Lord Shark, of course, I *shall* be the first.'

The Iron Orchid was amused. 'Shall we all, soon, be drawing one another's blood with those thin sticks of steel, extravagant duke?'

He laughed and kissed her cheek. 'Why not? I tire of "Cities", and even "Continents" pall. How long is it since we have had a primitive sport?'

'Nothing since the ballhead craze,' she confirmed.

'I shall learn all I can, and then I can teach others. When Jherek returns, we shall have something fresh for him to enjoy.'

'It will, at least, be in keeping with his current obsessions, as I understand them.'

Privately the Iron Orchid wondered if the Duke would, at last, be responsible for an entirely new fashion. She hoped, for his sake, that he would, but it was hard, at the moment, to see the creative possibilities of the medium. She was afraid that it would not catch on.

Chapter Three

Something of the History of Lord Shark the Unknown

If gloomy Mongrove, now touring what was left of the galaxy with the alien Yusharisp, had affected aloofness, then Lord Shark was, without question, genuinely reclusive. Absorbed in his duel, he had not noticed the approach of the Iron Orchid and the Duke of Queens, for if he had he would have made good his escape well before they could have hailed him. In all his life he had found pleasure in the company of only one human being: a short-lived time-traveller who had refused immortality and died many centuries since.

Lord Shark was not merely contemptuous of the society which presently occupied the planet, he was contemptuous of the very planet, the universe, of the whole of existence. Compared with him, Werther de Goethe was an optimist (as, indeed, secretly he was). Werther had once made overtures to Lord Shark, considering him a fellow spirit, but Lord Shark would have none of him, judging him to be as silly and as affected as all the others. Lord Shark was the last true cynic to come into being at the End of Time and found no pleasure in any pursuit save the pursuit of death, and in this he must be thought the unluckiest man in the world, for everything conspired to thwart him. Wounded, he refused to treat the wounds, and they healed. Injured, his injuries were never critical. He considered suicide, as such, to be unworthy of him, feeble, but dangers which would have brought certain death to others only seemed to bring Lord Shark at best some passing inconvenience.

As he returned home, Lord Shark could feel the pain in his shoulder already subsiding and he knew that it would not be long before there would only be a small scar to show where the sword blade had entered. He was regretting his bargain with the Duke of Queens. He was sure that the Duke would never attain the skill necessary to beat him, and, if he were not beaten, and killed, he would in his opinion have wasted his time. His pride now refused to let him go back on the bargain, for to do so would be to show him as feckless a fellow as any other and would threaten his confidence in his own superiority, his only consolation. It was the pride of the profoundly unimaginative man, for it was Lord Shark's lot to be without creative talent of any kind in a world where all were artists – good or bad, but artists, still. Even his mask was not of his own invention and had been made for him by his time-travelling friend shortly before that man's death (his name had come from the same source). He had taken both mask and name without humour, on good faith. It is perhaps unkind to speculate as to whether even this stalwart friend had been unable to resist playing one good joke upon poor Lord Shark, for it is a truism that those without humour find themselves the butts of all who possess even a spark of it themselves.

Whoever had created Lord Shark (and he had never been able to discover who his parents might be, perhaps because they were too embarrassed to claim him) might well have set out to create a perfect misanthrope, a person as unsuited to this particular society as was possible. If so, they had achieved their ambition absolutely. He had appeared in public only twice in the thousand or so years of his life, and the last time had been three hundred years ago at Mongrove's celebrated Black Ball. Lord Shark had stayed little more than half an hour at this, having rapidly reached the conclusion that it was as pointless as all the other social activities on the planet. He had considered time travel, as an escape, but every age he had studied seemed equally frivolous and he had soon ceased to entertain that scheme. He contented himself with his voluntary exile, his contempt, his conviction in the pointlessness of everything, and he continued to seek ways of dying suggested to him by his studies of history. His automata were created in his own image not from perversity, not from egocentricity, but because no other image presented itself to his mind.

Lord Shark trudged on, his grey-booted feet making the dust of his arid domain dance, giving the landscape a semblance of life, and came in a while to his rectangular domicile at the foot of those time-ground ridges, the ragged remains of the Rockies. Two guards, identical in appearance to each other and to Lord Shark, were positioned on either side of his single small door, and they remained rigid, only their eyes following him as he let himself in and marched up the long, straight, sparsely lit passage which passed through the centre of the internal grid (the house was divided into exactly equal sections, with rooms of exactly equal proportions) to the central chamber of the building in which he spent the greater part of his days. There he sat himself down upon a chair of grey metal and began to brood.

Regretfully, he must pursue his agreement with the Duke of Queens, but he felt no demand to hurry the business through; the longer it took, the better.

Chapter Four

In Which Unwilling Travellers Arrive at the End of Time

WALKING SLOWLY ACROSS the ceiling of his new palace, the Duke of Queens looked up to see that Bishop Castle had already arrived and was peering with some pleasure through a window. 'Shall we join him?' asked the Duke of the Iron Orchid and, at her nod of assent, turned a jewel on one of his rings. Elegantly they performed half a somersault so that they, too, were upside down and, from this new perspective, descending towards the floor. Bishop Castle hailed them. 'Such a simple idea, Duke, but beautiful.' He waved a white-gloved hand at the view. The sky now lay like a sea, spread out below, while inverted trees and gardens and lawns were overhead.

'It is refreshing,' confirmed the Duke, pleased. 'But I can take no credit. The idea was the Iron Orchid's.'

'Nonsense, most dashing of dukes. Actually,' she murmured to Bishop Castle, 'I borrowed it from Sweet Orb Mace. How is she, by the by?'

'Recovered completely, though the resurrection was a little late. I believe the snow helped preserve her, for all its heat.'

'We have just seen Lord Shark the Unknown,' she announced. 'And he challenged the Duke of Queens to, my lord bishop, a *duel*!'

'It was not exactly a challenge, luscious blossom. Merely an agreement to fight at some future date.'

'To fight?' Bishop Castle's large eyebrows rose, almost touching the rim of his tall crown. 'Would that involve "violence"?'

'A degree of it, I believe,' said the Duke demurely. 'Yes, blood will be spilled, if today's experience is typical. These little sticks...' He turned with a questioning frown to the Iron Orchid.

'Swords,' she said.

'Yes, swords – with points, you know, to pierce the flesh. You will have seen them in the old pictures and possibly wondered at their function. We have used them for decoration, of course, in the past – many believing them to be some sort of ancient totem, some symbol of rank – but it emerges that they were meant to kill.'

Bishop Castle was apologetic. 'The conceptions involved are a little difficult to grasp, as with so many of these ancient pastimes, though of course I have witnessed, in visitors to our age, the phenomena. Does it not involve "anger", however?'

'Not necessarily, from what little I know.'

The conversation turned to other subjects; they discussed their recent adventures and speculated upon the whereabouts of the Iron Orchid's son, Jherek Carnelian, of Mrs Underwood, whom he loved, of Lord Jagged of Canaria, and the uncouth alien musicians who had called themselves the Lat.

'Brannart Morphail, querulous as ever, refuses to discuss any part he might have played in the affair,' Bishop Castle told his friends. 'He merely hints at the dangers of "meddling with the fabric of time", but I cannot believe he is entirely objective, for he has always affected a somewhat proprietorial attitude towards time.'

'Nonetheless, it *is* puzzling,' said the Iron Orchid. 'And I regret the disappearance of so many entertaining people. Those space-travellers, the Lat, were they, do you think, "violent"?'

'That would explain the difficulties we had in communicating with them, certainly. But we can talk further when we see My Lady Charlotina.' Bishop Castle was evidently tiring of the discussion. 'Shall we go?'

As they drifted, still upside down, from the house, Bishop Castle complimented the Iron Orchid on her costume. It was dark blue and derived from the clothing of some of those she had encountered at the Café Royal, in the 19th century. The helmet suited her particularly, but Bishop Castle was not sure he liked the moustache.

Righting themselves, they all climbed into Bishop Castle's air carriage, a reproduction of a space vehicle of the 300th Icecream Empire, all red-gold curlicues and silver bodywork, and set off for Lake Billy the Kid, where My Lady Charlotina's reception (to celebrate, as she put it, their safe return) had already started.

They had gone no more than a few hundred miles when they encountered Werther de Goethe, magnificently pale in black, voluminous satin robes, riding upon his monstrous tombstone, a slab of purple marble, and evidently recovered from his recent affair with Mistress Christia, the Everlasting Concubine, in such good spirits that he deigned to acknowledge their presence as they put their heads through the portholes and waved to him. The slab swung gracefully over the tops of some tall pine trees and came to rest, hovering near them.

'Do you go to My Lady Charlotina's, moody Werther?' asked the Iron Orchid.

'Doubtless to be insulted again by her, but, yes, I go,' he confirmed. 'I suppose you have seen the newcomers already?'

'Newcomers?' The light breeze curled the Duke's feathers around his face. 'From space?'

'Who knows? They are humanoid. My Lady Charlotina has endomed them, near Lake Billy the Kid. Her whole party has gone to watch. I will see you there, then?'

'You shall, sorrowing son of Nature,' promised the Iron Orchid.

Werther was pleased with the appellation. He swept on. The spaceship turned to follow him.

Soon they saw the stretch of blue water which was My Lady Charlotina's home, the presence of her vast subaqueous palace marked only by a slight disturbance of the surface of the water in the middle of the lake where the energy-tube made its exit. They rose higher into the air, over the surrounding mountains, and at length saw the shimmering, green-tinted air indicating a force-dome. Descending, they saw that the dome, all but invisible, was surrounded by a large throng of people. They landed in the vicinity of a number of other air carriages of assorted designs and disembarked.

My Lady Charlotina, naked, with her skin coloured in alternate bands of black and white, saw them. She already had her arm through Werther's. 'Come and see what I have netted for my menagerie,' she called. 'Time-travellers. I have never seen so many at once.' She laughed. 'Brannart, of course, takes a very gloomy view, but I'm delighted! There isn't another set like it!'

Brannart Morphail, still in the traditional humpback and club-foot of the scientist, limped towards them. He shook a bony finger at the Iron Orchid. 'This is all your son's fault. And where is Lord Jagged to explain himself?'

'We have not seen him since our return,' she said. 'You fret so, Brannart. Think how entertaining life has become of late!'

'Not for long, delicate metal, fragile flower. Not for long.' Grumbling to himself, he hobbled past them. 'I must get my instruments.'

They made their way through the gathering until they reached the wall of the force-dome. The Iron Orchid put her hand to her lips in astonishment. 'Are they intelligent?'

'Oh, yes. Primitive, naturally, but otherwise…' My Lady Charlotina smiled. 'They growl and rave so! We have not yet had a proper talk with them.'

Orange fire splashed against the inner wall and spread across it, obscuring the scene within.

'They keep doing that,' explained My Lady Charlotina. 'I am not sure if they mean to burn us or the wall. A translator is in operation, though they are still a trifle incoherent. Their voices can be very loud.'

As the fire dissipated, the Iron Orchid stared curiously at the twenty or thirty men inside the dome. Their faces were bruised, bleeding and smudged with oil; they wore identical costumes of mottled green and brown; there were metal helmets on their heads, and what she supposed to be some sort of breathing apparatus (unused) on their backs. In their hands were artefacts consisting basically of a metal tube to which was fixed a handle, probably of plastic. It was from these tubes that the flames occasionally gouted.

'They look tired,' she said sympathetically. 'Their journey must have been difficult. Where are they from?'

'They were not clear. We put the dome up because they seemed ill at ease in the open; they kept burning things. Four of my guests had to be taken away for resurrection. I think they must calm down eventually, don't you, Duke of Queens?'

'They invariably do,' he agreed. 'They'll exhaust themselves, I suppose.'

'So many!' murmured Bishop Castle. He fingered the lobe of his ear.

'That is what makes them such a catch,' said the Duke of Queens. 'Well, Werther, you are an expert – what period would you say they were from?'

'Very early. The 20th century?'

'A little later?' suggested Bishop Castle.

'The 25th, then.'

Bishop Castle nodded. 'That seems right. Are any of your guests, My Lady Charlotina, from that age?'

'Not really. You know how few we get from those Dawn Age periods. Doctor Volospion might have one, but...'

Mistress Christia approached, her eyes wide, her lips wet. 'What *brutes*!' she gasped. 'Oh, I envy you, My Lady Charlotina. When did you find them?'

'Not long ago. But I've no idea how much time they've been here.'

More fire spread itself over the wall, but it seemed fainter. One of the time-travellers flung down his tube, growling and glaring. Some of the audience applauded.

'If only Jherek were here,' said the Iron Orchid. 'He understands these people so well! Where is their machine?'

'That's the odd thing, Brannart has been unable to find a trace of one. He insists that one exists. He thinks that it might have returned to its period of origin – that sometimes happens, I gather. But he says that no machine registered on his detectors, and it has caused him to become even more bad-tempered than usual.' My Lady Charlotina withdrew her arm from Werther's. 'Ah, Gaf the Horse in Tears, have you seen my new time-travellers yet?'

Gaf lifted his skirts. 'Have you seen my new *wheels*, My Lady Charlotina?'

They wandered away together.

Bishop Castle was trying to address one of the nearest of the time-travellers. 'How do you do?' he began politely. 'Welcome to the End of Time!'

The time-travellers said something to him which defeated the normally subtle translator.

'Where are you from?' asked the Iron Orchid of one.

Another of the time-travellers shouted to the man addressed. 'Remember, trooper. Name, rank and serial number. It's all you have to tell 'em.'

'Sarge, they must know we're from Earth.'

'Okay,' assented the other, 'you can tell 'em that, too.'

'Kevin O'Dwyer,' said the man, 'Trooper First Class, 0008859376.' He added, 'From Earth.'

'What year?' asked the Duke of Queens.

Trooper First Class Kevin O'Dwyer looked pleadingly at his sergeant. 'You're the ranking officer, sir. I shouldn't have to do this.'

'Let them do the talking,' snapped the sergeant. 'We'll do the fighting.'

'Fighting?' The Duke of Queens grinned with pleasure. 'Ah, you'll be able to help me. Are you soldiers, then?'

Again the translation was muddy.

'Soldiers?' asked Bishop Castle, in case they had not heard properly.

The sergeant sighed. 'What do you think, buddy?'

'This is splendid!' said the Duke of Queens.

Chapter Five
In Which the Duke of Queens Seeks Instruction

As soon as it was evident that the soldiers had used up all their fire, My Lady Charlotina released the one called 'sergeant', whose full name, on further enquiry, turned out to be Sergeant Henry Martinez, 0008832942. After listening in silence to their questions for a while he said:

'Look, I don't know what planet this is, or if you think you're fooling me with your disguise, but you're wasting your time. We're hip to every trick in the Alpha Centauran book.'

'Who are the Alpha Centaurans?' asked My Lady Charlotina, turning to Werther de Goethe.

'They existed even before the Dawn Age,' he explained. 'They were intelligent horses of some kind.'

'Very funny,' said Sergeant Martinez flatly. 'You know damn well who you are.'

'He thinks we're horses? Perhaps some optical disturbance, coupled with…' Bishop Castle creased his brow.

'Stow it, will you?' asked the sergeant firmly. 'We're prisoners of war. Now I know you guys don't pay too much attention to things like the Geneva Convention in Alpha Centauri, for all you –'

'It's a star system!' said Werther. 'I remember. I think it was used for something a long while ago. It doesn't exist any more, but there was a war between Earth and this other system in the 24th century – you are 24th-century, I take it, sir? – which went on for many years. These are typical warriors of the period. The Alpha Centaurans were, I thought, birdlike creatures…'

'The Vultures,' supplied Sergeant Martinez. 'That's what we call you.'

'I assure you, we're as human as you are, sergeant,' said My Lady Charlotina. 'You are an ancestor of ours. Don't you recognise the planet? And we have some of your near-contemporaries with us.

Li Pao? Where's Li Pao? He's from the 27th.' But the puritanical Chinaman had not yet arrived.

'If I'm not mistaken,' said Martinez patiently, 'you're trying to convince me that the blast which got us out there beyond Mercury sent us into the future. Well, it's a good try – we'd heard your interrogation methods were pretty subtle and pretty damn elaborate – but it's too fancy to work. Save your time. Put us in the camp, knock us off, or do whatever you normally do with prisoners. We're Troopers and we're too tough and too tired to play this kind of fool game. Besides, I can tell you for nothing, we don't *know* nothing – we get sent on missions. We do what we're told. We either succeed, or we die or, sometimes, we get captured. We got captured. That's what *we* know. There's nothing else we can tell you.'

Fascinated, the Iron Orchid and her friends listened attentively and were regretful when he stopped. He sighed. 'Bad Sugar!' he exclaimed. 'You're like kids, ain't you? Can you understand what I'm saying?'

'Not entirely,' Bishop Castle told him, 'but it's very interesting for us. To study you, you know.'

Muttering, Sergeant Martinez sat down on the ground.

'Aren't you going to say any more?' Mistress Christia was extremely disappointed. 'Would you like to make love to me, Sergeant Martinez?'

He offered her an expression of cynical contempt. 'We're up to that one, too,' he said.

She brightened, holding out her hand. 'Wonderful! You don't mind, do you, My Lady Charlotina?'

'Of course not.'

When Sergeant Martinez did not accept her hand, Mistress Christia sat down beside him and stroked his cropped head.

Firmly, he replaced the helmet he had been holding in his hands. Then he folded his arms across his broad chest and stared into the middle distance. His colour seemed to have changed. Mistress Christia stroked his arm. He jerked it away.

'I must have misunderstood you,' she said.

'I can take it or leave it alone,' he told her. 'You got it? Okay, I'll take it. When I want it. But if you expect to get any information from me that way, that's where you're wrong.'

'Perhaps you'd rather do it in private?'

A mirthless grin appeared on his battered features. 'Well, I sure ain't gonna do it out here, in front of all your friends, am I?'

'Oh, I see,' she said, confused. 'You must forgive me if I seem tactless, but it's so long since I entertained a time-traveller. We'll leave it for a bit, then.'

The Iron Orchid saw that some of the men inside the force-dome had stretched out on the ground and had shut their eyes. 'They probably need to rest,' she suggested, 'and to eat something. Shouldn't we feed them, My Lady Charlotina?'

'I'll transfer them to my menagerie,' agreed her hostess. 'They'll probably be more at ease there. Meanwhile, we can continue with the party.'

Some time went by; the world continued in pretty much its normal fashion, with parties, experiments, games and inventions. Eventually, so the Iron Orchid heard when she emerged from a particularly dull and enjoyable affair with Bishop Castle, the soldiers from the 24th century had become convinced that they had travelled into the future, but were not much reconciled. Some, it seemed, were claiming that they would rather have been captured by their enemies. No news came from Lord Shark, and the two or three messages the Duke of Queens had sent him had not been answered. Jherek Carnelian did not come back, and Lord Jagged of Canaria refused all visitors. Brannart Morphail bewailed the inconsistencies which he claimed had appeared in the fabric of time. Korghon of Soth created a sentient kind of mould which he trained to do tricks; Mistress Christia, having listened to an old tape, became obsessed with learning the language of the flowers and spent hour after hour listening to them, speaking to them in simple words; O'Kala Incarnadine became a sea lion and thereafter could not be found. The craze for 'Cities' and 'Continents' died and nothing replaced it. Visiting the Duke of Queens, the Iron Orchid mentioned this, and he revealed his growing impatience with Lord Shark. 'He promised he would send me an instructor. I have had to fall back on Trooper O'Dwyer, who knows a little about knives, but nothing at all about swords. This is the perfect moment for a new fashion. Lord Shark has let me down.'

Trooper O'Dwyer, ensconced in luxury at the Duke's palace, had agreed to assist the Duke, his sergeant having succumbed at last to the irresistible charms of Mistress Christia, but the Duke confided to the Iron Orchid that he was not at all sure if bayonet drill were the same as fencing.

'However,' he told her, 'I am getting the first principles. You decide, to start, that you are superior to someone else – that is that you have more of these primitive attributes than the other person or persons – love, hate, greed, generosity and so on...'

'Are not some of these opposites?' Her conversations with her son had told her that much.

'They are...'

'And you claim you have all of them?'

'*More* of them than someone else.'

'I see. Go on.'

'Patriotism is difficult. With that you identify yourself with a whole country. The trick is to see that country as yourself so that any attack on the country is an attack on you.'

'A bit like Werther's Nature?'

'Exactly. Patriotism, in Trooper O'Dwyer's case, can extend to the entire planet.'

'Something of a feat!'

'He accomplishes it easily. So do his companions. Well, armed with all these emotions and conceptions you begin a conflict – either by convincing yourself that you have been insulted by someone (who often has something you desire to own) or by goading him to believe that he has been insulted by you (there are subtle variations, but I do not thoroughly understand them as yet). You then try to kill that person – or that nation – or that planet – or as many members as possible. That is what Trooper O'Dwyer and the rest are currently attempting with Alpha Centauri.'

'They will succeed, according to Werther. But I understand that the rules do not allow resurrection.'

'They are *unable* to accomplish the trick, most delectable of blossoms, most marvellous of metals.'

'So the deaths are permanent?'

'Quite.'

'How odd.'

'They had much higher populations in those days.'

'I suppose that must explain it.'

'Yet, it appears, every time one of their members was killed, they grieved – a most unpleasant sensation, I gather. To rid themselves of this sense of grief, they killed more of the opposing forces, creating grief in them so that they would wish to kill more – and so on, and so on.'

'It all seems rather – well – unaesthetic.'

'I agree. But we must not dismiss their arts out of hand. One does not always come immediately to terms with the principles involved.'

'Is it even Art?'

'They describe it as such. They use the very word.'

One eyebrow expressed her astonishment. She turned as Trooper O'Dwyer shuffled into the room. He was eating a piece of brightly coloured fruit and he had an oddly shaped girl on his arm (created, whispered the Duke, to the trooper's exact specifications). He nodded at them. 'Duke,' he said. 'Lady.' His stomach had grown so that it hung over his belt. He wore the same clothes he had arrived in, but his wounds had healed and he no longer had the respiratory gear on his back.

'Shall we go to the – um – "gym", Trooper O'Dwyer?' asked the Duke in what was, in the Iron Orchid's opinion, a rather unnecessarily agreeable tone.

'Sure.'

'You must come and see this,' he told her.

The 'gym' was a large, bare room, designed by Trooper O'Dwyer, hung with various ropes, furnished with pieces of equipment whose function was, to her, unfathomable. For a while she watched as, enthusiastically, the Duke of Queens leapt wildly about, swinging from ropes, attacking large, stuffed objects with sharp sticks, yelling at the top of his voice, while, seated in the comfortable chair with the girl beside him, Trooper O'Dwyer called out guttural words in an alien tongue. The Iron Orchid did her best to be amused, to encourage the Duke, but she found it difficult. She was glad when she saw someone enter the hall by the far door. She went to greet the newcomer. 'Dear Lord Shark,' she said, 'the Duke has been so looking forward to your visit.'

The figure in the shark mask stopped dead, pausing for a moment or two before replying.

'I am not Lord Shark. I am his fencing automaton, programmed to teach the Duke of Queens the secrets of the duel.'

'I am very pleased you have come,' she said in genuine relief.

Chapter Six

Old-Fashioned Amusements

SERGEANT MARTINEZ AND his twenty-five troopers relaxed in the comparative luxury of a perfect reproduction of a partially ruined Martian bunker, created for them by My Lady Charlotina. It was better than they had expected, so they had not complained, particularly since few of them had spent much of their time in the menagerie.

'The point is,' Sergeant Martinez was saying, as he took a long toke on the large black Herodian cigar, 'that we're all going soft and we're forgetting our duty.'

'The war's over, sarge,' Trooper Gan Hok reminded him. He grinned. 'By a couple million years or so. Alpha Centauri's beaten.'

'That's what they're telling us,' said the sergeant darkly. 'And maybe they're right. But what if this *was* all a mirage we're in? An illusion created by the Vultures to make us *think* the war's over, so we make no attempt to escape.'

'You don't really believe that, do you, sarge?' enquired squat Trooper Pleckhanov. 'Nobody could make an illusion this good. Could they?'

'Probably not, trooper, but it's our duty to *assume* they could and get back to our own time.'

'That girl of yours dropped you, sarge?' enquired Trooper Denereaz, with the perspicacity for which he was loathed throughout the squad. Some of the others began to laugh, but stopped themselves as they noted the expression on the sergeant's face.

'Have you got a plan, sarge?' asked Trooper George diplomatically. 'Wouldn't we need a time machine?'

'They exist. You've all talked with that Morphail guy.'

'Right. But would he give us one?'

'He refused,' Sergeant Martinez told them. 'What does that suggest to you, Trooper Denereaz?'

'That they want us to remain here?' suggested Denereaz dutifully.

'Right.'

'Then how are we going to get hold of one, sarge?' asked Trooper Gan Hok.

'We got to use our brains,' he said sluggishly, staring hard at his cigar. 'We got one chance of a successful bust-out. We're gonna need some hardware, hostages maybe.' He yawned and slowly began to describe his scheme in broad outline while his men listened with different degrees of attention. Some of them were not at all happy with the sergeant's reminder of their duty.

Trooper O'Dwyer had not been present at the conference, but remained at the palace of the Duke of Queens, where he had become very comfortable. Occasionally he would stroll into the gym to see how the Duke's fencing lessons were progressing. He was fascinated by the robot instructing the Duke; it was programmed to respond to certain key commands, but within those terms could respond with rapid and subtle reflexes, while at the same time giving a commentary on the Duke's proficiency, which currently afforded Trooper O'Dwyer some easy amusement.

The words Lord Shark used in his programming were in the ancient language of Fransai, authentic and romantic (though the romance had certainly escaped Lord Shark). To begin a duel the Duke of Queens would cry:

'En tou rage!'

– and if struck (the robot was currently set not to wound) he would retort gracefully:

'Toujours gai, mon coeur!'

Trooper O'Dwyer thought that he had noted an improvement in the Duke's skill over the past week or so (not that weeks, as such, existed in this world, and he was having a hard time keeping track of days, let alone anything else) thanks, thought the trooper, to the original basic training. A good part of the Duke's time was spent with the robot, and he had lost interest in all other activities, all relationships, including that with Trooper O'Dwyer, who was content to remain at the palace, for he was given everything his heart desired.

A month or two passed (by Trooper O'Dwyer's reckoning) and

the Duke of Queens grew increasingly skilful. Now he cried 'En tou rage!' more often than 'Toujours gai!' and he confided, pantingly, one morning to the trooper that he felt he was almost ready to meet Lord Shark.

'You reckon you're as good as this other guy?' asked O'Dwyer.

'The automaton has taught me all it can. Soon I shall pay a visit to Lord Shark and display what I have learned.'

'I wouldn't mind getting a gander at Lord Shark myself,' said Trooper O'Dwyer, casually enough.

'Accompany me, by all means.'

'Okay, Duke.' Trooper O'Dwyer winked and nudged the Duke in the ribs. 'It'll break the monotony. Get me?'

The Duke of Queens, removing his fencing mask (fashioned in gold filigree to resemble a fanciful fox), blinked but made no answer. O'Dwyer could be interestingly cryptic sometimes, he thought. He noticed that the automaton was still poised in the ready position and he commanded it to come to attention. It did, its sword pointing upwards and almost touching its fishy snout.

The Duke drew O'Dwyer's attention to his new muscles. 'I had nothing to do with their appearance,' he said in delight. 'They came – quite naturally. It was most surprising!'

The trooper nodded and bit into a fruit, reflecting that the Duke now seemed to be in better shape than he was.

The Iron Orchid and My Lady Charlotina lay back upon the cushions of their slowly moving air carriage, which had been designed in the likeness of the long-extinct gryphon, and wondered where they might be. They had been making languid love. Eventually, My Lady Charlotina put her golden head over the edge of the gryphon's back and saw, not far off, the Duke of Queens' inverted palace. She suggested to her friend that they might visit the Duke; the Iron Orchid agreed. They adjusted their gravity rings and flew towards the topmost (or the lowest) door, leaving the gryphon behind.

'You seem unenthusiastic, my dear,' murmured My Lady Charlotina, 'about the Duke's current activities.'

'I suppose I am,' assented the Iron Orchid, brightening her silver skin a touch. 'He has such hopes of beginning a fashion.'

'And you think he will fail? I am quite looking forward to the – what is it – the fight?'

'The duel,' she said.

'And many others I know await it eagerly.' They floated down a long, curling passage whose walls were inset at regular intervals with cages containing pretty song-children. 'When is it to take place, do you know?'

'We must ask the Duke. I gather he practises wholeheartedly with the automaton Lord Shark sent him.'

'Lord Shark is so mysterious, is he not?' whispered My Lady Charlotina with relish. 'I suspect that the interest in the duel comes, as much as anything, from people's wish to inspect one so rarely seen in society. Is duelling his *only* pastime?'

'I know nothing at all of Lord Shark the Unknown, save that he affects a surly manner and that he is pleased to assume the rôle of a recluse. Ah, there is the "gym". Probably we shall find the Duke of Queens therein.'

They came upon the Duke as he divested himself of the last of his duelling costume.

'How handsome your body is, manly Master of Queens,' purred My Lady Charlotina. 'Have you altered it recently?'

He kissed her hand. 'It changed itself – a result of all my recent exercise.' He inspected it with pleasure. 'It is how they used to change their bodies, in the old days.'

'We wondered when your duel with Lord Shark the Unknown was to take place,' she said, 'and came to ask. Everyone is anxious to watch.'

He was flattered. 'I go today to visit Lord Shark. It is for him to name the time and the location.' The Duke indicated Trooper O'Dwyer, who lay half-hidden upon an ermine couch. 'Trooper O'Dwyer accompanies me. Would you care to come, too?'

'It is my understanding that Lord Shark does not encourage visitors,' said the Iron Orchid.

'You think you would not be welcome, then?'

'It is best to assume that.'

'Thank you, Iron Orchid, for saving me once again from a lapse of manners. I was ever tactless.' He smiled. 'It was that which led to this situation, really.'

'Trooper O'Dwyer!' My Lady Charlotina drifted towards the reclining warrior. 'Have you seen anything of your compatriots of late?'

'Nope. Have they gone missing?' He showed no great interest in his one-time mess-mates.

'They appear to have vanished, taking with them some power rings and a large air carriage I had given them for their own use. They have deserted my menagerie.'

'I guess they'll come back when they feel like it.'

'I do hope so. If they were not happy with their habitat they had only to tell me. Well,' turning with a smile to the Duke, 'we shall not keep you. I hope your encounter with Lord Shark is satisfactory today. And you must tell us, at once, if you agree place and time, so that we can tell everyone to make plans to be there.'

He bowed. 'You will be the first, My Lady Charlotina, Iron Orchid.'

'Is that your "sword"?'

'It is.'

She stroked the slender blade. 'I must get one for myself,' she said, 'and then you can teach me, too.'

As they returned to their gryphon, the Iron Orchid touched her friend's arm. 'You could not have said a more pleasing thing to him.'

My Lady Charlotina laughed. 'Oh, we live to indulge such honest souls as he. Do we not, Iron Orchid?'

'Do I detect a slightly archaic note in your choice of phrase?'

'You do, my dear. I have been studying, too, you see!'

Chapter Seven

The Terms of the Duel

LORD SHARK'S WARNING devices apprised him of the approach of an air car, and his screens revealed the nature of that car, a large kitelike contraption from which hung a gondola – in the gondola, two figures.

'Two,' murmured Lord Shark the Unknown to himself. Beneath his mask he frowned. The car drifted closer and was seen to contain the Duke of Queens and a plump individual in poorly fitting overalls of some description.

He instructed his automata, his servants, to admit the couple when they reached the building, then he sat back to wait.

Lord Shark's grey mind considered the information on the screens, but dismissed the questions raised until the Duke of Queens could supply answers. He hoped that the Duke had come to admit himself incapable of learning the skills of the duel and that he need not, therefore, be further bothered by the business which threatened to interrupt the routines of all the dull centuries of his existence. The only person on his planet who had not heard the news that the universe was coming to an end, he was the only one who would have been consoled by the knowledge or, indeed, even interested, for nobody else had paid it too much attention, save perhaps Lord Jagged of Canaria. Yet, even had Lord Shark known, he would still have preferred to await the end by following his conventional pursuits, being too much of a cynic to believe news until it had been confirmed by the event itself.

He heard footfalls in the passage. He counted thirty-four before they reached his door. He touched a stud. The door opened and there stood the Duke of Queens, in feathered finery, and lace, and gold, bowing with elaborate and meaningless courtesy.

'Lord Shark, I am here to receive your instructions!' He straightened, stroking his large black beard and looking about the room with a curiosity Lord Shark found offensive.

'This other? Is he your second?'

'Trooper O'Dwyer.'

'Of the 46th Star Squadron,' said Trooper O'Dwyer by way of embellishment. 'Nice to know you, Lord Shark.'

Lord Shark's small sigh was not heard by his visitors as he rose from behind his consoles. 'We shall talk in the gunroom,' he said. 'This way.'

He led them along a perfectly straight corridor into a perfectly square room which was lined with all the weapons his long-dead companion had collected in his lifetime.

'Phew!' said Trooper O'Dwyer. 'What an armoury!' He reached out and took down a heavy energy-rifle. 'I've seen these. We were hoping for an allocation.' He operated the moving parts, he sighted down the barrel. 'Is it charged?'

Lord Shark said tonelessly, 'I believe that they are all in working condition.' While Trooper O'Dwyer whistled and enthused, Lord Shark drew the Duke of Queens to the far end of the room where stood a rack of swords. 'If you feel that you wish to withdraw from our agreement, my lord Duke, I should like you to know that I would also be perfectly happy to forget –'

'No, no! May I?' The Duke of Queens wrapped his heavy cloak over his arm and selected an ancient sabre from the rack, flexing it and testing it for balance. 'Excellent!' He smiled. 'You see, Lord Shark, that I know my blades now! I am ready to meet you at any time, anywhere you decide. Your automaton proved an excellent instructor and can best me no longer. I am ready. Besides,' he added, 'it would not do to call off the duel. So many of my friends intend to watch. They would be disappointed.'

'Friends? Come to watch?' Lord Shark was in despair. The Duke of Queens was renowned for his vulgarity, but Lord Shark had not for a moment considered that he would turn such an event into a sideshow.

'So if you will name when and where…' the Duke of Queens replaced the sword in the rack.

'Very well. It might as easily be where we first met, on the plain, as anywhere.'

'Good. Good.'

'As to time – say a week from today?'

'A *week*? I know the expression. Let me think...'

'Seven days – seven rotations of the planet around the sun.'

'Ah, yes...' The Duke still seemed vague, so Lord Shark said impatiently:

'I will make you the loan of one of my chronometers. I will set it to indicate when you should leave to arrive at the appropriate time.'

'You are generous, Lord Shark.'

Lord Shark turned away. 'I will be glad when this is over,' he said. He glared at Trooper O'Dwyer, but the trooper was oblivious to his displeasure. He was now inspecting another weapon.

'I'd sure love the chance of trying one of these babies out,' he hinted.

Lord Shark ignored him.

'We shall fight, Duke of Queens, until one of us is killed. Does that suit you?'

'Certainly. It is what I expected.'

'You are not reluctant to die. I assumed...'

'I've died more than once, you know,' said the Duke airily. 'The resurrection is sometimes a little disorientating, but it doesn't take long to –'

'I shall not expect to be resurrected,' Lord Shark told him firmly. 'I intend to make that one of the terms of this duel. If killed – then it is final.'

'You are serious, sir?' The Duke of Queens was surprised.

'It is my nature to be ever serious, Duke of Queens.'

The Duke of Queens considered for a moment, stroking his beard. 'You would be annoyed with me if I did see to it that you were resurrected?'

'I would consider it extremely bad-mannered, sir.'

The Duke was conscious of his reputation for vulgarity. 'Then, of course, I must agree.'

'You may still withdraw.'

'No. I stand by your terms, Lord Shark. Absolutely.'

'You will accept the same terms for yourself, if I kill you?'

'Oh!'

'You will accept the same terms, sir?'

'To remain dead?'

Lord Shark was silent.

Then the Duke of Queens laughed. 'Why not? Think of the entertainment it will provide for our friends!'

'*Your* friends,' said Lord Shark the Unknown pointedly.

'Yes. It will give the duel an authentic flavour. And there would be no question that I would not have created a genuine stir, eh? Though, of course, I would not be in a position to enjoy my success.'

'I gather, then,' said Lord Shark in a peculiar voice, 'that you are willing to die for the sake of this frivolity?'

'I am, sir. Though "frivolity" is hardly the word. It is, at very least, an enjoyable jest – at best an act of original artistry. And that, I confide to you, Lord Shark, is what it has always been my ambition to achieve.'

'Then we are agreed. There is no more to say. Would you choose a sword?'

'I'll leave that to you, sir, for I respect your judgement better than my own. If I might continue to borrow your automaton until the appointed time...?'

'Of course.'

'Until then.' The Duke of Queens bowed. 'O'Dwyer?'

The trooper looked up from a gun he had partially dismantled. 'Duke?'

'We can leave now.'

Reluctantly, but with expert swiftness, Trooper O'Dwyer reassembled the weapon, cheerfully saluted Lord Shark and, as he left, said, 'I'd like to come back and have another look at these sometime.'

Lord Shark ignored him. Trooper O'Dwyer shrugged and followed the Duke of Queens from the room.

A little later, watching the great kite float into the distance, Lord Shark tried to debate with himself the mysteries of the temperament the Duke of Queens had revealed, but an answer was beyond him; he merely found himself confirmed in his opinion of the stupidity of the whole cosmos. It would do no great harm, he thought, to extinguish one small manifestation of that stupidity: the Duke of Queens certainly embodied everything Lord Shark most loathed about his world. And, if he himself, instead, were slain, then that would be an even greater consolation – though he believed the likelihood was remote.

Chapter Eight

Matters of Honour

NOT LONG AFTER the exchange between the Duke of Queens and Lord Shark, Trooper Kevin O'Dwyer, becoming conscious of his own lack of exercise, waddled out for a stroll in the sweet-smelling forest which lay to the west of the Duke's palace.

Trooper O'Dwyer was concerned for the Duke's safety. It had only just dawned on him what the stakes were to be. He took a kindly and patronising interest in the well-being of the Duke of Queens, regarding his host with the affection one might feel towards a large, stupid labrador, an amiable labrador. This was perhaps a naïve view of the Duke's character, but it suited the good-natured O'Dwyer to maintain it. Thus, he mulled the problem over as he sat down under a gigantic daffodil and rested a pair of legs which had become unused to walking.

The scent of the monstrous flowers was very heady and it made the already weary Trooper O'Dwyer rather drowsy, so that he had not accomplished very much thinking before he began to nod off, and would have fallen into a deep sleep had he not been tapped smartly on the shoulder. He opened his eyes with a grunt and looked into the gaunt features of his old comrade Trooper Gan Hok. With a gesture, Trooper Gan Hok cautioned O'Dwyer to silence, whispering, 'Is anyone else with you?'

'Only you.' Trooper O'Dwyer was pleased with his wit. He grinned.

'This is serious,' said Trooper Gan Hok, wriggling the rest of his thin body from the undergrowth. 'We've been trying to contact you for days. We're busting off. Sergeant Martinez sent me to find you. Didn't you know we'd escaped?'

'I heard you'd disappeared, but I didn't think much of it. Has something come up?'

'Nothing special, only we decided it was our duty to try to get back. Sergeant Martinez reckons that we're as good as deserters.'

'I thought we were as good as POWs?' said O'Dwyer reasonably. 'We can't get back. Only experienced time-travellers can even *attempt* it. We've been told.'

'Sergeant Martinez doesn't believe 'em.'

'Well,' said O'Dwyer, 'I do. Don't you?'

'That's not the point, trooper,' said Gan Hok primly. 'Anyway, it's time to rejoin your squad. I've come to take you back to our HQ. We've got a foxhole on the other side of this jungle, but time's running out, and so are our supplies. We can't work the power rings. We need food and we need weapons before we can put the rest of the sergeant's plan into operation.'

Through one of the gaps in his shirt Trooper O'Dwyer scratched his stomach. 'It sounds crazy. What's your opinion? Is Martinez in his right mind?'

'He's in command. That's all we have to know.'

Before he had become a guest of the Duke of Queens, Trooper O'Dwyer would have accepted this logic, but now he was not sure he found it palatable. 'Tell the sergeant I've decided to stay. Okay?'

'That *is* desertion. Look at you – you've been corrupted by the enemy!'

'They're not the enemy, they're our descendants.'

'And they wouldn't exist today if we hadn't done our duty and wiped out the Vultures – that's assuming what they say is true.' Gan Hok's voice took on the hysterical tones of the very hungry. 'If you don't come, you'll be treated as a deserter.' Meaningly, Trooper Gan Hok fingered the knife at his belt.

O'Dwyer considered his position and then replied. 'Okay, I'll come with you. There isn't any chance of this plan working anyhow.'

'The sergeant's got it figured, O'Dwyer. There's a good chance.'

With a sigh, Trooper O'Dwyer climbed to his feet and lumbered after Trooper Gan Hok as he moved with nervous stealth back into the forest.

*

'But, dearest of dukes, you cannot take such terms seriously!' The Iron Orchid's skin flickered through an entire spectrum of colour as, in agitation, she paced the floor of the 'gym'.

Embarrassed, he fingered the cloak of the dormant duelling automaton. 'I have agreed,' he said quietly. 'I thought you would find it amusing – you, in particular, my petalled pride.'

'I believe,' she replied, 'that I feel sad.'

'You must tell Werther. He will be curious. It is the emotion he most yearns to experience.'

'I would miss your company so much if Lord Shark kills you. And kill you he will, I am sure.'

'Nonsense. I am the match for his automaton, am I not?'

'Who knows how Lord Shark programmed the beast? He could be deceiving you.'

'Why should he? Like you, he tried to dissuade me from the duel.'

'It might be a trick.'

'Lord Shark is incapable of trickery. It is not in his nature to be devious.'

'What do you know of his nature? What do any of us know?'

'True. But I have my instincts.'

The Iron Orchid had a low opinion of those.

'If you wait,' he said consolingly, 'you will observe my skill. The automaton is programmed to respond to certain verbal commands. I intend, now, to allow it to try to wound me.' He turned, presented his sword at the ready and said to the automaton, 'We fight to wound.' Immediately the mechanical duellist prepared itself, balancing on the balls of its feet in readiness for the Duke's attack.

'Forgive me,' said the Iron Orchid coldly, 'if I do not watch. Farewell, Duke of Queens.'

He was baffled by her manner. 'Goodbye, lovely Iron Orchid.' His sword touched the automaton's; the automaton feinted; the Duke parried. The Iron Orchid fled from the hall.

Righting herself at the exit, she entered her little air car, the bird of paradise, and instructed it to carry her as rapidly as possible to the house of Lord Shark the Unknown. The car obeyed, flying over many partially built and partially destroyed scenes, several of them the Duke's own, of mountains, luscious sunrises, cities, landscapes of all descriptions, until the barren plain came in sight and beyond it the brown mountains, under the shadow of which lay Lord Shark's featureless dwelling.

The bird of paradise descended completely to the ground, its scintillating feathers brushing the dust; out of it climbed the Iron Orchid, walking determinedly to the door and knocking upon it.

A masked figure opened it immediately.

'Lord Shark, I have come to beg –'

'I am not Lord Shark,' said the figure in Lord Shark's voice. 'I am his servant. My master is in his duelling room. Is your business important?'

'It is.'

'Then I shall inform him of your presence.' The machine closed the door.

Impatient and astonished, for she had had no real experience of such behaviour, the Iron Orchid waited until, in a while, the door was opened again.

'Lord Shark will receive you,' the automaton told her. 'Follow me.'

She followed, remarking to herself on the unaesthetic symmetry of the interior. She was shown into a room furnished with a chair, a bench and a variety of ugly devices which she took to be crude machines. On one side of her stood Lord Shark the Unknown, a sword still in his gloved hand.

'You are the Iron Orchid?'

'You remember that we met when you challenged my friend the Duke of Queens?'

'I remember. But I did not challenge him. He asked how he might make amends for destroying the lichen I had been growing. He built his continent upon it.'

'His Afrique.'

'I do not know what he called it. I suggested a duel, because I wished to test my abilities against those of another mortal. I regretted this suggestion when I understood the light in which the Duke accepted it.'

'Then you would rather not continue with it?'

'It does not please me, madam, to be a clown, to be put to use for the entertainment of those foolish and capricious individuals you call your friends!'

'I do not understand you.'

'Doubtless you do not.'

'I regret, however, that you are displeased.'

'Why should you regret that?' He seemed genuinely puzzled. 'I regret only that my privacy has been disturbed. You are the *third* to visit me.'

'You have only to refuse to fight and you are saved from enduring that which disturbs you.'

The shark mask looked away from her. 'I must kill your Duke of Queens, as an example to the rest of you – as an example of the futility of all existence, particularly yours. If he should kill me, then I am satisfied, also. There is a question of honour involved.'

'Honour? What is that?'

'Your ignorance confirms my point.'

'So you intend to pursue this silly adventure to the bitter end?'

'Call it what you like.'

'The Duke's motives are not yours.'

'His motives do not interest me.'

'The Duke loves life. You hate it.'

'Then he can withdraw.'

'But you will not?'

'You have presented no arguments to convince me that I should.'

'But he seeks only to please his fellows. He agreed to the duel because he hoped it would please you.'

'Then he deserves death.'

'You are unkind, Lord Shark.'

'I am a man of intellect, madam, whose misfortune it is to find himself alone in an irrational universe. I do you all the credit of having the ability to see what I see, but I despise you for your unwillingness to accept the truth.'

'You see only one form of truth.'

'There *is* only one form of truth.' His grey shoulders shrugged. 'I see, too, that your reasons for visiting me were whimsical, after all. I would be grateful if you would leave.'

As she turned to go, something mechanical screamed from the

desk. She paused. With a murmur of displeasure, Lord Shark the Unknown hurried to his consoles.

'This is intolerable!' He stared into a screen. 'A horde has arrived! When you leave, please ask them to go away.'

She craned her neck to look at the screen. 'Why!' she exclaimed. 'It is My Lady Charlotina's missing time-travellers. What could their reason be, Lord Shark, for visiting you?'

Chapter Nine
Questions of Power

BRANNART MORPHAIL WAS not in a good temper. The scientist gesticulated at My Lady Charlotina, who had come to see him in his laboratories, which were attached to her own apartments at Below-the-Lake. 'Another time machine? Why should I waste one? I have so few left!'

'Surely you have one which you like less than the others?' she begged.

'Big enough to take twenty-five men? It is impossible!'

'But they are so destructive!'

'What serious harm can they do if their demands are simply ignored?'

'The Iron Orchid and Lord Shark are their prisoners. They have all those weapons of Lord Shark's. They have already destroyed the mountains in a most dramatic way.'

'I enjoyed the spectacle.'

'So did I, dear Brannart.'

'And if they destroy the Iron Orchid and Lord Shark, we can easily resurrect them again.'

'They intend to subject them to *pain*, Brannart, and I gather that pain is enjoyable only up to a point. Please agree.'

'The responsibility for those creatures was yours, My Lady Charlotina. You should not have let them wander about willy-nilly. Now look what has happened. They have invaded Lord Shark's home, captured both Lord Shark and the Iron Orchid (what on earth was she doing there?), seized those silly guns, and are now demanding a time machine in which to return to their own age. I have spoken to them already about the Morphail Effect, but they choose not to believe me.' He limped away from her. 'They shall not have a time machine.'

'Besides,' said My Lady Charlotina, 'Lord Shark is due, very shortly, to fight his duel with the Duke of Queens. We have all been looking forward to it so much. Think of the disappointment. I know you wanted to watch.'

His hump twitched. 'That's a better reason, I'd agree.' He frowned. 'There might be a solution.'

'Tell me what it is, most sagacious of scientists!'

Sergeant Martinez glared at Lord Shark and the Iron Orchid who, bound firmly, lay propped in a corner of the room. He and his men were armed with the pick of the weapons and they looked much more confident than when they had pushed past the Iron Orchid as she opened the door of Lord Shark's house.

'We don't like to do this,' said Sergeant Martinez, 'but we're running out of patience. Your friend Lady Charlotina is going to get your ear if someone doesn't deliver that time ship soon.'

'Why should she need it?' The Iron Orchid was enjoying herself. Her sense of boredom had lifted completely and she felt that if they continued to be prisoners for a little longer, the duel would have to be forgotten about. She wished, however, that Sergeant Martinez had not taken *all* her power rings from her fingers.

'Tell your robot to get us some more grub,' ordered the sergeant, digging Lord Shark in the ribs with the toe of his boot. Lord Shark complied. He seemed unmoved by what was happening; it rather confirmed his general view of an unreasonable and hostile universe. He felt vindicated.

A screen came to life. Trooper O'Dwyer, looking miserable, tuned the image with the manual control he had been playing with. 'It's the old crippled guy,' he informed his sergeant.

Sergeant Martinez said importantly, 'I'll take over, trooper. Hi,' he addressed Brannart Morphail. 'Have you agreed to give us a ship?'

'One is on its way to you.'

Sergeant Martinez looked pleased with himself. 'Okay. We get the ship and you get the hostages back.'

The Iron Orchid's heart sank. 'Do not give in to them, Brannart!' she cried. 'Let them do their worst!'

'I must warn you,' said Brannart Morphail, 'that it will do you little good. Time refuses paradox. You will not be able to return to your own age – or, at least, not for long. You would do better to forget this whole ridiculous venture…'

Sergeant Martinez switched him off.

'See?' he said to Trooper O'Dwyer. 'I told you it would work. Like a dream.'

'They must be treating it as a game,' said O'Dwyer. 'They've got nothing to fear. By using those power rings they could wipe us out in a second.'

Sergeant Martinez looked at the rings he had managed to get onto his little finger. 'I can't figure out why they don't work for me.'

'They are, in essence, biological,' said the Iron Orchid. 'They work only for the individual who owns them, translating his desires much as a hand does – without conscious thought.'

'Well, we'll see about that. What about the robots, will they obey anybody?'

'If so programmed,' said Lord Shark.

'Okay,' (of the automaton which had re-entered with a tray of food), 'tell that one to obey me.'

Lord Shark instructed the robot accordingly. 'You will obey the soldiers,' he said.

'There's some kind of vehicle arrived outside.' O'Dwyer looked up from the screen. He addressed Lord Shark. 'How come this equipment looks like it's out of a museum?'

'My companion,' explained Lord Shark, 'he built it.'

'Funny-looking thing. More like a space ship than a time ship.' Trooper Denereaz stared at the image: a long, tubular construction, tapering at both ends, hovering just above the ground.

'It's going to be good to get back amongst the cold, clean stars,' said Sergeant Martinez sentimentally, 'where the only things a man's got to trust is himself and a few buddies, and he knows he's fighting for something important. Maybe you people don't understand that. Maybe there's no need for you *to* understand. But it's because there are men like us, prepared to go out there and get their guts shot out of them in order to keep the universe a safe place to live in, that the rest of you sleep well in your beds at night, dreaming your nice, comfortable dreams…'

'Hadn't we better get going, sergeant?' asked Trooper O'Dwyer. 'If we're going.'

'It could be a trap,' said Sergeant Martinez grimly, 'so we'd better go out in groups of five. First five occupies the ship, checks for occupants, booby traps and so on, then signals to the next five, until we're all out. Trooper O'Dwyer, keep a watch on that screen until you see we're all aboard and nobody's shooting at us, then follow – oh, and bring that robot with you. We can use him.'

'Yes, sir.'

'And if there's any smell of a set-up, kill the hostages.'

'Yes, sir,' said Trooper O'Dwyer sceptically.

A bell began to ring.

'What does that mean?' demanded Sergeant Martinez.

'It means that I shall be able to keep my appointment with the Duke of Queens,' Lord Shark told him.

Chapter Ten
The Duel

THE REMAINS OF the Rocky Mountains were still smouldering in the background as, from a safe distance, the crowd watched the ship containing the troopers rise into the air. Behind the crowd, feeling a little upset by the lack of attention, the Duke of Queens stood, sword in hand, awaiting his antagonist. The Duke was early. He had no interest in these other events, which he regarded as an unwelcome interruption, threatening to diffuse the drama of his duel with Lord Shark the Unknown; he thought that Sergeant Martinez and his men had behaved rather badly. Certainly, at any other time, he would have been as diverted by their actions as anyone, but, as it was, they had confused the presentation and robbed it of some of its tension.

At last the Duke noticed that heads were beginning to turn in his direction, and he heard someone call:

'The Iron Orchid – Lord Shark – they emerge! They are saved!'

There came a chorus of self conscious exultation.

The ranks parted; now the Iron Orchid, her slender fingers bare of rings, walked with a self-satisfied air beside Lord Shark the Unknown, stiff, sworded and stern.

They confronted each other over a narrow fissure in the earth. The Duke of Queens bowed. Lord Shark the Unknown, after a second's hesitation, bowed.

The Iron Orchid seemed reconciled. She took a step back. 'May the best man win!' she said.

'My lord.' The Duke presented his sword. 'To the death!'

Silently, Lord Shark the Unknown replied to the courtesy.

'En tou rage, mon coeur!' The Duke of Queens adopted the traditional stance, balancing on the balls of his feet, his body poised, one hand upon his hip, ready for the lunge. Lord Shark's body fell into the same position as precisely as that of one of his own automata.

The crowd moved forward, but kept its distance.

Lord Shark lunged. The Duke of Queens parried, at the same time leaning back to avoid the point of the blade. Lord Shark continued his forward movement, crossing the fissure, lunged again, was parried again. This time the Duke of Queens lunged and was parried. For a short while it was possible for the spectators to follow the stylised movements of the duellists, but gradually, as the combatants familiarised themselves with each other's method of fighting, the speed increased, until it was often impossible to see the thin blades, save for a gleaming blur as they met, parted, and met again.

Back and forth across the dry, dancing dust of that plain the two men moved, the Duke's handsome, heavy features registering every escape, every minor victory, while the immobile mask of Lord Shark the Unknown gave no indication of how that strange, bleak recluse felt when his shoulder was grazed by the Duke's blade, or when he came within a fraction of an inch of skewering his opponent's rapidly beating heart.

At first some of the crowd would applaud a near-miss or gasp as one of the duellists turned his body aside from a lunge which seemed unerring; soon, however, they fell silent, realising that they must feel some of the tension the ancients had felt when they attended such games.

The Duke, refusing in homage to those same ancestors to allow himself any energy boosts, understood that he was tiring much more than he had tired during his tuition, but he understood, also, that Lord Shark the Unknown had patterned his automata entirely after himself, for Lord Shark fought in exactly the same manner as had his mechanical servant, and this made the Duke of Queens more hopeful. Dimly he became aware of the implications of his bargain with Lord Shark: to die and never to be resurrected, to forego the rich enjoyment of life, to become unconscious for ever. His attention wavered as these thoughts crept into his mind, he parried a lunge a little too late. He felt the sharp steel slide into his body. He knew pain. He gasped. Lord Shark the Unknown stepped back as the Duke of Queens staggered.

Lord Shark was expectant, and the Duke realised that he had forgotten to acknowledge the wound.

'Toujours gai, mon coeur!' He wondered if he were dying, but no, the pain faded and became an unpleasant ache. He was still able to continue. He drew himself upright, conscious of the Iron Orchid's high-pitched voice in the background.

'En tou rage!' he warned, and lunged before he had properly regained his balance, falling sideways against Lord Shark's sword, but able to step back in time, recall his training and position himself properly so that when Lord Shark lunged again, he parried the stroke, returned it, parried again and returned again.

The Duke of Queens wondered at the temperature changes in his body. He had felt uncomfortably warm and now he felt a chill throughout, from head to toe, with only his wound glowing hot, but no longer very painful.

And Lord Shark the Unknown pushed past the Duke's defence and the point of his sword gouged flesh from the Duke's left arm, just below the shoulder.

'Oh!' cried the Duke, and then, 'Toujours gai!'

In grim silence, Lord Shark the Unknown gave him a few moments in which to recover.

The Duke of Queens was surprised at his own reaction now, for he quickly resumed his stance, coolly gave his warning, and found that a new emotion directed him. He believed that the emotion must be 'fear'.

And his lunges became more precise, his parries swifter, firmer, so that Lord Shark the Unknown lost balance time after time and was hard-pressed to regain it. It seemed to some of those who watched that Lord Shark was nonplussed by this new, cold attack. He began to lose ground, backing further and further away under the momentum of the Duke's new-found energy.

And then the Duke of Queens, unthinking, merely a duellist, thrust once and struck Lord Shark the Unknown in the heart.

Although he must have been quite dead, Lord Shark stood erect for a little while, gradually lowering his sword and then falling, as stiff in death as he had been in life, onto the hard earth; his blood flooded from him, giving nourishment to the dust.

The Duke of Queens was astonished by what he had accomplished. Even as the Iron Orchid and his other friends came slowly towards him, he found that he was shaking.

The Duke dropped his blade. His natural reaction, at this time, would have made immediate arrangements for Lord Shark's resurrection, but Lord Shark had been firm, remorseless in his affirmation that if death came to him he must remain dead through the rest of time. The Duke wondered at the thoughts and feelings, all unfamiliar, which filled him.

He could not understand why the Iron Orchid smiled and kissed him and congratulated him, why My Lady Charlotina babbled of the excitement he had provided, why Bishop Castle and his old acquaintance Captain Oliphaunt clapped him on the back and reminded him of his wounds.

'You are a Hero, darling Duke!' cried the Everlasting Concubine. 'You must let me nurse you back to health!'

'A fine display, glamorous Lord of Queens!' heartily praised the captain. 'Not since "Cannibals" has there been such entertainment!'

'Indeed, the fashion begins already! Look!' Bishop Castle displayed a long and jewelled blade.

The Duke of Queens groaned and fell to his knees. 'I have killed Lord Shark,' he said. A tear appeared on his cheek.

In the reproduction of what had been either a space- or air-ship, part of the collection long since abandoned by the Duke of Queens, Sergeant Martinez and his men peered through portholes at the distant ground. The ship had ceased to rise but now was borne by the currents of the wind. No response came from the engines; propellers did not turn, rockets did not fire – even the little sails rigged along the upper hull would not unfurl when Sergeant Martinez sent a reluctant Denereaz out to climb the ladder which clung to the surface of what was either a gasbag or a fuel tank.

'We have been suckered,' announced Sergeant Martinez, after some thought. 'This is not a time machine.'

'Not so far,' agreed Trooper Gan Hok, helping himself to exotic food paste from a cabinet. The ship was well stocked with provisions, with alcohol and dope.

'We could be up here for ever,' said Sergeant Martinez.

'Well, for a good while,' agreed Trooper Smith. 'After all, sarge, what goes up must, eventually, come down – if we're still in this planet's gravity field, that is. Which we are.'

Only Trooper Kevin O'Dwyer appeared to have accepted the situation with equanimity. He lay on a divan of golden plush while the stolen automaton brought him the finest food from the cabinets.

'And what I'd like to know, O'Dwyer, is why that damn robot'll only respond to your commands,' said Sergeant Martinez darkly.

'Maybe it respects me, sarge?'

Without much conviction, Sergeant Martinez said: 'You ought to be disciplined for insubordination, O'Dwyer. You seem to be enjoying all this.'

'We ought to make the best of it, that's all,' said O'Dwyer. 'Do you think there's any way of getting in touch with the surface? We could ask them to send up some girls.'

'Be careful, O'Dwyer.' Sergeant Martinez lay back on his own couch and closed his eyes, taking a strong pull on his cigar. 'That sounds like fraternisation to me. Don't forget that those people have to be regarded as alien belligerents.'

'Sorry, sarge. Robot, bring me another drink of that green stuff, will you?'

The automaton seemed to hesitate.

'Hurry it up,' said O'Dwyer.

Returning with the drink, the automaton handed it to O'Dwyer and then hissed through its mask. 'What purpose is there any longer to this deception, O'Dwyer?'

O'Dwyer rose and took the robot by the arm, leading it from the main passenger lounge into the control chamber, now unoccupied. 'You must realise, Lord Shark, that if they realise I made a mistake and brought you up here instead of the robot, they'll use you as a bargaining counter.'

'Should I care?'

'That's for you to decide.'

'Your logic in substituting one of my automata for me and sending it out with the Iron Orchid to fight the Duke of Queens is still a mystery to me.'

'Well, it's pretty simple to explain, Sharko. The Duke was used to fighting robots – so I gave him a sporting chance. Also, when it's discovered it's a robot, and he's dead, they'll be able to bring him back to life – 'cause the rules will have been broken. Get it? If the robot's been put out of action, so what? Yeah?'

'Why should you have bothered to interfere?'

'I like the guy. I didn't want to see him killed. Besides, it was a favour to the Iron Orchid, too – and she looks like a lady who likes to return a favour. We worked it out between us.'

'I heard you. Releasing me from my bonds when it was too late for me to return, then suggesting to your comrades that I was an automaton. Well, I shall tell them that you have deceived them.'

'Go ahead. I'll deny it.'

Lord Shark the Unknown walked to the porthole, studying the peculiar purple clouds which someone had created in this part of the sky.

'All my life I have been unable to see the point of human activity,' he said. 'I have found every experience further proof of the foolishness of my fellows, of the absolute uselessness of existence. I thought that no expression of that stupidity could bewilder me again. Now I must admit that my assumptions, my opinions, my most profound beliefs seem to dissipate and leave me as confused as I was when I first came into this tired and decadent universe. You are an alien here yourself. Why should you help the Duke of Queens?'

'I told you. I like him. He doesn't know when to come in out of the rain. I fixed things so nobody lost. Is that bad?'

'You did all that, including risking the disapproval of your fellows, out of an emotion of – what – affection? – for that buffoon?'

'Call it enlightened self-interest. The fact is that the whole thing's de-fused. I didn't think we'd get off this planet, or out of this age, and I'm glad we haven't. I like it here. But Sergeant Martinez had to make the attempt, and I had to go along with him, to keep him happy. Don't worry, we'll soon be on-planet again.'

He gave Lord Shark the Unknown a friendly slap on the back. 'All honour satisfied, eh?'

And Lord Shark laughed.

Ancient Shadows

To Iain Sinclair

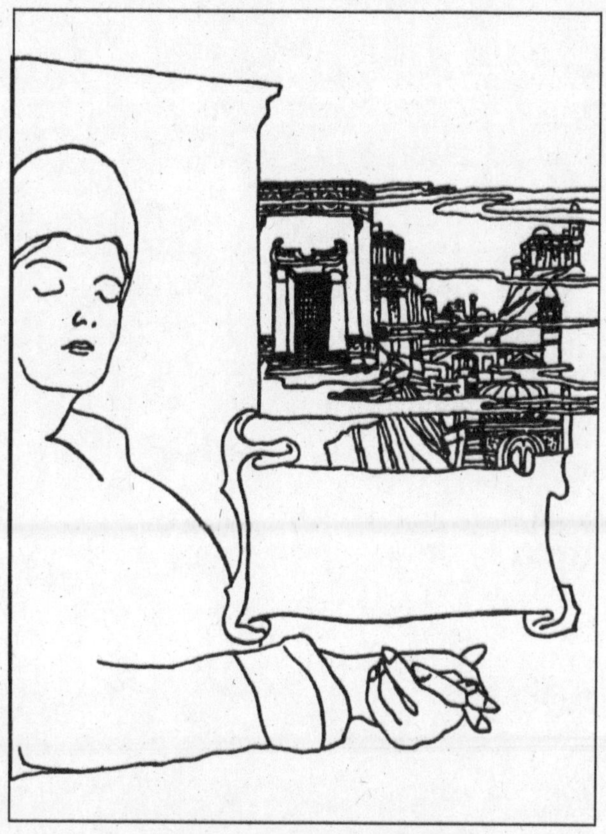

LEGEND THE THIRD

In ancient shadows and twilights
    Where childhood had stray'd,
    The world's great sorrows were born
And its heroes were made.
    In the lost boyhood of Judas
Christ was betray'd.

– G.W. Russell ('Æ'),
Germinal

Chapter One

A Stranger to the End of Time

UPON THE SHORE of a glowing chemical lake, peering through a visor of clouded perspex, a stranger stood, her dark features showing profound awe and some disapproval, while behind her there rustled and gibbered a city, half-organic in its decadence, palpitating with obscure colours, poisonous and powerful. And overhead, in the sallow sky, a small old sun spread withered light, parsimonious heat, across the planet's dissolute topography.

'Thus it ends,' murmured the stranger. She added, a little self-consciously, 'What pathetic monuments to mankind's Senility!'

As if for reassurance, she pressed a gloved hand to the surface of her time machine, which was unadorned and boxlike, smooth and spare, according to the fashions of her own age. Lifting apparently of its own volition, a lid at the top opened and a little freckled head emerged. With a frown she gestured her companion back, but then, changing her mind, she helped the child, which was clad in a small suit and helmet matching her own, from the hatch.

'Witness this shabby finale, my son. Could I begrudge it you?'

Guilelessly the child said, 'It is awfully pretty, Mama.'

It was not her way to contradict a child's judgement. She shrugged. 'I am fulfilled, I suppose, and unsurprised, though I had hoped, well, for Hope.' From the confusion of her private feelings she fled back to practicality. 'Your father will be anxious. If we return now we can at least report to the committee tonight. And report success!' A proud glove fell upon her son's shoulder. 'We have travelled the limit of the machine's capacity! Here, time has ceased to exist. The instruments say so, and their accuracy is unquestionable.' Her eye was caught by a shift of colour as the outline of one building appeared to merge with another, separate, and re-form. 'I had imagined it bleaker, true.'

The city coughed, like a giant in slumber, and was silent for a while.

The boy made to remove his helmet. She stopped him. 'The atmosphere! Noxious, Snuffles, without doubt. One breath could kill.'

It seemed for a moment that he would argue with her opinion. Eye met grey-blue eye; jaws set; he sighed, lowering his head and offering the side of the machine a petulant kick. From the festering city, a chuckle, causing the boy to whirl, defensive and astonished. A self-deprecating grin, the lips gleaming at the touch of the dampening tongue; a small gauntlet reaching for the large one. An indrawn breath.

'You are probably correct, Mama, in your assessment.'

She helped him back into their vessel, glanced once, broodingly, at the shimmering city, at the pulsing lake, then followed her son through the hatch until she stood again at her controls in the machine's green-lit and dim interior.

As she worked the dials and levers, she was studied by her son. Her curly brown hair was cut short at the nape, her up-curving lips gave an impression of amiability denied by the sobriety and intensity of her large, almond-shaped brown eyes. Her hands were small, well-formed, and, to a person from the 20th century, her body would have seemed slight, in proportion with those hands (though she was thought tall and shapely by her own folk). Moving efficiently, but with little instinctive feel for her many instruments, considering each action rapidly and intelligently and carrying it through in the manner of one who has learned a lesson thoroughly but unenthusiastically, she adjusted settings and figures. Her son seated himself in his padded chair, tucked beneath the main console at which his mother stood, and used his own small computer to make the simpler calculations required by her for the reprogramming of the machine so that it could return to the exact place and almost the exact time of its departure.

When she had finished, she withdrew a pace or two from the controls, appraised them and was satisfied. 'We are ready, Snuffles, to begin the journey home. Strap in, please.'

He was already safely buckled. She crossed to the chair facing him, arranged her own harness, spread gloved fingers across the seven buttons set into the arm of the chair, and pressed four of them in sequence. The green light danced across her visor and through it to her face as she smiled encouragement to her son. She betrayed no nervousness; her body and her features were mastered absolutely. It was left to her child to display some anxiety, the upper teeth caressing the lower lip, the eyes darting from mother to those dials visible to him, one hand tugging a trifle at a section of the webbing holding his body to the chair. The machine quivered and, barely audible, it hissed. The sound was unfamiliar. The boy's brows drew closer together. The green light became a faint pink. The machine signalled its perplexity. It had not moved a moment or a centimetre. There was no reason for this; all functions were in perfect operation.

Permitting herself no sign of a reaction, she reset the buttons. The green light returned. She repeated the preliminary code, whereupon the light grew a deeper pink and two blue lamps began to blink. She returned all functions to standby, pulled the harness from her body, rose to her feet and began to make her calculations from the beginning. Her original accuracy was confirmed. She went back to her seat, fastened her webbing, pressed the four buttons in sequence. And for the third time the machine stated its inability to carry out the basic return procedure.

'Is the time machine broken, Mama?'

'Impossible.'

'Then someone is preventing us from leaving.'

'The least welcome but the likeliest suggestion. We were unwise not to bring protection.'

'The baboons do not travel well.'

'It is our misfortune. But we had not expected any life at all at the End of Time.' She fingered her ear. 'We shall have to rule out metaphysical interference.'

'Of course.' He had been brought up to the highest standards. There were some things which were not mentioned, nor, better yet, considered, by the polite society of his day. And Snuffles was an aristocrat of boys.

She consulted the chronometer. 'We shall remain inside the

machine and make regular attempts to return at every hour out of twenty hours. If by then we have failed, we shall consider another plan.'

'You are not frightened, Mama?'

'Mystified, merely.'

Patiently, they settled down to let the first hour pass.

Chapter Two

An Exploratory Expedition

Hand in hand and cautiously they set their feet upon a pathway neither liquid nor adamantine, but apparently of a dense, purple gas which yielded only slightly as they stepped along it, passing between forms which could have been the remains either of buildings or of beasts.

'Oh, Mama!' The eyes of the boy were bright with unusual excitement. 'Shall we find monsters?'

'I doubt if it is life, in any true sense, that we witness here, Snuffles. There is only a moral. A lesson for you – and for myself.'

Streamers of pale red wound themselves around the whispering towers, like pennants about their poles. Gasping, he pointed, but she refused the sight more than a brief glance. 'Sensation, only,' she said. 'The appeal to the infantile imagination is obvious – the part of every adult that should properly be suppressed and which should not be encouraged too much in children.'

Blue winds blew and the buildings bent before them, crouching and changing shape, grumbling as they passed. Clusters of fragments, bloody marble, yellow-veined granite, lilac-coloured slate, frosted limestone, gathered like insects in the air; fires blazed and growled, and then where the pathway forked they saw human figures and stopped, watching.

It was an arrangement of gallants, all extravagant cloaks and jutted scabbards. It stuck legs and elbows at brave angles so the world should know its excellence and its self-contained beauty, so that the collective bow, upon the passing of a lady's carriage, should be accomplished with the precision of effect, swords raised, like so many tails, behind, heads bent low enough for doffed plumes to trail, and be soiled, upon the pavings.

Calling, she approached the group, but it had vanished, background, carriages and all, before she had taken three paces, to be replaced by exotic palms which forever linked and twisted their leaves and leaned one towards the other, as if in a love dance. She hesitated, thinking that she saw beyond the trees a plaza where stood a familiar old man, her father, but it was a statue, and then it was a pillar, then a fountain, and through the rainbow waters she saw three or four faces which she recognised, fellow children, known before her election to adult status, smiling at her, memories of an innocence she sometimes caught herself yearning for; a voice spoke, seemingly into her ear (she felt the breath, surely!): 'The Armatuce shall be Renowned through you, Dafnish…' Turning, clutching her son's hand, she discovered only four stately birds walking on broad, careful feet into a shaft of light which absorbed them. Elsewhere, voices sang in strange, delicate languages, of sadness, love, joy and death. A cry of pain. The tinkling of bells and lightly brushed harp strings. A groan and deep-throated laughter.

'Dreams,' said the boy. 'Like dreams, Mama. It is so wonderful.'

'Treachery,' she murmured. 'We are misled.' But she would not panic.

Once or twice more, in the next few moments, buildings shaped themselves into well-known scenes from her recent past. In the shifting light and the gas it was as if all that had ever existed existed again for a brief while.

She thought: 'If Time has ceased to be, then Space, too, becomes extinct – is all this simply illusion – a memory of a world? Do we walk a void, in reality? We must consider that a likelihood.'

She said to Snuffles: 'We had best return to our ship.'

A choir gave voice in the surrounding air, and the city swayed to the rhythm. A young man sang in a language she knew:

'Ten times thou saw'st the fleet fly by:
The skies illum'd in shining jet
And gold, and lapis lazuli.
How clear above the engines' cry
Thy voice of sweet bewilderment!
(Remember, Nalorna, remember the Night).'

Then, wistfully, the voice of an older woman:

'Could I but know such ecstasy again,
When all those many heroes of the air
Knel't down as one and call'd me fair,
Then I would judge Nalorna more than bless'd!
Immortal Lords immortal, too, made me!
(I am Nalorna, whom the flying godlings loved).'

And she paused to listen, against the nagging foreboding at the back of her brain, while an old man sang:

'Ah, Nalorna, so many that are dead loved thee!
Slain like wingèd game that falls beneath the hunter's shot.
First they rose up, and then with limbs outspread, they drop'd:
Through fiery Day they plung'd, their bodies bright;
Stain'd bloody scarlet in the sun's sweet mourning light.
(But Remember, Nalorna, remember only the Night).'

A little fainter, the young man's voice came again:

'Ten times, Nalorna, did the fleet sweep by!
Ten hands saluted thee, ten mouths
Ten garlands kiss't; ten silent sighs
Sailed down to thee. And then, in pride,
Thou rais'd soft arms and pointed South.
(Oh, Remember, Nalorna, only the Night).'

Telling herself that her interest was analytical, she bent her head to hear more, but though the singing continued, very faintly, the language had changed and was no longer in a tongue she could comprehend.

'Oh, Mama!' Snuffles glanced about him, as if seeking the source of the singing. 'They tell of a great air battle. Is it that which destroyed the folk of this city?'

'*... without which the third level is next to useless...*' said an entirely different voice in a matter-of-fact tone.

Rapidly, she shook her head, to clear it of the foolishness intimidating her habitual self-control. 'I doubt it, Snuffles. If you would seek a conqueror, then Self-Indulgence is the villain who held those last inhabitants in sway. Every sight we see confirms that fact. Oh, and Queen Sentimentality ruled here, too. The song is her testament – there were doubtless thousands of similar examples – books, plays, tapes – entertainments of every sort. The city reeks of uncontrolled emotionalism. What used to be called Art.'

'But we have Art, Mama, at home.'

'Purified – made functional. We have our machinemakers, our builders, our landscapers, our planners, our phrasemakers. Sophisticated and specific, our Art. This – all this – is coarse. Random fancies have been indulged, potential has been wasted...'

'You do not find it in any way attractive?'

'Of course not! My sensibility has long since been mastered. The intellects which left this city as their memorial were corrupt, diseased. Death is implicit in every image you see. As a festering wound will sometimes grow fluorescent, foreshadowing the end, so this city shines. I cannot find putrescence pleasing. By its existence this place denies the point of every effort, every self-sacrifice, every martyrdom of the noble Armatuce in the thousand years of its existence!'

'It is wrong of me, therefore, to like it, eh, Mama?'

'Such things attract the immature mind. Children once made up the only audience a senile old man could expect for his silly ravings, so I've heard. The parallel is obvious, but your response is forgivable. The child who would attain adult status among the Armatuce must learn to cultivate the mature view, however. In all you see today, my son, you will discover a multitude of examples of the aberrations which led mankind so close, so many times, to destruction.'

'They were evil, then, those people?'

'Unquestionably. Self-Indulgence is the enemy of Self-Interest. Do not the School Slogans say so?'

'And "Sentimentality Threatens Survival",' quoted the pious lad, who could recall perfectly every one of the Thousand Standard Maxims and several score of the Six Hundred Essential Slogans for Existence (which every child should know before he could even consider becoming an adult).

'Exactly.' Her pride in her son helped dispel her qualms, which had been increasing as a herd of monstrous stone reptiles lumbered past in single file while the city chanted, in what was evidently a version of her own tongue, something which seemed to be an involved scientific formula in verse form. But she shivered at the city's next remark:

'*... and Dissipation is Desecration and Dishonours All. Self-denial is a Seed which grows in the Sunlight of Purified something or other... Oh, well – I'll remember – I'll remember – just give me time – time... It is not much that a man can save. On the sands of life, in the straits of time, Who swims in sight of the great third wave that never a swimmer shall cross or climb. Some waif washed up with the strays and spars That ebb-tide shows to the shore and the stars; Weed from the water, grass from a grave, A broken blossom, a ruined rhyme... Rapid cooling can produce an effect apparently identical in every respect, and this leads us to assume that, that, that... Ah, yes, He who dies serves, but he who serves shall live for ever... I've got the rest somewhere. Available on Requisition Disc* AAA4. *Please use appropriate dialect when consulting this programme. Translations are available from most centres at reasonable swelgarter am floo-oo chardra werty...*'

'The Maxims, Mother! The city quotes the Maxims!'

'It mocks them, you mean! Come, we had best return to our craft.'

'Is the city mad, Mama?'

With an effort she reduced the rate of her heartbeat and increased the width of her stride, his hand firmly held.

'Perhaps,' he said, 'the city was not like this when Man lived here?'

'I must hope that.'

'Perhaps it pines.'

'The notion is ridiculous,' she said sharply. As she had feared, the place was beginning to have a deteriorating influence upon her son. 'Hurry.'

The hulls of three great ships, one in silver filigree, one in milk-jade, one in woven ebony, suddenly surrounded them, then faltered, then faded.

She considered an idea that she had not passed through time at all, but was being subjected by the Elders of Armatuce to a surprise

Test. She had experienced four such tests since she had become an adult, but none so rigorous, so complex.

She realised that she had lost the road. The purple pathway was nowhere to be seen; there was not a landmark which had retained its form since she had entered the city; the little niggardly sun had not, apparently, changed position, so offered no clue. Panic found a chink in the armour of her self-control and poked a teasing finger through.

She stopped dead. They stood together beside a river of boiling, jigging brown and yellow gas which bounded with what seemed a desperate gaiety towards a far-off pit which roared and howled and gulped it down. There was a slim bridge across this river. She placed a foot upon the first smooth step. The bridge was a coquette; it wriggled and giggled but allowed the pressure to remain. Slowly she and the boy ascended until they were crossing. The bridge made a salacious sound. She flushed, but marched on; she caught a trace of a smile upon her boy's lips. And she shivered for a second time. In silhouette, throbbing crimson, the city swayed, its buildings undulating as if they celebrated some primitive mass. Were the buildings actually creatures, then? If so, did they enjoy her discomfort? Did she and her son represent the sacrifice in some dreadful post-human ritual? Had the last of the city's inhabitants perished, mad, as she might soon be mad? Never before had she been possessed by such over-coloured terrors. If she found them a touch attractive, nothing of her conscious mind would admit it. The bridge was crossed, a meadow entered, of gilded grass, knee-high and harsh; the sounds of the city died away and peace, of sorts, replaced them. It was as if she had passed through a storm. In relief she hesitated, still untrusting but ready to accept any pause in order to recover her morale, and found that her hand was rising and falling upon her son's shoulder, patting it. She stopped. She was about to offer an appropriate word of comfort when she noted the gleam in his eye, the parted lips. He looked up at her through his little visor.

'Isn't this jolly, though, Mama?'

'J –?' Her mouth refused the word.

'What tales we'll have to tell. Who will believe us?'

'We must say nothing, save to the committee,' she warned. 'This is a secret you must bear for the rest of your boyhood, perhaps the rest of your life. And you must make every effort to – to expunge – to dismiss this – this...'

'Twa-la! The time-twavellers, doubtless. Even now Bwannaht seeks you out. Gweetings! Gweetings! Gweetings! Welcome, welcome, welcome to the fwutah!'

Looking to her right she drew in such a sharp gasp of oxygen that the respirator on her chest missed a motion and shivered; she could scarce credit the mincing young fantastico pressing a path for himself with his over-ornamented dandy pole through the grass, brushing at his drooping, elaborate eyebrows, which threatened to blind him, primping his thick, lank locks, patting at his pale, painted cheeks. He regarded her with mild, exaggerated eyes, fingering his pole as he paused.

'Can you undahstand me? I twust the twanslatah is doing its stuff. I'm always twisting the wong wing, y'know. I've seahched evewy one of the thiwty-six points of the compass without a hint of success. You haven't seen them, have you? A couple of lawge hunting buttahflies? So big.' He extended his arms. 'No? Then they've pwobably melted again.' He put index finger to tip of nose. 'They'd be yellah, y'know.'

A collection of little bells at his throat, wrists and knees began to tinkle. He looked suddenly skyward, but he was hopeless.

'Are you real?' asked Snuffles.

'As weal as I'll evah be.'

'And you live in this city?'

'Only ghosts, my deah, live in the cities. I am Sweet Ohb Mace. Cuwwently masculine!' His silks swelled, multicoloured balloons in parody of musculature.

'My name is Dafnish Armatuce. Of the Armatuce,' said she in a strangled tone. 'And this is Snuffles, my son.'

'A child!' The dreadful being's head lifted, like a swan's, and he peered. 'Why, the wohld becomes a kindehgahten! Of couwse, the otheh was actually Mistwess Chwistia. But weah! A gweat pwize foh someone!'

'I do not understand you, sir,' she said.

'Ah, then, it is the twanslatah.' He fingered one of his many rings. 'Shoroloh enafnisoo?'

'I meant that I failed to interpret your meaning,' said Dafnish Armatuce wearily.

Another movement of a ring. 'Is that bettah?'

She inclined her head. She was still less than certain that this was not merely another of the city's phantasms, for all that it addressed them and seemed aware that they had travelled through time, but she decided, nonetheless, to seek the help of Sweet Orb Mace.

'We are lost,' she informed him.

'In Djer?'

'That is the city's name?'

'Oah Shenalowgh, pewhaps. You wish to leave the city, at any wate?'

'If possible.'

'I shall be delighted to help.' Sweet Orb Mace waved his hands, made a further adjustment to a ring, and created something which shone sufficient to blind them for a moment. Of course they recognised the black, spare shape.

'Our time craft!' cried Snuffles.

'My povahty of imagination is wenowned, I feah,' said Sweet Orb Mace blithely. 'It's all I could come up with. Not the owiginal, of couwse, just a wepwoduction. But it will sehve us as an aih cah.'

They entered, all three, to find fantasy within. Gone were the instruments and the muted lights, the padded couches, the simple purity of design, the austere dials and indicators. Instead, caged birds lined the walls, shuffling and twittering, their plumage vulgar beyond imagining; there was a carpet which swamped the legs to the calves, glowing a violent lavender, a score of huge clocks with wagging pendulums, a profusion of brass, gold and dark teak.

Noting her expression, Sweet Orb Mace said humbly: 'I saw only the extewiah. I had hoped the inside would sehve foh the shoht time of ouah flight.'

With a sob, she collapsed into the carpet and sat there with her visor resting upon her gauntlets while Snuffles, insensitive to his mother's mood, waggled youthful fingers and tried to get a macaw to reveal its name to him.

'A mattah of moments!' Sweet Orb Mace assured her. He tapped at the clock with his cane and they were swinging upwards into the sky. 'Do not, I pway you, judge the wohld of the End of Time by yoah impwession of me. I am weckoned the most bohwing being on the planet. Soon you shall meet people much moah intewesting and intelligent than me!'

Chapter Three

A Social Lunch at the End of Time

'LOOK, MAMA! LOOK at the food!' The boy shuddered in his passion. 'Oh, look! Look!'

They descended from the reproduction time machine. They were in a long broad meadow of blue and white grass. The city lay several miles away, upon the horizon.

'An illusion, my dear.' Her voice softened in awe. 'Perhaps your desires project...'

He began to move forward, tugging at her hand, through the patchwork grass, with Sweet Orb Mace, bemused, behind, to where the long table stood alone, spread with dishes, with meats and fruits, pastes and breads. 'Food, Mama! I can almost smell it. Oh, Mama!'

He whimpered.

'Could it be real?' he entreated.

'Real or false, we cannot eat.' No amount of self-control could stem the saliva gathering upon her palate. She had never seen so much food at one time. 'We cannot remove our helmets, Snuffles.' For a second, her visor clouded at her breath. 'Oh...'

In the distance the city danced to a sudden fanfaronade, as if exulting in their wonderment.

'If you wish to begin...' murmured their guide, and he gestured at the food with his cane.

Her next word was moaned: 'Temptation...' It became a synonym, on her lips, for fulfilment. To eat – to eat and be replete for the first time in her life! To sit back from that table and note that there was still more to eat – more food than the whole of the Armatuce, if they ate absolutely nothing of their rations for a month, could save between them. 'Oh, such wickedness of over-production!'

'Mother?' Snuffles indicated the centre of the table.

'A pie.'

They stared. As the voices of the Sirens entranced the ancient Navigators, so were they entranced by flans.

'A vewy simple meal, I thought,' said Sweet Orb Mace, uncomfortable. 'You do not eat so much, in yoah age?'

'We would not,' she replied. 'To consume it, even if we produced it, would be disgusting to us.' Her knees were weak; resistance wavered. Of all the terrors she had anticipated in the future, this was one she could not possibly have visualised, so fearsome was it. She tried to avert her eyes. But she was human. She was only one woman, without the moral strength of the Armatuce to call on. The Armatuce and the world of the Armatuce lay a million or more years in the past. Her will drooped at this knowledge. A tear started.

'You cannot pwoduce it? Some disastah?'

'We could. Now, we could. But we do not. It would be the depths of decadence to do so!' She spoke through clenched teeth.

She and the boy remained transfixed, even when others arrived and spoke in reference to them.

'Time-travellers. Their uniforms proclaim their calling.'

'They could be from space.'

'They are hungry, it seems. Let them eat. You were speaking of your son, maternal Orchid. This other self, what?'

'He lives through her. He tells me that he lives *for* her, Jagged! Where does he borrow these notions? I fear for his – "health", is it?'

'You mean that you disapprove of his behaviour?'

'I suppose so. Jherek "goes too far".'

'I relish the sound of your words, Iron Orchid. I never thought to hear them here.'

'In Djer?'

'In any part of our world. My theories are confirmed. One small change in the accepted manners of a society and the result is hugely rich.'

'I cannot follow you, allusive lord. Neither shall I try… The strangers do not eat! They only stare!'

'The twanslatahs,' cautioned Mace. 'They opahwate even now.'

'I fear our visitors find us rude.'

Dafnish Armatuce felt a soft touch upon her shoulder and turned, almost with relief, from the food to look up into the patrician features of a very tall man, clothed in voluminous lemon-coloured lace which rose to his strong chin and framed his face. The grey eyes were friendly, but she would not respond (daughter to father) as her emotions dictated. She drew away. 'You, too, are real?'

'Ah. Call me so.'

'You are not one of the illusions of that city?'

'I suspect that I am at least as real as Sweet Orb Mace. He convinces you?'

She was mute.

'The city is old,' said the newcomer. 'Its whimsicalities proliferate. Yet, once, it had the finest of minds. During those agitated centuries, when beings rushed willy-nilly about the universe, all manner of visitors came to learn from it. It deserves respect, my dear time-traveller, if anything deserves it. Its memory is uncertain, of course, and it lacks a good sense of its identity, its function, but it continues to serve what remains of our species. Without it, I suspect that we should be extinct.'

'Perhaps you are,' she said quietly.

His shoulders moved in a lazy shrug and he smiled. 'Oh, perhaps, but there is better evidence supporting more entertaining theories.' His companion came closer, a woman. 'This is my friend the Iron Orchid. We await other friends. For lunch and so on. It is our lunch that you are admiring.'

'The food is real, then? So much?'

'You are obsessed with the question. Are you from one of the religious periods?'

She trusted that the child had not heard and continued hastily. 'The profusion.'

'We thought it simple.'

'Mama!' Tugging, Snuffles whispered, 'The lady's hand.'

The Iron Orchid, long-faced with huge brown eyes, hair that might have been silver filigree, peacock quills sprouting from shoulder blades and waist, had one hand of the conventional, five-fingered sort, but the other (which she flourished) was a white-petalled, murmuring goldimar poppy, having at the centre scarlet lips like welts of blood.

'And I am called here Lord Jagged of Canaria,' said the man in yellow.

'Mama!' An urgent hiss. But no, she would not allow the lapse, though it was with difficulty she redirected her own gaze away from the goldimar. 'Your manners, lad,' she said, and then, to the pair, 'This is my boy, Snuffles.'

The Iron Orchid was rapturous. 'A boy! What a shame you could not have arrived earlier. He would have been a playmate for my own son, Jherek.'

'He is not with you?'

'He wanders time. The womb, these days, cannot make claims. He is off about his own affairs and will listen to no-one, his mother least of all!'

'How old is your son?'

'Two hundred – three hundred – years old? Little more. Your own boy?'

'He is but sixty. My name is Dafnish Armatuce. Of the Armatuce. We...'

'And you have travelled through time to lunch with us.' Smiling, the Orchid bent her head towards the child. Stroking him with the hand that was a goldimar, she cooed. He scarcely flinched.

'We cannot lunch.' Dafnish Armatuce was determined to set an example, if only to herself. 'I thank you, however.'

'You are not hungry?'

'We dare not breathe your atmosphere, let alone taste your food. We wish merely to find our machine and depart.'

'If the atmosphere does not suit you, madam,' said Lord Jagged kindly, and with gentleness, 'it can be adapted.'

'And the food, too. The food, too!' eagerly declared the Iron Orchid, adding, *sotto voce*, 'though I thought it reproduced perfectly. You eat such things? In your own age?'

'Such things are eaten, yes.'

'The selection is not to your satisfaction?'

'Not at all.' Dafnish Armatuce permitted her curiosity a little rein. 'But how did you gather so much? How long did it take?'

The Iron Orchid was bewildered by the question. 'Gather? How long? It was made a few moments before we arrived.'

'Wustically wavishing!' carolled Sweet Orb Mace. 'A wondahfully wipping wuwal wepast!' He giggled.

'Two or three other time-travellers join us soon,' explained Lord Jagged. 'The choice of feast is primarily to please them.'

'Others?'

'They are inclined to accumulate here, you know, at the End of Time. From what age have you come?'

'The year was 1922.'

'Aha. Then Ming will be ideal.' He hesitated, looking deep into her face. 'You do not find us – sinister?'

'I had not expected to encounter people at all.' The perfection of his manners threw her into confusion. She was bent on defying his charm, yet the concern in his tone, the acuteness of his understanding, threatened to melt resolve. These characteristics were in conflict with the childish decadence of his costume, the corrupt grotesquerie of his surroundings, the idle insouciance of his conversation; she could not judge him, she could not sum him up. 'I had expected, at most, sterility...'

He had detected the tension in her. Another touch, upon her arm, and some of that tension dissipated. But she recovered her determination almost at once. Her own hand took her son's. How could such a creature of obvious caprice impress her so strongly of his respect both for her and for himself?

Watching them without curiosity, the Iron Orchid plucked up a plum and bit into it, the fruit and her lips a perfect match. Droplets of juice fell upon the gleaming grass, and clung.

Her eyes lifted; she smiled. 'This must be the first entrant.'

In the sky circled four gauzy rainbow shapes, dipping and banking.

'Mine weah the fiwst,' said Sweet Orb Mace, aggrieved, 'but they escaped. Or melted.'

'We play flying conceits today,' explained Lord Jagged. 'Aha, it is undoubtably Doctor Volospion. See, he has erected his pavilion.'

The large, be-flagged tent had not been on the far side of the field a moment ago, Dafnish Armatuce was sure; she would have marked its gaudy red, white and purple stripes.

'The entertainment begins.' Lord Jagged drew her attention to the table. 'Will you not trust us, Dafnish Armatuce? You cannot die at the End of Time, or at least cannot remain dead for very long. Try the atmosphere. You can always return to your armour.' He took a backward pace.

Good manners dictated her actions, she knew. But did he seduce her? Again Snuffles eagerly made to remove his helmet, but she restrained him, for she must be the first to take the risk. She raised hesitant hands. A sidelong glance at the dancing city, distant and, she thought, expectant, and then a decision. She twisted.

A gasp as air mingled with air, and she was breathing spice, her balance at risk. Three breaths and she was convinced; from the table drifted the aroma of pie, of apricots and avocados; she failed to restrain a sob, and tingling melancholy swept from toe to tight brown curl. Such profound feeling she had experienced only once before, at the birth of her Snuffles. The lad was even now wrenching his own helmet free – even as he was drawn towards the feast.

She cried 'Caution!' and stretched a hand, but he had seized a fowl and sunk soft, juvenile teeth into the breast. How could she refuse him? Perhaps this would be the only time in his life when he would know the luxury of abundance, and he must become an adult soon enough. She relented for him, but not for herself, yet even her indulgence of the child went hard against instinct.

Chewing, Snuffles presented her with a shining face, a greasy mouth, and eyes containing fires which had no business burning in one of his years. Feral, were they?

The Orchid trilled (artificial in all things, so thought Dafnish Armatuce): 'Children! Their appetites!' (Or was it irony Dafnish Armatuce detected? She dismissed any idea of challenge, placing her hands on her boy's shoulders, restraining her own lust): 'Food is scarce in Armatuce just now.'

'For how long?' Casually polite, the Iron Orchid raised a brow.

'The current shortage has lasted for about a century.'

'You have found no means of ending the shortage?'

'Oh, we have the means. But there is the moral question. Is it *good* for us to end the shortage?'

For a second there came a faint expression of puzzlement upon the Iron Orchid's face, and then, with a polite wave of an ortolan leg, she turned away.

'"Fatness is Faithlessness",' quoted Dafnish Armatuce. '"The Lean Alone Learn".' She realised then that these maxims were meaningless to them, but the zeal which touched the missionary touched her, and she continued: 'In Armatuce we believe that it is better to have less than to have enough, for those who have enough always feel the need for too much, whereas we only quell the yearning for sufficient, do you see?' She explained: '"Greed Kills". "Self-indulgence is Suicide". We stay hungry so that we shall never be tempted to eat more than we need and thus risk, again, the death of the planet. "Austerity is Equilibrium".'

'Your world recovers from disaster, then?' said Lord Jagged sympathetically.

'It has recovered, sir.' She was firm. 'Thanks to the ancestors of the Armatuce. Now the Armatuce holds what they achieved in trust. "Stable is He Who Stoic Shall Be".'

'You fear that without this morality you would reproduce the disaster?'

'We know it,' she said.

'Yet –' he spread his hands – 'you find a world still here when you did not expect it and no evidence that your philosophy has survived.'

She scarcely heard the words, but she recognised the sly, pernicious tone. She squared her shoulders. 'We would return now, if you please. The boy has eaten.'

'You will have nothing?'

'Will you show me to my ship?'

'Your ship will not work.'

'What? You refuse to let me leave?'

As succinctly as possible, Lord Jagged explained the Morphail Effect, concluding, 'Therefore you can never really return to your own age and, if you left this one, might well be killed or at very least stranded in a less congenial era.'

'You think I lack courage? That I would not take the risk?'

He pursed his lips and let his gaze fall upon the gorging boy. She followed his meaning and put two fingers softly upon her cheek.

'Eat now,' said the tall lord with a tender gesture.

Absently, she touched a morsel of mutton to her tongue.

A shadow moved across the field, cast by a beast, porcine and grey, which with lumbering grace performed a somersault or two in the sky. Overhead there were now several more objects and creatures pirouetting, diving, spiralling – a small red biplane, a monstrous mosquito, a winged black-and-white cat, a pale green stingray – while below the owners of these entrants jostled, laughed and talked: a motley of races (some earthly beasts, others extraterrestrial; but mostly humanoid), clothed and decorated in all manner of fanciful array. On the edges of the blue-and-white field there had sprouted marquees, flagpoles, lines of bunting, crowded together and waving boisterously, so that she could no longer see beyond their confines. She let the mutton melt, took one plum and consumed it, drank an inch of water from a goblet, and her meal was done, though the effort of will involved in resisting a leaf of lettuce only by a fraction succeeded in balancing the guilt experienced at having allowed herself to eat the second half of the fruit. Meanwhile Snuffles's jaws continued to move with dedicated precision.

Several large, fiery wheels went by, a score of feet above her head, drowning with their hissing the loud babble of the crowd.

'Cwumbs!' exclaimed Sweet Orb Mace, with a knowing wink at her, as if they shared a secret. 'Goah Blimey!'

The words were meaningless, but he appeared to be under the impression that she would understand them.

Deliberately, she guided her glance elsewhere. Everyone was applauding.

'Chariots of Fire!' bellowed a deep, proprietorial voice. 'Chariots of Fire! Number Seventy-Eight!'

'We shan't forget, dear Duke of Queens,' sang a lady whose gilded skin clashed sickeningly with her green mouth and glowing, emerald eyes.

'My Lady Charlotina of Below-the-Lake,' murmured Lord Jagged. 'Would you like to meet her?'

'Can she be of help to me? Can she give me practical advice?' The rhetoric rang false, even in her own ears.

'She is the patron of Brannart Morphail, our greatest, maddest scientist, who knows more about the nature of time than anyone else in history, so he tells us. He will probably want to interview you shortly.'

'Why should one of your folk require a patron?' she asked with genuine interest.

'We seek traditions wherever we can find them. We are glad to get them. They help us order our lives, I suppose. Doubtless Brannart dug his tradition up from some ancient tape and took a fancy to it. Of late, because of the enthusiasm of the Iron Orchid's son, Jherek, we have all become *obsessed* with morality...'

'I see little evidence of that.'

'We are still having difficulty defining what it is,' he told her. 'My Lady Charlotina – our latest time-travellers – Mother and Son – Dafnish and Snuffles Armatuce.'

'How charming. How unusual. Tell me, delightful Dafnish, are you claimed yet?'

'Claimed?' Dafnish Armatuce looked back at the departing Jagged.

'We vie with one another to be hosts to new arrivals,' he called. His wave was a little on the airy side. 'You are "claimed", however, as my guests. I will see you anon.'

'Greedy Jagged! Does he restock his menagerie?' My Lady Charlotina of Below-the-Lake stroked her crochet snood as her eyes swept up from Dafnish's toes and locked with Dafnish's eyes for a moment. 'Your figure? Is it your own, my dear?'

'I fail to understand you.'

'Then it is! Ha, ha!' Mood changed, My Lady Charlotina made a curtsey. 'I will find you some friends. My talent, they say, is as a Catalyst!'

'You are modest, cherubic Charlotina! You have all the talents in the catalogue!' In doublet and hose reminiscent of pre-cataclysm decadence, extravagantly swollen, catachrestically slashed and galooned, bearing buttons the size of cabbages, the shoes with toes a yard or two long and curled to the knees, the cap peaked to jut more than a foot from the face, beruffed and bedecked with thin brass chains, a big-buckled belt somewhere below the waist so as, in whole, to make Sweet Orb Mace seem mother naked, a youth bent a calculated leg before continuing with his catechism of compliment. 'Let me cast myself beneath the cataract of your thousand major virtues, your myriad minor qualities, O mistress of my soul, for though I am considered clever, I am nought but your lowliest catechumen, seeking only to absorb the smallest scraps of your wisdom so that I may, for one so small, be whole!' Whereupon he flung himself to the grass on velvet knees and raised powdered, imploring hands.

'Good afternoon, Doctor Volospion.' She relished the flattery, but paused no longer, saying over her shoulder, 'You smell very well today.'

Unconcerned, Doctor Volospion raised himself to his feet, his cap undulating, his chains jingling, and his rouged lips curved in a friendly smile as he saw Dafnish Armatuce.

'I seek a lover,' he explained, peeling a blade of blue grass from his inner thigh. 'A woman to whom I can give my All. It is late in the season to begin, perhaps, with so many exquisite Romances already under way or even completed (as in Werther's case), but I am having difficulty in finding a suitable recipient.' His expression, as he stared at her, became speculative. 'May I ask your sex, at present?'

'I am a woman, sir, and a mother. An Armatuce, mate to a cousin of the Armatuce, sworn to suffer and to serve together until my son shall be ready to suffer and to serve in my place.'

'You would not like to link your fate with mine, to give yourself body and soul to me until the End of Time (which, of course, is not far off, I hear)?'

'I would not.'

'I came late to the fashion, you see, and now most are already bored with it, I understand. But there is, surely, the fulfilment of abandonment. Is it not delicious to throw oneself upon another's mercy – to make him or her the absolute master of one's fate?' He took a step closer, peering into her immobile countenance, his eye sparkling. 'Ah! Do I tempt you? I see that I do!'

'You do not!'

'Your tone lacks conviction.'

'You are deceived, Doctor Volospion.'

'Could we have our bodies so engineered as to produce another child?'

'My operation is past. I have my child. No more can bloom.'

She turned to search for Snuffles, fearing suddenly for the safety of his person as well as for his mind, for she was now aware that this folk had no scruples, no decency, no proper inhibitions even where that most sacrosanct of subjects was concerned. 'Snuffles!'

'Here, Mama!'

The boy was in conversation with a tall, thin individual wearing a crenellated crown as tall as himself.

'To me!'

He came reluctantly, waddling, snatching a piece of pastry from the table as he passed, wheezing, his little protective suit bearing a patina of creams and gravies, his hair sticky with confectionery, his face rich with the traces of his feast.

Someone had begun to build cloud-shapes, interweaving colours and kinds and creating the most unlikely configurations. She seized his sweetened hand, tempted to remonstrate, to read him a lesson, to forbid further food, but she knew the dangers of identifying her own demands upon herself with what she expected from her son. Too often, she had learned, had ancient parents forbidden their children food merely because they could not or would not eat themselves, forbidden children childish pleasures because those pleasures tempted them, too. She would not transfer. Let the boy, at least, enjoy the experience. His training would save him, should they ever return. A lesson would be learned. And if they did not return, well, it would not profit him to retain habits which put him at odds with the expectations of society. And should it seem inevitable that they were permanently marooned, she could decide when he would be mature enough to become an adult, grant him that status herself and so put an end to her own misery.

The crowd seemed to close in on her. Doctor Volospion had already wandered away, but there were others – every one of whom was a living, mocking parody of all she held to be admirable in Man. Her heart beat faster, at last unchecked. She sought for the only being in that whole unnatural, fatuous farrago who might help her escape, but Lord Jagged was gone.

And My Lady Charlotina broke through the throng, Death's Harlequin, grinning and triumphant, drawing another woman with her. 'A contemporary, dear Dafnish. Mutual reminiscence is now possible!'

'I must go…' began the time-traveller. 'Snuffles wearies. We can sleep in our ship.'

'No, no! The air fête is hardly begun. You shall stay and converse with Miss Ming.'

Miss Ming, at first bored, brightened, giving Dafnish Armatuce a quick glance which was at once questioning and appraising, warm and calculating. Miss Ming was a heavily built young woman whose long fair hair had been carefully brushed but had acquired no more of a lustre than her pale, unwholesome skin. She wore, for this age, a simple costume, tight dungarees of glowing orange and a shirt and short jacket of pale blue. Now Dafnish Armatuce had her whole attention, was granted Miss Ming's smile of knowing and insincere sympathy.

'Your year?' My Lady Charlotina creased her golden forehead. 'You said…'

'1922.'

'Miss Ming is from 2067. Until recently she lived at Doctor Volospion's menagerie. One of the few human survivors, in fact.'

Miss Ming's abrupt, monotonous voice might have seemed surly had it not been for the eagerness with which she imparted meaningless (to Dafnish Armatuce) confidences, coming closer than was necessary and placing intimate fingers upon her shoulder to say: 'Some of Mongrove's diseases escaped and struck down half the inhabitants of Doctor Volospion's menagerie. By the time the discovery was made, resurrection was out of the question. Mongrove refuses to apologise. Doctor Volospion shuns him. I didn't know time travel was discovered in 1922. And,' a girlish pout, 'they told me that I was the first woman to go into time.'

Surely, Dafnish thought, she sensed aggression here.

'An all-woman team launched the craft.' Miss Ming spoke significantly. 'I was the first.'

And Dafnish Armatuce, her boy hard alongside, chanted at this threat: 'Time travel, Miss Ming, is the creation and the copyright of the Armatuce. We built the first backward-shifting ships two years ago, in 1920. This year, in 1922, I was chosen to go forward.'

Miss Ming pursed lips which became thin and downturned at the corners, giving her a slight leonine look, but she did not seek conflict. 'Can we both be deluded? I am an historian, after all! I cannot be wrong. Aha! Illumination. AD?'

'I regret…'

'From what event does your calendar run?'

'From the First Birth.'

'Of Christ?'

'Of a child, following the catastrophe in which all became barren. A method was discovered whereby –'

'There you have the answer! We are not even from the same millennium. Nonetheless,' Miss Ming linked an arm through hers before she could react, and held it tight, 'it needn't stop friendship. How delicate you are. How exquisite. Almost,' insinuatingly, 'a child yourself.'

Dafnish pulled free. 'Snuffles.' She began to dab at his face with her wetted glove. The little boy turned resigned eyes upward and watched the circling machines and beasts. The crowd sighed and swayed, and they were jostled.

'You are married?' implacably continued Miss Ming. 'In your own age?'

'To a cousin of the Armatuce, yes.' Dafnish's manner became more distant as she tried to move on, but Miss Ming's warm hand slipped again into the crook of her elbow. The fingers pressed into her flesh. She was chilled.

Three white bats swooped by, performing acrobatics in unison, their twenty-foot wings making the air hiss. A trumpet sounded. There was applause.

'I was divorced, before my journey.' Miss Ming paused, perhaps in the hope of some morbid revelation from her new friend, then continued, girl to girl: 'His name was Donny Stevens. He was well thought of as a scientist – a popular and powerful family, too – very old – in Iowa. Rich. But he was like all men. You know. They think they're doing you a favour if they can get to your cubicle once a month, and if it's once a week, they're Casanova! No thanks!

Someone said – Betty Stern, I think – that he had that quality of aggressive stupidity which so many women find attractive in a man: they think it's strength of character and, once they've committed themselves to that judgement, maintain it against all the evidence. Betty said dozens of the happiest marriages are based on it. (I idolised Betty.) Unfortunately, I realised my mistake. If I hadn't, I wouldn't be here, though. I joined an all-woman team – know what I mean? – anyway we got the first big breakthrough and made those dogs look sick when they saw what the bitches could do. And this age suits me now. Anything goes, if you know what I mean – I mean, really! Wow! What kind of guys do you like, honey?'

She did not want Miss Ming's attentions. Again she cast about for Jagged and, as a rent appeared for a second in the ranks, saw him talking to a small, serious-faced yellow man, clad in discreet denim (the first sensible costume she had observed thus far). Hampered both by reluctant, sleepy son and clinging Ming, she pushed her way through posturing gallants and sparkling frillocks, to home slowly on Jagged who saw her and smiled, bending to murmur a word or two to his companion. Then, as she closed: 'Li Pao, this is Dafnish Armatuce of the Armatuce. Dafnish, I introduce Li Pao from the 27th century.'

'She won't know what you're talking about!' crowed the unshakeable Miss Ming. 'Her dates go from something she calls the First Birth. 1922. I was baffled myself.'

Lord Jagged's eyes became hooded.

Li Pao bowed a neat bow. 'I gather you find this age disturbing, Comrade Armatuce?'

Her expression confirmed his assumption.

Li Pao's small mouth moved with soft, sardonic deliberation. 'I, too, found it so, upon arrival. But there is little need to feel afraid, for, as you will discover, the rich are never malevolent, unless their security is threatened, and here there is no such threat. If they seem to waste their days, do not judge them too harshly; they know no better. They are without hungers or frustrations. Nature has long since been conquered by Art. Their resources are limitless, for they feed upon the whole universe (what remains of it). These cities suck power from any available part of the galaxy and transfer it to them so that they may play. Stars die so that on old Earth someone might change the colour of his robe.' There was irony in his tone, but he spoke without censure.

Snuffles cried out as something vast and metallic appeared to drop upon the throng, but it stopped a few feet up, hovered, then drifted away, and the crowd became noisy again.

'The First Birth period?' Lord Jagged made a calculation. 'That would place you in the year 9478 AD. We find the Dawn Age reckoning most convenient here. I understand your dismay. You are reconstituting your entire planet, are you not? From the core, virtually, outward, eh?'

She was grateful for his erudition. Now he and Li Pao seemed allies in this fearful world. She was able to steady her heart and recover something of her self-possession. 'It has been hard work, Lord Jagged. The Armatuce have been fortunate in winning respect for their several sacrifices.'

'Sacrifice!' Li Pao was nostalgic. 'A joy impossible to experience here, where the gift of the self to the common cause would go unremarked. They would not know.'

'Then they are, indeed, unfortunate,' she said. 'There is a price they pay for their pleasure, after all.'

'You find our conceits shallow, then?' Lord Jagged wished to know.

'I do. I grieve. Everywhere is waste and decay – the last stages of the Romantic disease whose symptoms are a wild, mindless seeking after superficial sensation for its own sake, effect piled upon effect, until mind and body disintegrate completely, whose cure is nothing else but death. Here, all is display – your fantasies appear the harmless play of children, but they disguise the emptiness of your lives. You colour corpses and think yourselves creative. But I am not deceived.'

'Well,' he replied equably enough, 'visions vary. To one who cannot conceive of such things, another's terrors and appetites, his day-to-day phantasms, are, indeed, poor conceits, intended merely to display their possessor's originality and to dismay his fellows. But some of us have our joys, even our profundities, you know, and we cherish them.'

She felt a little shame. She had offended him, perhaps, with her candour. She lowered her eyes.

'Yet,' continued Jagged, 'to one of us (one who bothers to contemplate such things at all, and there are few) your way of life might seem singularly dull, denying your humanity. He could claim that you are without any sort of real passion, that you deliberately close your consciousness to the glowing images which thrive on every side, thus making yourself less than half alive. He might not realise that you, or this dour fellow Li Pao here, have other excitements. Li Pao celebrates Logic! A clearly stated formula is, for him, exquisite delight. He feels the same frisson from his theorems that I might feel for a well-turned aphorism. I am fulfilled if I give pleasure with a paradox, while he would seek fulfilment if he could order a silly world, build, comfort, complete a pattern and fix it, to banish the very Chaos he has never tasted but which is our familiar environment, and precious to us as air, or as water to the fish. For to us it is not Chaos. It is Life, varied, stimulating, rich with vast dangers and tremendous consolations. Our world sings and shimmers. Its light can blind with a thousand shapes and colours. Its darkness is always populated, never still, until death's own darkness swoops and obliterates all. We inhabit one sphere, but that sphere contains as many worlds as there are individuals on its surface. Are we shallow because we refuse to hold a single point of view?'

Li Pao was appreciative of the argument, but something puzzled him. 'You speak, Lord Jagged, as you sometimes do, as one from an earlier age than this, for few here think in such terms, though they might speak as you did if they bothered to consider their position at all.'

'Oh, well. I have travelled a little, you know.'

'Are there none here,' asked Dafnish Armatuce, 'who have the will to work, to serve others?'

Lord Jagged laughed. 'We seek to serve our fellows with our wit, our entertainments. But some would serve in what you would call practical ways.' He paused, serious for a second, as if his thoughts had become a little private. He drew breath, continuing: 'Werther de Goethe, perhaps, might have had such a will, had he lived in a different age. Li Pao's, for instance. Where another sees dreams and beauty, Li Pao sees only disorder. If he could, or dared, he would make our rotting cities stable, clarify and formalise the architecture, populate his tidy buildings with workers, honest and humane, to whom Peace of Mind is a chance of worthy promotion and the prospect of an adequate pension, to whom Adventure is a visit to the sea or a thunderstorm during a picnic – and Passion is Comfort's equal, Prosperity's cohort. But shall I judge his vision dull? No! It is not to him, or to those who think as he, in his own age, in your own age, Dafnish Armatuce.' Lord Jagged teased at his fine nose. 'We are all what our society makes of us.'

'When in Rome…' murmured Miss Ming piously. Something flapped by and received a cheer.

Jagged was impatient with Miss Ming. 'Indeed.' His cloak billowed in a wind of his own subtle summons, and he looked kindly down on Dafnish Armatuce. 'Explore all attitudes, my dear. Honour them, every one, but be slippery – never let them hold you, else you fail to enjoy the benefits and be saddled only with the liabilities. It's true that canvas against the skin can be as sensual as silk, and milk a sweeter drink than wine, but feel everything, taste everything, for its own sake, and for your own sake, then no one thing shall be judged better or worse than another, no person shall be so judged, and nothing can ensnare you!'

'Your advice is well-meant, sir, I know,' said Dafnish Armatuce, 'and would probably be good advice if I intended to stay in your world. But I do not.'

'You have no choice,' said Miss Ming with satisfaction.

He shrugged. 'I have told you of the Morphail Effect.'

'There are other means of escape.'

Miss Ming, by her superior smirk, felt she had found a flaw in Lord Jagged's argument. 'Cancer?' she demanded. 'Could we love cancer?'

He rose to it willingly enough, replying lightly: 'You are obscure, Miss Ming, for there is no physical disease at the End of Time. But, yes, we could – for what it taught us – the comparisons it offered. Perhaps that is why some of our number seek discomfort – in order to comfort their souls.'

Miss Ming simpered. 'You argue cunningly, Lord Jagged, but I suspect your logic.'

'Is it so dignified, my conversation, as to be termed Logic? I am flattered.' One hand pressed gently against Dafnish Armatuce's back and the other against Li Pao's, rescuing them both. Miss Ming hesitated and then retreated at last.

Eight dragons waltzed the skies above while faraway music played; the crowd grew quieter as it watched, and even Dafnish Armatuce admitted, to herself, that it was a delicate beauty they witnessed.

She sighed. 'So this is Utopia, Lord Jagged, for you? You are satisfied?'

'Could I expect more? Many think the days of our universe numbered. Yet, do you find concern amongst us?'

'You sport to forget the inevitable?'

He shook his head. 'We sported thus before we knew. We have not changed our lives at all, most of us.'

'You must sense tension. You cannot live so mindlessly.'

'I do not think we live as you describe. Do you not strive, in your age, for a world without fear?'

'Of course.'

'There is no fear here, Dafnish Armatuce, even of total extinction.'

'Which suggests you are far divorced from reality. You speak of the atrophy of natural instinct.'

'I suppose that I do. There are few such instincts to be found among those who are native to the End of Time. You have no philosophers among your own folk who argue that those natural instincts might be the cause of the tragedy once described, I believe, as the Human Condition?'

'Of course. It is part of our creed. But we ensure that the tragedy shall never be played again, for we encourage the virtues of self-sacrifice and consideration of the common good, and we discourage the vices.'

'Which suggests that they continue to exist. Here, they do not; there is no necessity for either vice or virtue.'

'Yet if Hate dies, surely Love dies, too?'

'I think it has been rediscovered, lately. Love.'

'A fad. I spoke with your Doctor Volospion. An affectation,

JCAWTHORN74

nothing more.' She gasped and shut her eyes, for two great suns had appeared, side by side, glaring scarlet, and drenched the gathering with their light.

Almost at once the suns began to grow smaller, rising away from the Earth. She blinked and recovered her composure, though weariness threatened her thoughts. 'And Love of the sort you describe is no Love at all, for its attendants are Jealousy and Despair, and in Despair lies the most destructive quality of all, Cynicism.'

'You think us cynical, then?'

She looked about her at the chattering press. One of their number, tall, bulky and bearded, festooned in feathers and furs, was being congratulated for what doubtless had been his display. 'I thought so at first.'

'And now?'

She changed the subject. 'I have the impression, Lord Jagged, that you are trying to make this world palatable to me. What if I agree that there is something to be said for your way of life and turn the conversation to a problem rather closer to my heart? My husband, cousin to the Armatuce, and a Grinash on his mother's side, cares for me, as he cares for Snuffles, our son, and eagerly awaits our return, as does the committee which I serve (and which elected me to accomplish my voyage). I would go back to that age, which you would find grim, no doubt, but which is home, familiar, security for us. You tell me that I cannot, so I must consider my position accordingly. Could I not send a message, at least, or return for a second to assure them of my physical safety?'

'You speak of caring for the common cause,' interrupted Li Pao. 'If you do, you will not make the attempt, for time disrupts. Morphail warns us. And you risk death. If you tried to go back you might succeed, but you would in all probability flicker for only a moment, unseen, before being flung out again. The time stream would suck you up and deposit you anywhere in your future, in any one of a million less pleasant ages than this, or you could be killed outright (which has happened more than once). The Laws of Time are cruel.'

'I would risk any danger,' she said, 'were it not for –'

'– the child,' softly said Lord Jagged.

'We are used to sacrifice, the Armatuce. But our children are precious. We exist for them.'

Darkness fell and ivory clashed and rattled above her as a great ship, made all of bone, its sections strung loosely together, its wings beating erratically, staggered upon a sea of faintly glowing clouds.

'What a splendid ending,' she heard Lord Jagged say.

Chapter Four

An Apology and an Explanation from Your Auditor

YOUR AUDITOR, FOR the most part a mere ear, a humble recorder of that which he is privileged to hear, apologises if he interrupts the reader's flow with a few words of his own, but it is his aim to speed the narrative on by condensing somewhat the events immediately following Dafnish Armatuce's introduction to the society at the End of Time.

Her reaction was a familiar one (familiar to you who have followed this compilation of legends, gossip, rumours and accredited reminiscence thus far) and to detail it further would risk repetition. Suffice: she was convinced of the Morphail Effect. Time had thrown her (as a shipwrecked English tar of old might have been thrown on the shores of the Caliph's Land) upon the mercies of an alien and self-satisfied culture which considered her an amusing prize. Her protestations? They were not serious. Her warnings? Irrelevant fancies. And her sensitivities? Meaningless to those who luxuriated in the inherited riches of an entire race's history; to whom Grief was a charming affectation and Anxiety an archaic word whose meaning had been lost. They were pleased to listen to her in so far as she remained entertaining, but even as their enthusiasms waxed and waned, mayfly swift, so did their favours shift from visitor to visitor.

Ah, if they had known how cruel they were, how they might have explored the sensation – but they were feline, phantasmagorical, and, like careless cats, they played with the poor creatures they trapped until one of them wearied of the game, for even those denizens at the End of Time who claimed to have known pain knew only the play-actor's pain, that grandiose anguish which, at its most profound, resolves itself as hurt pride.

Dafnish Armatuce knew great pain – though she herself would not admit it – particularly where her maternal instincts were involved. Children, like all else, were scarce in Armatuce, and she had worked for half her life to be permitted one. Now her ambition was that her boy be elected to adult status among the Armatuce and take her place so that she might, at last, rest from service, content and proud. For sixty years, since Snuffles's birth, she had looked forward to the day when he would be chosen (she had been certain that he would be) and had known that his voyage through time would have been a guarantee of early promotion. But here she was, stranded, thwarted of all she had striven for, unable and unwilling to give service to a community which had no needs; thus it is no wonder that she pined and schemed alternately while she remained a guest of Lord Jagged of Canaria, and fought to retain the standards of the Armatuce against every temptation.

However, though she remained rigorously self-disciplined, she indulged the boy, refusing to impose upon him the demands she made of herself. She allowed him a certain amount of decoration in his clothing; she let him eat, within reason, what he wished to eat. And she took him on journeys to see this world, so similar, in much of its topography, to the deserts of their own. Ruined it might be, wasted and tortured, covered with the half-finished abandoned projects of its feckless inhabitants, but it was beautiful, too.

And it was on these trips that she could find a certain peace she had never known before. While Snuffles climbed the remains of mountains, crying out in delight whenever he made a discovery, she would sit upon a rock and stare at the pale, faded sky, the eroded landscape through which dust and the wind sang with quiet melancholy, and she would think the world new and herself its first inhabitant, perhaps its only inhabitant. As an Armatuce, in Armatuce, she had never once spent a full hour alone, and here, at the End of Time, she realised that it was what she had always wanted, that perhaps this was why she had looked forward so much to her commission, that she had secretly hoped for the cold peace of a lifeless planet. Then she would turn brooding eyes upon her son, as he scrambled, ran or climbed, and she would consider her duty and her love and wonder if she had, after all, been prepared to risk his life, as well as her own, in this quest for loneliness. Such thoughts would throw her into a further crisis of conscience and make her more than ever determined to ensure that he should not suffer as a result of her desires.

But if there was a Devil in this dying Eden, then it came in the shape of Miss Ming, who sought out Dafnish Armatuce wherever she went. Lord Jagged was gone from his cage-shaped castle, either to work in his hidden laboratories or else embarked upon a journey. Dafnish did not know, and with him had gone his protection. Miss Ming found excuse after excuse for visiting her, each one increasingly unlikely. And there was no solitude which Miss Ming might not interrupt, in whatever obscure corner of the globe Dafnish flew her little air boat (a gift of Lord Jagged). Miss Ming had observations on every aspect of life; she had gossip concerning every individual in the world; she made criticism of all she met or saw, from Doctor Volospion's new manikin to the shade of the sky hanging over the Ottawa monuments; but in particular Miss Ming had advice for Dafnish Armatuce, on the care of her skin, her clothes, the upbringing of children (she had had none of her own), her diet, her choice of scenery and of residence.

'I wish,' Miss Ming would say, 'only to help, dear, for you're bound to have difficulty getting used to a world like this. We expatriates must stick together. If we don't, we're in trouble. Don't let it get to you. Don't mope. Don't get morbid.'

And if Dafnish Armatuce would make an excuse, suggesting that Snuffles must be put to bed, perhaps, Miss Ming would exclaim. 'There! You'll do harm to the boy. You must let him grow up, stand on his own feet. You're afraid of experience – you're using him to protect yourself from what this world can offer. While he remains a child, he gives you an excuse to turn away from your own responsibilities as an adult. You're too possessive, Dafnish! Is it doing any good to either of you? He's got to develop his personality, and so have you.'

At last, Dafnish Armatuce turned on the intolerable Ming. She would ask her, direct, to leave. She would say that she found Miss Ming's company unwelcome. She would ask Miss Ming never to return, but Miss Ming knew how to respond to this.

'Menstrual tension,' she would say, sympathetically, undeterred by Dafnish Armatuce's reiteration of the fact that she had never experienced the menstrual cycle. 'You're not yourself today.' Or she would smile a sickly smile and suggest that Dafnish Armatuce get a better night's rest, that she would call tomorrow, in the hope of finding her in an improved mood. Or: 'Something's worrying you about the boy. Let him have his head. Lead your own life.' Or: 'You're frustrated, dear. You need a friend like me, who understands. A woman knows what a woman needs.' And a clammy, white, red-tipped hand would fall upon Dafnish's knee, like a hungry spider.

That Miss Ming wanted her for a lover, Dafnish Armatuce understood quite early, but love-making, even between man and woman, was discouraged in Armatuce; it was thought vulgar, and some would have it that the old sexual drive had been another central cause of the disaster which had nearly succeeded in destroying the whole race. The new methods of creating children, originally developed from necessity, were seen to contain virtues previously unconsidered. Besides, there was plainly no Armatuce blood in Miss Ming, and there was a strong taboo about forming liaisons beyond the clan.

Thus, no matter how lonely she might sometimes feel, Dafnish Armatuce remained unswervingly contemptuous of Miss Ming's advances, which would sometimes bring the accusation from that poor, smitten, unlovely woman that Dafnish Armatuce was 'playing hard to get' and shouldn't 'toy with someone's affections the way you do'.

Scarcely for a day did Miss Ming lift her siege. She tried to dress like Dafnish Armatuce, or impress her with her own coarse taste. She would appear in fanciful frocks or stern tweed; several times she arrived stark naked, and once she had her body engineered so that it was a near-copy of Dafnish's own.

Even Miss Ming's determinedly self-centred consciousness must have understood that the look on Dafnish Armatuce's face, when she witnessed the travesty of her own form, was an expression of revulsion, for the invader did not stay long in that guise.

Harried, horrified and exasperated by Miss Ming's obsessive suit, Dafnish Armatuce began to accept invitations to the various functions arranged by those who were this world's social leaders, for if she could not find peace of mind in the great, silent spaces, then at least she might find some comfort in surrounding herself by a wall of noise, of empty conversation or useless display. To these balls, fêtes and exhibitions she sometimes took her Snuffles, but on other occasions she would trust his security to the sophisticated mechanical servants Lord Jagged had placed at her disposal. Here she would often encounter Miss Ming, but here, at least, there was often someone to rescue her – the Iron Orchid or Sweet Orb Mace or, more rarely and much more welcome, Li Pao. Dafnish Armatuce resented Miss Ming mightily, but since this world placed no premium on privacy, there was no other way to avoid her – and Dafnish resented Miss Ming for that, too: for forcing her into a society with which she had no sympathy, for which she often felt active disgust, and which she suspected might be corrupting the values she was determined to maintain against a day when, in spite of constant confirmation of the impossibility, she might return to Armatuce.

Moreover, it must be said, since she made no effort to adapt herself to the world at the End of Time, she often felt an unwelcome loneliness at the gatherings, for the others found her conversation limited, her descriptions of Armatuce dull, her observations without much wit and her sobriety scarcely worth playing upon; she made a poor topic. Her boy was more attractive, for he was a better novelty; but she baulked any effort of theirs to draw him out, to pet him, to (in their terms) improve him. As a result both would find themselves generally ignored (save by the ubiquitous Ming). There was not even food for malicious gossip in her – she was too likeable. She was intelligent and she understood what made her unacceptable to them, that the fault (if fault it were) lay in her, but the treatment she received hardened her, laid her prey to that most destructive of all the demons which threaten the tender, vulnerable human psyche, the Demon of Cynicism. She resisted him, for her son's sake, if not her own, but the struggle was exhausting and took up her time increasingly. Like us all, she desired approval, but, like rather fewer of us, she refused to seek it by relinquishing her own standards. Her son, she knew, had yet to learn this pride, for it was of a kind unattractive in a child, a kind that can only be earned, not imitated. So she did not show active disapproval if he occasionally warmed to some paradox-quoting, clown-costumed fop, or repeated a vulgar rhyme he had overheard, or even criticised her for her dour appearance.

How could she know, then, that all these efforts of hers to maintain a balance between dignity and tolerance would have such tragic results for them both, that her nobility, her fine pride, would be the very instruments of their mutual ruin?

Not that disaster is inherent in these qualities; it required another factor to achieve it, and that factor took the form of the despairing, miserable Miss Ming, a creature without ideals, self-knowledge or common sense (which might well be mutually encouraging characteristics), a creature of Lust which called itself Love and Greed masquerading as Concern, and one who was, incidentally, somewhat typical of her era. But now we race too fast to our Conclusion. Your auditor stands back, once again no more than an observing listener, and allows the narrative to carry you on.

Chapter Five
In Which Snuffles Finds a Playmate

THE DUKE OF Queens, in cloth-of-gold bulked and hung about with lace; pearls in his full black beard, complicated boots upon his large feet, a natural, guttering flambeau in his hand, led his party through his new caverns ('Underground' was the current fad, following the recent discovery of a lost nursery-warren, there since the time of the Tyrant Producers) bellowing cheerfully as he pointed out little grottoes, his stalagmites ('Prison-children in the ancient Grautt tongues – a pretty, if unsuitable, name!'), his scuttling troglodytes, his murky rivers full of white reptiles and colourless fish, while flame made shadows which changed shape as the fluttering wind changed and strange echoes distorted their speech.

'They must stretch for miles!' hissed Miss Ming, hesitant between Dafnish and Snuffles and the host she admired. 'Aren't they altogether gloomier than Bishop Castle's, eerier than Guru Guru's?'

'They seem very similar to me,' coldly said Dafnish Armatuce, looking hungrily about her for a branching tunnel down which, with luck, she might escape for a short while.

'Oh, you judge without seeing properly. You close your eyes, as always, to the experience.'

Dafnish Armatuce wondered, momentarily, how much of her self-esteem she might have to relinquish to purchase the good will of a potential ally, someone willing to rescue her from her remorseless leech, but she dismissed the notion, knowing herself incapable of paying the price.

'Snuffles is enjoying himself – aren't you, dear?' said Miss Ming pointedly.

Snuffles nodded.

'You think they're the best you've seen, don't you?'

Again, he nodded.

'A child's eye!' She became mystical. 'They take for granted what we have to train ourselves to look at. Oh, how I *wish* I was a little girl again!'

Sweet Orb Mace, in loose, navy-blue draperies, waved his torch expansively as he recognised Dafnish Armatuce and her son. His accent had changed completely since their last meeting and he had dropped his lisp. 'Good afternoon, time-travellers. The twists and turns of these tunnels, are they not tremendously tantalising? Such a tangle of intricate transits!' The caverns echoed his alliterative 't's so as to seem filled with the ticking of a thousand tiny clocks. A bow; he offered her his arm. Desperate, she took it, uncaring, just then, that Snuffles remained behind with Miss Ming. She needed a respite, for both their sakes. 'And how do you find the grottoes?' he enquired.

'Grotesque,' she said.

'Aha!' He brightened. 'You see! You learn! Shall we ogle the gorgeous gulfs together?'

She failed to take his meaning. He paused, waiting for her response. None came. His sigh was politely stifled. The passage widened and became higher. There was a murmur of compliment, but the Duke of Queens silenced it with a modest hand.

'This is a discovery, not an invention. I came upon it while I worked. You'll note it's limestone, and natural limestone was thought extinct.'

Their fingers went to the smooth, damp rock and it received a reverential stroke.

Sometimes in silhouette, sometimes gleaming and dramatic in the flamelight, the Duke of Queens indicated rock formations which must have lain here since before the Dawn Age: ghastly, smooth, rounded, almost organic in appearance, the limestone dripped with moisture, exuding a musty smell which reminded Dafnish Armatuce, and only Dafnish Armatuce, of a mouldering cadaver, as if this was all that remained of the original Earth, rotting and forgotten. It began to occur to her that it would be long before they were able to leave the caverns; the walls seemed, suddenly, to exert a pressure of their own, and she experienced something of the panic she had felt before, when the crowd had become too dense. She clung to Sweet Orb Mace, who would rather have gone on. She knew that she bored him, but she must have some reassurance, some sort of anchor. The party moved: she felt that it pushed her where she did not want to go. She had a strong desire to turn back, to seek the place where they had entered the maze; she did a half-turn, but was confronted by the grinning face of Miss Ming so she allowed herself to be carried forward.

Sweet Orb Mace had made an effort to resume the conversation, on different lines. '... would not believe how jealous Brannart Morphail was. But he shall not have it. I was the first to discover it – and you – and while he is welcome to make a reproduction, I shall hold the original. There are few like it.'

'Like it?'

'Your time machine.'

'You have it?'

'I have always had it. It's in my collection.'

'I assumed it lost or destroyed. When I went back to seek it, it had gone, and no-one knew where.'

'I must admit to a certain deception, for I knew how desperately Brannart would want it for himself. I hid it. But now it is the pride of my collection and on display.'

'The machine is the property of the Armatuce,' she said gently. 'By rights it should be in my care.'

'But you have no further use for it, surely!'

She did not possess sufficient strength for argument. She allowed him his assumption. From behind her there came an unexpected giggle. She dared to look. Miss Ming was bent low, showing Snuffles a fragment of rock she had picked up. Snuffles beamed and shook with laughter as Miss Ming indicated features in the piece of rock.

'Isn't it the image of Doctor Volospion?'

Snuffles saw that his mother watched. 'Look, Mama! Doctor Volospion to the life!'

She failed to note the resemblance. The rock was oddly shaped, certainly, and she supposed that it might, if held at an angle, roughly resemble a human face.

'I hadn't realised Doctor Volospion was so old!' giggled Ming, and Snuffles exploded with laughter.

'Can't you see it, Mama?'

Her face softened; she smiled, not at the joke (for there was none, in her view), but in response to his innocent joy. Miss Ming's sense of humour was evidently completely compatible with her son's: the unbearable woman had succeeded in making the boy happy, perhaps for the first time since their arrival. All at once Dafnish Armatuce felt grateful to Miss Ming. The woman had some virtue if she could make a child laugh so thoroughly, so boisterously.

The caverns took up the sound of the laughter so that it grew first louder, then softer, until finally it faded in some deep and far-off gallery.

Now Miss Ming was dancing with the boy, singing some sort of nonsense song, also concerning Doctor Volospion. And Snuffles chuckled and gasped and all but wept with delight, and whispered jokes which made Miss Ming, in turn, scream with laughter. 'Ooh! You *naughty* boy!' She noticed that Mother observed them. 'Your son – he's sharper than you think, Dafnish!'

Infected, Dafnish Armatuce found that she smiled still more. She realised that hers was not only a smile of maternal pleasure but a smile of relief. She felt free of Ming. Having transferred her attentions to the boy, the woman acquired an altogether pleasanter personality. Perhaps because she was so immature Miss Ming was one of those who only relaxed in the company of children. Whatever the cause of this change, Dafnish Armatuce was profoundly grateful for it. She, too, relaxed.

Stronger light lay ahead as the cavern grew wider. Now they all stood in a vast chamber whose curved roof was a canopy of milky green jade through which sunlight (filtered, delicate, subtly coloured) fell, illuminating rock-carved chairs and benches of the subtlest marble and richest obsidian, while luminous moss and ivy mingled on the walls and floor, revealing little clusters of pale blue and yellow primroses.

'What a *perfect* spot for a fairy feast!' cried Miss Ming, hand in hand with Snuffles. 'We can have fun here, can't we, Prince Snuffles?' Her heavy body was almost graceful as she danced, her green and purple petticoats frothing over sparkling, diamanté stockings. 'I'm the Elf Queen. Ask me what you wish and it shall be granted.'

Buoyed by her exuberance, Snuffles was beside himself with glee. Dafnish Armatuce stood back with a deep sigh, quietly revelling in the sight of her son's flushed, jolly cheeks, his darting eyes. It had concerned her that Snuffles had no children with whom he could play. Now he had found someone. If only Miss Ming had earlier discovered her affinity – what was evidently her real affinity – with Snuffles, how much better it might have been for everyone, thought Dafnish.

Her attention was drawn to Doctor Volospion. In a costume of, for him, unusual simplicity (black and silver) he capered upon one of the tables with the leopard-spotted woman called Mistress Christia, while the rest of the guests, the Duke of Queens amongst them, clapped in time to the music of the jig Doctor Volospion played upon some archaic stringed instrument tucked under his goateed chin.

Unusually light-hearted, Dafnish Armatuce was tempted to join them, but she checked the impulse, tolerantly enough, contenting herself with her silent pleasure at the sight of Snuffles and Miss Ming who, even now, were climbing upon the table. Soon all but Dafnish were dancing.

Chapter Six
In Which Dafnish Armatuce Enjoys a Little Freedom

HAVING PERMITTED HER boy a generous frolic with his new-found friend, Dafnish Armatuce expressed genuine thanks to Miss Ming for devoting so much of her time to the lad's pleasure.

As flushed and happy as Snuffles, looking almost as attractive, Miss Ming declared: 'Nonsense! It was Snuffles who entertained me. He made me feel young again.' She hugged him. 'Thank you for a lovely day, Snuffles.'

'Shall I see you tomorrow, Miss Ming?'

'That's up to Mama.'

'I had planned a visit to the Uranian Remains…' began Dafnish. 'However, I suppose –'

'Why don't you visit your dull old Remains on your own and let Snuffles and me go out to play together.' Miss Ming became embarrassing again as she made a little-girl face and curtseyed. 'If you please, Mrs Armatuce.'

'He'll exhaust you, surely.'

'Not at all. He makes me feel properly, fully alive.'

Dafnish Armatuce tried to disguise the slightly condescending note which crept into her voice, for it now became poignantly plain that the poor creature had never really wanted to grow up at all. Understanding this, Dafnish could allow herself to be kind. 'Perhaps for an hour or two, then.'

'Wonderful! Would you like that, Snuffles?'

'Oh, yes! Thank you, Miss Ming!'

'You are doing him good, Miss Ming, I think.'

'He's doing *me* good, Dafnish. And it will give *you* a chance to be by yourself and relax for a bit, eh?' Her tone of criticism, of false concern, did not offend Dafnish as much as usual. She inclined her head.

'That's settled, then. I'll pick you up tomorrow, Snuffles. And I'll be thinking of some jolly games we can play, eh?'

'Oh, yes!'

They strolled across the undulating turf to where the air cars waited. Most of the other guests had already gone. Dafnish Armatuce helped her son into their car, which was fashioned in the shape of a huge apple-half, red and green, and, astonished that the woman had made no attempt to return with them to Canaria, bade Miss Ming a friendly farewell.

Snuffles leaned from the car as it rose into the pink and amber sky, waving to Miss Ming until she was out of sight.

'You are happy, Snuffles?' asked Dafnish as he settled himself into his cushions.

'I never had a nicer day, Mama. It's funny, isn't it, but I used not to like Miss Ming at all, when she kept hanging around us. I thought she wanted to be your friend, but really she wanted to be mine. Do you think that's so?'

'It seems to be true. I'm glad you enjoyed today, and you shall play with Miss Ming often. But I beg you to remember, my boy, that you are an Armatuce: One day you must become an adult and take my place, and serve.'

His laughter was frankly astonished. 'Oh, Mama! You don't really think we'll ever go back to Armatuce, do you? It's impossible. Anyway, it's nicer here. There's a lot more to do. It's more exciting. And there's plenty to eat.'

'I have always seen the attraction this world holds for a boy, Snuffles. However, when you are mature you will recognise it for what it is. I have your good at heart. Your moral development is my responsibility (though I grant you your right to enjoy the delights of childhood while you may), but I feel that you are forgetting...'

'I shan't forget, Mama.' He dismissed her fears. They were passing over the tops of some blue-black clouds shot through with strands of gleaming grey. He studied them. 'Don't you think Miss Ming a marvellous lady, though?'

'She has an affinity with children, obviously. I should not have suspected that side to her character. I have modified my opinion of her.'

Dafnish did not let Snuffles see her frown as she contemplated her motives in allowing him freedom that would be sheer licence in Armatuce. Events must take their own course, for a while; then she might determine how good or bad were the effects of Miss Ming's company upon her son.

The mesa, red sandstone and tall, on which stood golden, cage-shaped Castle Canaria, came into view; the air car lost height, speeding a few feet above the waving, yellow corn which grew here the year round, aiming for the dark entrance at the base of the cliff.

'You must try to remember, Snuffles,' she added, while the car took its old place in the row of oddly assorted companions (none of which Lord Jagged ever seemed to use), 'that Miss Ming regrets becoming an adult. That she wishes she was still, like you, a child. You may find, therefore, a tendency in her to try to make you suppress your maturer thoughts. In my company, I feel, you thought too much as an adult – but in hers you may come to think too much as a child. Do you follow me?'

But Snuffles, played out, had fallen asleep. Tenderly she raised him in her arms and began to walk (she refused to fly) up the ramp towards the main part of the castle.

Through rooms hung in draperies of different shades of soft brown or yellow, through the great Hall of Antiquities, she carried her child, until she came to her own apartments, where mechanical servants received the boy, changed his clothes for night attire and put him to bed. She sat on a chair beside him, watching the servants move gently about the room, and she tenderly stroked his fair curls, so, save for colour, like her own (as was his face), and yearned a trifle for Armatuce and home. It was as she rose to go to her chamber, adjoining his, that she saw a figure standing in the entrance. She knew a second's alarm, then laughed. 'Lord Jagged. You are back!'

He bowed. There was a weariness in his face she had never noted before.

'Was your journey hard?'

'It had its interests. The fabric of time, those Laws we have always regarded as immutable…' He hesitated, perhaps realising that he spoke to himself.

He was dressed in clothes of a pearly grey colour, of stiffer material than he usually preferred. She felt that they suited him better, were more in keeping with the temperament she detected behind the insouciant exterior. Did he stagger as he walked? She put out a hand to help, but he did not notice it.

'You have been travelling in time? How can that be?'

'Those of us who are indigenous to the End of Time are more fortunate than most. Chronos tolerates us, perhaps because we have no preconceptions of what the past should be. No, I am weary. It is an easier matter to go back to a chosen point from one's own era. If one goes forward, one can never go all the way back. Oh, I babble. I should not be speaking at all. I would tempt you.'

'Tempt me?'

'To try to return. The dangers are the same, but the checks against those dangers are less rigid. I'll say no more. Forgive me. I will *not* say more.'

She walked beside him, past her own rooms, down the brown-and-yellow corridor, eager for further information. But he was silent and determined to remain so. At his door he paused, leaning with one hand against the lintel, head bowed. 'Forgive me,' he said again. 'I wish you good night.'

She could not in all humanity detain him, no matter how great her curiosity. But the morning would come: here, at Canaria, the morning would come, for Lord Jagged chose to regulate his hours according to the age-old movements of the Earth and the Sun, and when it did she would demand her right to know if there was any possibility of return to Armatuce.

Thus it was that she slept scarcely at all that night and rose early, with the first vermilion flush of dawn, to note that Snuffles still slept soundly, to hover close by Jagged's door in the hope that he would rise early – though the evidence of last night denied this hope, she knew. Robot servants prowled past her, preparing the great house for the morning, ignoring her as she paced impatiently to the breakfast room with its wide windows and its views of fields, hills and trees, so like a world that had existed before Cataclysm, before Armatuce, and which none of her folk would ever have expected to see again. In most things Lord Jagged's tastes harked to the planet's youth.

The morning grew late. Snuffles appeared, hungry for the Dawn Age food the robots produced at his command, and proceeded to eat the equivalent of an Armatuce's monthly provisions. She had to restrain her impulse to stop him, to warn him that he must look forward to changing his habits, that his holiday could well be over. Dawn Age *kipper* followed antique *kedgeree*, to be succeeded by *sausages* and *cheese*, the whole washed down with primitive *tea*. She felt unusually hungry, but the time for her daily meal was still hours away. Still Jagged did not come, although she knew it was ever his custom, when at Canaria, to breakfast each morning (he had always eaten solid food, even before the fashion for it). She returned to the passage, saw that his door was open, dared to glance in, saw no-one.

'Where is Master?' she enquired of an entering servant.

The machine hesitated. 'Lord Jagged has returned to his work, my lady. To his laboratories. His engines.'

'And where are they?'

'I do not know.'

So Jagged was gone again. Elusive Jagged had disappeared, bearing with him the knowledge which could mean escape to Armatuce.

She found that she was clenching her hands in the folds of the white smock she wore. She relaxed her fingers, took possession of her emotions. Very well, she would wait. And, in the meantime, she had her new freedom.

Dafnish Armatuce returned to the breakfast room and saw that Miss Ming had arrived and was arranging sausages and broccoli on a plate to make some sort of caricature. Snuffles, mouth stuffed, spluttered. Miss Ming snorted through her nose.

'Good morning, good morning!' she trilled as she saw Dafnish. For an instant she stared at bare shoulders and nightdress with her old, heated expression, but it was swiftly banished. 'We're going swimming today, my boyfriend and me!'

'You'll be careful.' She touched her son's cheek. She was warmed by his warmth; she was happy.

'What can happen to him here?' Miss Ming smiled. 'Don't worry. I'll look after him – and he'll look after me – won't you, my little man?'

Snuffles grinned. 'Fear not, princess, you are safe with me.'

She clasped her hands together, piping, 'Oh, sir, you are so *strong*!'

Dafnish Armatuce shook her head, more amused than disturbed

by her antics. She found herself thinking of Miss Ming as a child, rather than as an adult; she could no longer condemn her.

They left in the apple-shaped air car, flying south towards the sea. Dafnish watched until they were out of sight before she returned to her apartments. As she changed her clothes she listened obsessively for a hint of Lord Jagged's return. She was tempted to remain at Canaria and wait for him, to beg him to aid her find Armatuce again, if only for a moment, so that she might warn others of their danger and show those nearest to her that she lived. But she resisted the impulse; it would be foolish to waste perhaps the only opportunity she had to seek the silent and remote places and be alone.

Walking down to where the air cars lay, she reflected upon the irony of her situation. Without apparent subtlety Miss Ming had first denied her the freedom she was now granting. Dafnish was impressed by the woman's power. But she lacked the inclination to brood on the matter at this time; instead, she relished her freedom.

She climbed into a boat shaped like a swooping, sand-coloured sphinx. Miss Ming and Snuffles had gone south. She spoke to the boat, a single word: 'North.'

And northward it took her, over the sentient, senile cities, the dusty plains, the ground-down mountains, the decaying forests, the ruins and the crumbling follies, to settle in a green valley through which a silver river ran and whose flanks were spotted with hawthorn and rowan and where a few beasts (what if they were mechanical?) grazed on grass which crunched as they pulled it from the soft earth, the sound all but drowned by the splashing of small waterfalls, sighing as the river made its winding way to a miniature and secluded lake at the far end of the valley.

Here she lay with her back against the turf, spreadeagled and displayed to the grey sky through which the sun's rays weakly filtered. And she sang one of the simple hymns of the Armatuce she had learned as a child and which she thought forgotten by her. And then, unobserved, she allowed herself to weep.

Chapter Seven
In Which a Man Is Made

LORD JAGGED REMAINED away from Canaria for many days, but Dafnish Armatuce was patient. Every morning Miss Ming, punctual in arriving, would take Snuffles on some new jaunt, and she was careful to return at the agreed hour, when a joyful boy would be reunited with a mother who was perhaps not so unrelaxed as she had once been; then Miss Ming, with the air of one who has performed a pleasant duty, would retire, leaving them to spend the remainder of the afternoon together. If Dafnish Armatuce thought she detected an unwelcome change in her son's attitude to certain values she held dear, she told herself that this was unreasonable fear, that she would be harming the boy's development if she interfered too much with his ideas. She hardly listened to his words as he described his latest escapades with his friend, but the animation in his voice was music and the sparkle in his eye was sweet to see, and experience, she told herself, would teach him reverence.

She returned to her private valley time after time, glad that whoever had created it had forgotten it or had, for some reason, omitted to dissimilate it. Here, and only here, could she show the whole Dafnish Armatuce to the world, for here there was none to judge her, to quiz her as to why she spoke or sang, laughed or wept. Her favourite maxims she told to trees; her secret fears were confided to flocks of sheep; and stones were audience to her hopes or dreams. Long for Armatuce she might, but she did not despair.

Her confidence repaired, she was able to visit those she chose, and most frequently she visited Sweet Orb Mace, who welcomed her, observing to his friends that she was much improved, that she had learned to accept what life at the End of Time could offer. A few fellow time-travellers, also noticing this improvement, guessed that she had found a lover and that her lover was none other than haughty Lord Jagged. As a consequence she was often questioned as to her host's whereabouts (for there was always such speculation where Lord Jagged was concerned). But, while she was not aware of the rumours, she kept her own counsel and added no flax to Dame Gossip's wheel. She courted Sweet Orb Mace (another, but less heavily backed contender for the title of Lover) for the simple reason that he possessed her time machine. He allowed her to inspect it, to linger in its cabin when she wished. She reassured him: she could not attempt to use it, her concern for Snuffles's well-being overriding any desire she might have to return to Armatuce. But, privately, she hoped; and should it be foolish to hope against all evidence, then Dafnish Armatuce was foolish.

If she had not found happiness, she had found a certain contentment, during the month which passed, and this gave her greater tolerance for herself, as well as for their society. Two more time-travellers arrived in that month, and, perhaps unluckier than she, were snapped up, one for Doctor Volospion's menagerie, which he was patiently restocking, one for My Lady Charlotina's great collection. Dafnish spoke to both, and both agreed that they had little difficulty reaching the Future but that the Past (meaning their own period) had been denied them. She refused to be depressed by the information, consoling herself with the prospect of Jagged's help.

This equilibrium might have been maintained for many more such months had not Miss Ming betrayed (in Dafnish's terms) her trust.

It happened that Dafnish Armatuce, returning from visiting Brannart Morphail, the scientist (a visit cut short by the old misanthrope himself), passed in her air car over an area of parkland still occupied by the remnants of small Gothic palaces and towns which had been constructed, during a recent fad for miniatures, by the Duke of Queens. And there she observed two figures, which she recognised as those of Snuffles and Miss Ming, doubtless playing one of their fanciful games. Noting that it was almost time for Miss Ming to bring Snuffles home, Dafnish decided that she would save Miss Ming the trouble and collect him there and then. So the sphinx-car sank to earth at her command and she crossed a flower-strewn lawn to bend and enter the dim interior of the little chateau into which she had seen them go as she landed.

Having no wish to take them by surprise, she called out, but came upon them almost immediately, to discover Miss Ming dabbing hastily at Snuffles's face. In the poor light it was difficult to see why she dabbed, but Dafnish assumed that the lad had, as usual, been eating some confection of which she might have disapproved.

She chuckled. 'Oh, dear. What have you two been up to while my back was turned?' (This whimsicality more for Miss Ming's sake than her son's). She reached out her hand to the boy, whose guilty glance at Miss Ming seemed more imploring than was necessary, and led him into the sunlight.

She quelled the distaste she felt for the long red robes of velvet and lace in which Miss Ming had clothed him (Miss Ming herself wore tights and doublet) but could not resist a light: 'What would they make of you in Armatuce?' and wondered why he kept his face from her.

Turning to Miss Ming, who had a peculiar expression upon her own features, she began, 'I'll take him –' And then her voice died as she saw the smeared rouge, the mascara, the eye shadow, the paint with which Miss Ming had turned the child's face into a parody of a female adult's.

Shocked, she trembled, unable to speak, staring at Miss Ming in accusation and horror.

Miss Ming tried to laugh. 'We were playing Princes and Princesses. There was no harm meant…'

The boy began to protest. 'Mama, it was only a game.'

All she could do was gasp, 'Too far. Too far,' as she dragged him to the air car. She pushed him roughly in, climbed in herself and stood confronting the ridiculous woman. She tensed herself to reduce the shaking in her body and she drew a deep breath. 'Miss Ming,' she said carefully, 'you need not call tomorrow.'

'I hardly think,' said Miss Ming. 'I mean, I feel you're over-reacting, aren't you? What's wrong with a little fantasy?'

'This,' indicating the cosmetics on the frightened face, 'is not what children do!'

'Of course they do. They love to dress up and play at being big people.'

'I thought, Miss Ming, you played at children. You are a corrupt, foolish woman. I concede that you are unaware of your folly, but I cannot have my child influenced any longer by it. I admit my own stupidity, also. I have been lazy. I allowed myself to believe that your nonsense could do Snuffles no harm.'

'Harm? You're overstating...'

'I am not. I saw you. I saw the guilt. And I saw guilt on my boy's face. There was never guilt there before, in all the years of his life.'

'I've nothing to be ashamed of!' protested Miss Ming as the air car rose over her head. 'You're reacting like some frustrated old maid. What's the matter, isn't Lord Jagged –?' The rest faded and they were on course again for Canaria.

Metal servants gently bathed the boy as soon as they arrived. Slowly the cosmetics disappeared from his skin, and Dafnish Armatuce looked at him with new eyes. She saw a pale boy, a boy who had become too fat; she saw lines of self-indulgence in his face; she detected signs of greed and arrogance in his defiant gaze. Had all this been put there by Miss Ming? No, she could not blame the silly woman. The fault was her own. Careful not to impose upon him the strictures which she imposed upon herself, she had allowed him to indulge appetites which, perhaps, she secretly wished to indulge. In the name of Love and Tolerance she, not Ming, had betrayed Trust.

'I have been unfair,' she murmured as the robots wrapped him in towels. 'I have not done my duty to you, Snuffles.'

'You'll let me play with Miss Ming tomorrow, Mama?'

She strove to see in him that virtue she had always cherished, but it was gone. Had it gone from her, too?

'No,' she said quietly.

The boy became savage. 'Mama! You must! She's my only friend!'

'She is no friend.'

'She loves me. You do not!'

'You are that part of myself I am allowed to love,' she said. 'That is the way of the Armatuce. But perhaps you speak truth, perhaps I do not really love anything.' She sighed and lowered her head. She had, she thought, become too used to crying. Now the tears threatened when they had no right to come.

He wheedled. 'Then you will let me play with Miss Ming?'

'I must restore your character,' she said firmly. 'Miss Ming is banished.'

'No!'

'My duty –'

'Your duty is to yourself, not to me. Let me go free!'

'You *are* myself. The only way in which I could give you freedom is to let you come to adult status…'

'Then do so. Give me my life-right.'

'I cannot. It serves the Armatuce. The race. We have to go back. At least we must try.'

'You go. Leave me.'

'That is impossible. If I were to perish, you would have no means of sustenance. Without me, you would die!'

'You are selfish, Mama! We can never go back to Armatuce.'

'Oh, Snuffles! Do you feel nothing for that part of you which is your mother?'

He shrugged. 'Why don't you let me play with Miss Ming?'

'Because she will turn you into a copy of her fatuous, silly self.'

'And you would rather I was a copy of a prude like you. Miss Ming is right. You should find yourself a friend and forget me. If I am doomed to remain a child, then at least let me spend my days with whom I choose!'

'You will sleep now, Snuffles. If you wish to continue this debate, we shall do so in the morning.'

He sulked, but the argument, the effort of thinking in this way, had tired him. He allowed the robots to lead him off.

Dafnish Armatuce was also tired. Already she was debating the wisdom of allowing herself to react as she had done. No good was served by insulting the self-justifying Miss Ming; the boy lacked real understanding of the principles involved. She had been guilty of uncontrolled behaviour. She had failed, after all, to maintain her determination, her ideals. In Armatuce there would be no question of her next decision, she would have applied for adult status for her son and, if it had been granted, so settled the matter. But here…

And was she justified in judging Miss Ming a worse influence than herself? Perhaps Miss Ming, in this world, prepared Snuffles for survival? But she could not support such an essentially cynical view. Miss Ming was disliked by all, renowned for her stupidity. Lord Jagged would make a better mentor; Sweet Orb Mace, indeed, would make a better mentor than Miss Ming.

All the old confusion swam back into her mind, and she regretted bitterly her misguided tolerance in allowing Miss Ming to influence the boy. But still she felt no conviction; she wondered whether self-interest, loneliness – even jealousy – had dictated her actions. Never before had she known such turmoil of conscience.

That night the sleep of Dafnish Armatuce was again disturbed and there were dreams, vague, prophetic and terrible, from which she woke into a reality scarcely less frightening. Before dawn she fell asleep again, dreaming of her husband and her co-workers in Armatuce. Did they condemn her? It seemed so.

She became aware, as she slept, that there was pressure on her legs. She tried to move them, but something blocked them. She opened her eyes, sought the obstruction, and saw that Miss Ming sat there. She was prim today. She wore black and blue; muted, apologetic colours. Her eyes were downcast. She twisted at a cuff.

'I came to apologise,' said Miss Ming.

'There is no need.' Her head ached; the muscles in her back were knotted. She rubbed her face. 'It was my fault, not yours.'

'I was carried away. It was so delightful, you see, for me. As a girl I had no chums.'

'I understand. But,' more gently, 'you still intrude, Miss Ming.'

'I know you, too, must be very lonely. Perhaps you resent the fact that your son has a friend in me. I don't mean to be rude, but I've thought it over lots. I feel I should speak out. You shouldn't be unkind to Snuffles.'

'I have been. I shall not be in future.'

Miss Ming frowned. 'I thought of a way to help. It would give you more freedom to live your own life. And I'm sure Snuffles would be pleased...'

'I know what to do, Miss Ming.'

'You wouldn't punish him! Surely!'

'There is no such thing as punishment in Armatuce. But I must strengthen his character.'

A tear gleamed. Miss Ming let it fall. 'It's all my fault. But we were good friends, Dafnish, just as you and I could be good friends, if you'd only...'

'I need no friends. I have Armatuce.'

'You need me!' The woman lurched forward, making a clumsy attempt to embrace her. 'You need me!'

The wail was pathetic and Dafnish Armatuce was moved to pity as she pushed Miss Ming by her shoulders until she had resumed her original position on the bed. 'I do not, Miss Ming.'

'The boy stands between us. If only you'd let him grow up normally!'

'Is that what you were trying to achieve?'

'No! We were both misguided. I sought to please *you*, don't you see? You're so proud, such an egotist. And this is what I get. Oh, yes, I was a fool.'

'The customs of the Armatuce are such,' said Dafnish evenly, 'that special procedures must be taken before a child is allowed adult status. There is no waste in Armatuce.'

'But this is *not* Armatuce.' Miss Ming was sobbing violently. 'You could be happy here, with me, if you'd only let me love you. I don't ask much. I don't expect love in return, not yet. But, in time...'

'The thought is revolting to me!'

'You suppress your normal emotions, that's all!'

She said gently: 'I am an Armatuce. That means much to me. I should be obliged, Miss Ming, if...'

'I'm going!' The woman rose, dabbing at her eyes. 'I could help. Doctor Volospion would help us both. I could...'

'Please, Miss Ming.'

Miss Ming looked up imploringly. 'Could I see Snuffles? One last time?'

Dafnish relented. 'To say goodbye to the child? Yes. Perhaps you could help me –'

'Anything!'

'Tell him to remember his destiny. The destiny of an Armatuce.'

'Will he understand?'

'I hope so.'

'I'll help. I *want* to help.'

'Thank you.'

Miss Ming walked unsteadily from the room. Dafnish Armatuce heard her footsteps in the corridor, heard her enter Snuffles's chamber, heard the child's exclamation of pleasure. She drew a deep breath and let it leave her slowly. With considerable effort she got up, washed and dressed, judging, now, that Miss Ming had had a fair allotment of time with the boy.

As she entered the brown-and-yellow hall, she glanced across to Lord Jagged's door. It was open. She hesitated, and as she did so, Lord Jagged appeared, looking less tired than he had before, but more thoughtful.

'Lord Jagged!'

'Aha, the admirable Dafnish!' His smile was soft, almost melancholy. 'Do you enjoy your stay at Canaria? Is all to your liking?'

'It is perfect, Lord Jagged, but I would go home.'

'You cannot. Are you still unconvinced?'

'When we last met – that night – you said something concerning the fabric of time. The Laws, hitherto regarded as immutable, were not operating as expected?'

'I was weary. I should not have spoken.'

'But you did. Therefore can I not request a fuller explanation?'

'I would raise hope where none should be permitted.'

'Can I not judge?'

He shrugged, his high, grey collar almost swallowing the lower half of his face. His slim hands fingered his lower lip. 'Very well, but I must ask secrecy from you.'

'You have it. I am an Armatuce.'

'There is little I can tell you, save this: Of late the sturdy, relentless structure of time, which has always, so far as we know, obeyed certain grim laws of its own, has begun to show instabilities. Men *have* returned to the past and remained there for much longer periods than was thought possible. By contravening the Laws of Time, they have further weakened them. There are disruptions – distortions – anomalies. I hope to discover the true cause, but every passage through time threatens the fabric further, producing paradoxes which, previously, time refused to allow. So far no major disaster has occurred – history remains history – but there is a danger that history itself will be distorted and then – well, we all might suddenly vanish as if we had never been!'

'Is that possible? I have listened to such speculation, but it has always seemed pointless.'

'Who knows if it is possible? But can we take the risk? If, say, you were to return to Armatuce and tell them what the future held, would that not alter the future? You are familiar with these arguments, of course.'

'Of course. But I would tell them nothing of your world. It would be too disturbing.'

'And your boy? Children are not so discreet.'

'He is an Armatuce. He would be silent.'

'No, no. You risk your lives by moving against the current.'

'Our lives are for Armatuce. They serve no purpose here.'

'That is a difficult philosophy for one such as I to comprehend.'

'Let me try!'

'Your boy would go with you?'

'Of course. He would have to.'

'You'd subject him to the same dangers?'

'Here, his soul is endangered. Soon he will be incapable of giving service. His life will be worthless.'

'It is a harsh, materialist assessment of worth, surely?'

'It is the way of the Armatuce.'

'Besides, there is the question of a time vessel.'

'My own is ready. I have access to it.'

'There are only certain opportunities, when the structure wavers...'

'I should wait for one. In the machine.'

'Could you not leave the child, at any rate?'

'He would not be able to exist without me. I grant his life-right. He is part of me.'

'Maternal instincts...'

'More than that!'

'If you say so.' He shook his head. 'It is not my nature to influence another's decisions, in the normal course of things. Besides, no two consciences are alike, particularly when divorced by a million or two years.' He shook his head. 'The fabric is already unstable.'

'Let me take my son and leave! Now! Now!'

'You fear something more than the strangeness of our world.' He looked shrewdly into her face, 'What is it that you fear, Dafnish Armatuce?'

'I do not know. Myself? Miss Ming? It cannot be. I do not know, Lord Jagged.'

'Miss Ming? What harm could that woman do but bore you to distraction? Miss Ming?'

'She – she has been paying court to me. And, in a way, to my child. In my mind she has become the greatest threat upon the face of this planet. It is monstrous of me to permit such notions to flourish, but I do. And because she inspires them, I hate her. And because I hate her, why, I detect something in myself which must resemble her. And if I resemble her, how can I judge her? I, Dafnish Armatuce of the Armatuce, must be at fault.'

'This is complicated reasoning. Perhaps too complicated for sanity.'

'Oh, yes, Lord Jagged, I could be mad. I have considered the possibility. It's a likely one. But mad by whose standards? If I can go back to Armatuce, let Armatuce judge me. It is what I rely upon.'

'I'll agree to debate this further,' he said. 'You are in great pain, are you not, Dafnish Armatuce?'

'In moral agony. I admit it.'

He licked his upper lip, deliberating. 'So strange, to us. I had looked forward to conversations with you.'

'You should have stayed here, then, at Canaria.'

'I would have liked that, but there are certain very pressing matters, you know. Some of us serve, Dafnish Armatuce, in our individual ways, to the best of our poor abilities.' His quiet laughter was self-deprecating. 'Shall we breakfast together?'

'Snuffles?'

'Let him join us when it suits him.'

'Miss Ming is with him. They say their farewells.'

'Then give them the time they need.'

She was uncertain of the wisdom of this, but with the hope of escape, she could afford to be more generous to Miss Ming. 'Very well.'

As they sat together in the breakfast room, she said, 'You do not believe that Miss Ming is evil, do you, Lord Jagged?' She watched him eat, having contented herself with the treat of a slice of toast.

'Evil is a word, an idea, which has very little resonance at the End of Time, I'm afraid. Crime does not exist for us.'

'But crime exists here.'

'For you, Dafnish Armatuce, perhaps. But not for us.'

She looked up. She thought she had seen something move past the window, but she was tired; her eyes were faulty. She gave him her attention again. He had finished his breakfast and was rising, wiping his lips. 'There must be victims, you see,' he added.

She could not follow his arguments. He had become elusive once more, almost introspective. His mind considered different, to him more important, problems.

'I must go to the boy,' she said.

All at once she had his full attention. His grey, intelligent eyes penetrated her. 'I have been privileged, Dafnish Armatuce,' he said soberly, 'to entertain you as my guest.'

Did she blush then? She had never blushed before.

He did not accompany her back to the apartments, but made his apologies and entered the bowels of the building, about his own business again. She went swiftly to the room, but it was empty.

'Snuffles!' She called out as she made her way to her own chamber. 'Miss Ming.'

They were gone.

She returned to the breakfast room. They were not there. She ran, panting, to the air-car hangar. She ran through it into the open, standing waist-high in the corn, questing for Miss Ming's own car. The blue sky was deserted. She knew, as she had really known since finding her son's room absented, that she had seen them leaving, seen the car as it flashed past the window.

She calmed herself. Reason told her that Miss Ming was merely taking Snuffles on a last impulsive expedition. It was, of course, what she might have suspected of the silly woman. But the dread would not dissipate. An image of the boy's painted features became almost tangible before her eyes. Her lips twisted, conquering her ability to arrange them, and it seemed that frost ate at the marrow of her bones. Fingers caught in hair, legs shook. Her glance was everywhere and she saw nothing but that painted face.

'Snuffles!'

There was a sound. She wheeled. A robot went by bearing the remains of the breakfast.

'Lord Jagged!'

She was alone.

She began to run through the yellow-and-brown corridors until she reached the hangar. She climbed into her air car and sat there, unable to give it instructions, unable to decide in which direction she should search first. The miniature palaces of yesterday? Were they not a favourite playground for the pair? She told the car its destination, ordered maximum speed.

But the Gothic village was deserted. She searched every turret, every hall into which she could squeeze her body, and she called their names until her voice cracked. At last she clambered back into her car. She recalled that Miss Ming was still resident at Doctor Volospion's menagerie.

'Doctor Volospion's,' she told the car.

Doctor Volospion's dwelling stood upon several cliffs of white marble and blue basalt, its various wings linked by slender, curving bridges of the same materials. Minarets, domes, conical towers, skyscraper blocks, sloping roofs and windows filled with some reflective but transparent material gave it an appearance of considerable antiquity, though it was actually only a few days old. Dafnish Armatuce had seen it once before, but she had never visited it, and now her difficulty lay in discovering the appropriate entrance.

It took many panic-filled minutes of circling about before she was hailed, from the roof of one of the skyscrapers, by Doctor Volospion himself, resplendent in rippling green silks, his skin coloured to match. 'Dafnish Armatuce! Have you come to accept my tryst? O, rarest of beauties, my heart is cast already – see – at your feet.' And he gestured, twisting a ring. She looked down, kicking

the pulsing, bloody thing aside. 'I seek my Snuffles,' she cried. 'And Miss Ming. Are they here?'

'They were. To arrange your surprise. You'll be pleased. You'll be pleased. But have patience – come to me, splendid one.'

'Surprise? What have they done?'

'Oh, I cannot tell you. It would spoil it for you. I was able to help. I once specialised in engineering, you know. Sweet Orb Mace owes much to me.'

'Explain yourself, Doctor Volospion.'

'Perhaps, when the confidences of the bedchamber are exchanged...'

'Where did they go?'

'Back. To Canaria. It was for you. Miss Ming was overjoyed by what I was able to accomplish. The work of a moment, of course, but the skill is in the swiftness.' With a wave of his hand he changed his costume to roaring red. The light of the flames flooded his face with shadow. But she had left him.

As she fled back to Canaria, she thought she heard Doctor Volospion's laughter; and she knew that her mind could not be her own if she detected mockery in his mirth.

On her right the insubstantial buildings of Djer streamed past, writhing with gloomy colour, muttering to themselves as they strove to recall some forgotten function, some lost experience, recreating, from a memory partially disintegrated, indistinct outlines of buildings, beasts or men, calling out fragments of song or scientific formulae; almost piteous, this place, which had once served Man proudly, in the spirit with which she served the Armatuce, so that she permitted herself a pang of understanding, for she and the city shared a common grief.

'Ah, how much better it might have been had we stayed there,' she said aloud.

The city cried out to her as if in reply, as if imploringly:

'The world is too much with us; late and soon,
Getting and spending, we lay waste our powers:
Little we see in Nature that is ours;
We have given our hearts away, a sordid boon!'

She did not understand the meaning of the words, but she replied: 'You could have helped me, but I was afraid of you. I feared your variety, your wealth.' Then the car had borne her on, and soon Canaria's graceful cage loomed into view, glittering in sparse sunshine, its gold all pale.

With tense impatience she stood stiffly in the car while it docked, until she could leap free, running up the great ramp, through the dwarfing portals, down halls which echoed a magnified voice, calling for her boy.

It was when she had pushed open the heavy doors of Lord Jagged's Hall of Antiquities that she saw three figures standing at the far end, beneath a wall mounted with a hundred examples of heavy Dawn Age furniture. They appeared to be discussing a large piece in dark wood, set with mirrors, brass and mother-of-pearl, full of small drawers and pigeonholes from which imitation doves poked their little heads and crooned. Elsewhere were displayed fabrics, cooking utensils, vehicles, weapons, technical apparatus, entertainment structures, musical instruments, clothing from mankind's first few thousand years of true planetary dominance.

The three she saw were all adults, and she guessed initially that they might, themselves, be exhibits, but as she approached she saw, with lifting heart, that one of them was Lord Jagged and another was Miss Ming. Her anger with Miss Ming turned to annoyance and she experienced growing relief. The third figure she did not recognise. He was typical of those who inhabited the End of Time; a foppish, overdressed, posturing youth, doubtless some acquaintance of Lord Jagged's.

'Miss Ming!'

Three heads turned.

'You took Snuffles. Where is he now?'

'We went to visit Doctor Volospion, dearest Dafnish. We thought you would not notice. You yourself gave me the idea when you told me to remind Snuffles of his destiny. It's my present to you.' She fluttered winsome lashes. 'Because I care so much for you. A tribute of my admiration for the wonderful way you've tried to do your best for your son. Well, Dafnish, I have put your misery at an end. No more sacrifices for you!'

Dafnish Armatuce did not listen, for the tone was as familiar to her as it was distasteful. 'Where is Snuffles now?' she repeated.

The youth, standing behind Miss Ming, laughed, but Lord Jagged was frowning.

Miss Ming's oversweet smile spread across her pallid face. 'I have done you a favour, Dafnish. It's a surprise, dear.' Two clammy hands tried to fold themselves around one of Dafnish's, but she pulled away. Miss Ming had to be content with clinging to an arm. 'I know you'll be pleased. It's what you've looked forward to, what you've worked for. And it means real freedom for us.'

'Freedom? What do you mean? Where is my Snuffles?'

Again the stranger laughed, spreading his arms wide, showing off exotic garments – blue moleskin tabard stitched with silver, shirt of brown velvet with brocaded cuffs, puffed out at the shoulders to a height of at least two feet, hose which curled with snakes of varicoloured light, boots whose feet were the heads of living, glaring dragons, the whole smelling strongly of musk – and pouting in his peacock pride. 'Here, Mama!'

She stared.

The youth waltzed forward, the smile languid, the eyes half-closed. 'I am your son! It is my destiny come to fulfilment at last. Miss Ming has made a man of me!'

Miss Ming preened herself, murmuring with false modesty: 'With Doctor Volospion's help. My idea – his execution.'

Dafnish Armatuce swayed on her feet as she stared. The face was longer, more effeminate, the eyes large, darker, luminous, the hair pure blond; but something of Snuffles, something of herself, was still there. There were emeralds in his lobes. His brows had been slimmed and their line exaggerated; the lips, though naturally red, were too full and too bright.

Dafnish Armatuce groaned and her fingers fled to cover her face. A hand touched her shoulder. She shook it off and Lord Jagged apologised.

Miss Ming's voice celebrated the spirit of comfiness: 'It's a shock, of course, at first, until you understand what it means. You don't have to die!'

'Die?' She looked with loathing upon Miss Ming's complacent features.

'He is a man and you are free. Snuffles explained something of your customs to me.'

'Customs! It is more than custom, Miss Ming. How can this be? What of his life-right? He has no soul!'

'Such superstitions,' declared Miss Ming, 'are of little consequence at the End of Time.'

'I have not transferred the life-right! He remains a shadow until that day! But even that is scarcely important at this moment – look what you have made of him! Look!'

'You really are very silly, Mother,' said Snuffles, his voice softening in something close to kindness. 'They can do anything here. They can change their shapes to whatever they wish. They can be children, if they want to be, or beasts, or even plants. Whatever fancy dictates. I am the same personality, but I have grown up, at last! Sixty years was too long. I have earned my maturity.'

'You remain an infant!' she spoke through her teeth. 'Like your fatuous and self-called friend. Miss Ming, he must be restored to his proper body. We leave, as soon as we may, for Armatuce.'

Miss Ming was openly incredulous and condescending. 'Leave? To be killed or stranded?'

Snuffles affected superciliousness. 'Leave?' he echoed. 'For Armatuce? Mother, it's impossible. Besides, I have no intention of returning.' He leaned against the rusted remains of a Nash Rambler and shared (or thought he shared) a conspiratorial wink with Miss Ming and Lord Jagged. 'I shall stay.'

'But –' her lips were dry – 'your life-right…'

'Here, I do not need my life-right. Keep it, Mother. I do not want your personality, your ridiculous prejudices. Why should I wish to inherit them, when I have seen so much? Here, at the End of Time, I can be myself – an individual, not an Armatuce!'

'His destiny?' Dafnish rounded on Miss Ming. 'You thought I meant *that*?'

'Oh, you…' Miss Ming's blue eyes, bovine and dazed, began to fill.

'I could change him to his original shape,' began Lord Jagged, but Dafnish Armatuce shook her head in misery.

'It is too late, Lord Jagged. What is there left?'

'But this is intolerable for you.' There was a hint of unusual emotion in Lord Jagged's voice. 'This woman is not one of us. She acts without wit or intelligence. There is no resonance in these actions of hers.'

'You would still say evil does not exist here?'

'If vulgar imitation of art is "evil", then perhaps I agree with you.'

Dafnish Armatuce was drained. She could not move. Her shoulder twitched a little in what might have been a shrug. 'Responsibility leaves me,' she said, 'and I feel the loss. Who knows but that I did use it as armour against experience.' She sighed, addressing her son. 'If adult you be, then make an adult's decision. Be an Armatuce, recall your Maxims, consider your Duty.' She was pleading and she could not keep her voice steady. 'Will you return with me to Armatuce? To Serve?'

'To serve fools? That would make a fool of me, would it not? Look about you! This is the way the race is destined to live, Mother. Here –' he spread decorated hands to indicate the world – 'here is my destiny, too!'

'Oh, Snuffles…' Her head fell forward and her body trembled with her silent sobbing. *'Snuffles!'*

'That name's offensive to me, Mother. Snuffles is dead. I am now the Margrave of Wolverhampton, who shall wander the world, impressing his magnificence on All! My own choice, the name, with Miss Ming's assistance concerning the details. A fine name, an excellent ambition. Thus I take my place in society, my only duty to delight my friends, my only maxim "Extravagance in Everything!" and I shall give service to myself alone! I shall amaze everyone with my inventions and events. You shall learn to be proud of me, Mama!'

She shook her head. 'All my pride is gone.'

Several ancient clocks began to chime at once, and through the din she heard Lord Jagged's voice murmuring in her ear. 'The fabric of time is particularly weak now. Your chances are at their best.'

She knew that this was mercy, but she sighed. 'If he came, what point? My whole life has been dedicated to preparing for the moment when my son would become an adult, taking my knowledge, my experience, my Duty. Shall I present our Armatuce with – with what he is now?'

The youth had heard some of this and now he raised a contemptuous shoulder to her while Miss Ming said urgently: 'You cannot go! You must not! I did it for you, so that you could be happy. So that we could enjoy a full friendship. There is no obstacle.'

Dafnish's laughter drove the woman back. Fingers in mouth, Miss Ming cracked a nail with her teeth, and the shadow of terror came and went across her face.

Dafnish spoke in an undertone. 'You have killed my son, Miss Ming. You have made of my whole life a travesty. Whether that shell you call "my son" survives or not, whether it should be moulded once more into the original likeness, it is of no importance any longer. I am the Armatuce and the Armatuce is me. You have poisoned at least one branch of that tree which is the Armatuce, whose roots bind the world, but I am not disconsolate; I know other branches will grow. Yet I must protect the roots, lest they be poisoned. I have a responsibility now which supersedes all others. I must return. I must warn my folk never to send another Armatuce to the End of Time. It is evident that our time-travelling experiments threaten our survival, our security. You assure me that – that the boy can live without his life-right, that remaining part of my being which, at my death, I would pass on to him, so that he could live. Very well, I leave him to you and depart.'

Miss Ming wailed: 'You can't! You'll be killed! I love you!'

The youth held some kind of hayfork at arm's length, inspecting its balance and workmanship, apparently unconcerned. Dafnish took a step towards him. 'Snuffles…'

'I am not "Snuffles".'

'Then, stranger, I bid you farewell.' She had recovered something of her dignity. Her small body was still tense, her oval face still pale. She controlled herself. She was an Armatuce again.

'You'll be *killed*!' shrieked Miss Ming, but Dafnish ignored her. 'At best, time will fling you back to us. What good will the journey do you?'

'The Armatuce shall be warned. There is a chance of that?' The question was for Lord Jagged.

'A slight one. Only because the Laws of Time have already been transgressed. I have learned something of a great conjunction, of other layers of reality which intersect with ours, which suggests you might return, for a moment, anyway, since the Laws need not be so firmly enforced.'

'Then I go now.'

He raised a warning hand. 'But, Dafnish Armatuce, Miss Ming is right. There is little probability time will let you survive.'

'I must try. I presume that Sweet Orb Mace, who has my time ship, knows nothing of this disruption, will take no precautions to keep me in your age?'

'Oh, certainly! Nothing.'

'Then I thank you, Lord Jagged, for your hospitality. I'll require it no longer and you may let Snuffles go to Doctor Volospion's. You are a good man. You would make a worthy Armatuce.'

He bowed. 'You flatter me…'

'Flattery is unknown in Armatuce. Farewell.'

She began to walk back the way she had come, past row upon row, rank upon rank of antiquities, past the collected mementoes of a score of ages, as if, already, she marched, resolute and noble, through time itself.

Lord Jagged seemed about to speak, but then he fell silent, his expression unusually immobile, his eyes narrowed as he watched her march. Slowly, he reached a fine hand to his long cheek and his fingers explored his face, just below the eye, as if he sought something there but failed to find it.

Miss Ming blew her nose and bawled:

'Oh, I've ruined everything. She was looking forward to the day you grew up, Snuffles! I *know* she was!'

'Margrave,' he murmured, to correct her. He made as if to take a step in pursuit, but changed his mind. He smoothed the pile of his tabard. 'She'll be back.'

'She'll realise her mistake?' Saucer eyes begged comfort from their owner's creation.

The Margrave of Wolverhampton had found a mirror in a silver frame. He was pleased with what he saw. He spoke absently to his companion.

'Possibly. And if she should reach Armatuce, she'll be better off. You have me for a friend, instead. Shall I call you Mother?'

Mavis Ming uttered a wordless yelp. Impatiently the Margrave of Wolverhampton stroked her lank hair. 'She would never know how to enjoy herself. No Armatuce would. I am the first. Why should sacrifices be made pointlessly?'

Lord Jagged turned and confronted him. Lord Jagged was grim. 'She has much, your mother, that is of value. You shall never have that now.'

'My inheritance, you mean?' The Margrave's sneer was not altogether accomplished. 'My life-right? What use is it here? Thanks, old man, but no thanks!' It was one of Miss Ming's expressions. The Margrave acknowledged the origin by grinning at her for approval. She laughed through tears, but then, again, was seized:

'What if she dies!'

'She would have had to give it up, for me, when we returned. She loses nothing.'

'She passes her whole life to you?' said Jagged, revelation dawning. 'Her *whole* life?'

'Yes. In Armatuce but not here. I don't need the life-force. There she would be absorbed into me, then I would change, becoming a man, but incorporating her "soul". What was of use to me in her body would also be used. Nothing is wasted in Armatuce. But this way is much better, for now only a small part of her is in me – the part she infused when I was made – and I become an individual. We both have freedom, though it will take her time to realise it.'

'You are symbiotes?'

'Of sorts, yes.'

'But surely,' said Jagged, 'if she dies before she transfers the life-right to you, you are still dependent on the life-force emanating from her being?'

'I would be, in Armatuce. But here, I'm my own man.'

Miss Ming said accusingly, 'You should have tried to stop her, Lord Jagged.'

'You said yourself she was free, Miss Ming.'

'Not to destroy herself!' A fresh wail.

'But to become your slave?'

'Oh, that's nonsense, Lord Jagged.' Another noisy blowing of the nose. 'Your trouble is, you don't understand real emotions at all.'

His smile as he looked down at her was twisted and strange.

'I loved her,' said Miss Ming defiantly.

Chapter Eight

The Return to Armatuce

ALONE IN HER machine, her helmet once more upon her head, her protective suit once again armouring her body, Dafnish Armatuce quelled pain, at the sight of Snuffles's empty chair, and concentrated upon her instruments. All was ready.

She adjusted her harness, tightening it. She reached for the seven buttons inset on the chair's arm; she pressed a sequence of four. Green light rolled in waves across her vision, subtly altering to blue and then to black. Dials sang out their information, a murmuring rose to a shout: the ship was moving. She was going back through time.

She watched for the pink light and the red, which would warn her that the ship was malfunctioning or that it was off course: the colours did not falter. She moved steadily towards her goal. Her head ached, but that was to be expected; neuralgia consumed her body (also anticipated); but the peculiar sense of unease was new, and her stare went too frequently to the small chair beneath the main console. To distract her attention, she brought in the vision screen earlier than was absolutely necessary. Outside was a predominantly grey mist, broken occasionally by bright flashes or patches of blackness; sometimes she thought she could distinguish objects for fractions of a second, but they never stayed long enough for her to identify them. The instruments were more interesting. They showed that she moved back through time at a rate of one minute to the thousand years. The instruments were crude, she knew, but she had already traversed seven thousand years and it would be many more minutes before she came to Armatuce. The machine had automatic devices built into it so that it would return to its original resting place a few moments after it had, so far as the observers in Armatuce were aware, departed. As best she could, she refused to let her thoughts dwell on her return. She would have to lie, and she had never lied before. She would have to admit to having abandoned her boy and she would know disgrace; she would no longer be required to serve. Yet she knew that she *would* serve, if only she were allowed to warn them against further expeditions into the future. She would be content. Yet still her heart remained heavy. It was obvious that she, too, had been corrupted. She would demand isolation, in Armatuce, so that she would not corrupt others.

A shadow darkened the vision screens for a few seconds, then the grey, sparkling mist came back.

She heard herself speaking. 'It was not betrayal. He, too, was betrayed. I must not blame him.'

She had become selfish; she wanted her boy for herself, for comfort. Therefore, she reasoned, she did not deserve him. She must forget…

The machine shuddered, but no pink light came. Physical agony made her bite her lip, but the machine maintained its backward course.

It became difficult to breathe. At first she blamed the respirator, but she saw that it functioned perfectly. With considerable effort she made herself breathe more slowly, felt her heartbeat resume its normal rhythm. Why did she persist in experiencing that same panic she had first experienced at the End of Time – the sense of being trapped? No-one had known claustrophobia in Armatuce for centuries. How could they? Such phobias had been eliminated.

Ten minutes passed. She was tempted to increase the machine's speed, but such a step would be dangerous. For the sake of the Armatuce, she must not risk her chances of getting home.

She recalled her son's disdainful words, remembered all the others who had told her that the sacrifices of the Armatuce were no longer valid. They had been valid once; they had saved the world, continued the race, passing life to life, building a huge fund of wisdom and knowledge. Like ants, she thought. Well, the ants survived. They and Man were virtually all that had survived the cataclysm. Was it not arrogant to assume that Man had any more to offer than the ant?

Five more minutes went by. The pain was worse, but it was not so sharp. Her sight was a little blurred, but she was able to see that the machine's passage through time was steady.

Her moods seemed to change rapidly. One moment she was consoled and hopeful; at another she would sink into despair and be forced to fight against such useless emotions as regret and anger. She could not carry such things back to Armatuce! It would be Sin. She strove to recall some suitable Maxim, but none came to her.

The machine lurched, paused, and then it continued. Another six minutes had gone by. The pain suddenly became so intense that she lost consciousness. She had expected nothing else.

She awoke, her ears filled with the protesting whining of the time ship. She opened her eyes to pink, oscillating light. She blinked and peered at the instruments. All were at zero. It meant that she was back.

Hastily, with clumsy fingers, she freed herself of her harness. The vision screen showed the white laboratory, the pale-faced, black-clad figures of her compatriots. They were very still.

She opened the mechanism to raise the hatch, climbed urgently through, crying out: 'Armatuce! Armatuce! Beware of the Future!' She was desperate to warn them in case time snatched her from her own age before she could complete her chosen task, her last Service.

'Armatuce! The Future holds Despair! Send no more ships!' She stood half out of the hatch, waving to attract their attention, but they remained absolutely immobile. None saw her, none heard her, none breathed. Yet they were not statues. She recognised her husband among them. They lived, yet they were frozen!

'Armatuce! Beware the Future!'

The machine began to shake. The scene wavered and she thought she detected the faintest light of recognition in her husband's eye.

'We both live!' she cried, anxious to give him hope.

Then the machine lurched and she lost her footing, was swallowed by it. The hatch slammed shut above her head. She crawled to the speaking apparatus. 'Armatuce! Send no more ships!' The pink light flared to red. Heat increased. The machine roared.

Her mouth became so dry that she could hardly speak at all. She whispered, 'Beware the Future…' and then she was burning, shivering, and the red light was fading to pink, then to green, as the machine surged forward again, leaving Armatuce behind.

She screamed. They had not seen her. Time had stopped. She dragged herself back to the chair and flung herself into it. She tried to pull her harness round her, but she lacked the strength. She pressed the four buttons to reverse the machine's impetus, forcing it against that remorseless current.

'Oh, Armatuce…'

She knew, then, that she could survive if she allowed the machine to float, as it were, upon the forward flow of time, but her loyalty to Armatuce was too great. Again she pressed the buttons, bringing a return of the pink light, but she saw the indicators begin to reverse.

She staggered from her chair, each breath like liquid fire, and adjusted every subsidiary control to the reverse position. The machine shrieked at her, as if it pleaded for its own life, but it obeyed. Again the laboratory flashed upon the vision screen. She saw her husband. He was moving sluggishly.

Something seemed to burst in her atrophied womb; tears etched her skin like corrosive acid. Her hair was on fire.

She found the speaking apparatus again. 'Snuffles,' she whispered. 'Armatuce. Future.'

And she looked back to the screen; it was filled with crimson. Then she felt her bones tearing through her flesh, her organs rupturing, and she gave herself up, in peace, to the pain.

Chapter Nine
In Which Miss Ming Claims a Keepsake

'ADAPTABILITY, SURELY, IS the real secret of survival?' The new Margrave of Wolverhampton seemed anxious to impress his unwilling host. Lord Jagged had been silent since Dafnish Armatuce's departure. 'I mean, that's why people like my mother are doomed,' continued the youth. 'They can't bear change. She could have been perfectly content here, if she'd listened to reason. Couldn't she, Lord Jagged?'

Lord Jagged was sprawled in an ancient steel armchair, refusing to give his affirmation to these protestations. Miss Ming had at last dried her eyes, hopefully for the final time. She inspected a 40th-century wall hanging, feeling the delicate cloth with thumb and forefinger.

'I mean, that whole business about controlling the population. It wasn't necessary in Armatuce. It hadn't been for hundreds of years. There was wealth everywhere, but we weren't allowed to touch it. We never had enough to *eat*!' This last, plaintive, remark caused Lord Jagged to look up. Encouraged, the Margrave became expansive: 'The symbiosis, the ritual passing on of the life-force from one to another. It came about because children couldn't be produced naturally. I was made in a metal tub! She threw in a bit of her – what? – soul? Her "self"? Call it what you like. And there I was – forced to remain, once I'd grown a little, a child for sixty years! Oh, I was content enough, certainly, until I came here and saw what life could be like. If it hadn't been for Miss Ming...'

Lord Jagged sighed and closed his eyes.

'Think what you like!' The Margrave's silks rustled as he put a defiant hand to his hip. 'Miss Ming's done me a lot of good, and could have done Mother good, too. Whose fault is it? I was doomed to be linked to her until some complacent, ludicrous committee decided I could become an adult; but my mama would have to die so that I could inherit the precious – and probably non-existent – life-force! I'd have been a copy of her, little more. Great for her ego, eh? Lousy for mine.'

'And now you utter the coarse rhetoric of a Miss Ming!' Lord Jagged rose from his chair, an unusual bitterness in his tone. 'You substitute the Maxims of the Armatuce for the catchphrases which support a conspiracy of selfishness and greed. There is dignity here, at the End of Time, but you do not ape that, because your mother also had dignity. You are vulgar now, little Snuffles, as no child can ever be vulgar. Do you not sense it? Can you not see how that wretched inhabitant of Doctor Volospion's third-rate menagerie has used you, to further her own stupid, short-sighted ambitions? She lusted for Dafnish Armatuce and thought you stood between her and the object of her desires. So she turned you into this travesty of maturity, with no more wit or originality or intelligence than she, herself, possesses.'

'Oh!' Miss Ming was sneering now. She caught at the young Margrave's arm. 'He's jealous because he wanted her for himself. He's never kept guests here before. Don't take it out on the lad, Lord Jagged, or on me!'

He began to walk away. She crowed. 'The truth hurts, doesn't it?'

Without looking back, he paused. 'When couched in your terms, Miss Ming, it must always hurt.'

'Aha! You see!' She was triumphant. She embraced her monster. 'Time to go, Snuffles, dear.'

The youth was unresponsive. The ruby lips had turned the colour of ivory, the lustre had gone from the huge eyes. He staggered, clutching at his head. He moaned.

'Snuffles?'

'Marg – I am dizzy. I am hot. My body shakes.'

'A mistake in the engineering? Doctor Volospion can't have… We must get you back to him, in case…'

'Oh, I feel the flesh fading. My substance…' His face had crumpled in pain. He lurched forward. A dry, retching noise came from a throat which had acquired the wrinkles of extreme old age. He fell to his knees. His skin began to crack. She tried to pull him to his feet.

'Lord Jagged!' cried Miss Ming. 'Help me. He's ill. Oh, why should this happen to me? No-one can be ill at the End of Time. Do something with one of your rings. Draw strength from the city.'

Lord Jagged had been watching, but he did not choose to move.

'Mother,' gasped the creature on the floor. 'My life-right...'

'He's dying! Help him, Lord Jagged! Save him!'

Lord Jagged seemed to be measuring his steps as he advanced slowly towards them. He stopped and looked without pity at Snuffles as he moved feebly in clothes too large for him. 'They were completely symbiotic, then,' mused Jagged. 'See, Miss Ming – Dafnish Armatuce must be dead – killed somewhere on the megaflow – escaping from this world. Or was she driven from it? Dafnish Armatuce is dead – and that part of her which was her son – a shadow, as she said – dies, too. Snuffles was never an individual, as we understand it.'

'It can't be. He's all I have left! Oh!' She leaned forward in horror, for the body was disintegrating rapidly, becoming fine, brown dust, leaving nothing but an empty suit of moleskin, velvet and brocade. The hose ceased to writhe with light; the dragon shoes scarcely hissed.

She looked up anxiously at the tall man. 'But you can resurrect him, Lord Jagged.'

'I am not sure I could. Besides, I see no reason to do so. There is little there to bring back to life. It is not Dafnish Armatuce. If it were, I would not hesitate. But her body burns somewhere between the end of one moment and the beginning of the next – and this, this is all we have of her now. Dying, she reclaims her son.'

Miss Ming shuddered with frustration. She glared at Lord Jagged, hating him, tensed as if, physically, she might attack him. But she had no courage.

Lord Jagged pursed his lips, then drew a deep breath of the musty air. He left her in his Hall of Antiquities, returning to his mysterious labours.

Later, Miss Ming stood up and unclenched her hand. On her palm lay a little pile of brown dust. She put it in her pocket, for a keepsake.

Constant Fire

A little something for Alfie Bester

LEGEND THE FOURTH

Kindle me to constant fire,
Lest the nail be but a nail!
Give me wings of great desire,
Lest I look within and fail!

... Red of heat to white of heat,
Roll we to the Godhead's feet!
Beat, beat! white of heat,
Red of heat, beat, beat!

– George Meredith,
The Song of Theodolinda

Chapter One

In Which Your Auditor Gives Credit to His Sources

THE INCIDENTS INVOLVING Mr Jherek Carnelian and Mrs Amelia Underwood, their adventures in time, the machinations of, among others, the Lord of Canaria, are already familiar to those of us who follow avidly any fragment of gossip coming back from the End of Time.

We know, too, why it is impossible to learn further details of how life progresses there since the inception of Lord Jagged's grand (and some think pointless) scheme, details of which have been published in the three volumes jointly entitled *The Dancers at the End of Time*.

Time-travellers, of course, still visit the periods immediately preceding the inception of the scheme. They bring us back those scraps of scandal, speculation, probable fact and likely lies which form the bases for the admittedly fanciful reconstructions I choose to term my 'legends from the future' – stories which doubtless would cause much amusement if those I write about were ever to read them (happily, there is no evidence that the tales survive our present century, let alone the next few million years).

If this particular tale seems more outrageous and less likely than any of the others, it is because I was gullible enough to believe the sketch of it I had from an acquaintance who does not normally journey so far into the future. A colleague of Mrs Una Persson in the Guild of Temporal Adventurers, he does not wish me to reveal his name and this, fortunately, allows me to be rather more frank about him than would have been possible.

My friend's stories are always interesting, but they are consistently highly coloured; his exploits have been bizarre and his claims incredible. If he is to be believed, he has been present at a good many of the best-known key events in history, including the crucifixion of Christ, the massacre at My Lai, the assassination of Naomi Jacobsen in Paris and so on, and has often played a major rôle.

From his base in West London (20th century, Sectors 3 and 4) my friend has ranged what he terms the 'chronoflow', visiting periods of the past and future of this Earth as well as those of other Earths which, he would have us accept, coexist with ours in a complex system of intersecting dimensions making up something called the 'multiverse'.

Of all the temporal adventurers I have known, my friend is the most ready to describe his exploits to anyone who will listen. Presumably, he is not subject to the Morphail Effect (which causes most travellers to exercise the greatest caution regarding their actions and conversations in any of the periods they visit) mainly because few but the simple-minded, and those whose logical faculties have been ruined by drink, drugs or other forms of dissipation, will take him seriously.

My friend's own explanation is that he is not affected by such details; he describes himself rather wildly as a 'chronic outlaw' (a self-view which might give the reader some insight into his character). You might think he charmed me into believing the tale he told me of Miss Mavis Ming and Mr Emmanuel Bloom, and yet there is something about the essence of the story that inclined me to believe it – for all that it is, in many ways, one of the most incredible I have heard. It cannot, of course, be verified readily (certainly so far as the final chapters are concerned) but it is supported by other rumours I have heard, as well as my own previous knowledge of Mr Bloom (whose earlier incarnation appeared in a tale, told to me by one of my friend's fellow Guild members, published variously as *The Fireclown* and *The Winds of Limbo*, some years ago).

The events recorded here follow directly upon those recorded in 'Ancient Shadows' and take up Miss Ming's story where we left it after her encounter with Dafnish Armatuce and her son Snuffles.

As usual, the basic events described are as I had them from my source. I have rearranged certain things, to maintain narrative tensions, and added to an earlier, less complete, draft of my own which was written hastily, before all the information was known to me.

The 'fleshing-out' of the narrative, the interpretations where they occur, many of the details of conversations, and so on, must be blamed entirely on your auditor.

In the account previous to this one, I have already retailed something of that peculiar relationship existing between Miss Ming and Doctor Volospion: the unbearable bore and that ostentatious misanthrope.

Why Doctor Volospion continued to take perverse pleasure in the woman's miserable company, why she allowed him to insult her in the most profound of ways – she who spent the greater part of her days avoiding any sort of pain – we cannot tell. Suffice to say that relationships of this sort exist in our own society and can be equally puzzling.

Perhaps Doctor Volospion found confirmation of all his misanthropy in her; perhaps she preferred this intense, if unpleasant, attention to no attention at all. She confirmed his view of life, while he confirmed her very existence.

But it is the purpose of a novel, not a romance, to speculate in this way and it is no part of my intention to dwell too much upon such thoughts.

Here, then, for the reader's own interpretation (if one is needed), is the tale of Miss Ming's transformation and the part which both Doctor Volospion and Emmanuel Bloom had in it.

Chapter Two
In Which Miss Mavis Ming Experiences a Familiar Discomfort

THE PECULIAR EFFECT of one sun rising just as another set, causing shadows to waver, making objects appear to shift shape and position, went more or less entirely unobserved by the great crowd of people who stood, enjoying a party, in the foothills of a rather poorly finished range of mountains erected some little time ago by Werther de Goethe during one of his periodic phases of attempting to re-create the landscape, faithful to the last detail, of Holman Hunt, an ancient painter Werther had discovered in one of the rotting cities.

Werther, it is fair to say, had not been the first to make such an attempt. However, he held to the creed that an artist should, so far as his powers allowed, put up everything exactly as he saw it in the painting. Werther was a purist. Werther volubly denied the criticisms of those who found such literal work bereft of what they regarded as true artistic inspiration. Werther's theories of Fidelity to Art had enjoyed a short-lived vogue (for a time the Duke of Queens had been an earnest acolyte) but his fellows had soon tired of such narrow disciplines.

Werther, alone, refused to renounce them.

As the party progressed, another of the suns eventually vanished while the other rose rapidly, reached zenith and stopped. The light became golden, autumnal, misty. Of the guests but three had paused to observe the phenomenon: they were Miss Mavis Ming, plump and eager in her new dress; Li Pao, bland in puritanical denim; and Abu Thaleb, their host, svelte and opulent, splendidly overdressed.

'Whose suns?' murmured Abu Thaleb appreciatively. 'How pretty! And subtle. Rivals, perhaps...'

'To your own creations?' asked Li Pao.

'No, no – to one another.'

'They could be Werther's,' suggested Miss Ming, anxious to return to their interrupted topic. 'He hasn't arrived yet. Go on, Li Pao. You were saying something about Doctor Volospion.'

A fingered ear betrayed Li Pao's embarrassment. 'I spoke of no-one specifically, Miss Ming.' His round Chinese face became expressionless.

'By association,' Abu Thaleb prompted, a somewhat sly smile manifesting itself within his pointed beard, 'you spoke of Volospion.'

'Ah! You would make a gossip of me. I disdain such impulses. I merely observed that only the weak hate weakness; only the wounded condemn the pain of others.' He wiped a stain of juice from his severe blouse and turned his back on the tiny sun.

Miss Ming was arch. 'But you *meant* Doctor Volospion, Li Pao. You were *suggesting*...'

A tide of guests flowed by, its noise drowning what remained of her remark, and when it had passed, Li Pao (perhaps piqued by an element of truth) chose to show impatience. 'I do not share your obsession with your protector, Miss Ming. I generalised. The thought can scarcely be considered a specific one, nor an original one. I regret it. If you prefer, I retract it.'

'I wasn't *criticising*, Li Pao. I was just *interested* in how you saw him. I mean, he has been very *kind* to me, and I wouldn't like anybody to think I wasn't aware of all he's *done* for me. I could still be in his menagerie, couldn't I? But he showed his respect for me by letting me go – that is, asking me to be his *guest* rather than – well, whatever you'd call it.'

'He is a model of chivalry.' Abu Thaleb stroked an eyebrow and hid his face with his hand. 'Well, if you will excuse me, I must see to my monsters. To my guests.' He departed, to be swallowed by his party, while Li Pao's imploring look went unnoticed.

Miss Ming smoothed the front of Li Pao's blouse. 'So you see,' she said, 'I was only curious. It certainly wasn't *gossip* I wanted to hear. But I respect your opinions, Li Pao. We are fellow "prisoners", after all, in this world. Both of us would probably prefer to be back in the past, where we belong – you in the 27th century, to take your rightful position as chairman or whatever of China, and me in the 21st, to, to…' Inspiration left her momentarily. She contented herself with a coy wink. 'You mustn't pay any attention to little Mavis. There's no malice in her.'

'Aha.' Li Pao closed his eyes and drew a deep breath.

Miss Ming's sky-blue nail traced patterns on the more restrained blue of his chest. 'It's not in Mavis's nature to think naughty thoughts. Well, not that sort of naughty thought, at any rate!' She giggled.

'Yaha?' It was almost inaudible.

From somewhere overhead came the distant strains of one of Abu Thaleb's beasts. Li Pao raised his head as if to seek the source. He contemplated heaven.

Miss Ming, too, looked up. 'Nothing,' she said. 'It must have come from over there.' She pointed and, to her chagrin, her finger indicated the approaching figure of Ron Ron Ron who was, like herself and Li Pao, an expatriate (although in his case from the 140th century). 'Oh, look out, Li Pao. It's that bore Ron coming over…'

She was surprised when Li Pao expressed enthusiastic delight. 'My old friend!'

She was sure that Li Pao found Ron Ron Ron just as awful as everyone else but, for his sake, she smiled as sweetly as she could. 'How *nice* to see you!'

Ron Ron Ron had an expression of hauteur on his perfectly oval face. This was his usual expression. He, too, seemed just a little surprised by Li Pao's effusion. 'Um?'

The two men contemplated one another. Mavis plainly felt that it was up to her to break the ice. 'Li Pao was just saying – *not* about Doctor Volospion or anybody in particular – that the weak hate weakness and won't – what was it, Li Pao?'

'It was not important, Miss Ming. I must…' He offered Ron Ron Ron a thin smile.

Ron Ron Ron cleared his throat. 'No, please…'

'It was very *profound*,' said Miss Ming. 'I thought.'

Ron Ron Ron adjusted his peculiar jerkin so that the edges were exactly in line. He fussed at a button. 'Then you must repeat it for me, Li Pao.' The shoulders of his jerkin were straight-edged and the whole garment was made to the exact proportions of a square. His trousers were identical oblongs; his shoes, too, were exactly square. The fingers of his hands were all of the same length.

'Only the weak hate weakness...' murmured Miss Ming encouragingly, 'and...'

Li Pao's voice was almost a shriek: '... only the wounded condemn the pain of others. You see, Ron Ron Ron, I was not –'

'An interesting observation.' Ron Ron Ron put his hands together under his chin. 'Yes, yes, yes. I see.'

'No!' Li Pao took a desperate step forwards, as if to leave.

'By the same argument, Li Pao,' began Ron Ron Ron, and Li Pao became passive, 'you would imply that a strong person who exercised that strength is, in fact, revealing a weakness in his character, eh?'

'No. I...'

'Oh, but we must have a look at this.' Ron Ron Ron became almost animated. 'It suggests, you see, that indirectly you condemn my efforts as leader of the Symmetrical Fundamentalist Movement in attempting to seize power during the Anarchist Beekeeper period.'

'I assure you that I was not...' Li Pao's voice had diminished to a whisper.

'Certainly we were strong enough,' continued Ron Ron Ron. 'If the planet had not, in the meantime, been utilised as a strike-base by some superior alien military force (whose name we never did learn), which killed virtually all opposition and enslaved the remaining third of the human race during the duration of its occupation – not much more than twenty years, admittedly – before they vanished again, either because our part of the galaxy was no longer of strategic importance to them or because their enemies had defeated them, who knows what we could have achieved.'

'Wonders,' gasped Li Pao. 'Wonders, I am sure.'

'You are kind. As it was, Earth was left in a state of semi-barbarism which had no need, I suppose, for the refinements either of

Autonomous Hiveism or Symmetrical Fundamentalism, but given the chance I could have –'

'I am sure. I am sure.' Li Pao's voice had taken on the quality of a labouring steam engine.

'Still,' Ron Ron Ron went on, 'I digress. You see, because of my efforts to parley with the aliens, my motives were misinterpreted –'

'Certainly. Certainly.'

'– and I was forced to use the experimental time craft to flee here. However, my point is this…'

'Quite, quite, quite…'

Miss Ming shook her head. 'Oh, you men and your politics. I…'

But she had not been forceful enough. Ron Ron Ron's (or Ron's Ron's Ron's, as he would have preferred us to write) voice droned on, punctuated by Li Pao's little gasps and sighs. She could not understand Li Pao's allowing himself to be trapped in this awful situation. She had done her best, when he seemed to want to talk to Ron Ron Ron, to begin a conversation that would interest them both, knowing that the only thing the two men had in common was a past taste for political activity and a present tendency, in their impotence, to criticise the shortcomings of their fellows here at the End of Time. But now Li Pao showed no inclination at all to take Ron Ron Ron up on any of his points, which were certainly of no interest to anyone but the Symmetrical Fundamentalist himself. She knew what it was like with some people; if a string was pulled in them, they couldn't stop themselves going on and on. A lot of those she had known, back home in 21st-century Iowa, had been like that.

Again, thought Mavis, it was up to her to change the subject. For Li Pao's sake as well as her own.

'… they never did separate properly, you see,' said Ron Ron Ron.

'Separate?' Miss Ming seized the chance given her by the pause in his monologue. She spoke brightly. 'Properly? Why, that's like my Swiss cheese plant. The one I used to have in my office? It grew so big! But the leaves wouldn't separate properly. Is that what happened to yours, Ron Ron Ron?'

'We were discussing strength,' said Ron Ron Ron in some bewilderment.

'Strength! You should have met my ex. I've mentioned him before? Donny Stevens, the heel. Now say what you like about him, but he was *strong*! Betty – you know, that's the friend I told you about? – *more* than a friend really…' she winked. '… Betty used to say that Donny Stevens was prouder of his pectorals than he was of his prick! Eh?' She shook with laughter.

The two men looked at her in silence.

Li Pao sucked his lower lip.

'And that was saying a lot, where Donny was concerned,' Mavis added.

'Ushshsh…' said Li Pao.

'Really?' Ron Ron Ron spoke in a peculiar tone.

The silence returned at once. Dutifully, Mavis tried to fill it. She put a hand on Ron Ron Ron's tubular sleeve.

'I shouldn't tell you this, what with my convictions and all – I was polarised in '65, became an all-woman woman, if you get me, after my divorce – but I miss that bastard of a bull sometimes.'

'Well…' Ron Ron Ron hesitated.

'What this world needs,' said Mavis as she got into her stride, 'if you ask me, is a few more real men. You know? Real men. The girls around here have got more balls than the guys. One real man and, boy, you'd find my tastes changing just like that…' She tried, unsuccessfully, to snap her fingers.

'Ssssss…' said Li Pao.

'Anyway,' Mavis was anxious to reassure him that she had not lost track of the original topic, 'It's the same with Swiss cheese plants. They're strong. Any conditions will suit them and they'll strangle anything that gets in their way. They use – they *used* to use, I should say – the big ones to fell other trees in Paraguay. I think it's Paraguay. But when it comes to getting the leaves to separate, well, all you can say is that they're bastards to train. Like strong men, I guess. In the end you have to take 'em or leave 'em as they come.'

Mavis laughed again, waiting for their responding laughter, which did not materialise. She was valiant:

'I stayed with my house plants, but I left that stud to play in his own stable. And how he'd been playing! Betty said if I tried to count the number of mares he'd serviced while I thought he was stuck late at the lab I'd need a computer!'

Li Pao and Ron Ron Ron now stood side by side, staring at her.

'*Two* computers!' She had definitely injected a bit of wit into the conversation and given Li Pao a chance to get onto a subject he preferred but evidently neither of them had much of a sense of humour. Li Pao now glanced at his feet. Ron Ron Ron had a silly fixed grin on his face and was just grunting at her, even though she had stopped speaking.

Miss Ming decided to soldier on:

'Did I tell you about the busy Lizzie that turned out to be poison ivy? We were out in the country one day, this was before my divorce – it must have been just after we got married – either '60 or '61 – no, it must have been '61 definitely because it was spring – probably May…'

'*Look!*'

Li Pao's voice was so loud that it startled Mavis.

'What?'

'There's Doctor Volospion.' He waved towards where the crowd was thickest. 'He was signalling to you, Miss Ming. Over there!'

The news heartened her. This would be her excuse to get away. But she could not, of course, show Li Pao how pleased she was. So she smiled indulgently. 'Oh, let him wait. Just because he's my host here doesn't mean I have to be at his beck and call the whole time!'

'Please,' said Ron Ron Ron, removing a small, pink, even-fingered hand from a perfectly square pocket. 'You must not let us, Miss Ming, monopolise your time.'

'Oh, well…' She was relieved. 'I'll see you later, perhaps. Byee.' Her wink was cute; she waggled her fingers at them. But as she turned to seek out Doctor Volospion it seemed that he had disappeared. She turned back and to her surprise saw Li Pao sprinting away from Ron Ron Ron towards the foot of one of Abu Thaleb's monsters, perhaps because he had seen someone to whom he wished to speak. She avoided Ron Ron Ron's eye and set off in the general direction indicated by Li Pao, making her way between guests and wandering elephants who were here in more or less equal numbers.

'At least I did my best,' she said. 'They're very difficult men to talk to.'

She yawned. She was already beginning to be just a trifle bored with the party.

Chapter Three

In Which Miss Ming Fails to Find Consolation

THE ELEPHANTS, ALTHOUGH the most numerous, were not the largest beasts providing the party's entertainment; its chief feature being the seven monstrous animals who sat on green-brown haunches and raised their heavy heads in mournful song.

These beasts were the pride of Abu Thaleb's collection. They were perfect reproductions of the singing gargantua of Justine IV, a planet long since vanished in the general dissipation of the cosmos (Earth, the reader will remember, had used up a good many other star systems to rejuvenate its own energies).

Abu Thaleb's enthusiasm for elephants, and all that was elephantine, was so great that he had changed his name to that of the ancient Commissar of Bengal solely because one of that legendary dignitary's other titles had been Lord of All Elephants.

The gargantua were more in the nature of huge baboons, their heads resembling those of Airedale terriers (now, of course, long-extinct) and were so large that the guests standing closest to them could not see them as a whole at all. Moreover, so high were these shaggy heads above the party that the beautiful music of their voices was barely audible.

Elsewhere, the commissar's guests ate from trays carried upon the backs of baby mammoths, or leaned against the leather hides of hippopotami which kneeled here and there about the grounds of Abu Thaleb's vast palace, itself fashioned in the shape of two marble elephants standing forehead to forehead, with trunks entwined.

Mavis Ming paused beside a resting oryx and pulled a tiny savoury doughnut or two from its left horn, munching absently as the beast's huge eyes regarded her. 'You look,' she remarked to it, 'as fed up as I feel.' She could find no-one to keep her company in that whole cheerful throng. Almost everyone she knew had seemed to turn aside just as she had been about to greet them and Doctor Volospion himself was nowhere to be seen.

'This party,' she continued, 'is definitely tedious.'

'What a supehb fwock, Miss Ming! So fwothy! So yellah!'

Sweet Orb Mace, in flounces and folds of different shades of grey, presented himself before her, smiling and languid. His eyebrows were elaborately arched; his hair incredibly ringleted, his cheeks exquisitely rouged. He made a leg.

The short-skirted yellow dress, with its several petticoats, its baby-blue trimmings (to match her eyes, her best feature), was certainly, Mavis felt, the sexiest thing she had worn for a long while, so she was not surprised by his compliment.

She gave one of her little-girl trills of laughter and pirouetted for him.

'I thought,' she told him, 'that it was high time I felt feminine again. Do you like the bow?' The big blue bow in her honey-blonde hair was trimmed with yellow and matched the smaller bows on her yellow shoes.

'Wondahful!' pronounced Sweet Orb Mace. 'It is quite without compahe!'

She was suddenly much happier. She blew him a kiss and fluttered her lashes. She warmed to Sweet Orb Mace, who could sometimes be such good company (whether as a man or a woman, for his moods varied from day to day) and she took his arm, confiding: 'You know how to flatter a girl. I suppose you, of all people, *should* know. I'll tell you a secret. I've been a bit cunning, you see, in wearing a full skirt. It makes my waist look a little slimmer. I'm the first to admit that I'm not the thinnest girl in the world, but I'm not about to emphasise the fact, am I?'

'Wemahkable.'

Amiably, Sweet Orb Mace strolled in harness while Mavis whispered further secrets. She told him of the polka-dot elephant she had had when she was seven. She had kept it for years, she said, until it had been run over by a truck, when Donny Stevens had thrown it through the apartment window into the street, during one of their rows.

'I could have taken almost anything else,' she said.

Sweet Orb Mace nodded and murmured little exclamations, but he scarcely seemed to have heard the anecdote. If he had a drawback as a companion, it was his vagueness; his attention wavered so.

'He accused *me* of being childish,' exclaimed Mavis putting, as it were, twice the energy into the conversation, to make up for his failings. 'Ha! He had the mental age of a dirty-minded eleven-year-old! But there you go. I got more love from that elephant than I ever got from Donny Stevens. It's always the people who try to be nice who come in for the nasty treatment, isn't it?'

'Wather!'

'He blamed me for everything. Little Mavis *always* gets the blame! Ever since I was a kid. Everybody's whipping boy, that's Mavis Ming! My father...'

'Weally?'

She abandoned this line, thinking better of it, and remained with her original sentiment. 'If you don't stand up for yourself, someone'll always step on you. The things I've done for people in the past. And you know what almost always happens?'

'Natuwally...'

'They turn round and say the cruellest things to you. They always blame you when they should really be blaming themselves. That woman – Dafnish Armatuce – *well*...'

'Twagic.'

'Doctor Volospion said I'd been too easy-going with her. I looked after that kid of hers as if it had been my own! It makes you want to give up sometimes, Sweet Orb. But you've got to keep on trying, haven't you? Some of us are fated to suffer...'

Sweet Orb Mace paused beside a towering mass of ill-smelling hairy flesh which moved rhythmically and shook the surrounding ground so that little fissures appeared. It was the gently tapping toe of one of Abu Thaleb's singing gargantua. Sweet Orb Mace stared gravely up, unable to see the head of the beast. 'Oh, cehtainly,' he agreed. 'Pwetty tune, don't you think?'

She lifted an ear, but shrugged. 'No, I don't.'

He was mildly surprised.

'Too much like a dirge for my taste,' she said. 'I like something catchy.' She sighed, her mood returning to its former state. 'Oh, dear! This is a very boring party.'

He became astonished.

'This pwofusion of pachyderms bohwing? Oh, no! I find it fascinating, Miss Ming. An extwavagance of elephants, a genewosity of giants!'

She could not agree. Her eye, perhaps, was jaundiced.

Sweet Orb Mace, sensing her displeasure, became anxious. 'Still,' he added, 'evewyone knows how easily impwessed I am. Such a poah imagination of my own, you know.'

She sighed. 'I expected more.'

'Monsters?' He glanced about, as if to find her some. 'Awgonheart Po has yet to make his contwibution! He is wumouhed to be supplying the main feast.'

'I didn't know.' She sighed again. 'It's not that. I was hoping to meet some nice person. Someone – you know – I could have a real relationship with. I guess I expected too much from that Dafnish and her kid – but it's, well, turned me on to the *idea*. I'm unfulfilled as a woman, Sweet Orb Mace, if you want the raw truth of it.'

She looked expectantly at her elegantly poised escort.

'Tut,' said Sweet Orb Mace abstractedly. 'Tut, tut.' He still stared skywards.

She raised her voice. 'You're not, I guess, in the mood yourself. I'm going to go home if things don't perk up. If you feel like coming back now – or dropping round later...? I'm still staying at Doctor Volospion's.'

'Weally?'

She laughed at herself. 'I should try to sound more positive, shouldn't I? Nobody's going to respond well to a faltering approach like that. Well, Sweet Orb Mace, what about it?'

'It?'

She was actually depressed now.

'I meant...'

'I pwomised to meet O'Kala Incarnadine heah,' said Sweet Orb Mace. 'I was suah – ah – and theah he is!' carolled her companion. 'If you will excuse me, Miss Ming...' Another elaborate bending of the body, a sweep of the hand.

'Oh, sure,' she murmured.

Sweet Orb Mace rose a few feet into the air and drifted towards O'Kala Incarnadine, who had come as a rhinoceros.

'The way I'm beginning to feel,' said Miss Ming to herself, 'even O'Kala Incarnadine's looking attractive. Bye, bye, Sweet Orb. No sweat. Oh, Christ! This boredom is *killing*!'

And then she had seen her protector, her host, her mentor, her guardian angel and, with a grateful 'Hi!', she flew.

Doctor Volospion was sighted at last! He seemed at times like this her only stability. He it was who had first found her when, in her time machine, dazed and frightened, she had arrived at the End of Time. Doctor Volospion had claimed her for his menagerie, thinking from her conversation that she belonged to some religious order (she had been delirious) and had discovered only later that she was a simple historian who believed that she had returned to the past, to the Middle Ages. He had been disappointed but had treated her courteously and now allowed her the full run of his house. She did not fit into his menagerie which was religious in emphasis, consisting of nuns, prophets, gods, demons and so forth. She could have founded her own establishment, had she wished, but she preferred the security of his sometimes dolorous domicile.

She slowed her pace. Doctor Volospion was hailing the Commissar of Bengal, whose howdah-shaped golden air car was drifting back to the ground (apparently, Abu Thaleb had been feeding his gigantic pets).

'Coo-ee!' cried Miss Ming as she approached.

But Doctor Volospion had not heard her.

'Coo-ee.'

He joined in conversation with Abu Thaleb.

'Coo-ee, Doctor!'

Now the sardonic, saturnine features turned to regard her. The sleek black head moved in a kind of bow and the corners of the thin, red mouth lifted.

She was panting as she reached them. 'It's only little me!'

Abu Thaleb was avuncular. 'Miss Ming, again we meet. Scheherazade come among us.' The dusky commissar was one of the few regular visitors to Doctor Volospion's, perhaps the only friend of the Doctor's to treat her kindly. 'You enjoy the entertainment, I hope?'

'It's a great party if you like elephants,' she said. But the joke had misfired; Abu Thaleb was frowning. So she added with some eagerness: 'I personally love elephants.'

'I did not know we had that in common.'

'Oh, yes. When I was a little girl I used to go for rides at the zoo whenever I could. At least once a year, on my birthday. My daddy would try to take me, no matter what else was happening…'

'I must join in the compliments.' Doctor Volospion cast a glinting eye from her toes to her bow. 'You outshine us all, Miss Ming. Such taste! Such elegance! We, in our poor garb, are mere flickering candles to your supernova!'

Her giggle of response was hesitant, as if she suspected him of satire, but then an expression almost of tranquillity passed across her features. His flattery appeared to have a euphoric effect upon her. She became a fondled cat.

'Oh, you always do it to me, Doctor Volospion. Here I am trying to be brittle and witty, cool and dignified, and you make me grin and blush like a schoolgirl.'

'Forgive me.'

She frowned, finger to lips. 'I'm trying to think of a witticism to please you.'

'Your presence is uniquely pleasing, Miss Ming.'

Doctor Volospion moved his thin arms which were hardly able to bear the weight of the sleeves of his black-and-gold brocade gown.

'But…'

Doctor Volospion turned to Abu Thaleb. 'You bring us a world of gentle monsters, exquisite commissar. Gross of frame, mild of manner, delicate of spirit. Your paradoxical pachyderms!'

'They are very *practical* beasts, Doctor Volospion.' Abu Thaleb spoke defensively, as if he, too, suspected irony.

People would often respond in this way to Doctor Volospion's remarks which were almost always, on the surface at least, bland enough.

'Oh, indeed!' Doctor Volospion eyed a passing calf which had paused and was tentatively extending its trunk to accept a piece of fruit from the commissar's open palm. 'Servants of man since the beginning of time.'

'Worshipped as gods in many eras and climes...' added Abu Thaleb.

'Gods! True. Ganesh...'

Abu Thaleb had lost his reservations:

'I have re-created examples of every known species! The English, the Bulgarian, the Chinese, and of course the Indian...'

'You have a favourite?' Volospion heaved at a sleeve and scratched an eyebrow.

'My favourites are the Swiss Alpine elephants. There is one now. Notice its oddly shaped hoofs. These were the famous white elephants of Sitting Bull, used in the liberation of Chicago in the 50th century.'

Miss Ming felt bound to interrupt. 'Are you absolutely certain of that, commissar? The story sounds a bit familiar, but isn't quite right. I am an historian, after all, if not a very good one. You're not thinking of Carthage...?' She became confused, apparently afraid that she had offended him again. 'I'm sorry. I shouldn't have butted in. You know what a silly little ignoramus I am...'

'I am absolutely certain, my dear,' said Abu Thaleb kindly. 'I had most of the information from an old tape which Jherek Carnelian found for me in one of the rotting cities. The translation might not have been perfect, but...'

'Ah, so Carthage could have sounded like Chicago, particularly after it has been through a number of transcriptions. You see *Sitting* Bull could have been –'

Doctor Volospion broke in on her speculations. 'What romantic times those must have been! Your own stories, Miss Ming, are redolent with the atmosphere of our glorious and vanished past!' He looked at Abu Thaleb as he spoke. Abu Thaleb moved uncomfortably.

Mavis Ming laughed. 'Well, it wasn't all fun, you know.' She sighed with pleasure, addressing Abu Thaleb. 'The thing I like about Doctor Volospion is the way he always lets me talk. He's always *interested*...'

Abu Thaleb avoided both their eyes.

'Say what you like about him,' she continued, 'Doctor Volospion's a gentleman!' She became serious. 'No, in a lot of ways the past was hell, though I must say there were satisfactions I never realised I'd miss till now. Sex, for instance.'

'You mean sexual pleasure?' The Commissar of Bengal drew a banana from his quilted cuff and began to peel it.

Miss Ming appeared to be taken aback by this gesture. Her voice was distant. 'I certainly do mean that.'

'Oh, surely...' murmured Doctor Volospion.

Miss Ming found her old voice. 'Nobody around here ever seems to be interested. I mean, really interested. If that's what's meant by an ancient race, give me what you call the Dawn Ages – my time – any day of the week! Well, not that you have days or weeks, but you know what I mean. Real sex!'

She seemed to realise that she was in danger of becoming intense and she tried to lighten the effect of her speech by breaking into what, in the Dawn Age, might have been a musical laugh.

When her laughter had died away, Doctor Volospion touched his right index finger to his left eyelid. 'Can this be true, Miss Ming?'

'Oh, you're a sweetie, Doctor Volospion. You make a girl feel really foolish sometimes. It's not your fault. You've got what we used to call an "unfortunate tone" – it seems to make a mockery of everything. I know what it is. You don't have to tell me. You're really quite shy, like me. I've lived with you long enough to know...'

'I am honoured, as always, by your interpretation of my character. But I am genuinely curious. I can think of so many who concern themselves with little else but sexual gratification. My Lady Charlotina, O'Kala Incarnadine, Gaf the Horse in Tears and, of course, Mistress Christia, the Everlasting Concubine.' He cast an eye over the surrounding guests. 'Jherek Carnelian *crucifies* himself in pursuit of his sexual object...'

'It's not what I meant,' she explained. 'You see, they only *play* at it. They're not really *motivated* by it. It's hard to explain.' She became coy. 'Anyway, I don't think any of those are my types, actually.'

The Commissar of Bengal finished feeding his banana to a

passing pachyderm. 'I seem to recall that you were quite struck by My Lady Charlotina at one time, Miss Ming.' he said.

'Oh, that was –'

Doctor Volospion studied something beyond her left shoulder. 'And then there was that other lady. The time-traveller, who I rather took to, myself. Why, we were almost rivals for a while. *You* were in love, you said, Miss Ming.'

'Oh, now you're being cruel! I'd rather you didn't mention...'

'Of course.' Now he looked beyond her right shoulder. 'A tragedy.'

'It's not that I – I mean, I don't like to think. I was badly let down by Dafnish – and by Snuffles, in particular. How was I to know that... Well, if you hadn't consoled me then, I don't know what I'd have done. But I wish you wouldn't bring it up. Not here, at least. Oh, people can be so *baffling* sometimes. I'm not perfect, I know, but I do my best to be tactful. To look on the bright side. To help others. Betty used to say that I ought to think more of my *own* interests. She said I wasn't selfish enough. Oh, dear – people must think me a terrible fool. When they think of me at *all*!' She sniffed. 'I'm sorry...'

She craned to look back, following Doctor Volospion's gaze.

Li Pao was nearby, bowing briefly to Doctor Volospion, making as if to pass on, for he was apparently in some haste, but Doctor Volospion smilingly called him over.

'I was complimenting our host on his collection,' he explained to Li Pao.

Abu Thaleb made a modest gesture.

Miss Ming bit her lip.

Li Pao cleared his throat.

'Aren't they fine?' said Doctor Volospion.

'It is pleasant to see the beasts working,' Li Pao said pointedly, 'if only for the delight of these drones.'

Doctor Volospion's smile broadened. 'Ah, Li Pao, as usual you refuse amusement! Still, that's your recreation, I suppose, or you would not attend so many of our parties.'

Li Pao bridled. 'I come, Doctor Volospion, on principle. Occasionally, there is one who will listen to me for a few moments. My conscience drives me here. One day perhaps I will begin to convince you of the value of moral struggle.'

An affectionate trunk nuzzled his oriental ear. He moved his head.

Doctor Volospion was placatory. 'I *am* convinced, Li Pao, my dear friend. Its value to the 27th century is immeasurable. But here we are at the End of Time and we have quite different needs. Our future is uncertain, to say the least. The cosmos contracts and perishes and soon we must perish with it. Will industry put a stop to the dissolution of the universe? I think not.'

Miss Ming patted at a blonde curl.

'Then you fear the end?' Li Pao said with some satisfaction.

Doctor Volospion affected a yawn. 'Fear? What is that?'

Li Pao's chuckle was grim. 'Oh, it's rare enough here, but I think you reveal at least a touch of it, Doctor Volospion.'

'Fear!' Doctor Volospion's nostrils developed a contemptuous flare. 'You suggest that I –? But this is such a baseless observation. An accusation, even!'

'I do not accuse, Doctor Volospion. I do not denigrate. Fear, where real danger threatens, is surely a sane enough response? A healthy one? Is it insane to ignore the knife which strikes for the heart?'

'Knife? Heart?' Abu Thaleb lured the persistent elephant towards him, holding a bunch of grapes. 'Do forgive me, Li Pao...'

Doctor Volospion said softly: 'I think, Li Pao, that you will have to consider me insane.'

Li Pao would not relent. 'No! You are afraid. Your denials display it, your posture pronounces it!'

Doctor Volospion moved an overloaded shoulder. 'Such instincts, you see, have atrophied at the End of Time. You credit your own feelings to me, I think.'

Li Pao's gaze was steady. 'I am not deceived, Doctor Volospion. What are you? Time-traveller or space-traveller? You are no more born of this age than am I, or Miss Ming, here.'

'What –?' Doctor Volospion was alerted.

'You say that you do not fear,' continued the Chinese. 'Yet you hate well enough, that's plain. Your hatred of Lord Jagged, for instance, is patent. And you exhibit jealousies and vanities that are unknown, say, to the Duke of Queens. If these are innocent of true guile, you are not. It is why I know there is a point in my talking to you.'

'I will not be condescended to!' Doctor Volospion glared.

'I repeat – I praise these emotions. In their place –'

'Praise?' Doctor Volospion raised both his hands, palms outward, to bring a pause. His voice, almost a whisper, threatened. 'Strange flattery, indeed! You go too far, Li Pao. The manners of your own time would never allow such insults.'

'I do think you've gone just a teeny bit too far, Li Pao.' Mavis Ming was anxious to reduce the tension. 'Why are you so bent on baiting Doctor Volospion? He's done nothing to you.'

'You refuse to admit it,' Li Pao continued relentlessly, 'but we face the death of everything. Thus I justify my directness.'

'Shall we die gracelessly, then? Pining for hope when there is none? Whining for salvation when we are beyond help? You are offensive at every level, Li Pao.'

Miss Ming was desperate to destroy this atmosphere. 'Oh, look over there!' she cried. 'Can it be Argonheart Po arrived at last, with the food?'

'He *is* late,' said Abu Thaleb, looking up from his elephant.

Li Pao and Doctor Volospion both ignored this sidetracking.

'There *is* hope, if we work,' said Li Pao.

'What? This is unbelievable.' Doctor Volospion sought an ally but found only the anxious eyes of Mavis Ming. He avoided them. 'The end looms – the inevitable beckons. Death comes stalking over the horizon. Mortality returns to the Earth after an absence of millennia. And you speak of what? Of work? Work!' Doctor Volospion's laugh was harsh. 'Work? For what? This age is called the End of Time for good reason, Li Pao! We have run our race. Soon we shall all be ash on the cosmic wind.'

'But if a few of us were to consider…'

'Forgive me, Li Pao, but you bore me. I have had my fill of bores today.'

'You boys should really stop squabbling like this.' Determinedly, Mavis Ming adopted a matronly rôle. 'Silly, gloomy talk. You're making me feel quite depressed. What possible good can it do for anyone? Let's have a bit more cheerfulness, eh? Did I ever tell you about the time I – well, I was about fourteen, and I'd done it for a dare – we got caught in the church by the Reverend Kovac – I'd told Sandy, that was my friend –'

Doctor Volospion's temper was not improved. An expression of pure horror bloomed on her round face as she realised that she had made another misjudgement and caused her protector to turn on her.

He was vicious. 'The rôle of diplomat, Miss Ming, does not greatly suit you.'

'Oh!'

Abu Thaleb became aware, at last, of the ambience. 'Come now…'

'You will be kind enough not to interfere, not to interject your absurd and pointless anecdotes into the conversation, Miss Ming!'

'*Doctor Volospion!*' It was a shriek of betrayal. Miss Ming took a step backwards. She became afraid.

'Oh, she meant no harm…' Li Pao was in no position to mediate.

'How,' enquired Doctor Volospion of the shaking creature, 'would you suggest we settle our dispute, Miss Ming? With swords, like Lord Shark and the Duke of Queens? With pistols? Reverb-guns? Flame lances?'

Her throat quivered. 'I didn't mean…'

'Well? Hm?' His long chin pointed at her throat. 'Speak up, my portly referee. Tell us!'

She had become very pale and yet her cheeks flamed with humiliation and she did not dare look at any of them. 'I was only trying to help. You were so angry, both of you, and there's no need to lose your tempers…'

'Angry? You are witless, madam. Could you not see that we jested?'

There was no evidence. Miss Ming became confused.

Li Pao's lips were pursed, his cheeks were as pale as hers were red. Doctor Volospion's eyes were hard and fiery. Abu Thaleb gave vent to a troubled muttering.

Miss Ming seemed fixed in her position by a terrible fascination. Mindlessly, she stared at the eyes of her accuser. It seemed that her urge to flee was balanced by her compulsion to stay, to fan these flames, to produce the holocaust that would consume her, and her mouth opened and words fled out of it, high and frightened:

'Not a very funny joke, I must say, calling someone fat and stupid. Make up your mind, Doctor Volospion. Only a minute or two ago you said how nice I looked. Don't pick on little Mavis, just because you're losing your argument!' She panted. 'Oh!'

She cast about for friends, but all eyes were averted, save Volospion's, and those pierced.

'Oh!' she said again.

Doctor Volospion parted his teeth a fraction, to hiss:

'I should be more than grateful, Miss Ming, if you would be silent. For once in your life I suggest that you reflect on your own singular lack of sensitivity –'

'Oh!'

'– on your inability to interpret the slightest nuance of social intercourse save in your own unsavoury terms.'

'O-oh!'

'A psychic cripple, Miss Ming, has no business swimming in the fast-running rivers of philosophical discussion.'

'Volospion!' Li Pao made a hesitant movement.

Perhaps Miss Ming did not hear his words at all, perhaps she only experienced his tone, his vicious stance. 'You *are* in a bad mood today…' she began, and then words gave way to her strangled, half-checked sobs.

'Volospion! Volospion! You round on that wretch because you cannot answer me!'

'Ha!' Doctor Volospion turned slowly, hampered by his robes.

Abu Thaleb had been observing Miss Ming. He spoke conversationally, leaning forward to stare at her face, his huge, feathered turban nodding. 'Are those tears, my dear?'

She snorted.

'I had heard of elephants weeping,' said Abu Thaleb with some animation. 'Or was it giraffes? – but I never thought to have the chance to witness…'

His tone produced a partial recovery in her. She lifted a wounded face. 'Oh, be quiet! You and your stupid elephants.'

'So, all our time-travellers are blessed with the same brand of good manners, it seems.' Volospion had become cool. 'I fear we have yet to grasp the essence of your social customs, madam.'

She trembled.

'Childish irony…' said Li Pao.

'Oh, stop it, Li Pao!' Mavis flinched away from him. 'You started all this.'

'Well, perhaps…'

Abu Thaleb put a puzzled tongue to his lower lip. 'If…'

'Oh,' she sobbed, 'I'm so *sorry*, commissar. I'm sorry, Doctor Volospion. I didn't mean to…'

'It is we who are in the wrong,' Li Pao told her. 'I should have known better. You are a troubled young girl at heart…'

Her weeping grew mightier.

Doctor Volospion, Abu Thaleb and Li Pao now stood around her, looking down at her.

'Come, come,' said Abu Thaleb. He patted the crown of her head.

'Oh, I'm sorry. I was only trying to help… Why does it always have to be me…?'

Doctor Volospion at last placed a hand on her arm. 'Perhaps I had best escort you home?' He was magnanimous. 'You should rest.'

'Oh!' She moved to him, as if to be comforted, and then withdrew. 'Oh, you're right! You're right! I'm fat. I'm stupid. I'm ugly.' She pulled away from him.

'No, no…' murmured Abu Thaleb. 'I think that you are immensely attractive…'

She raised a trembling chin. 'It's all right.' She swallowed. 'I'm fine now.'

Abu Thaleb gave a sigh of relief. The other two, however, continued to watch her.

She sniffed. 'I just didn't want to see anyone having a bad time, hurting one another. Yes, you're right, Doctor Volospion. I shouldn't have come. I'll go home.'

Doctor Volospion replaced his hand, to steady her. His voice was low and calming. 'Good. I will take you in my air car.'

'No. You stay and enjoy yourself. It's my fault. I'm very sorry.'

'You are too distraught.'

'Perhaps I should take her,' said Li Pao. 'After all, I introduced the original argument.'

'We all relieve the boredom in one way or another,' said Doctor Volospion quietly. 'I should not have responded as I did.'

'Nonsense. You had every reason...'

'Boo-hoo,' said Miss Ming. She had broken down again.

Abu Thaleb said coaxingly: 'Would you like one of my little flying elephants, my dear, for your very own? You could take it with you.'

'Oh-ah-ha-ha...'

'Poor thing,' said Abu Thaleb. 'I think she would have been better off in a menagerie, Doctor Volospion. Some of them feel much safer there, you know. Our world is too difficult for them to grasp. Now, if I were you...'

Doctor Volospion tightened his grip.

'Oh!'

'You are too sensitive, Miss Ming,' said Li Pao. 'You must not take us seriously.'

Doctor Volospion laughed. 'Is that so, Li Pao?'

'I meant...'

'Ah, look!' Doctor Volospion raised a hand to point. 'Here's your friend, Miss Ming.'

'Friend?' Red eyes were raised. Another sniff.

'Your friend, the cook.'

It was Argonheart Po, in smock and cap of dark brown and scarlet, so corpulent as to make Miss Ming look slim. He advanced towards them with monumental dignity, pushing small elephants from his path. With a brief bow he acknowledged the company and then addressed Abu Thaleb.

'I have come to apologise, epicurean commissar, for the lateness of my contribution.'

'No, no...' Abu Thaleb seemed weary of what appeared to be a welter of regrets.

'There is an internal fault in my recipe,' explained the Master Chef, 'which I am loath to disguise by any artifice...'

The Commissar of Bengal waved a white-gloved hand. 'You are too modest, Kaiser of Kitchens. You are too much a perfectionist. I am certain that none of us would detect any discrepancy...'

Argonheart Po acknowledged the compliment with a smile. 'Possibly. But I would know.' He confided to the others: 'The cry of the artist, I fear, down the ages. I hope, Abu Thaleb, that things will right themselves before long. If not, I shall bring you those confections which have been successful, but I will abandon the rest.'

'Drastic...' Abu Thaleb lowered his eyes and shook his head. 'Can we not help in some way?'

'The very reason I came. I hoped to gain an opinion. If there is someone who could find it within themselves to leave the party for a short while, to return with me and sample my creations, not so much for their flavour as for their consistency. It would not require much time, nor would it require a particularly sophisticated palate, but...'

'Miss Ming!' said Doctor Volospion.

'Me,' she said.

'Here is your chance to be of service.'

'Well,' she began, 'as everyone knows, I'm no gourmet. Not that I don't enjoy my chow, and, of course, Argonheart's is always excellent, but I'd like to help out, if I can.' She was twice the woman.

'It is not a gourmet's opinion I seek,' Argonheart Po told her. 'You will do excellently, Miss Ming, if you can spare a little time.'

'You would be delighted, wouldn't you, Miss Ming?' said Abu Thaleb sympathetically.

'Delighted,' she confirmed. She cast a wary glance at Doctor Volospion. 'You wouldn't mind?'

'Certainly not!' He was almost effusive.

'A splendid idea,' said Li Pao, blatantly relieved.

'Well, then, I shall be your taster, Argonheart.' She linked her arm in the cook's. 'And I really am sorry for that silly fuss, everybody.'

They shook their heads. They waved their fingers.

She smiled. 'It did clear the air, anyway, didn't it? You're all friends again now.'

'Absolutely,' said Li Pao.

'Well, that's fine.'

'And you won't be wanting the little elephant?' Abu Thaleb asked. 'I can always create another.'

'I'd *love* one, Abu. Another time, perhaps when I have a menagerie of my own. And power rings of my own and everything. I've nowhere to keep it while I stay with Doctor Volospion.'

'Ah, well.' Abu Thaleb also seemed relieved.

'I think,' said Argonheart Po, 'that we should go as quickly as possible.'

'Of course,' she said, 'You really must take me in hand, Argonheart, and tell me exactly what you expect me to do.'

'An opinion, I assure you, is all I seek.'

They made their adieux.

'*Well*,' she confided to Argonheart as they left, 'I must say you turned up at just the right moment. Honestly, I've never *seen* such a display of temper! You're so calm, Argonheart. So unshakeably dignified, you know? I did my best, of course, to calm everyone down, but they were just *determined* to have a row! Of course, I do blame Li Pao. Doctor Volospion had a perfectly understandable point of view, but would Li Pao listen to him? Not a bit of it. I suspect that Li Pao never listens to anyone but himself. He can be so thoughtless sometimes, don't you find that?'

The Master Chef smacked his lips.

Chapter Four

In Which Mavis Ming Is Once Again Disappointed in Her Ambitions

ARGONHEART PO DIPPED his fingers into his rainbow plesiosaurus (sixty distinct flavours of gelatine) and withdrew it as the beast turned its long neck round to investigate, mildly, the source of the irritation.

The great cook put a hand to mouth, sucked, and sighed.

'What a shame! Such an excellent taste.'

Argonheart Po's creature, lumbering on massive legs that were still somewhat wobbly, having failed to set at the same time as the rest of its bulk, moved to rejoin the herd grazing some distance away on the especially prepared trees of pastry and angelica he had designed to occupy them until it was time to drive them to the party which was only a mile or two off (the gargantua were plainly visible on the horizon).

'You agree, then, Miss Ming? The legs lack coherence.' He licked a disappointed mouth.

'Isn't there something you could add?' she suggested. 'Those flippers were really meant for the sea, you know...'

'Mm?'

'It's not your fault, not strictly speaking. The design of the creature itself is wrong. You must be able to do *something*, Argonheart, dear.'

'Oh, indeed. A twist of a power ring and all would be well, but I should continue to be haunted by the mystery. Was the temperature too high, for instance? You see, I allow for all the possibilities. My researches show that the animal could move on land. I wonder if the weight of the beast alters the atomic structure of the gelatine. If so, I should have prepared for it in my original recipe. There is no time to begin again.'

'But Argonheart...'

He shook his huge head. 'I must cull the herd of the failures and present, I am afraid, only a partial spectacle.'

'Abu Thaleb will still be pleased, I'm sure.'

'I hope so.' He voiced a stupendous and sultry sigh.

'It is nice to be out of the hurly-burly for a bit,' she told him, her mind moving on to other topics.

'If you would care to rejoin the party now?'

'No. I want to be here with you. That is, if you have no objection to little Mavis watching a real artist at work.'

'Of course.'

She smiled at him. 'It's such a relief, you see, to be out here alone with a real man. With someone who *does* something.' She simpered. 'What I mean is, Argonheart, is that I've always wanted...'

She gasped as he jumped, his hands flailing, to taste a passing pterodactyl. He missed it by several inches, staggered and fell to one knee.

'Cunning beasts, those.' He picked himself up. 'My fault. I should have made them easier to catch. Too much sherry and not enough blancmange.'

She sidled up to him again. 'My husband, Donny Stevens, was a real man, for all his faults.'

Argonheart returned suddenly to his knees. He cupped his hands around something which wobbled, glinting green and yellow in the pale sunshine. 'Oh, this makes up for everything. See what it is, Miss Ming?'

'A dollop of jello?'

'Dollop? *Dollop*!' He breathed upon it. He fondled the rounded, quivering surface. He spoke reverently. 'This is an egg, Miss Ming. One of my creations has actually laid an egg. Good heavens! I could breed them. What an achievement!' His expression became seraphic.

'A man like you is capable of anything, Argonheart. I often felt Donny was like that. I never thought I'd miss the bastard.'

He was searching the ground for more eggs.

'You remind me of him a little,' she said softly. 'You are *real*, Argonheart.'

Argonheart Po's only weakness was for metaphysical speculation.

Miss Ming had captured his attention. Stroking his egg, he looked round. 'Mm?'

Her breast rose and fell rapidly. 'A real man.'

He was curious. 'You believe everyone else imaginary, then? But why should I be real when the others are not? Why should *you* be real? Reality, after all, can be the syllabub that melts upon the tongue, leaving not even a flavour of memory…'

Her breathing became calmer. She turned to contemplate the half-melted remains of a completely unsuccessful stegosaurus.

'I meant,' she said, 'that Donny was a manly man. Stupid and vain, of course. But that's all part of it. And obsessed with his work – well, when he wasn't screwing his assistants.' She laid her hand upon his trembling egg. 'I like you, Argonheart. Have you ever thought…?'

But the chef's attention was wavering again as he bent to scoop up a little iguanodon. He placed his egg carefully upon a slab of marzipan rock and held the iguanodon out to her for her inspection.

With a frustrated sigh she licked the beast's slippery neck. 'Too much lime for my taste.' She gave a theatrical shudder and laughed. 'Far too bitter for me, Argonheart, dear.'

'But the texture? It was the texture, alone, I needed to know about.'

The iguanodon struggled, squawking rather like a chicken, and was released. It ran, glistening, semi-transparent, green and orange, in a crazy path towards the nearby cola lake.

'Perfect,' she said. 'Firm and juicy.'

He nodded sadly. 'The small ones are by far the most successful. But that will scarcely satisfy Abu Thaleb. I meant the monsters for him. The little beasts were only to set off the large ones – to set the scale, do you see? I was too ambitious, Miss Ming. I tried to produce too much and too many.' His fat brow wrinkled.

'You haven't been listening, Argonheart, dear,' she chided. 'Argonheart?'

Reluctantly he withdrew from his regrets. 'We were discussing the nature of reality.'

'No.'

'You were discussing what? Men?'

She patted at the yellow flounces of her frock. 'Or their absence?' She chuckled. 'I could do with one…'

He had picked up a ladle in his plump, gloved hand. She followed him as he approached his lake, bent on a final taste.

'A man? What could you do with one?' He sipped.

'I need one.'

'A special kind?'

'A real one.'

'Couldn't you make something – someone, I mean – to suit you? Doctor Volospion would help.' He looked across the tranquil surface, like molten amber. 'Delicious!'

She seemed pained. 'There's no need, dear, to throw that particular episode in my face.'

'Um. Yet, I'm indulging myself, I fear.' He stooped, dipped his ladle, drew it to his red lips, sampled self-critically and nodded his head. 'Yes. The conception was too grandiose. Given another day I could put everything to rights, but poor Abu Thaleb expects… Ah, well!'

'Forget all about that for a moment.' Lust was mounting in her. She slipped a hand along his massive thigh. 'Make love to me, Argonheart. I've been so unhappy.'

He rubbed his several chins. 'Oh, I see.'

'You knew all along, didn't you? What I wanted?'

'Um.'

'You're so proud, Argonheart. So masculine. A lot of girls don't like fat men, but I do.' She giggled. 'It's what they used to say about me. All the more to get hold of. Please, Argonheart, please!'

'My confections,' he murmured lamely.

'You can spare a few minutes, surely?' She dug her nails into his chest. 'Argonheart!'

'They could –'

'You must relax sometime. You have to relax. It gives you a new perspective.'

'Well, yes, that's true.'

'Argonheart!' She moved against him.

'I certainly cannot improve anything now. Perhaps you are right. Yes…'

'Yes! You'll feel so much better. And I will, too.'

'Possibly…'

'Definitely!'

She pulled him towards a pile of discarded dark brown straw. 'Here's a good place.' She sank into it, tugging at his gloved hand.

'What?' he murmured. 'In the vermicelli?'

It was already beginning to stick to her sweating arms, but it was plain that such considerations were no longer important. 'Why not? Why not? Oh, my darling. Oh, Argonheart!'

He drew off his gloves. He reached down and removed a strand or two of the vermicelli from her elbow and placed it neatly on her neck. He stood back.

She writhed in the chocolate.

'Argonheart!' She mewed.

With a shrug, he fell beside her in the chocolate.

It was at the point where she had helped him to drag the tight scarlet smock up to his navel while wriggling her own blue lace knickers to just below her knees that they heard a shriek that filled the sky and saw the crimson spaceship falling through the dark blue heavens in an aura of multicoloured flame.

Argonheart's belly quivered against her as he paused.

'Golly!' said Mavis Ming.

Argonheart licked her shoulder, but his attention was no longer with her. He glanced back. The spaceship was still falling. The noise was immense.

'Don't stop,' she said. 'There's still time. It won't take long.'

But Argonheart was already rolling over in the vermicelli, pulling his smock back into position. He stood up. Shreds of half-melted confectionery dropped from his legs.

A dreadful wail escaped Miss Ming. It was drowned by the roar of the ship.

With her fist she pounded at the vermicelli. It flew in all directions. She appeared to be swearing. And then, when the ship's noise had dropped momentarily to a muted howl, and as Mavis Ming drew up her underwear, her voice, disappointed, despairing, could be heard again.

'What a moment to pick! Poor old Mavis. Isn't it just your luck.'

Chapter Five

In Which Certain Denizens at the End of Time Indulge Themselves in Speculation As To the Nature of the Visitor from Space

It was a spaceship from some mythical antiquity, all fins and flutes and glittering bubbles, tapering at the nose, bulbous at the base, where its rockets roared. It slowed as they watched, falling with a peculiar swaying motion, as if its engines malfunctioned, the vents first on one side and then on the other sputtering, gouting, sputtering again until, just before the ship reached the ground, the rockets flared in unison, bouncing the machine like a ball on a water jet, gradually subsiding until it had settled to earth.

Miss Ming, observing it from her nest of chocolate worms, tightened her lips.

Even after the ship had landed, flame still rolled around its hull, sensuous flame caressing the scarlet metal.

The surrounding terrain sent up heavy black smoke, crackling as if to protest. The smoke curled close to the ground, moving towards the ship: eels attracted to wreckage.

Miss Ming was in no temper to admire the machine; she glared at it.

'It has a certain authority, the ship,' murmured Argonheart Po.

'A fine sense of timing, I must say! A little love-making would have improved my spirits no end and taken away the nasty taste of Doctor Volospion's tantrum. It isn't as if I get the chance every day and I haven't had a man for ages. I don't even know if one can still give me what I need! Even you, Argonheart…'

She pouted, brushing at the nasty sticky stuff clinging to her petticoats. 'I'm too furious to speak!'

Argonheart Po helped her from the pile and, perhaps moved by unconscious chivalry, pecked her upon the cheek. The smell of burning filled the air.

'Ugh,' she said. 'What a *stink*, too!'

'It is the least attractive of odours,' Argonheart said.

'It's horrible. Surely it can't just be coming from that ship?'

The heat from the vessel was heavy on their skins. Argonheart Po, had his body been so fashioned, would have been sweating quite as much as Miss Ming. His sensitive nose twitched.

'There is something familiar about it,' he agreed, 'which I would not normally identify with hot metal.' He perused the landscape. His cry of horror echoed over it.

'Ah! Look what it has done! Look! Oh, it is too bad!'

Miss Ming looked and saw nothing. 'What?'

Argonheart was in anguish. His hands clenched, his eyes blazed.

'It has melted half my dinosaurs. That is what is making the smoke!'

Argonheart Po began to roll rapidly in the direction of the ship, Mavis Ming forgotten.

'Hey!' she cried. 'What if there's danger?'

He had not heard her.

With a whimper, she followed him.

'Murderer!' cried the distressed chef. 'Philistine!' He shook his fist at the ship. He danced about it, forced back by its heat. He attempted to kick it and failed.

'Locust!' he raved. 'Ravager! Insensitive despoiler!'

His energy dissipated, he fell to his knees in the glutinous mess. He wept. 'Oh, my monsters! My jellies!'

Mavis Ming hovered a short distance away. She wore the pout of someone who considered themselves abandoned in their hour of need.

'Argonheart!' she called.

'Burned! All burned!'

'Argonheart, we don't know what sort of creatures are *in* that spaceship. They could mean us harm!'

'Ruin, ruin, ruin…'

'Argonheart. I think we should go and warn someone, don't you?' She discovered that her lovely shoes were stuck. As she lifted her feet, long strands of toffeelike stuff came with them. She waded back to a patch of dust still free of melted dinosaur.

Her attention focused upon the ship as curiosity conquered caution. 'I've seen alien spacecraft before,' she said. 'Lots of them. But this doesn't look alien at all. It's got a distinctly human look to it, in fact.'

Argonheart Po raised his mighty body to its feet and, with shoulders bowed, mourned his dead creations.

'Argonheart, don't you think it's got a rather *romantic* appearance, really?'

Argonheart Po turned his back on the source of his anger and folded his arms across his chest. He wore a martyred air, yet his dignity increased.

Mavis Ming continued to inspect the spaceship. A strange smile had replaced the expression of anxiety she had worn earlier. 'Come to think of it, it's just the sort of ship I used to read about when I was a little girl. All the space-heroes had ships like that.' She became fey. 'Perhaps at long last my prayers have been answered, Argonheart.'

The Master Chef grunted. He was lost in profundity.

Miss Ming uttered her trilling laugh. 'Has my handsome space-knight arrived to carry me off, do you think? To the wonderful planet of Paradise V?'

From Argonheart there issued a deep, violent rumbling, as of an angry volcano. 'Villain! Villain!'

She put a hand to her mouth. 'You could be right. It could easily carry a villain. Some pirate captain and his cut-throat crew.' She became reminiscent. 'My two favourite authors, you know, when I was young – well, I'd still read them now, if I could – were J.R.R. Tolkien and A.A. Milne. Well, this is more like the *movie* versions, of course, but still... Oooh! Could they be *rapists* and *slavers*, Argonheart?'

She took his silence for disapproval. 'Not that I really want anything nasty to happen to us. Not really. But it's *thrilling*, isn't it, wondering?'

'I –' said Argonheart Po. 'I –'

Miss Ming, as she anticipated the occupants of the ship, seemed torn between poles represented in her fantasies by the evil, fascinating Sauron and the soft, jolly Winnie-the-Pooh.

'Will they be fierce, do you think, Argonheart? Or cuddly?' She bit her lower lip. 'Better still, they might be fierce *and* cuddly!'

'Aaaaaah,' breathed Argonheart.

She looked at him in surprise. She appeared to make an effort to retrieve herself from sentiment which, she had doubtless learned, was not always socially acceptable in this world. She achieved the retrieval by a return to her previous alternative, her vein of heavy cynicism. 'I was only joking,' she said.

'Sadist,' hissed Argonheart. 'This might have been deliberately engineered.'

'Well,' she said, having determined her new attitude, 'at least it might be someone to relieve the awful *boredom* of this bloody planet!'

Still bowed, her baffled and grieving escort turned from the blackened fragments of his culinary dreams to stare wistfully after his surviving stegosauri and tyrannosauri which, startled by the ship, were in rapid and uncertain flight in all directions.

His self-control returned. He became a fatalist. His little shrug went virtually unnoticed by her.

'It is fate,' declared the Master Chef. 'At least I am no longer in a dilemma. The decision has been taken from me.'

He began to wade, as best the sticky glue would allow him, towards her.

'Couldn't you round them up?' she asked. 'The ones who survived?'

'And make only a paltry contribution? No. I shall find Abu Thaleb and tell him he must create something for himself. A few turns of a power ring, of course, and he will have a feast of sorts, though it will lack the inspiration of anything I could have prepared for him.' A certain guilt, it seemed, inspired him to resent the object of his guilt and therefore made him feel somewhat aggressive towards Abu Thaleb.

He reached Miss Ming's side. 'Shall we return to the party together?'

'But what of the ship?'

'It has done its terrible work.'

'But the people who came in it?'

'I forgive them,' said Argonheart with grandiose magnanimity.

'I mean – don't you want to see what they look like?'

'I bear them no ill will. They were not aware of the horror they brought. It is ever thus.'

'They might be interesting.'

'*Interesting*?' Argonheart Po was incredulous.

'They might have some news, or something.'

Argonheart Po looked again upon the spaceship. 'They are scarcely likely to be anything but crude, ill-mannered rogues, Miss Ming. Surely, they must have seen, by means of their instruments, my herds?'

'It could be a crash-landing.'

'Perhaps.' Argonheart Po was a fair-minded chef. He did his best to see her point. 'Perhaps.'

'They might need help.'

He cast one final glance about the smoking detritus and said, with not a little violence, 'Well, I hope that they find it.'

'Shouldn't we…?'

'I return to find Abu Thaleb and tell him of the disaster.'

'Oh, very well, I suppose I shall have to come with you. But, really, Argonheart, you're looking at this in a rather selfish way, aren't you? This could be a great event. Remember those other aliens who turned up recently? They were trying to help us, too, weren't they? It would be lovely to have some *nice* news for a change…'

She reached for his arm, so that he might escort her through the glutinous pools.

At that moment there came a grinding noise from the vessel. Both looked back.

A circular section in the hull was turning.

'The airlock,' she gasped. 'It's opening.'

The door of the airlock swung back, apparently on old-fashioned hinges, to reveal a dark hole from which, for a few seconds, flames poured.

'They can't be human,' she said. 'Not if they live in fire.'

No further flames issued from within the ship but from the darkness of the interior there came at intervals tiny flashes of light.

'Like fireflies,' whispered Mavis Ming.

'Or eyes,' said Argonheart, his attention held for the moment.

'The feral eyes of wild invaders.' Miss Ming seemed to be quoting from one of her girlhood texts.

An engine murmured and the ship shivered. Then, from somewhere inside the airlock, a wide band of metal began to emerge.

'A ramp,' said Mavis Ming. 'They're letting down a ramp.'

The ramp slid slowly to the ground, making a bridge between airlock and earth, but still no occupant emerged.

Mavis cupped her hands around her mouth. 'Greetings!' she cried. 'The peaceful people of Earth welcome you!'

There was still no acknowledgement from the ship. Grainy dust drifted past. There was silence.

'They might be afraid of us,' suggested Mavis.

'Most probably they are ashamed,' said Argonheart Po. 'Too abashed to display themselves.'

'Oh, Argonheart! They probably didn't even see your dinosaurs!'

'Is that an excuse?'

'Well…'

Now a muffled, querulous voice sounded from within the airlock, but the language it used was unintelligible.

'We have no translators.' Argonheart Po consulted his power rings. 'I have no means of making him speak any sort of tongue I'll understand. Neither have I the means to understand him. We must go. Lord Jagged of Canaria usually has a translation ring. Or the Duke of Queens. Or Doctor Volospion. Anyone who keeps a menagerie will…'

'Sssh,' she said. 'The odd thing is, Argonheart, that while I can't actually understand the words, the language *does* seem familiar. It's like – well, it's like English – the language I used to speak before I came here.'

'You cannot speak it now?'

'Obviously not. I'm speaking this one, whatever it is, aren't I?'

The voice came again. It was high-pitched. It tended to trill, like birdsong, and yet it was human.

'It's not unpleasant,' she said, 'but it's not what I would have called *manly.*' She was kind: 'Still, the pitch might be affected by a change in the atmosphere, mightn't it?'

'Possibly.' Argonheart peered. 'Hm. One of them seems to be coming out.'

At last a space-traveller emerged at the top of the ramp.

'Oh, dear,' murmured Miss Ming. 'What a disappointment! I hope they're not all like him.'

Although undoubtedly humanoid, the stranger had a distinctly birdlike air to him. There was a wild crest of bright auburn hair, which rose all around his head and created a kind of ruff about his neck; there was a sharp pointed nose; there were vivid blue eyes which bulged and blinked in the light; there was a head which craned forward on an elongated neck and which would sometimes jerk back a little, like a chicken's as it searched for grain amid the farmyard's dust; there was a tiny body which also moved in rapid, poorly co-ordinated jerks and twitches; there were two arms, held stiffly at the sides of the body, like clipped wings. And then there was the plaintive, questioning cry, like a puzzled gull's:

'Eh? Eh? Eh?'

The eyes darted this way and that and then fixed suddenly upon Mavis Ming and Argonheart Po. They received the creature's whole attention.

'Eh?'

He blinked imperiously at them. He trilled a few words.

Argonheart Po waited until the newcomer had finished before announcing gravely:

'You have ruined the Commissar of Bengal's dinner, sir.'

'Eh?'

'You have reduced a carefully planned feast to a rabble of side dishes!'

'Fallerunnerstanja,' said the visitor from space. He reached back into the airlock and produced a black frock-coat dating from a period at least a hundred and fifty years before Mavis Ming's own. He drew the coat over his shirt and buttoned it all the way down. 'Eh?'

'It's not very clean,' said Mavis, 'that coat. Is it?'

Argonheart had not noticed the stranger's clothes. He was

regretting his outburst and trying to recover his composure, his normal amiability.

'Welcome,' he said, 'to the End of Time.'

'Eh?'

The space-traveller frowned and consulted a bulky instrument in his right hand. He tapped it, shook it and held it up to his ear.

'Well,' said Mavis with a sniff. '*He* isn't much, is he? I wonder if they're all like him.'

'He could be the only one,' suggested Argonheart Po.

'Like that?'

'The only one at all.'

'I hope not!'

As if in response to her criticism the creature waved both his arms in a sort of windmilling motion. It seemed for a moment as if he were trying to fly. Then, with stiff movements, reminiscent of a poorly controlled marionette, the creature retreated back into his ship.

'Did we frighten him, do you think?' asked Argonheart Po in some concern.

'Quite likely. What a weedy little creep!'

'Mm?'

'What a rotten specimen! He doesn't go with the ship at all. I was expecting someone tanned, brawny, handsome...'

'Why so? You know these ships? You have met those who normally use them?'

'Only in my dreams,' she said.

Argonheart made no further effort to follow her. 'He is humanoid, at least. It makes a change, don't you think, Miss Ming, from all those others?'

'Not much of one though.' She shifted a gluey foot. 'Ah, well! Shall we return, as you suggested?'

'You don't think we should remain?'

'There's no point, is there? Let someone else deal with him. Someone who wants a curiosity for their menagerie.'

Argonheart Po offered his arm again. They began to wade towards the dusty shore.

As they reached the higher ground they heard a familiar voice from overhead. They looked up.

Abu Thaleb's howdah hovered there.

'Aha!' said the Commissar of Bengal. His face, with its beard carefully curled and divided into two parts, set with pearls and rubies, after the original, peered over the edge of the air car. 'I thought so.' He addressed another occupant, invisible to their eyes. 'You see, Volospion, I was right.'

'Oh, dear.' Mavis tried to rearrange her disordered dress. 'Doctor Volospion, too...'

Volospion's tired tones issued from the howdah. 'Yes, indeed. You were quite right, Abu Thaleb. I apologise. It is a spaceship. Well, if you feel you would like to descend, I shall not object.'

The howdah came down to earth beside Argonheart Po and Miss Ming. Within, it was lined with dark green and blue plush.

Doctor Volospion lay among cushions, still in black and gold, his tight hood covering his skull and framing his pale face. He made no attempt to move. He scarcely acknowledged Miss Ming's presence as he addressed Argonheart Po:

'Forgive this intrusion, great Prince of Pies. The Commissar of Bengal is bent on satisfying his curiosity.'

Argonheart Po made to speak but Abu Thaleb had already begun again:

'What a peculiar odour it has – sweet, yet bitter...'

'My creations...' said Argonheart.

'Like death,' pronounced Doctor Volospion.

'The smell is all that is left,' insisted Argonheart now, 'of the dinner I was preparing for your party, Abu Thaleb. The ship's landing destroyed almost all of it.'

Climbing from his howdah the slender commissar clapped the chef upon his broad back. 'Dear Argonheart, how sad! But another time, I hope, you will be able to re-create all that you have lost today.'

'It is true that there were imperfections,' Argonheart told him, 'and I would relish the opportunity to begin afresh.'

'Soon, soon, soon. What a lovely little ship it is!' Abu Thaleb's plumes bounced upon his turban. 'I had yearnings, you see, to embellish my menagerie, but I fear the ship is too small to accommodate the kind of prize I seek.'

Mavis Ming said: 'You'd be even more disappointed than me, Abu Thaleb. You should see the little squirt we saw just before you turned up. He –'

Doctor Volospion, so it seemed, had not heard her begin to speak. He called from his cushions:

'Your menagerie is already a marvel, Belle of Bengal. The most refined collection in the world. Splendid, specialised, so much more sophisticated than the scrambled skelter of species scraped together by certain so-called connoisseurs whose zoos surpass yours only in size but never in superiority of sensitive selection!'

Mavis Ming displayed confusion. Although Doctor Volospion appeared to address Abu Thaleb he seemed to be speaking for her benefit. She looked from one to the other, wondering if she should form a smile.

Doctor Volospion winked at her.

Mavis grinned. She had been forgiven for her outburst. The joke was at Abu Thaleb's expense.

She began to giggle.

'Go on, Doctor Volospion. I'm sure Abu Thaleb enjoys your flattery,' she said.

'In taste, salutary commissar, you are assured of supremacy, until our planet passes at last into that limbo of silence and non-existence which must soon, we are told, be its fate.'

Abu Thaleb's back was to Miss Ming and she seemed glad of this. She held her breath. She went deep red. She made a muted, spluttering noise.

But now the Commissar of Bengal was looking back at Doctor Volospion. 'Oh, really, my friend!' He was good-natured. 'You are capable of subtler mockery than this!'

'But I am a true showman, Abu Thaleb. I relate properly to my audience.'

'Can that be so?' Abu Thaleb turned to Mavis. 'You have seen the visitors, then, Miss Ming?'

'Briefly,' she said. 'Actually, there only seems to be one.'

Abu Thaleb stroked his beard, his pearls and rubies. 'He is not in any way, I suppose, um – elephantoid?'

She was prepared to allow herself a giggle now. She glanced sidelong towards the lounging Volospion.

'Not a trace of a trunk, I'm afraid.' She looked for approval from her protector. 'Not even a touch of a tusk. He couldn't be less like a jumbo, although his nose is long enough, I suppose. He's more like one of those little birds, Abu Thaleb, who pick stuff out of elephant's teeth.'

'Excellent!' applauded Doctor Volospion. 'Ha, ha, ha!'

Abu Thaleb turned and regarded her with mysterious gravity. 'Teeth?'

She giggled again. 'Don't they have teeth, then, any more?'

Argonheart Po seemed much embarrassed. His glance at Doctor Volospion was almost disapproving. 'I must away to my thoughts,' he said. 'I shall leave this sad scene. There is nothing I can save. Not now. So I'll wish you all farewell.'

'Are we to be denied even a taste of your palatable treasure, Argonheart?' Doctor Volospion used much the same voice as the one he had used to speak to Abu Thaleb. 'Hm?'

Argonheart Po cleared his throat. He shook his head. He glanced at the ground. 'I think so.'

'Oh, but Argonheart, you still have a few dinosaurs left. Can't I see one now? On the horizon.' Miss Ming clutched at his hand but failed to engage.

'No more, no more,' said the Master Chef.

Doctor Volospion spoke again. 'Ah, mighty Lord of the Larder, how haughty you can sometimes be! Just a morsel of mastodon, perhaps, to whet our appetites?'

'I made no mastodons!' bellowed Argonheart Po, and now he was striding away. 'Goodbye to you!'

Doctor Volospion stirred in his cushion. 'Well, well. Obsessive people can be very boorish sometimes, I think.'

Mavis Ming said: 'He was more interested in his confectionery than any opportunity for contact with another intelligence. Still, he *was* upset.'

'Then you are the only one of us to have tasted his preparations.' Abu Thaleb looked doubtfully at the congealing lake between him and the spaceship.

'How were his dishes, by the by, Miss Ming?' Doctor Volospion wished to know. 'You sampled them, eh?'

Miss Ming adopted something of a worldly air for Doctor Volospion's approval. She uttered a light, amused laugh. 'Oh, a bit over-flavoured, really, if the truth be told.'

His thin tongue ran the line of his lips. 'Too strong, the taste?'

'He's not as good as they say he is, if you ask me. All this –' she rotated a wrist – 'all these big ideas.'

Abu Thaleb would not allow such malice. 'Argonheart Po is the greatest culinary genius in the history of the world!'

'Perhaps our world has not been well favoured with cooks…' suggested Doctor Volospion slyly.

'And he is the most good-hearted of fellows! The *time* he must have spent preparing the feast for today!'

'Time?' enquired Volospion in some disbelief. 'Time? Time?'

'His presents are famous. Not long since, he made me a savoury mammoth that was the most delicious thing I have ever eaten. An arrangement of flavours defeating description, and yet possessing a unity of taste that was inevitable!' Abu Thaleb was displaying unusual vivacity.

Doctor Volospion was incapable of diplomacy now. He was as one who has hooked his shark and refuses to cut the line, no matter what damage may ensue to both boat and man.

'Perhaps you confuse the subject matter with the art, admirable Abu?'

Mavis Ming would also take hold of the rod, secure in the approval of her protector, inspired by his wit. 'One man's elephant steak, after all, is another man's bicarbonate of soda!'

And now it was as if rod and line snapped over the side to be borne to the depths.

Abu Thaleb stared at her in frank bewilderment.

Doctor Volospion turned from his prey, his grey face controlled. There was a pause. His expression changed. A secretive smile, for himself more than for her.

The Commissar of Bengal had been saved from conflict and as a result became confused. 'Well,' he said weakly, 'I for one am always astonished by his invention.'

Miss Ming became aware of the atmosphere. Such an atmosphere often followed her funniest observations. 'I'm being too subtle and obscure. I'm sorry. No – Argonheart can be very clever. Very clever indeed. He's very nice. He's always made me feel very much at home. Oh, dear! Do I always manage to spoil things? It can't be me, can it?'

Doctor Volospion, for reasons of his own, had cast a fresh line. 'My dear Miss Ming, you are being too kind again!'

He raised a long hand, the fingers curled forwards to form a claw. 'Do not let this clever commissar confuse you into compromising your opinions. Be true to your own convictions. If you find Argonheart's work unsatisfactory, not up to the demands of your palate, then say so.'

Abu Thaleb this time ignored the bait. 'Volospion, you mock us both too much,' he protested. 'Leave Miss Ming, at least, alone!'

'Oh, he's not mocking *me*,' Miss Ming observed.

'I?' Doctor Volospion moved his brows in apparent astonishment. 'Mock?'

'Yes. Mock.' Abu Thaleb studied the spaceship.

'You do me too much credit, my friend.'

'Hum,' said Abu Thaleb.

Mavis Ming laughed amiably. 'You never know when he's being serious or when he's joking, do you, commissar?'

Abu Thaleb was brief. 'Well, Miss Ming, if you are not discomforted, then –'

He was interrupted by Doctor Volospion, who pointed to the ship.

'Ha! Our guest emerges!'

Chapter Six
In Which Mr Emmanuel Bloom Lays Claim to His Kingdom

Once more he stood before them, his head bent forwards, his bright blue eyes glittering, his stiff arms at his sides, his red hair flaring to frame his face. He remained for some while at the top of the ramp. He watched them, not with caution but with dispassionate curiosity.

He had changed his clothes.

Now he had on a suit of crumpled black velvet, a shirt whose stiff, high collar rose as if to support his chin, whose cuffs covered his clenched hands to the knuckles. His feet were small and there were tiny, shining pumps on them. He leaned so far over the ramp that he threatened to topple straight down it.

'What an altogether ridiculous figure,' hissed Miss Ming to Doctor Volospion. 'Don't you think?'

She would have said more but, for the moment, she evidently felt the compelling authority of those bulging blue eyes.

'Not from space at all,' complained the Commissar of Bengal. 'He's a time-traveller. His clothes…'

'Oh, no.' Miss Ming was adamant. 'We saw him arrive. The ship came from space.'

'From the *sky*, perhaps, but not from space.' Abu Thaleb pushed pearls away from his mouth. 'Now –'

But the newcomer had struck a strange pose, arms stiffly extended before him, little mouth smiling, head held up. He spoke in fluting musical tones that were this time completely comprehensible to them all.

'I welcome you, people of Earth, to my presence. I cannot say how moved I am to be among you again and I appreciate your own feelings on this wonderful day. For the Hero of your greatest legends returns to you. Ah, but how you must have yearned for me.

How you must have prayed for me to come back to you! To bring you Life. To bring you Reassurance. To bring you that Tranquillity that can only be achieved by Pain! Well, dear people of Earth, I am back. At long last I am back!'

'Back...?' grunted Abu Thaleb.

'Oh, the journey has demented him,' suggested Mavis Ming.

Abu Thaleb cleared his throat. 'I believe you have the advantage, sir...'

'We missed the name,' explained Doctor Volospion, his voice a fraction animated.

A sweet smile appeared upon the creature's ruby lips. 'But you *must* recognise me!'

'Not a stirring of memory, for my part,' said Doctor Volospion.

'A picture, perhaps, in the old cities. But no...' said Abu Thaleb.

'You *do* look like someone. Some old writer or other,' said Miss Ming. 'I never did literature.'

He frowned. He turned his palms inwards. He looked down at his strange body. His voice trilled on. 'Yes. Yes. I suppose it is possible that you do not recognise this particular manifestation.'

'Perhaps you could offer a clue.' Doctor Volospion sat up in his cushions for the first time.

He was ignored. The newcomer was patting at his chest. 'I have changed my physical appearance so many times that I have forgotten how I looked at first. The body has probably diminished quite a lot. The hands are certainly of a different shape. Once, as I recall, I was fat. As fat as your friend – ah, he's gone! – the one who was here when I first emerged and whose language I couldn't understand – the translator is working fine now, eh? Good, good. Oh, yes! Quite as fat as him. Fatter. And tall, I think, too. Much taller than any of you. But I leant towards economy. I had the opportunity to change. To be more comfortable in the confines of my ship. I caused my physique to be altered. Irreversibly. This form was modelled after a hero of my own whose name and achievements I forget.' He drew a deep breath. 'Still, the form is immaterial. I am here, as I say, to bring you Fulfilment.'

'I am sure that we are all grateful,' said Doctor Volospion.

'But your name, sir?' Abu Thaleb reminded him.

'Name? Names! Names! Names! I have so many!' He flung back his head and gave forth a warbling laugh. 'Names!'

'Just one would help...' said Abu Thaleb without irony.

'Names?' His blue eyes fixed them. He gestured. 'Names? How would you have me called? For I am the Phoenix! I am the Sun's Eagle! I am the Sun's Revenge!' He strutted to the very edge of the ramp but still did not descend. He leaned against the airlock opening. 'You shall know me. You shall! For I am the claws, come to take back the heart you stole from the centre of that great furnace that is my Lord and my Slave. Eh? Do you recall me now, as I remind you of your crimes?'

'Quite mad,' said Miss Ming in a low, tense voice. 'I think we'd better...' But her companions were fascinated.

'Here I am!' He spread his legs and arms, to fill the airlock: X. 'Magus, clown and prophet, I – Master of the World! Witness!'

Mavis Ming gasped as flames shot from his fingertips. Flames danced in his hair. Flames flickered from his nostrils. 'Clownly, kingly, priestly eater and disgorger of fire! Ha!'

He laughed and gestured and balls of flame surrounded him.

'I have no ambiguities, no ambitions – I *am* all things! Man and woman, god and beast, child and ancient – all are compatible and all coexist in me.'

A huge sheet of fire seemed to engulf the whole ship and then vanish, leaving the newcomer standing there at the airlock, his high voice piping, his blue eyes full of pride.

'I am Mankind! I am the Multiverse! I am Life and Death and Limbo, too. I am Peace, Strife and Equilibrium. I am Damnation and Salvation. I am all that exists. And I am *you*!'

He threw back his little head and began to laugh while the three people stared at him in silent astonishment. For the first time he walked a little way down the ramp, balancing on the balls of his feet, extending his arms at his sides. And he began to sing:

'For I am GOD – and SATAN, too!
PHOENIX, FAUST and FOOL!
My MADNESS is DIVINE, and COOL my SENSE!
I am your DOOM, your PROVIDENCE!'

'We are still, I fear, at a loss…' murmured Doctor Volospion, but he could not be heard by that singing creature whose attention was suddenly, as if for the first time, on Mavis Ming.

Miss Ming retreated a step or two. 'Oo! What do you think you're looking at, chum!'

He stopped his singing. His features became eager. He bent to regard her.

'Ah! What a *splendid* woman!'

He moved still further down the ramp and he was sighing with pleasure.

'Oh, Madonna of Lust. Ah, my Tigress, my Temptation. Mm! Never have I seen such beauty! But this is Ultimate Femininity!'

'I've had enough,' said Miss Ming severely, and she began to edge away.

He did not follow, but his eyes enchained her. His high, sing-song voice became ecstatic.

'What Beauty! Ah – I will bring great wings to beat upon your breast.' His hands clenched at air. 'Tearing talons your talents shall grasp! Claws of blood and sinew shall catch the silver strings of your cool harp! Ha! I'll have you, madam, never fear! Ho! I'll bring your blood to the surface of your skin! Hei! It shall pulse there – in service to my sin!'

'I'm not hanging around,' she said, but she did not move.

The other two watched, forgotten by both, as the strange, mad figure pranced upon his ramp, paying court to the fat, bewildered lady in blue and yellow below.

'You shall be mine, madam. You shall be mine! This is worth all those millennia when I was denied any form of consolation, any sort of human company. I have crossed galaxies and dimensions to find my reward! Now I know my twofold mission. To save this world and to win this woman!'

'No chance,' she breathed. 'Ugh!' She panted but could not flee.

He ignored her, or else had not heard her, his attention drawn back to Doctor Volospion. 'You asked my name. Now do you recognise me?'

'Not specifically.' Even Doctor Volospion was impressed by the intensity of the newcomer's speech. 'Um – perhaps another clue?'

Bang! A stream of flame had shot from the man's hand and destroyed one of Werther's unfinished mountains.

Boom! The sky darkened and thunder shook the landscape while lightning struck all about them. Chaos swirled around the ship and out of it stared the newcomer's face shouting:

'There! Is that enough to tell you?'

Abu Thaleb demurred. 'That was one of a set of mountains manufactured by someone who was hoping...'

'Manufactured?'

The thunder stopped. The lightning ceased. The sky became clear again.

'Manufactured? You *make* these pathetic landscapes? From *choice*? Pah!'

'There are other things we make...'

'And what puny conceits! Paint! I use all that is real for *my* canvases. Fire, water, earth and air – and human souls!'

'We can sometimes achieve quite interesting effects,' continued Abu Thaleb manfully, 'by...'

'Nonsense! Know you this – that I am the Controller of your Destinies! Reborn, I come among you to give you New Life! I offer the Universe!'

'We have had the universe,' said Doctor Volospion. 'That is partly why we are in our current predicament. It is all used up.'

'Bah! Well, well, well. So I must take it upon myself again to rescue the race. I shall not betray you – as you have betrayed me in the past. Again I give you the opportunity. Follow me!'

The Commissar of Bengal passed a hand over the gleaming corkscrew curls of his blue-black beard; he tugged at the red Star of India decorating his left earlobe; he fingered a feather of his turban.

'Follow you? By Allah, sir, I'm confounded! Follow you? Not a word, I fear. Not a syllable.'

'That is not what I meant.'

'I think,' interposed Doctor Volospion, 'that our visitor regards himself as a prophet – a chosen spokesman for some religion or other. The phrase he uses is more than familiar to me. Doubtless he wishes to convert us to the worship of his god.'

'God? God! God! I am no servant of a Higher Power!' The visitor's neck flashed back in shock. 'Unless, as can fairly be said, I serve myself – and mankind, of course...'

Doctor Volospion casually changed the colour of his robes to dark green and silver, then to crimson and black. He sighed. He became all black.

The visitor watched this process with some contempt. 'What have we here? A jester to my clown?'

Doctor Volospion glanced up. 'Forgive me if I seem unmannerly. I was seeking an appropriate colour for my mood.'

Abu Thaleb was dogged. 'Sir, if you could introduce yourself, perhaps a little more formally...?'

The stranger regarded him through a milder eye, as if giving the commissar's remark weighty consideration.

'A name? Just one,' coaxed the Lord of All Elephants. 'It might jog our memories, d'you see?'

'I am your Messiah.'

'There!' cried Doctor Volospion, pleased with his earlier interpretation.

The Messiah raised inflexible arms towards the skies. 'I am the Prophet of the Sun! Flamebringer, call me!'

Still more animated, even amused, Doctor Volospion turned his attention away from his cuffs (now of purple lace) to remark: 'The name is not familiar, sir. Where are you from?'

'Earth! I am from Earth!' The prophet gripped the lapels of his velvet coat. 'You must know me. I have given you every hint.'

'But when did you *leave* Earth?' Abu Thaleb put in, intending help. 'Perhaps we are further in your future than you realise. This planet, you see, is millions, billions, of years old. Why, there is every evidence that it would have perished a long time ago – so far as supporting human life was concerned, at any rate – if we had not, with the aid of our great, old cities, maintained it. You could be from a past so distant that no memory remains of you. The cities, of course, do remember a great deal, and it is possible that one of *them* might know you. Or there are time-travellers here, like Miss Ming, with better memories of earlier times than even the cities possess. What I am trying to say, sir, is that we are not being deliberately obtuse. We should be only too willing to show you proper respect if we knew who you were and how we should show it. It is on you, the onus, I regret.'

The head jerked from side to side; a curious cockatoo. 'Eh?'

'Name, rank and serial number!' Miss Ming guffawed.

'Eh?'

'We are an ancient and ignorant people,' Abu Thaleb apologised. 'Well, at least, I speak for myself. I am very ancient and extremely ignorant. Except, I should explain, in the matter of elephants, where I am something of an expert.'

'Elephants?'

The stranger's blue eyes glittered. 'So this is what you have become? Dilettantes! Fops! Dandies! Cynics! Quasi-realists!'

'We have become all things at the End of Time,' said Doctor Volospion. 'Variety flourishes, if originality does not.'

'Pah! I call you lifeless bones. But fear not. I am returned to resurrect you. I am Power. I am the forgotten Spirit of Mankind. I am Possibility.'

'Quite so,' said Doctor Volospion agreeably. 'But I think, sir, that you underestimate the degree of our sophistication.'

'We have really considered the matter quite closely, some of us,' Abu Thaleb wished the stranger to know. 'We are definitely, it seems, doomed.'

'Not now! Not now!' The little man jerked his hand and fire began to roar upon Argonheart Po's cola lake. It was a bright, unlikely red. There was heat.

'Delightful,' murmured Doctor Volospion. 'But if I may demonstrate...' He turned a sapphire ring on his right finger. Pale blue clouds formed over the lake. A light rain fell. The fire guttered. It died. 'You will see,' added Doctor Volospion quickly, noting the stranger's expression, 'that we enjoy a certain amount of control over the elements.' He turned another ring. The fire returned.

'I am not here to match conjuring tricks with you, my jackal-eyed friend!' The stranger gestured and a halo of bright flame appeared around his head. He swept his arms about and black clouds filled the sky once more and thunder boomed again; lightning crashed. 'I use my mastery merely to demonstrate my moral purpose.'

Doctor Volospion raised a delighted hand to his mouth. 'I did not realise…'

'Well, you shall! You shall know me! I shall awaken the memory dreaming in the forgotten places of your minds. Then, how gladly you will welcome me! For I am Salvation.' He struck a pose and his high, musical voice very nearly sang his next speech:

'Oh, call me Satan, for I am cast down from Heaven! The teeming worlds of the multiverse have been my domicile till now; but here I am, come back to you, at long last. You do not know me now – but you shall know me soon. I am He for whom you have been waiting. I am the Sun Eagle. Ah, now shall this old world blossom with my fire. For I shall be triumphant, the terrible, intolerant Master of your Globe.'

He paused only for a second to review his audience, his head on one side. Then he filled his lungs and continued with his litany:

'This is my birthright, my duty, my desire. I claim the World. I claim all its denizens as my subjects. I shall instruct you in the glories of the Spirit. You sleep now. You have forgotten how to fly on the wild winds that blow from Heaven and from Hell, for now you cower beneath a mere breeze that is the cold Wind of Limbo. It flattens you, deadens you, and you abase yourselves passively before it, because you know no other wind.'

His hands settled upon his hips. 'But I am the wind. I am the air and the fire to resurrect your Spirit. You two, you bewildered men, shall be my first disciples. And you, woman, shall be my glorious consort.'

Mavis Ming gave a little shudder and confided to Abu Thaleb: 'I couldn't think of anything worse. What a bombastic little idiot! Isn't one of you going to put him in his place?'

'Oh, he is entertaining, you know,' said Abu Thaleb tolerantly.

'Charming,' agreed Doctor Volospion. 'You should be flattered, Miss Ming.'

'What? Because he hasn't seen another woman in a thousand years?'

Doctor Volospion smiled. 'You do yourself discredit.'

The stranger did not seem upset by the lack of immediate effect he had on them. He turned grave, intense eyes upon her. Mavis

Ming might have blushed. He spoke with thrilling authority, for all his pre-pubescent pitch:

'Beautiful and proud you may be, woman, yet you shall bend to me when the time comes. You shall not then react with callow cynicism.'

'I think you've got rather old-fashioned ideas about women, my friend,' said Miss Ming staunchly.

'Your true soul is buried now. But I shall reveal it to you.'

The sky began to clear. A flock of transparent pteranodons sailed unsteadily overhead, fleeing the sun. Miss Ming pretended an interest in the flying creatures. But it was plain that the stranger had her attention.

'I am Life,' he said, 'and you are Death.'

'Well...' she began, offended.

He explained: 'At this moment everything is Death that is not me.'

'I'm beginning to pity you,' said Mavis Ming in an artificial voice. 'It's obvious that you've been so long in space, whatever your name is, that you've gone completely mad!' She made nervous tuggings and pullings at her costume. 'And if you're trying to scare me, or turn my stomach, or make fun of me, I can assure you that I've dealt with much tougher customers than you in my time. All right?'

'So,' he said, in tones meant only for her, 'your mind resists me. Your training resists me. Your mother and your father and your society resist me. Perhaps even your body resists me. But your soul does not. Your soul listens. Your soul pines for me. How many years have you refused to listen to its promptings? How many years of discomfort, of sorrow, of depravity and degradation? How many nights have you battled against your dreams and your true desires? Soon you shall kneel before me and know your own power, your own strength.'

Miss Ming took a deep breath. She looked to Doctor Volospion for help, but his expression was bland, mildly curious. Abu Thaleb seemed only embarrassed.

'Listen, you,' she said. 'Where I come from women have had the vote for a hundred and fifty years. They've had equal rights for almost a hundred. There are probably more women in administrative jobs than there are men and more than fifty per cent of all leading politicians are women and when I left we hadn't had a big war for ten years, and we know all about dictators, sexual chauvinists and old-fashioned seducers. I did a History of Sexism course as part of my post-graduate studies, so I know what I'm talking about.'

He listened attentively enough to all this before replying. 'You speak of Rights and Precedents, woman. You refer to Choice and Education. But what if these are the very chains which enslave the spirit? I offer you neither security nor responsibility – save the security of knowing your own identity and the responsibility of maintaining it. I offer you Dignity.'

Miss Ming opened her mouth.

'I note that you are a romantic, sir,' said Doctor Volospion with some relish.

The stranger no longer seemed aware of his presence, but continued to stare at Mavis Ming who frowned and cast about in her troubled skull for appropriate defence. She failed and instead sought the aid of her protector.

'Can we go now?' she whispered to Doctor Volospion. 'He might do something dangerous.'

Doctor Volospion lowered his voice only a trifle. 'If my reading of our friend's character is correct, he shares a preference with all those of his type for words and dramatic but unspecific actions. I find him quite stimulating. You know my interests...'

'Do not reject my gifts, woman,' warned the stranger. 'Others have offered you Liberty (if that is what it is) but I offer you nothing less than yourself – your whole self.'

Miss Ming tried to bridle and, unsuccessful, turned away. 'Really, Doctor Volospion,' she began urgently, 'I've had enough...'

Abu Thaleb attempted intercession. 'Sir, we have few established customs, though we have enjoyed and continue to enjoy many fashions in manners, but it would seem to me that, since you are a guest in our age...'

'Guest!' The little man was astonished. 'I am not your guest, sir, I am your Saviour.'

'Be that as it may...'

'There is no more to be said. There is no question of my calling!'

'Be that as it may, you are disturbing this lady, who is not of our time and is therefore perhaps more sensitive to your remarks than if she were, um, indigenous to the age. I think "stress" is the word I seek, though I am not too certain of how "stress" manifests itself. Miss Ming?' He begged for illumination.

'He's a pain in the neck, if that's what you mean,' said Miss Ming boldly. 'But you get used to that here.' She drew herself up.

'As a gentleman, sir –' continued Abu Thaleb.

'Gentleman? I have never claimed to be a "gentleman". Unless by that you mean I am a man – a throbbing, ardent, lover of women – of one woman, now – of *that* woman!' His quivering finger pointed.

Miss Ming turned her back full on him and clambered into Abu Thaleb's howdah. She sat, stiff-necked, upon the cushions, her arms folded in front of her.

The stranger smiled almost tenderly. 'Ah, she is so beautiful! So feminine! Ah!'

'Doctor Volospion,' Miss Ming's voice was flat and cold. 'I should like to go home now.'

Doctor Volospion laughed.

'Nonsense, my dear Miss Ming.' He bowed a fraction to the stranger, as if to apologise. 'It has been an eternity since we entertained such a glorious guest. I am eager to hear his views. You know my interest in ancient religions – my collection, my menagerie, my investigations – well, here we have a genuine prophet.' A deeper bow to the stranger. 'A preacher who shows Li Pao up for the parsimonious hair-splitter that he is. If we are to be berated for our sins, then let it be full-bloodedly, with threats of fire and brimstone!'

'I said nothing of brimstone,' said the stranger.

'Forgive me.'

Miss Ming leaned from the howdah to put her lips to Doctor Volospion's ear. 'You think he's genuine, then?'

He stroked his chin. 'Your meaning is misty, Miss Ming.'

'Oh, I give up,' she said. 'It's all right for everybody else, but that madman's more or less announced his firm decision to rape me at the earliest opportunity.'

'Nonsense,' objected Doctor Volospion. 'He has been nothing but chivalrous.'

'It would be like being raped by a pigeon,' she added. She withdrew into herself.

Doctor Volospion's last glance in her direction was calculating but when he next addressed the stranger he was all hospitality. 'Your own introduction, sir, has been perhaps a mite vague. May I be more specific in my presentation of myself and my friends. This lovely lady, whose beauty has understandably made such an impression upon you, is Miss Mavis Ming. This gentleman is Abu Thaleb, Commissar of Bengal –'

'– and Lord of All Elephants,' modestly appended the commissar.

'– while I, your humble servant, am called Doctor Volospion. I think we share similar tastes, for I have long studied the religions and the faiths of the past and judge myself something of a connoisseur of Belief. You would be interested, I think, in my collection, and I would greatly value your inspection of it for, in truth, there are few fellow spirits in this world-weary age of ours.'

The stranger's red lips formed a haughty smile. 'I am no theologian, Doctor Volospion. At least, only in the sense that I am, of course, All Things…'

'Of course, of course, but –'

'And I see you for a trickster, a poseur.'

'I assure you –'

'I know you for a poor ghost of a creature, seeking in bad casuistry, to give a dead mind some semblance of life. You are cold, sir, and the cruelties by means of which you attempt to warm your own blood are petty things, the products of a niggardly imagination and some small, but ill-trained, intelligence. Only the generous can be truly cruel, for they know also what it is to be truly charitable.'

'You object to casuistry, and yet you do not disdain the use of empty paradox, I note.' Doctor Volospion remained, so it appeared, in good humour. 'I am sure, sir, when we are better acquainted, you will not be so wary of me.'

'Wary? I should be wary? Ha! If that is how you would misrepresent my nature, to comfort yourself, then I give you full permission. But know this – in giving that permission I am allowing you to remain in the grave when it might have been that you could have known true life again.'

'I am impressed...'

'No more! I am your Master, whether you acknowledge it or no, whether I care or no, and that is unquestionable. I'll waste no more energy in debate with you, manikin.'

'Manikin!' Miss Ming snorted. 'That's a good one.'

Doctor Volospion put a finger on his lips. 'Please, Miss Ming. I would continue this conversation.'

'After he's insulted you –'

'He speaks his mind, that is all. He does not know our preferences for euphemism and ornament, and so –'

'Exactly,' said Abu Thaleb, relieved. 'He will come to understand our ways soon.'

'Be certain,' fluted the stranger, 'that it is you who will come to understand my ways. I have no respect for customs, manners, fashions, for I am Bloom the Eternal. I am Bloom, who has experienced all. I am Emmanuel Bloom, whom Time cannot touch, whom Space cannot suppress!'

'A name at last,' said Doctor Volospion in apparent delight. 'We greet you, Mr Bloom.'

'That's funny,' said Miss Ming, 'you don't look Jewish.'

Chapter Seven

In Which Doctor Volospion Becomes Eager to Offer Mr Bloom His Hospitality

Mr Emmanuel Bloom seemed for the moment to have lost interest in them. He stood upon the ramp of his spaceship and stared beyond Argonheart Po's cola lake (still bearing a wisp or two of flame) towards the barren horizon. He shook his head in some despair. 'My poor, poor planet. What have they made of it in my absence?'

'Do you think we could go now?' complained Miss Ming to Doctor Volospion and Abu Thaleb. 'If you really want to see him again you could tell him where to find you.' She had an inspiration. 'Or invite him to your party, Abu Thaleb, to make up for what he did to Argonheart's feast!'

'He would be welcome, of course,' said the commissar doubtfully.

'His conversation would be refreshing, I think,' said Doctor Volospion. He plucked at his ruff and then, with a motion of a ring, disposed of it altogether. He was once again in green and silver, his cap tight about his head, emphasising the angularity of his white features. 'There are many there who would respond rather better than can I to the tone of his pronouncements. Werther de Goethe, for instance, with his special yearning for sin? Or even Jherek Carnelian, if he is still with us, with his pursuit of the meaning of morality. Or Mongrove, who shares something of his monumental millennialism. Mongrove is back from space, is he not?'

'With his aliens,' Abu Thaleb confirmed.

'Well, then, perhaps you should invite him now, courteous commissar?'

'We could tell him that the party was in his honour,' suggested Abu Thaleb. 'That would please him, don't you think? If we humour him…'

'Can't he hear us?' hissed Miss Ming.

'I think he only listens to us when it interests him to do so,' guessed Doctor Volospion. 'His mind appears on other things at present.'

'This is all very uncomfortable for me,' said Mavis Ming, 'though I suppose I shouldn't complain. Not that there's a lot of point, because nobody ever listens to little Mavis. It's too much to expect, isn't it? But, mark my words, he's going to make trouble for all of us, and especially for me. We shouldn't be wondering about inviting him to parties. We should tell him he's not welcome. We should give him his marching orders. Tell him to leave!'

'It is traditional to welcome all visitors to our world, Miss Ming,' said Abu Thaleb. 'Even the dullest has something to offer and we, in turn, can often offer sanctuary. This Mr Bloom, while I agree with you he seems a little deluded as to his importance to us, must have had many experiences of interest. He has travelled, he tells us, through Time and through Space. He has knowledge of numerous different societies. There will be many here who will be glad to meet him. Lord Jagged of Canaria, I am sure –'

'Jagged is gone from us again,' said Volospion somewhat sharply. 'Fled, some say, back into time – to avoid disaster.'

'Well, there are women, too, who would delight in meeting one so passionate. My Lady Charlotina, Mistress Christia, the Iron Orchid…'

'They're welcome,' said Mavis Ming. 'More than welcome. Though what any woman would see in the little creep, I don't know.'

'Once he meets other ladies, doubtless his own infatuation for you will subside,' said Abu Thaleb encouragingly. 'As you say, you are probably the first woman he has seen for many a long year and he has had no opportunity to select from all our many, wonderful women one who pleases him even more than you do at present. He is evidently a man of great passion. One might almost call it elephantine in its grandeur.'

Miss Ming put her chin on her fist.

There was a bang. Pensively, Mr Bloom had blown up the rest of Werther's mountains. He continued to remain with his hands on his hips, contemplating the distance.

'Miss Ming. As a student of history have you any knowledge of Mr Bloom?' Doctor Volospion came and sat next to her in the howdah.

'None,' she said. 'Not even a legend. He must be after my time.'

'A near-contemporary, I would have thought, judging by his dress.'

'He said himself he'd taken on someone else's appearance. Someone he'd admired.'

'Ah, yes. Another prophet, do you think?'

'From the 19th century? Who was there? Karl Marx? Nietzsche? Wagner? Maybe he looks a bit like Wagner. No. Someone like that, though. English? It's just not my period, Doctor Volospion. And religion was never my strong subject. The Middle Ages were my own favourite, because people lived such simpler lives, then. I could get quite nostalgic about the Middle Ages, even now. That's probably why I originally started doing history. When I was a little girl you couldn't get me away from all those stories of brave knights and fair ladies. I guess I was like a lot of kids, but I just hung on to that interest, until I went to university, where I got more interested in the politics, well, that was Betty, really, who was the political nut, you know. But she really had some strong ideas about politics – good ideas. She –'

'But you do not recognise Mr Bloom?'

'You couldn't fail to, could you, once you'd seen him? No. Doctor Volospion, can't you send me home on my own?' pleaded Miss Ming. 'If I had a power ring, even a little one, I could...'

She had hinted to him before that if she were equipped with a power ring or two she would be less of a nuisance to him. Few time-travellers, however, were given the rings which tapped the energy of the old cities, certainly not when, like Miss Ming, they were comparative newcomers to the End of Time. As Doctor Volospion had explained to her before, there was a certain discipline of mind – or at least a habit of mind – which had to be learned before they could be used. Also they were not one of the artefacts which could be reproduced at will. There was a relatively limited number of them. Miss Ming had never been quite convinced by Doctor Volospion's arguments against her having her own power ring, but there was little she could do save hope that one day he would relent.

'Regretfully...' He gestured. 'Not yet, Miss Ming.' It was not clear to which of her suggestions he was referring. She allowed her disappointment to show on her plump face.

'Hm,' said Mr Bloom from above, 'it is evident that the entire planet will have to be consumed so that, from the ashes, a purer place may prosper.'

'Mr Bloom!' cried Abu Thaleb. 'I would remind you, sir, that while you are a most honoured guest to our world, you will inconvenience a great many people if you burn them up.'

Bloom blinked as he looked down at Abu Thaleb. 'Oh, they will not die. I shall resurrect them.'

'They are perfectly capable of resurrecting one another, Mr Bloom. That is not my point. You see, many of us have embarked on schemes – oh, menageries, collections, creations of various kinds – and if you were to destroy them they would be seriously disappointed. It would be the height of bad manners, don't you think?'

'You have already heard my opinion of manners.'

'But –'

'It is for your own good,' Bloom told him.

'Aha! The authentic voice of the prophet!' cried Doctor Volospion. 'Sir, you must be my guest!'

'You begin to irritate me, Doctor Volospion,' piped Emmanuel Bloom, 'with your constant references to me as a guest. I am not a guest. I am the rightful inheritor of this world, controller of the destinies of all who dwell in it, sole Saviour of your souls.'

'Quite,' apologised Doctor Volospion. 'I should imagine, however, that your spaceship, however grandly furnished and with whatever fine amenities, palls on you as a domicile after so many centuries. Perhaps if you would allow me to put my own humble house at your disposal until a suitable palace – or temple, perhaps – can be built for you, I should be greatly flattered.'

'Your feeble attempts at guile begin to irritate me, Doctor Volospion. I am Emmanuel Bloom.'

'So you have told us…'

'I am Emmanuel Bloom and I can see into every soul.'

'Naturally. I merely…'

'And this priestly fawning only makes me despair of you still further. If you would defy me, defy me with some dignity.'

'Mr Bloom, I am simply attempting to make you welcome. Your ideas, your language, your attitudes, they are all decidedly unfashionable now. It was my intention to offer you a dwelling from which you may observe the age at the End of Time, and make plans for its specific salvation – at your leisure.'

'My plans are simple enough. They can apply to any age. I shall destroy everything. Then I shall create it afresh. Your identity will not only be preserved, it will be fully alive, perhaps for the first time since you were born.'

'Most of us,' Abu Thaleb wished to point out, 'were not actually born at all, Mr Bloom…'

'That is immaterial. You exist now. I shall help you find yourselves.'

'Most of us are content…'

'You think you are content. Are you never restless? Do you never wake from slumber recalling a dream of something lost, something finer than anything you have ever experienced before?'

'As a matter of fact I have not slept for many a long year. The fashion died, with most people, even before I became interested in elephants.'

'Do not seek to confuse the issue, Abu Thaleb.'

'Mr Bloom, I *am* confused. I have no wish to have my precious pachyderms destroyed by you. My enthusiasm is at its height. I am sure the same can be said for at least half the population, small though it is, of this planet.'

'I cannot heed you,' said Emmanuel Bloom, feeling in the pockets of his velvet suit. 'You will be grateful when it is done.'

'At least you might canvass the opinion of a few more people, Mr Bloom.' Abu Thaleb begged. 'I mean to say, for all I know, most people might think the idea a splendid one! It would make a dramatic change, at least…'

'And besides,' said Doctor Volospion, 'we certainly have the means to resist you, Mr Bloom, should you begin seriously to discommode us.'

Emmanuel Bloom began to stride up the ramp of his spaceship. 'I am weary of all this. Woman, do you come with me now?'

Miss Ming maintained silence.

'Please reconsider, Mr Bloom,' Doctor Volospion said spiritedly, 'as my guest you would share the roof with many great philosophers and prophets, with messiahs and reformers of every description.'

'It sounds,' piped Mr Bloom, 'like Hell.'

'And there are things you should see. Souvenirs of a million faiths. Miraculous artefacts of every kind.'

Emmanuel Bloom seemed mildly interested. 'Eh?'

'Magical swords, relics, supernatural stones – my collection is justly famous.'

Emmanuel Bloom continued on his way.

'You would, as well as enjoying this fabulous company, be sharing the same roof as Miss Ming, who is another guest of mine,' said Doctor Volospion.

'Miss Ming comes with me. Now.'

'Oh, no I don't,' exclaimed Miss Ming.

'What?' Emmanuel Bloom paused again.

'Miss Ming stays with me,' said Doctor Volospion. 'If you wish to visit her, you may visit her at my dwelling.'

'Oh, don't bother with him!' said Mavis Ming.

'You will come to me, in Time, Mavis Ming,' said Emmanuel Bloom.

'That's the funniest thing I've ever heard,' she told him. She said to Doctor Volospion: 'It's a bit insensitive of you, isn't it, Doctor Volospion, to use me as bait? Why do you want him so badly?'

Doctor Volospion ignored the question.

'You would be very comfortable at Castle Volospion,' he told Mr Bloom. 'Everything you could desire – food, wine, luxurious furniture, women, boys, any animal of your taste…'

'I need no luxuries and I desire only one woman. She shall be mine soon enough.'

'It would make Miss Ming happy, I am sure, if you became my g… if you used my house.'

'You are determined, I think, to misunderstand my mission upon this world. I have come to re-fire the Earth, as its Leader and its Hero. To restore Love and Madness and Idealism to their proper eminence. To infuse your blood with the stuff that makes it race, that makes the heart beat and the head swim! Look about you, manikin, and tell me if you see any heroes. You no longer have heroes – and you have such paltry villains!'

'It does not seem reasonable of you to judge by we three alone,' said Abu Thaleb.

'Three's enough. Enough to tell the general condition of the whole. Your society is revealed in your language, your gestures, your costumes, your landscapes! Oh, how sad, how ruined, how unfulfilled you are! Ah, how you must have longed, in your secret thoughts, those thoughts hidden even from yourselves, for me to return. And look now – you still do not realise it.'

He smiled benevolently down on them standing near the entrance to his ship.

'But that realisation shall dawn anon, be sure of that. You ask me to live in one of your houses – in a tomb, I say. And could I bear to leave my ship behind? My much-named ship, the *Golden Hind*? Or *Firedrake* call her, or *Virgin Flame – Pi-meson* or the *Magdelaine* – sailing out of Carthage, Tyre, Old Bristol or Bombay: Captain Emmanuel Bloom, late of Jerusalem, founder of the Mayan faith, builder of pyramids, called Ra or Raleigh, dependent on your taste – Kubla Khan or Prester John, Baldur, Mithras, Zoroaster – the Sun's Fool, for I bring you Flame in which to drown! I am blooming Bloom, blunderer through the million planes – I am Bloom, the booming drum of destiny. I am Bloom – the Fireclown! Aha! Now you know me!'

The three faces stared blankly up.

He leaned with his hand against the entrance to the airlock, his head on his shoulder, his eye beady and intelligent. 'Eh?'

Doctor Volospion remained uncharacteristically placatory. 'Perhaps you could enlighten us over a meal? You must be hungry. We can offer the choicest foods, to suit the most demanding of tastes. Please, Mr Bloom, I ask again that you reconsider…'

'No.'

'You feel I have misinterpreted you, I know. But I am an earnest student. I remain a mite confused. Your penchant for metaphor…'

The Fireclown clapped a tiny hand to a tiny knee. He frowned at

Doctor Volospion. 'One metaphor is worth a million of your euphemisms, Doctor Volospion. I have problems to consider and must seek solitude. I have poetry to write – or to recall – I forget which – and need time for meditation. I should accept your invitation for it is my duty to broaden your mind – but that duty can wait.'

He turned again to regard the woman.

'You'll join me now, Miss Ming?'

His huge blue eyes flashed suddenly with an intelligence, a humour, which shocked her completely from her hard-won composure.

'What?' The response was mindless.

He stretched out a hand. 'Come with me now. I offer you pain and knowledge, lust and freedom. Hm?'

She began to rise, as if mesmerised. She seemed to be shivering. Then she sat down. 'Certainly not!'

Emmanuel Bloom laughed. 'You'll come.' He returned his attention to Doctor Volospion. 'And I would advise you, sir, to save your breath in this meaningless and puny Temptation. Your hatred of me is patent, whether you admit it to yourself or not. I would warn you to cease your irritation.'

'You still refuse to believe my good faith, Mr Bloom. So be it.' Doctor Volospion bowed low.

The ramp was withdrawn. The airlock shut.

No further sound escaped the ship.

Chapter Eight

In Which Miss Ming Begins to Feel a Certain Curiosity Concerning the Intentions of Emmanuel Bloom

IF ANYONE AT the End of Time expected Mr Bloom to begin immediately to exercise his particular plans for bringing Salvation to the planet they were to be disappointed, for his extravagant spaceship (which the fashion of the moment declared to be in hideous taste) remained where it landed and Emmanuël Bloom, the Fireclown, did not re-emerge. A few sightseers came to view the ship – the usual sensation-seekers like the Duke of Queens (who wanted to put the ship at once into his collection of ancient flying machines), My Lady Charlotina of Below-the-Lake, O'Kala Incarnadine, Sweet Orb Mace, the Iron Orchid, Bishop Castle and their various followers, imitators and hangers-on – but in spite of all sorts of hallooings, bangings, catcalls, lettings-off of fireworks, obscene displays (on the part of the ladies who were curious to see what Miss Ming's most ardent suitor really looked like) and the rest, the great Saviour of Mankind refused to reveal himself; nothing occurred which could be interpreted as action on the Fireclown's part. No fires swept the Earth, no thunders or lightnings broke the calm of the skies, there was no destruction of artefacts nor any further demolition of landscapes. Indeed, it was singularly peaceful, even for the End of Time, and certain people became almost resentful of Mr Bloom's refusal to attempt, at least, a miracle or two.

'Doctor Volospion exaggerated!' pronounced My Lady Charlotina, all in blue and sage, the colours of dreams, as she lunched on a green and recently constructed hillside overlooking the ship (it now stood in clouds of daisies, a memento of the Duke of Queens' pastoral phase which had lasted scarcely the equivalent of an ancient Earth summer) and raised a turnip (another memento) to her ethereal lips. 'You know his obsessions, my dear O'Kala. His taste for monks and gurus and the like.'

O'Kala Incarnadine, currently a gigantic field mouse, nibbled at the lemon he held in both front paws. 'I am not familiar with the creatures,' he said.

'They are not creatures, exactly. They are a kind of person. Lord Jagged was good enough to inform me about them, although, of course, I have forgotten most of what he said. My point is, O'Kala, that Doctor Volospion *wished* this Mr Bloom to be like a guru and so interpreted his words accordingly.'

'But Miss Ming confirmed...'

'Miss Ming!'

O'Kala shrugged his mousy shoulders in assent.

'Miss Ming's bias was blatant. Who could express such excessive ardour of anyone, let alone Miss Ming?' My Lady Charlotina wiped the white juice of the turnip from her chin.

'Jherek – he pursues his Amelia with much the same enthusiasm.'

'Amelia is an ideal – she is slender, beautiful, unattainable – everything an ideal should be. There is nothing unseemly in Jherek's passion for such a woman.' My Lady Charlotina was unaware of anything contradictory in her remarks. After her brief experience in the Dawn Age she had developed a taste for propriety which had not yet altogether vanished.

'In certain guises,' timidly offered O'Kala, 'I have lusted for Miss Ming myself, so...'

'That is quite different. But this Mr Bloom is a *man*.'

'Abu Thaleb's tale was not dissimilar to Doctor Volospion's.'

'Abu Thaleb is impressionable. On elephants he is unequalled, but he is no expert on prophets.'

'Is anyone?'

'Lord Jagged. That is why Doctor Volospion apes him. You know of the great rivalry Volospion feels for Lord Jagged, surely? For some reason, he identifies with Jagged. Once he used to emulate him in everything, or sought to. Jagged showed no interest. Gave no praise. Since then – oh, so long ago my memory barely grants me the bones of it – Doctor Volospion has set himself up as a sort of contra-Jagged. There are rumours – no more than that, for you know how secretive Jagged can be – rumours of a sexual desire which flourished between them for a while, until Jagged tired of it. Now that Lord Jagged has disappeared, I suspect that Doctor Volospion would take his place in our society, for Jagged has the knack of making us all curious about his activities. You have my opinion in a nutshell – Volospion makes much of this Bloom in an effort to pique our interest, to gossip about him in lieu of Jagged.'

O'Kala Incarnadine wiped his whiskers. 'Then he has succeeded.'

'For the moment, I grant you, but unsubtly. It will not last.'

My Lady Charlotina sighed and sucked at a celery stalk, letting her gaze wander to the scarlet spaceship. 'Our curiosity is still with Jagged. Where can he be? This,' she indicated the vessel with her vegetable, 'is no more than a diversion.'

'It would be amusing, though, if Mr Bloom did begin to lay waste the world.'

'There is no logic to it. The world will be finished soon enough, as everyone knows. The very universe in which our planet hangs is on the point of vanishing for ever. Mr Bloom has brought his salvation at altogether the wrong moment and at a time when salvation itself is unfashionable, even as a topic of conversation.'

'The reasons are obvious...' began O'Kala, in a rare and philosophical mood, '... for who would wish to discuss such matters, now that we know –?'

'Quite.' My Lady Charlotina waved. An air car was approaching. It was the shape of a great winged man, its bronze head flashing in the red light of the sun, its blind eyes glaring, its twisted mouth roaring as if in agony. The Duke of Queens had modelled his latest car after some image recently discovered by him in one of the rotting cities.

The car landed nearby and from it trooped many of My Lady Charlotina's most intimate friends. From his saddle behind the head of the winged man the Duke of Queens raised his hand in a salute. He had on an ancient astronaut's jacket, in silver-tipped black fur, puffed pantaloons of mauve and ivory stripes, knee-boots of orange lurex hide, a broad-brimmed hat of panda ears, all sewn together in the most fanciful way.

'My Lady Charlotina! We saw you and had to greet you. We are on our way to enjoy the new boys Florence Fawkes had made for her latest entertainment. Will you come with us?'

'Perhaps, but boys…' She lifted a corner of her mouth.

My Lady Charlotina noted that Doctor Volospion and Mavis Ming were among those pouring from the body of the winged man. She greeted Sweet Orb Mace with a small kiss, laid a sincere hand upon the arm of Bishop Castle, winked at Mistress Christia and smiled charmingly at Miss Ming.

'Aha! The beauty for whom Mr Bloom crossed the galaxies. Miss Ming, you are the focus of all our envy!'

'Have you seen Mr Bloom?' asked Miss Ming.

'Not yet, not yet.'

'Then wait before you envy me,' she said.

Doctor Volospion's cunning eye glittered. 'There is nothing more certain to attract the attention of a lady to a gentleman, even in these weary times of ours, than the passion of that gentleman for another lady.'

'How perceptive you are, dear Doctor Volospion! It must be admitted. In fact, I believe I already admitted it, when I first greeted you.'

Doctor Volospion bowed his head.

'You are looking at your best,' she continued, for it was true. 'You are always elegant, Doctor Volospion.' He had on a long, full-sleeved robe of bottle-green, trimmed with mellow gold, the neck high, to frame his sharp face, a matching tight-fitting cap upon his head, buttoned beneath the pointed chin.

'You are kind, My Lady Charlotina.'

'Ever truthful, Doctor Volospion.' She gave her attention to Miss Ming's white frills. 'And this dress. You must feel so much younger in it.'

'Much,' agreed Miss Ming. 'How clever of you to understand what it was to be like me! How many hundreds of years can it have been?'

'More than that, Miss Ming. Thousands, almost certainly. I see, at any rate, that your would-be ravisher has yet to come out of his little lair again.'

'He can stay there for ever as far as I'm concerned.'

'I have made one or two attempts to rouse him,' said Doctor Volospion. 'I sought to shift the ship, too, but it is protected now by a singularly intractable force-field. Nothing I possess can dissipate that field.'

'So he does have the power he boasted of, eh?' Bishop Castle in his familiar tall *tête* which cast a shadow over half the company, looked without much interest at the spaceship.

'Apparently,' said Doctor Volospion.

'But why doesn't he *use* it?' The Duke of Queens joined them. 'Has he perished in there, do you think. In his own mad flames?'

'We should have smelled something, at least,' said O'Kala Incarnadine.

'Well,' Sweet Orb Mace was now a pretty blonde in a black sari, '*you* would have smelled something, O'Kala, with your nose.'

O'Kala wrinkled his current one.

'He's playing cat and mouse with me, that's what I think,' said Mavis Ming with a nervous glance at the vessel. 'Oh, I'm sorry, O'Kala, I didn't mean to suggest...'

O'Kala Incarnadine made a toothy grin. 'I pity any ordinary cat who met a mouse like me!'

'He's hoping I'll give in and go to him. That's typical of some men, isn't it? Well, I had enough of crawling with Donny Stevens. Never again, I told my friend Betty. And never again it was!'

'But you have been tempted, eh?' My Lady Charlotina became intimate.

'Not once.'

My Lady Charlotina let disappointment show.

'I wish,' said Mavis Ming, 'that he'd either start something or else just go away. It must have been weeks and weeks he's been waiting there! It's getting on my nerves, you know.'

'Of course, it must be, my dear,' said Sweet Orb Mace.

'Well,' the Duke of Queens reminded them all, 'Florence Fawkes awaits us. Will you come, My Lady Charlotina? O'Kala?'

'I have a project,' said My Lady Charlotina, by way of an excuse, 'to finish. Of course, it is very hard to tell if it is properly finished or not. An invisible city populated with invisible androids. You must come and feel it soon.'

'A lovely notion,' said Bishop Castle. 'Are the androids of all sexes?'

'All.'

'And it is possible to –?'

'Absolutely possible.'

'It would be interesting –'

'It is.'

'Aha!' Bishop Castle tilted his *tête*. 'Then I look forward to visiting you at the earliest chance, My Lady Charlotina. What entertainments you do invent for us!' He bowed, almost toppled by his headgear.

The Duke of Queens had resumed his saddle. 'All aboard!' he cried enthusiastically.

It was then that there came a squeak from the space vessel below. The airlock opened. All heads turned.

Emmanuel Bloom's bright blue eyes regarded them. His high-pitched voice drifted up to them.

'So you have come to me,' he said.

'I?' said the Duke of Queens in astonishment.

'I have waited,' Emmanuel Bloom said, 'for you, Miss Ming. So that you may share my joy.'

Miss Ming drew back into the main part of the gathering. 'I was only passing…' she began.

'Come.' He extended a stiff hand from the interior of the ship. 'Come.'

'Certainly not!' She hid behind Doctor Volospion.

'So, the one with the jackal eyes holds you still. And against your will, I am sure.'

'Nothing of the sort! Doctor Volospion is my host, that is all.'

'You are too afraid to tell me the truth.'

'She speaks the truth, sir,' said Volospion in an offhand tone. 'She is free to come and go from my house as she pleases.'

'Some pathetic enchantment, no doubt, keeps her there. Well, woman, never fear. The moment I know that you need me I shall rescue you, wherever you may be hidden.'

'I don't *need* rescuing,' declared Miss Ming.

'Oh, but you do. So badly do you need it that you dare not tell yourself!'

My Lady Charlotina cried: 'Excuse me, sir, for intruding, but we were wondering if your plans for the destruction of the world were completely formulated. I, for one, would appreciate a little notice.'

'My meditations are not yet completed,' he told her. He still stared at Miss Ming. 'Will you come to me now?'

'Never!'

'Remember my oath.'

Doctor Volospion stepped forward. 'I would remind you, sir, that this lady is under my protection. Should you make any further attempt to annoy her then I must warn you that I shall defend her to the death!'

Miss Ming was taken aback by this sudden about-face. 'Oh, Doctor Volospion! How *noble*!'

'What's this?' said Bloom, blinking rapidly. 'More posturing?'

'I give fair warning, that is all.'

Doctor Volospion folded his arms across his chest and stared full into the eyes of Emmanuel Bloom.

Bloom remained unimpressed. 'So you do keep her prisoner, as I suspected. She believes she has her liberty, but you know better!'

'I shall accept no more insults.' Doctor Volospion lifted his chin in defiance.

'This is not mere braggadocio, I can tell. It is calculated. But what do you plan?'

'Any more of this, sir,' said Doctor Volospion in ringing tones, 'and I shall have to demand satisfaction of you.'

The Fireclown laughed. 'I shall free the woman soon.'

The airlock shut with a click.

'How extraordinary!' murmured My Lady Charlotina. 'How exceptional of you, Doctor Volospion! Miss Ming must feel quite moved by your defence of her.'

'I am, I am.' Miss Ming's small eyes were shining. 'Doctor Volospion. I never *knew*…'

Doctor Volospion strode for the air car. 'Let us leave this wretched place.'

Miss Ming tripped behind him. It was as if she had found her true knight at last.

Chapter Nine
In Which the Fireclown Brings Some Small Salvation to the End of Time

IT WAS, AS it happened, My Lady Charlotina who first experienced the fiery wrath of Emmanuel Bloom.

Tiring (for reasons described elsewhere) of her apartments under Lake Billy the Kid, she had begun a new palace which was to be constructed in an arrangement of clouds above the site of the lake, so that it hovered over the water, reflecting both this and the sun. It was to be primarily white but with some other pale colours here and there, perhaps for flanking towers. She had spent considerable thought upon the palace and it was still by no means complete, for My Lady Charlotina was not one of those who could create a complete conception with the mere twist of a power ring; she must consider, she must alter, she must build piece by piece. Thus, in the clouds over Lake Billy the Kid, there were half-raised towers, towers without tops, domes with spires and domes that were turreted; there were gaps where halls had been, there were whole patches of space representing apartments which, at a whim, she had returned to their original particles.

After resting, My Lady Charlotina emerged from Lake Billy the Kid and stood upon the shore, surrounded by comfortable oaks and cypresses. She arranged the mist upon the water into more satisfactory configurations, making it drift so high that it mingled with the clouds on which her new palace was settled, and she was about to eradicate a tower which offended, now, her sense of symmetry, when there came a loud roaring sound and the whole edifice burst into flame.

My Lady Charlotina gasped with indignation. Her first thought was that one of her friends had misjudged an experiment and accidentally set fire to her palace, but she soon guessed the true cause of the blaze.

'The lunatic incendiary!' she cried, and she flung herself into the sky, not to go to her crackling palace (which was beyond salvaging) but to look down upon the world and discover the whereabouts of the Fireclown.

He was not a mile from the conflagration, standing on top of a great plinth meant to support a statue of himself which the Duke of Queens had never bothered to complete. He wore his black velvet, his bow tie, his shirt with its ruffles. He rested upon the plinth like a parrot upon its pedestal, shifting from side to side and flapping his arms at his sides as he studied his handiwork. He did not see My Lady Charlotina as, in golden gauze, she fluttered down towards him.

She paused, to hover a few feet above his head; she waited, watching him, until he became aware of her presence. She listened to him as he spoke to himself.

'Quite good. A fitting symbol. It will look well in any legends, I think. It is best for the first few miracles to be spectacular and not directed at individuals. I should not leave it too late, however, before rescuing the remains of any residents and resurrecting them.'

She could not contain herself.

'I, sir, might have been the only resident of that castle in the clouds. Happily, I had not arrived at it before you began your fire-raising!'

His little head jerked here and there. At last he looked up. 'So!'

'The palace was to be my new home, Mr Bloom. It was impolite of you to destroy it.'

'There were no inhabitants?'

'Not yet.'

'Well, then, I shall be on my way.'

'You make no attempt to apologise?'

Mr Bloom was amused. 'I can scarcely apologise for something so calculating. You ask me to lie? I am the Fireclown. Why should I lie?'

She was speechless. Mr Bloom began to climb down a ladder he had placed against the plinth. 'I bid you good morning, madam.'

'Good *morning*?'

'Or good afternoon – you keep no proper hours on this planet at all. It is hard to know. That will be changed,' he smiled, 'in Time.'

'Mr Bloom, your purposes here are quite without point. Are we to be impressed by such displays?' She waved her hand towards the blazing palace. Her clouds had turned brown at the edges. 'Time, Mr Bloom, is not what it was. Times, Mr Bloom, have changed since those primitive Dawn Ages when such "miracles" might have provoked interest, even surprise, in the inhabitants of this world. Watch!' She turned a power ring. The fire vanished. An entire, if uninspired, fairy palace glittered again in pristine clouds.

'Hum,' said Mr Bloom, still on his ladder. He began to climb back to the top of the plinth. 'I see. So Volospion is not the only conjuror here.'

'We all have that power. Or most of us. It is our birthright.'

'Birthright? What of my birthright?'

'You have one?'

'It is the world. I explained to Doctor Volospion, madam…' He was aggrieved. 'Did he speak to no-one of my mission here?'

'He told us what you had said, yes.'

'And you are not yet spiritually prepared, it seems. I left you plenty of time for contemplation of your fate. It is the accepted method, where Salvation is to be achieved.'

'We have no need of Salvation, Mr Bloom. We are immortal, we control the universe – what's left of it – we are, most of us, without fear (if I understand the term properly).' My Lady Charlotina was making an untypical effort to meet Emmanuel Bloom halfway. It was probably because she had no strong wish to be at odds with him, since she was curious to know better the man who courted Miss Ming with such determination. 'Really, Mr Bloom, you have arrived too late. Even a few hundred years ago, before we heard of the dissolution of the universe, there might have been some enjoyment for all, but not now. Not now, Mr Bloom.'

'Hum.' He frowned. He lifted a hand to his face and appeared to peck at his cuff. 'But I have no other rôle, you see. I am a Saviour. It is all I can do.'

'Must you save a whole world? Aren't there a few individuals you could concentrate on?'

'It hardly seems worthwhile. I am, to be more specific, a World Saviour – a Saver of Worlds. I have ranged the multiverse saving them. From all sorts of things, physical and spiritual. And I always leave the places that I have saved spiritually regenerated. Ask any of them. They will all tell you the same. I am loved throughout the teeming dimensions.'

'Then perhaps you could find another world...'

'No, this is the last. I left it long ago, promising that I would return and save it, as my final action.'

'Well, you are too late.'

'Really, madam, I cannot take your word for it. I am the greatest authority on such matters in the universe, to say the least. I am the Champion Eternal, Hero of a million legends. When Law battles Chaos, I am always called. When civilisations are threatened with total extermination, it is to me that they turn for rescue. And when decadence and despair rule an otherwise secure and prosperous world, it is for Emmanuel Bloom, the Fireclown, Time's Jester, that they yearn. And I come.'

'But we did not call you, we require no rescuing. We are not yearning, I assure you, even a fraction.'

'Miss Ming is yearning.'

'Miss Ming's yearning is hardly spiritual.'

'So you think. I know better.'

'Well, then, I'll grant you that Miss Ming is yearning. But I am not yearning. Doctor Volospion is incapable, I am sure, of yearning. Yearning, all in all, Mr Bloom, is extinct in this age.'

'Forgotten, hidden, unheeded, but I know it is there. I know. A deep, unadmitted sadness. A demand for Romance. A pining for Ideals.'

'We take up Romance from time to time, and we have an interest, on occasion, in Ideals – but these are passing enthusiasms, Mr Bloom. Even those of us most obsessed with such things show no particular misery when circumstances or changing fashion require that they be dropped.'

'How shallow are those who dwell here now! All, that is, save Miss Ming.'

'Some think her the shallowest of us all.' My Lady Charlotina regretted her spite, for she did not wish to seem malicious in Mr Bloom's eyes.

'It is often the case,' he said, 'with those who cannot see beyond flesh and into the soul.'

'I doubt if there are many souls remaining among us,' said My Lady Charlotina. 'Since we are almost every one of us self-made creatures. There is even some speculation that we are not human at all, but sophisticated androids.'

'It could be the explanation,' he mused.

'I hope you will not be wholly frustrated,' she said sympathetically, watching him climb down his ladder. 'I can imagine what it is like to possess only one rôle.'

She settled, like a butterfly, upon the vacated plinth.

He reached the ground and peered up at her, arms held stiffly, as usual, by his side, red hair flaring. 'I assure you, madam,' he piped, 'that I am not in the least impressed by what you have told me.'

'But I speak the truth.'

'Unlike Volospion, who lies, lies, lies. I agree that you believe, as does Miss Ming, that you speak the truth. But I see decadence. And where there is decadence, there is misery. And where there is misery, then must come the Fireclown, to bring laughter, joy, terror, to banish all anxieties.'

'Your logic is, I fear, obsolete, Mr Bloom. There is no misery here, to speak of. And,' she added, 'there is no joy. Instead, we have a comfortable balance. It enables us to contemplate our own end with a certain grace.'

'Hum.'

'Surely, this equilibrium is what all human morality and philosophy has striven for over the millennia?' she said, seating herself on the edge of the plinth and arranging her gold gauze about her legs. 'Would you set the see-saw swinging again?'

He frowned. 'No heights or depths here, eh?'

'For most of us, no.'

'No Heaven and Hell?'

'Only those we create for our own amusement.'

'No terror and no ecstasy?'

'Scarcely a scrap.'

'How can you bear it?'

'It is the ultimate achievement of our race. We enjoy it.'

'Are there none who –?'

'Those time-travellers, space-travellers, a few who have induced special anachronistic tendencies in themselves. Yes, there are some who might respond to you. A good few of them are not with us at present, however. The Iron Orchid's little son, Jherek Carnelian, his great love Amelia Underwood, his mentor Lord Jagged of Canaria and perhaps a few others, one loses track. Doctor Volospion? Perhaps, for it is rumoured that he is not of this age at all. Li Pao and various aliens who have visited us and stayed… Yes, from these you could derive a certain satisfaction. Some would undoubtedly welcome you, for one reason or another…'

'It is usually for one reason or another,' said the Fireclown frankly. 'Men see me as many things. It is because I *am* many things.'

'And all of them excellent, I am sure.'

'But I must do what I must do,' he said. 'It is all I know. For I am Bloom the Destroyer, Bloom the Builder, Bloom the Bringer of Brightness, Bloom who Blooms Forever! And my mission is to save you all.'

'I thought we had at least removed ourselves from generalities, Mr Bloom,' she said, a little chidingly.

He turned away disconsolately, so My Lady Charlotina thought.

'Generalities, madam, are all I deal in. They are my stock-in-trade. It is the gift I bring – to remove petty anxieties, momentary considerations, and to replace them with grandeur, with huge, simple, glorious Ideals.'

'It is not a simple problem,' she said. 'I can see that.'

'It must be a *simple* problem!' he complained. 'All problems are simple. All!'

He disappeared into the soft trees surrounding the plinth. She heard his voice muttering for some while, but he made no formal farewell, for he was too much lost in his own concerns. A short time later she saw a distant tree burst into flame and subside almost at once. She saw a rather feeble bolt of lightning crash and split a trunk. Then he was gone away.

My Lady Charlotina remained on the plinth, for she was enjoying a rare sense of melancholy and was reluctant to let the mood pass.

Chapter Ten

In Which the Fireclown Attempts to Deny any Suggestion so far Made that He Is an Anachronism

My Lady Charlotina's words had failed, as was soon to be shown, to convince Mr Bloom. Yet there was something pathetic in his acts of destruction, something almost sad about the way he demolished the Duke of Queens' 'City of Tulips' (each dwelling a separate flower) or laid waste Florence Fawkes's delightful little 'Sodom' with all its inhabitants, including Florence Fawkes who was never, due to an oversight, resurrected. It was in a half-abstracted mood that he brought a rain of molten lava to disrupt the party which Bishop Castle was giving for moody Werther de Goethe (and which, as it happened, was received with approval by all concerned, since Werther was one of the few to appreciate the Fireclown's point of view and died screaming of repentance and the like. Though when he was resurrected, almost immediately, he did complain that the consistency of the lava was not all that it might have been – too lumpy, he thought). The Fireclown rarely appeared personally on any of these occasions. He seemed to have lost the will to enjoy intercourse with his fellows. Moreover, there was scarcely anyone who found him very entertaining, after the first demolition or two, largely because his wrath always took exactly the same form. Werther de Goethe sought him out and enthused. He found, he said, Mr Bloom deeply refreshing, and he offered himself as an acolyte. Mr Bloom had informed him that he would let Werther know when acolytes were needed, if at all. Lord Mongrove also visited the Fireclown, hoping for conversation, but the Fireclown told him frankly that his talk was depressing. My Lady Charlotina visited him, too, and came away refusing to tell anyone what had passed between herself and Mr Bloom, though she seemed upset. And when Mistress Christia followed close in the footsteps of her friend and was also rebuffed, Mr Bloom told her sombrely that he waited for one woman and one alone – the beautiful Mavis Ming.

Upon hearing this, Miss Ming shuddered and suggested that someone destroy the Fireclown before he did any more damage to the world.

If it had not been for the immense and unshakeable force-field around the Fireclown's ship, there is no doubt that some of the denizens at the End of Time would have at least made an attempt to halt the Fireclown's inconveniencing activities. It was of a type unfamiliar even to the rotting cities, who did their best to analyse it and produce a formula for coping with it, but failed, forgetting the purpose of half their experiments before they were completed and drawing no conclusions from those they did complete, for the same reason. In most cases they took a childish delight in the more spectacular effects of their experiments and would play with the energies they had created until, growing tired and petty, they refused to help any further.

The Fireclown had been unable to bring quite the holocaust he had promised, for things were rebuilt as soon as he had destroyed them, but he had at least become a large flea upon the flanks of society, wrecking carefully planned picnics, entertainments, artistic creations and games, so that precautions had to be taken against him which spoiled the general effect intended. Force-fields had to be produced to protect property for the first time in untold thousands of years and even the Duke of Queens, that most charitable of immortals, agreed that his ordinary enjoyment of life was being detrimentally influenced by Mr Bloom, particularly since the destruction of his menagerie, the resurrection of which had greatly discommoded him.

There came such a twittering of protest as had never been heard at the End of Time and plans were discussed interminably for ridding the world of this pest. Deputations were sent to his ship and were ignored, polite notes left at his airlock's entrance were either burned on the spot or allowed to drift away on the wind.

'It is quite ridiculous,' said My Lady Charlotina, 'that this puny prophet should be allowed to figure so largely in our lives. If only Lord Jagged were here, he would surely find a solution.'

She spoke spitefully, for she knew that Doctor Volospion was in earshot. They were both attending the same reception, given on Sweet Orb Mace's new lawns which surrounded his mansion, modelled on one of the baroque juvenile slaughterhouses of the late 200,006th century. From within sounded the most authentic screams, causing all to compliment Sweet Orb Mace on an unprecedented, for her, effort of imagination.

'Lord Jagged has undoubtedly found that his interests are not best served by remaining at the End of Time,' said Doctor Volospion from behind her.

She pretended surprise, 'How do you do, Doctor Volospion?' She inspected his costume – another long-sleeved robe, this one of maroon and white. 'Hm.'

'I am well, My Lady Charlotina.'

'The Fireclown has made no attack upon you, yet? That is strange. Of all of us, it is you whom he actually appears to dislike.'

Doctor Volospion lowered his eyes and smiled. 'He would not harm Miss Ming, my guest.'

'Of course!'

She swept silky skirts of brown and blue about her and made to move on, but Volospion stayed her. 'I gather there has been much debate about this Fireclown.'

'Far too much.'

'He would be a marvellous prize for my menagerie.'

'So that is why he mistrusts you!'

'I think not. It is because my logic defeats him.'

'I did not know.'

'Yes. I have probably had the longest debate of anyone at the End of Time with Bloom. He found that he could not best me in argument. It is sheer revenge, the rest. Or so I suspect.'

'Aha?' My Lady Charlotina turned her fine and scented head so that she could smile pleasantly upon the Duke of Queens, strutting past in living koalas. 'Then surely you can conceive a means of halting his activities, Doctor Volospion?'

'I believe that I have done so, madam.'

She laughed, almost rudely. 'But you decide to keep it to yourself.'

'The Fireclown has a certain sensitivity. For all I know he has the means to overhear us.'

'I should not have thought that, temperamentally, he was an ordinary eavesdropper.'

'But I feel, nonetheless, that I should be cautious.'

'So you'll not illuminate me?'

'To my regret.'

'Well, I wish you luck with your plan, Doctor Volospion.' She looked here and there. 'Where is your guest, the Fireclown's quarry? Where is Miss Ming?'

He expressed secret glee. 'Not here.'

'Not here? She travels to meet her suitor at last?'

'No. On the contrary…'

'Then what?' My Lady Charlotina expressed cool impatience.

'Wait,' said Doctor Volospion. 'I protect her, as I promised. I am her true knight. You heard me called that. Well, I am doing my duty, My Lady Charlotina.'

'You are vague, Doctor Volospion.'

'Oh, madam, recall that encounter when we stood upon the cliff above Mr Bloom's ship!'

She drew her beautiful brows together. 'You acted uncharacteristically, as I remember.'

'You thought so.'

'Oh,' she was again impatient. 'Yes, yes…'

'Mr Bloom noticed, do you think?'

'He remarked on it, did he not?'

Doctor Volospion brought his hands together at his groin, his maroon and white sleeves swirling. He had an expression upon his pale, ascetic features of extreme self-satisfaction. 'Miss Ming,' he said, 'is safe in my castle. A force-field, quite as strong as the Fireclown's, surrounds it. For her own good, she cannot leave its confines.'

'You have locked her up?'

'For her own good. She agreed, for she fears the Fireclown greatly. I merely pointed out to her that it was the best way of ensuring that she would never encounter him.'

'In your menagerie?'

'She is comfortable, secure and, doubtless, happy,' said Doctor Volospion.

'True knight, say you? Sorcerer, more accurately!' My Lady Charlotina for the first time showed admiration of Doctor Volospion's cunning. 'I see! Excellent!'

Doctor Volospion's thin smile was almost joyous. His cold eyes sparkled. 'I shall show you, I think, that I am no mere shadow of Jagged.'

'Did anyone suggest…?'

'If anyone did suggest such a thing, they shall be proved in error.'

She pursed her lips and looked first at one of her feet and then the other. 'If the plan works…'

'It will work. The art of conflict is to turn the antagonist's own strengths against him and to draw out his weaknesses.'

'It is one interpretation of the art. There have been so many, down all these millions of days.'

'You shall see, madam.'

'The Fireclown knows what you have done?'

'He has already accused me of it.'

'Well, you shall have the gratitude of each of us if you succeed, Doctor Volospion.'

'It is all I wish.'

The ground shook. They both turned, to see a magnificent pink pachyderm lumbering towards them. The beast bore a swaying howdah in which were seated both Abu Thaleb and Argonheart Po.

Abu Thaleb, in quilted silks of rose and sable, leaned down to greet them. 'My Lady Charlotina! I see music! And my old friend, Volospion. It has been so long…'

'I will leave you to this reunion,' murmured My Lady Charlotina, and with a curtsey to the Commissar of Bengal she departed.

'Have you been all this time in your castle, Volospion?' asked Abu Thaleb. 'We have not met since that time when we were all three together, Argonheart, you and I, when Mr Bloom's ship had first landed. I have looked for you at many a gathering.'

'My attention, for my sins, has been much taken up with our current problem,' said Doctor Volospion.

'Ah, if only there were a solution,' rumbled Argonheart Po. 'We should have realised, when my dinosaurs were incinerated...'

'It was the moment to act, of course,' agreed Doctor Volospion. His neck grew stiff with craning and he lowered his head.

'It needs only Miss Ming,' said Abu Thaleb, lowering himself over the side of the howdah and beginning to descend by means of a golden rope ladder the side of his great beast, 'to complete the original quartet.'

'She cannot be with us. She remains in safety in my castle.'

'Probably wise.' Abu Thaleb reached the ground. He signed for Argonheart Po that his way was now clear. The monstrous chef heaved his bulk gingerly to the edge and put a tentative foot upon a golden rung. Doctor Volospion watched with some fascination as the corpulent figure, swathed in white, came down the pink expanse.

'It is my duty to protect the lady from any danger,' Doctor Volospion said with a certain semblance of piety.

'She must be very much pleased by your thoughtfulness. She is so lacking in inner tranquillity that the trappings of security, physical and tactile, must mean much to her.'

'I think so.'

'Of course,' said Abu Thaleb doubtfully, 'this will confirm Mr Bloom's suspicions of you. Are you sure –?'

'I shall have to bear those suspicions, as a gentleman. I do my duty. If my actions are misinterpreted, particularly by Mr Bloom, that is no fault of mine.'

'Naturally.' Abu Thaleb dismissed his elephant. 'But if Mr Bloom were to take it into his head to – um – rescue Miss Ming?'

'I am prepared.'

Argonheart Po grunted. 'You are looking paler than ever, Doctor Volospion. You should eat more.'

'More? I do not eat at all.'

'There is more to eating than merely sustaining the flesh,' said Argonheart Po pointedly. 'If it comes to that, none of us *needs* to eat, there are so many quicker ways of absorbing energy, but there is a certain instinctive relish to such old-fashioned activities which it is as well to enjoy. After all, we are all human. Well, most of us.'

Abu Thaleb was upset by what seemed to him to be one friend's criticism of another. 'Argonheart, my dear, we all have preferences. Doctor Volospion enjoys rather more intellectual pastimes than do we. We must respect his tastes.'

Argonheart Po was quick to apologise. 'I did not mean to infer...'

'I detected no inference,' said Doctor Volospion with an extravagant wave of his hand. 'My interests, as you must know, are specialised. I study ancient faiths and have little time for anything else. It is perhaps because I would wish to believe in something supernatural. However, in all my studies I have yet to find something which cannot be explained or dismissed either as natural or as delusion. I do, admittedly, possess one or two miraculous artefacts which would *seem* to possess qualities not easily defined by science, but I fear it is only lack of knowledge on my part, and that these, too, will be shown to be the products of man's ingenuity.'

Argonheart Po smiled. 'If, one day, you will let me, I shall produce a culinary miracle for you and defy you to detect all the flavours and textures I shall put into it.'

'One day, perhaps, I should be honoured, mighty King of the Kitchen.'

And to Abu Thaleb's relief, the two parted amicably.

Doctor Volospion, alone for the moment, glanced about him. He seemed unusually content. A little sigh of pleasure passed between his normally tight-pressed lips. He could, upon occasions, produce in himself a semblance of gaiety and now there was a lightness to his step as he moved to greet Mistress Christia, the Everlasting Concubine, changing his costume as he went, to brilliant damson doublet and hose, curling shoes, a hat with a high crown and an elongated peak which could be doffed to brush the turf with a flourish as he bowed low. 'Beautiful Christia, queen of my heart, how I have longed for this opportunity to see you alone!'

Mistress Christia wore ringlets today of light red-gold, a translucent gown of sea-green antique rayon, bracelets of live lizards, their tails held between their tiny forepaws.

'Oh, Doctor Volospion, how you flatter me! I have heard that you keep the most sought-after beauty in the world imprisoned in one of your gloomy towers!'

'You have heard? Already? It is true.' He pretended shame. 'I cannot help it. I am sworn to do so.'

'It is fitting, then, that you dally with me – for my reputation –'

'Is enviable,' he said.

She kissed his chilly cheek. 'But I know you to be heartless.'

'It is you, Mistress Christia, who gives me a heart.'

'But you will lay it at another's feet, I know. It is my fate, always.'

His attention was distracted, all at once. Sweet Orb Mace's juvenile slaughterhouse was blazing. And a look of joy crossed Doctor Volospion's face.

Mistress Christia was bemused. 'You seem pleased at this? Poor Sweet Orb Mace and his lovely little house.'

'Oh, no, no, that is not it, at all.' He moved like a moth for the flames, his face lit by them. And then fire licked his body again and he was naked. There came a chorus from all around. Everyone was likewise unclad.

From out of the inferno stepped Emmanuel Bloom. He wore a black-and-white pierrot costume.

'I have come,' he trilled amiably, 'to be worshipped. I strip you naked. Thus I will strip your souls.' He looked at their bare bodies and seemed rather confounded by some of the sights.

Fussing, a number of the guests were already replenishing themselves. Costumes blossomed on flesh again.

'No matter,' said the Fireclown, 'I have made my moral point.'

With a caress Doctor Volospion brought rippling velvet to his body, dark reds and greens glowed upon him. 'Shall you never tire of these demonstrations?' he asked.

Emmanuel Bloom shrugged. 'Why should I? It is my way of preaching to you. There are many excellent precedents for the method. A miracle and a parable or two work, as it were, wonders.'

'You have converted no-one, sir,' said My Lady Charlotina, in a huge china bell, decorated with little flowers. Her voice tended to echo.

The Fireclown agreed with her. 'It is taking longer than I

expected, madam. But I am persistent, by nature. And patient, in my way.'

'Well, sir, we lose patience,' said Abu Thaleb. 'I regret to say it, but it is true.' He turned for confirmation to his friends. All nodded. 'You see?'

'Is consensus truth?' the Fireclown wished to know. 'Agree what you like between yourselves, for it will not alter what is so.'

'It could be said that that which all are agreed upon is truth,' mildly proposed Argonheart Po, who saw the chance of a metaphysical spat. 'Do we not make the truth from the stuff of Chaos?'

'If the will is strong enough, perhaps,' said Emmanuel Bloom. 'But your wills are nothing. Mine is immeasurably powerful. You use gadgetry for your miracles. Do you see me using anything else but the power of my mind?'

'Your ship's force-field...' suggested Doctor Volospion.

'That, too, is controlled by my mind.'

Doctor Volospion seemed unhappy with this information.

'And where is my soul mate?' enquired Mr Bloom. 'Where is my consort? Where are you hiding her, Volospion? Eh, manikin? Speak!' He glared up at his smiling adversary.

'She is protected,' said Volospion, 'from you.'

'Protected? She needs no protection from Emmanuel Bloom. So, you imprison her.'

'For her own safety,' said My Lady Charlotina. 'It is what Miss Ming wants.'

'She is deluded.' The Fireclown displayed irritation. 'Deluded by this conjuror and his jesuitry. Give her up to me. I demand it. If I can save no other soul in this whole world, I shall save hers, I swear!'

'Never,' said Doctor Volospion, 'would I give another human creature into your keeping. How could I justify my conscience?'

'Conscience! Pah!'

'She is secure,' My Lady Charlotina glanced once at Doctor Volospion, 'is she not? Locked in your deepest dungeon?'

'Well...' Doctor Volospion's shrug was modest.

'Ah, I cannot bear it! Know this, creeping jackal, sniggering quasi-priest, that I shall release her. I shall rescue her from any prison you may conceive. Why do you do this? Do you bargain with me?'

'Bargain?' said Doctor Volospion. 'What have you that I should wish to bargain?'

'What do you wish from me?' The Fireclown had become agitated. 'Tell me!'

'Nothing. You have heard my reasons for keeping Miss Ming safe from your threats...'

'Threats? When did I threaten?'

'You have frightened the poor woman. She is not very intelligent. She has scant self-confidence...'

'I offer her all of that and more. It is promises, not threats, I make! Bah!' The Fireclown set the lawn to smouldering and, as a consequence, many of the guests to dancing. At length everyone withdrew a few feet into the air, though still disturbed by rich smoke. Only the Fireclown remained on the ground, careless of the heat. 'I can give that woman everything. You take from her what little pride she still has. I can give her beauty and love and eternal life...'

'The secret of eternal life, Mr Bloom, is already known to us,' said My Lady Charlotina from above. She had some difficulty in seeing him through the smoke, which grew steadily thicker.

'This? It is a state of eternal death. You have no true enthusiasms any longer. The secret of eternal life, madam, is enthusiasm, nothing more or less.'

'Enough?' said a distant Argonheart Po. 'To sustain us physically?'

'To relish everything to the full, for its own sake, that's the answer.' Mr Bloom's black-and-white pierrot costume was almost invisible now in the boiling smoke. 'Away with your charms and potions, your Shangri-Las, your planets of youth, of frozen cells and brain transfers! – many's the entity I've seen last little more than a thousand years before boredom shrivels up his soul and kills him.'

'Kills him?' Argonheart's voice was even fainter.

'Oh, his body may live. But one way or another, boredom kills him!'

'Your ideas remain somewhat out of date,' said My Lady

Charlotina. 'Immortality is no longer a matter of potions, enchantments or surgery…'

'I speak of the soul, madam.'

'Then you speak of nothing at all,' said Doctor Volospion.

There was no reply.

The Fireclown was gone.

Chapter Eleven

In Which Doctor Volospion Is Subjected to a Siege and Attempts to Parley

Miss Ming was neither chained nor bound, neither did she languish in a dungeon, but she did confine herself, at Doctor Volospion's request, to her own apartments, furnished by him to her exact requirements, and at first she was content to accept this security. But as time passed she came to pine for human company, for even Doctor Volospion hardly ever visited her, and her only exchanges were with mechanical servants. When she did encounter her dark-minded host she would beg for news of Bloom, praying that by now he would have abandoned his plans and left the planet.

She saw Doctor Volospion soon after the party at Sweet Orb Mace's, where the house and lawn had been burned.

'He is still, I fear, here,' Volospion informed her, seating himself on a pink, quilted pouf. 'His determination to save the world has weakened just a little, I would say.'

'So he will go soon?'

'His determination to win your hand, Miss Ming, is if anything stronger than ever.'

'So he remains...' She sank upon a satin cushion.

'Everyone shares your dismay. Indeed, I have been deputised to rid the world of the madman, in an informal way, and I have racked my brains to conceive a plan, but none comes. Can you think of anything?'

'Me? Little Mavis? I am very honoured, Doctor Volospion, but...' She played with the neck of her blue lace négligée. 'If you have failed, how can *I* help?'

'I thought you might have a better understanding of your suitor's mentality. He loves you very much. He told me so again, at the party. He accused me of keeping you here against your will.'

She uttered her familiar tinkling laugh. 'Against my will? What does he intend to do, but carry me off!' She shuddered.

'Quite.'

'I still can't believe he was serious,' she said. 'Can you?'

'He is deeply serious. He is a man of much experience. That we know. He has considerable learning and his powers are impressive. As a lover, you could know worse, Miss Ming.'

'He's repulsive.'

Doctor Volospion rose from the pouf. 'As you say. Well – why, what is that beyond the window?'

The window to which he pointed was large but filled with small panels of thick glass, obscured, moreover, by the frothy blue curtains on either side of it, reminiscent of the ornament on a baby's cradle, the ribbons being pink and yellow.

It seemed that a small nova flared above the dour landscape of brooding trees and rocks surrounding Castle Volospion. The light approached them and then began to fall, just short of the force-field which protected the whole vast building (or series of buildings, as they actually were). Its colour changed from white to glowing red and it became identifiable as Emmanuel Bloom's baroque spacecraft.

'Oh, no!' wailed Miss Ming.

'Rest assured,' said Doctor Volospion. 'My force-field, like his own, is impregnable. He cannot enter.'

The vessel landed, destroying a tree or two as it did so and turning rocks to a pool of black glass.

Miss Ming fled hastily to the window and drew the curtains. 'There! This is torment, Doctor Volospion. I'm so unhappy!' She began to weep.

'I will do what I can,' he said, 'to dissuade him, but I can make no promises. He is so dedicated.'

'You'll go to see him?' She snuffled. Her blue eyes begged. 'You'll make him go away?'

'As I said –'

'Oh! Can't you kill him? Can't you?'

'Kill? What a waste that would be of such an authentic messiah…'

'You're still thinking of yourself. What about me?'

'Of course, I know that you are feeling some stress but, perhaps with your help, I could solve our problem.'

'You could?' She dried her eyes upon her lacy sleeve.

'It would demand from you, Miss Ming, considerable courage, but the end would, I assure you, be worthwhile to us all.'

'What?'

'I shall tell you if and when the opportunity arises.'

'Not now?'

'Not yet.'

'I'll do anything,' she said, 'to be rid of him.'

'Good,' he said. He left her apartments.

Doctor Volospion strode, in ornamental green and black, through the candlelight of his corridors, climbing stairs of grey-brown stone until he had reached a roof. Into the late evening air, which he favoured, he stepped, upon his battlements, to peruse the Fireclown's ship.

Doctor Volospion laughed and his joy was mysterious. 'So, sir, you lay siege to my castle!'

His voice echoed from many parts of his stronghold, from massive towers, from steeples and from eaves. A cool breeze blew at his robes as he stood there in his pride and his mockery. Behind him stretched bridges without function, buttresses which gave support to nothing, domes which sheltered only empty air. Above were dark masses of cloud in a sky the colour of steel. Below, lurid and out of key with all these surroundings, stood the spaceship.

'I warn you, sir, you shall be resisted!' continued Doctor Volospion.

But there was still no reply.

'Miss Ming is in my charge. I have sworn an oath to protect her!'

The airlock hatch swung back. Little tongues of flame came forth and dissipated in the dank air. The ramp licked out and touched the glassy rock and the Fireclown made his appearance. He wore a scarlet cap and a jerkin of red and yellow stripes. One leg was amber and the other orange, one foot, with bell-toed shoes, matched the red of his jerkin and the other matched the yellow. He had painted his face so that it was now the ridiculous mask of a traditional clown of antiquity and yet, withal, Doctor Volospion received the impression that Emmanuel Bloom was dressed for battle. Doctor Volospion smiled.

The thin, birdlike voice rose to the battlements. 'Let the woman go free!'

'She fears you, sir,' said Doctor Volospion equably. 'She begs me to slay you.'

'Of course, of course. It is because, like so many mortals, she is terror-struck by some hint of what I can release in her. But that is of no consequence, at this moment. You must remove yourself from the position you have taken between us.'

Emmanuel Bloom walked in poorly co-ordinated strides down his ramp, crossed the grass and was halted by the force-field. 'Remove this,' he commanded.

'I cannot,' Doctor Volospion told him.

'You must!'

'My pledge to Miss Ming...'

'Is meaningless, as well you know. You serve only yourself. It is your doom ever to serve yourself and thus never to know true life!'

'You invent a rôle for me as you invent one for Miss Ming. Even your own rôle is invented. Your imagination, sir, is disordered. I advise you, with all courtesy, to leave, or change your ways, or alter your ambitions. This masquerade of yours will bring you only misery.' Doctor Volospion adopted the voice of sympathy.

'Must I suffer further examples of your hypocrisy, manikin? Let down this screen and show me to my soul mate.' Emmanuel Bloom banged a small fist upon the field, causing it to shimmer somewhat. His mad blue eyes were fierce and paradoxical in their setting of paint.

'Your "soul mate" sir, reviles you.'

'Your interpretations are of no interest to me. Let me see her!'

'If you saw her, she would confirm my words.'

'Her voice, perhaps, but not her soul.'

'I'll indulge you no further, sir.' Doctor Volospion turned from the battlements.

Behind him there came a most terrible tumult. He felt heat upon his back. He whirled. The Fireclown could not be seen, for now a wall of flame reared in place of the force-field. And the wall screamed.

Doctor Volospion touched a power ring and the flames became transparent ice through which he could just make out the silhouette of the Fireclown.

'Mr Bloom!' he called. 'We can play thus for many a century and consume all our energies. If I admitted you, would you give me your word that you would use no violence against either myself or Miss Ming, that you would not attempt to achieve your ends with force?'

'I never use force. I use my power to produce living parables, that is all, and so convince those who would oppose me.'

'But you would give your word?'

'If you require it, you have it.' And then the Fireclown raised his shadowy fist again and struck at the ice which shattered. He strode through the hole he had made. 'But you see how easily I can dispose of your protection!'

Doctor Volospion hid his mouth behind his hand. 'Ah, I had not realised...' He lowered his lids so that his eyes might not be seen yet it might have been that a cunning humour glittered there for a moment.

'Will you admit me to your castle, Doctor Volospion, so that I may see Miss Ming for myself?'

'Give me a little while so that I may prepare the lady for your visit. You will dine with me?'

'I will undergo any ritual you wish, but when I leave, it shall be with Mavis Ming, my love.'

'You gave your word...'

'I gave my word and I shall keep it.'

Doctor Volospion quit his battlements.

Chapter Twelve

In Which Doctor Volospion Gives a Tour of His Museum and His Menagerie of Forgotten Faiths

MAVIS MING WAS desolate.

'Oh, you have betrayed me!'

'Betrayed?' Doctor Volospion laid a hand upon her trembling shoulder. 'Nothing of the sort. This is all part of my plan. I beg you to become an actress, Miss Ming. Show, as best you can, some little sympathy for your suitor. It will benefit you in the end.'

'You're laying a trap for him, aren't you?'

'I can only say, now, that you will soon be free of him.'

'You're certain.'

'Certain.'

'I'm not sure I could keep it up.'

'Trust me. I have so far proved myself your loyal protector, have I not?'

'Of course. I didn't mean to imply...' She was hasty to give him reassurance.

'Then dress yourself and join us, as soon as you can, for dinner.'

'You'll be eating? You never –'

'It is the ceremony which is important.'

She nodded. 'All right.'

He crossed to the door. She said: 'He's not really very intelligent, is he?'

'I think not.'

'And you're very clever indeed.'

'You are kind.'

'What I mean is, I'm sure you *can* trick him, Doctor Volospion, if that's what you mean to do.'

'I appreciate your encouragement, Miss Ming.' He went out.

Mavis looked to her wardrobe. She dragged from it an evening dress of green and purple silk. She passed to her mirror and looked with displeasure upon her red-rimmed eyes, her bedraggled hair. 'Chin up, Mavis,' she said, 'it'll all be over soon. And it means you can go visiting again. What a relief that'll be! And if I play my part right, they'll have me to thank, as well as Doctor Volospion. I'll get a bit of respect.' She settled to her toilet.

It was to her credit that she made the most of herself, in her own eyes. She curled her hair so that it hung in blonde waves upon her shoulders. She applied plenty of mascara, to make her eyes look larger. She was relatively subtle with her rouge and she touched her best perfumed deodorant to all those parts of her body which, in her opinion, might require it (her cosmetics were largely 20th-century, created for her by Doctor Volospion at her own request, for she considered the cosmetics of her own time to be crude and synthetic by comparison). She arranged an everlasting orchid upon her dress; she donned diamond earrings, a matching necklace, bracelets. 'Good enough to dine with the Emperor of Africa,' she said of herself, when she was ready.

She left her apartments and began her journey through passages which, in her opinion, Doctor Volospion kept unnecessarily dark, although, as she knew, it was done for the artistic effect he favoured.

At last she reached the great, gloomy hall where Doctor Volospion normally entertained his guests. Hard-faced metal servants already waited on the long table at one end of which sat dignified Doctor Volospion, and the pipsqueak Bloom, dressed in the silliest outfit Mavis Ming had ever seen. Strips of ancient neon, blue-white, illuminated this particular part of the castle, though they had been designed to malfunction and so flickered on and off, creating sudden shadows and brilliances which always disturbed Miss Ming. The walls were of undressed stone and bore no decoration save the tall portrait of Doctor Volospion over the massive fireplace in which a small electric fire had been positioned. The fire was also an antique, designed to simulate burning coal.

Becoming aware of her entrance, both men rose from their seats.

'My madonna!' breathed Bloom.

'Good evening, Miss Ming.' Doctor Volospion bowed.

Emmanuel Bloom seemed to be making an effort to contain himself. He sat down again.

'Good evening, gentlemen.' She responded to this effort with one of her own. 'How nice to see you again, Mr Bloom!'

'Oh!' He lifted a chop to his grease-painted mouth.

Simple food was placed by servants before her. She sat at Doctor Volospion's left. She had no appetite, but she made some show of eating, noting that Doctor Volospion did the same. She hoped that Bloom would not subject them to any more of his megalomaniacal monologues. It was still difficult to understand why a man of Doctor Volospion's intelligence indulged Bloom at all, and yet they seemed to converse readily enough.

'You deal, sir, in Ideals,' Doctor Volospion was saying, 'I, in Realities: though I remain fascinated by the trappings by means of which men seek to give credence to their dreamings.'

'The trappings are all you can ever know,' said the Fireclown, 'for you can never experience the ecstasy of Faith. You are too empty.'

'You continue to be hard on me, sir, while I try –'

'I speak the truth.'

'Ah, well. I suppose you do read me aright, Mr Bloom.'

'Of course, I do. I gave my word only that I should not take Miss Ming from here by force. I did not agree to join in your courtesies, your hypocrisies. What are your manners when seen in the light of the great unchangeable realities of the multiverse?'

'Your belief in the permanence of anything, Mr Bloom, is incredible to me. Everything is transitory. Can the experience of a billion years have taught you nothing?'

'On the contrary, Doctor Volospion.' He did not amplify. He chewed at his chop.

'Has experience left you untouched? Were you ever the same?'

'I suppose my character has changed little. I have known the punishments of Prometheus, but I have been that god's persecutor, too – for Bloom has bloomed everywhere, in every guise...'

'More peas?' interrupted Miss Ming.

Emmanuel Bloom shook his head.

'But creed has followed creed, movement followed movement,

down all the centuries,' continued Doctor Volospion, 'and not one important change in any of them, though millions have lost their lives over some slight interpretation. Are men not fools to destroy themselves thus? Questing after impossibilities, golden dreams, romantic fancies, perfect…'

'Oh, certainly. Clowns, all of them. Like me.'

Doctor Volospion did not know what to make of this.

'You agree?'

'The clown weeps, laughs, knows joy and sorrow. It is not enough to look at his costume and laugh and say – here is mankind revealed. Irony is nothing by itself. Irony is a modifier, not a protection. We live our lives because we have only our lives to live.'

'Um,' said Doctor Volospion. 'I think I should show you my collection. I possess mementoes of a million creeds.' He pointed with his thumb at the floor. 'Down there.'

'I doubt that they will be unfamiliar to me,' said Bloom. 'What do you hope to prove?'

'That you are not original, I suppose.'

'And by this means you think you will encourage me to leave your planet without a single pledge fulfilled?'

Doctor Volospion made a gesture. 'You read me so well, Mr Bloom.'

'I'll inspect this stuff, if you wish. I am curious. I am respectful, too, of all prophets and all objects of devotion, but as to my originality…'

'Well,' said Doctor Volospion, 'we shall see. If you will allow me to conduct you upon a brief tour of my collection, I shall hope to convince you.'

'Miss Ming will accompany us?'

'Oh, I'd love to,' said Miss Ming courageously. She hated Doctor Volospion's treasures.

'I think my collection is the greatest in the universe,' continued Doctor Volospion. 'No better has existed, certainly in Earth's history. Many missionaries have come this way. Most have made attempts to – um – save us. As you have. They have not been, in the main, as spectacular, I will admit, nor have they claimed as much as you claim. However…' He took a pea upon his fork. There was something in the gesture to make Miss Ming suspect that he planned something more than a mere tour of his treasures. '... you would agree that your arguments are scarcely subtle. They allow for no nuance.'

Now nothing would stop the Fireclown. He rose from the table, his birdlike movements even more exaggerated than usual. He strutted the length of the table. He strutted back again. 'A pox on nuance! Seize the substance, beak and claws, and leave the chitterlings for the carrion! Let crows and storks squabble over the scraps, these subtleties – the eagle takes the main carcass, as much or as little as he needs!' He fixed his gaze upon Miss Ming. 'Forget your quibbling scruples, madonna! Come with me now. Together we'll leave the planet to its fate. Their souls gutter like dying candles. The whole world reeks of inertia. If they will not have my Ideals, then I shall bestow *all* my gifts on you!'

Mavis Ming said in strangled tones: 'You are very kind, Mr Bloom, but...'

'Perhaps that particular matter can be discussed later,' proposed Doctor Volospion, tightening his cap about his head and face. 'Now, sir, if you will come?'

'Miss Ming, too?'

'Miss Ming.'

The trio left the hall, with Miss Ming reluctantly trailing behind. She desperately hoped that Doctor Volospion was not playing one of his games at her expense. He had been so nice to her lately, she thought, that he was evidently mellowing her, yet she hated in herself that slight lingering suspicion of him, that voice which had told her, on more than one occasion, that if someone liked her, then that someone could have no taste at all and was therefore not worth knowing.

They descended and they descended, for it was Doctor Volospion's pleasure to bury his collection in the bowels of his castle. Murky corridor followed murky corridor, lit by flambeaux, candles, rush torches, oil lamps, anything that would give the minimum of light and cast the maximum number of shadows.

'You have,' said Mr Bloom after some while of this tramping, 'an unexceptional imagination, Doctor Volospion.'

'I do not concern myself with the lust for variation enjoyed by most of my fellows at the End of Time,' remarked the lean man. 'I follow but a few simple obsessions. And in that, I think, we share something, Mr Bloom.'

'Well –' began the Fireclown.

But then Doctor Volospion had stopped at an iron-bound door. 'Here we are!' He flung the door wide. The light from within seemed intense.

The Fireclown strutted, stiff-limbed as ever, into the high vaulted hall. He blinked in the light. He sniffed the warm, heavy air. For almost as far as the eye could see there were rows and rows of cabinets, pedestals, display domes; Doctor Volospion's museum.

'What's this?' enquired Mr Bloom.

'My collection of devotional objects, culled from all ages. From all the planets of the universe.' Doctor Volospion was proud.

It was difficult to see if Mr Bloom was impressed, for his clown's paint hid most expression.

Doctor Volospion paused beside a little table. 'Only the best have been preserved. I have discarded or destroyed the rest. Here is a history of folly!' He looked down at the table. On it lay a dusty scrap of skin to which clung a few faded feathers. Doctor Volospion plucked it up. 'Do you recognise that, Mr Bloom, with all your experience of Time and Space?'

The long neck came forwards to inspect the thing. 'The remains of a fowl?' suggested Mr Bloom. 'A chicken, perhaps?'

Miss Ming wrinkled her nose and backed away from them. 'I never liked this part of the castle. It's creepy. I don't know how –' She pulled herself together.

'Eh?' said Mr Bloom.

Doctor Volospion permitted a dark smile. 'It is all that remains of Yawk, Saviour of Shakah, founder of a religion which spread through fourteen star systems and eighty planets and lasted some seven thousand years until it became the subject of a jihad.'

'Hm,' said Mr Bloom noncommittally.

'I had this,' confided Doctor Volospion, 'from the last living being to retain his faith in Yawk. He regarded himself as the only guardian of the relic, carried it across countless light years, preaching the gospel of Yawk (and a fine, poetic tale it is), until he reached Earth.'

'And then?' Bloom reverently replaced the piece of skin.

'He is now a guest of mine. You will meet him later.'

A smile appeared momentarily on Miss Ming's lips. She believed that she had guessed what her host had in mind.

'Aha,' murmured the Fireclown. 'And what would this be?' He moved on through the hall, pausing beside a cabinet containing an oddly wrought artefact made of something resembling green marble.

'A weapon,' said Volospion. 'The very gun which slew Marchbanks, the Martyr of Mars, during the revival, in the 25th century (AD, of course), of the famous Kangaroo Cult which had swept the solar system about a hundred years previously, before it was superseded by some atheistic political doctrine. You know how one is prone to follow the other. Nothing, Mr Bloom, changes very much, either in the fundamentals or the rhetoric of religions and political creeds. I hope I am not depressing you?'

Bloom snorted. 'How could you? None of these others has experienced what I have experienced. None has had the knowledge I have gained and, admittedly, half-forgotten. Do not confuse me with these, I warn you, Doctor Volospion, if you wish to continue to converse with me. I could destroy all this in a moment, if I wished, and it would make no difference…'

'You threaten?'

'What?' The little man removed his clown's cap and ran his fingers through the tangles of his auburn hair. 'Eh? Threaten? Don't be foolish. I gave my word. I was merely lending emphasis to my statement.'

'Besides,' said Doctor Volospion smoothly. 'You could do little now, I suspect, for there are several force-fields lying between you and your ship now – they protect my museum – and I suspect that your ship is the main source of your power, for all you claim it derives entirely from your mind.'

Emmanuel Bloom chuckled. 'You have found me out, Doctor Volospion, I see.' He seemed undisturbed. 'Now, then, what other pathetic monuments to the nobility of the human spirit have you locked up here?'

Doctor Volospion extended his arms. 'What would you see?' He pointed in one direction. 'A wheel from Krishna's chariot?' He pointed in another. 'A tooth said to belong to the Buddha? A fragment of the true cross? The Holy Grail? Mohammed's sword? Bunter's bottle? The sacred crown of the Kennedys? Hitler's nail? There,' he tapped a dome, 'you'll find them all in that case. Or over here,' a sweep of a green-and-black arm, 'the finger-bones of Karl Marx, the kneecap of Mao Tse-tung, a mummified testicle belonging to Heffner, the skeleton of Maluk Khan, the tongue of Suhulu. Or what of these? Filp's loincloth, Xiombarg's napkin, Teglardin's peach rag. Then there are the coins of Bibb-Nardrop, the silver wands of Er and Er, the towels of Ich – all the way from a world within the Crab Nebula. And most of these, in this section here, are only from the Dawn Age. Farther along are relics from all other ages of this world and the universe. Rags and bones, Mr Bloom. Rags and bones.'

'I am moved,' said Emmanuel Bloom.

'All that is left,' said Doctor Volospion, 'of a million mighty causes. And all, at core, that those causes ever were!'

The clown's face was grave as he moved among the cases.

Mavis Ming was shivering. 'This place really *does* depress me,' she whispered to her guardian. 'I know it's my fault, but I've always hated places like this. They seem ghoulish. Not that I'm criticising, Doctor Volospion, but I've never been able to understand why a man like you could indulge in such a strange hobby. It's all research material, of course. We have to do research, don't we? Well, at least, you do. It's nice that someone does. I mean this is your area of research, isn't it, this particular aspect of the galaxy's past? It's why I'll never make a first-rank historian, I suppose. It's the same, you know, when I lived with Donny Stevens. It was the cold-blooded killing of those sweet little rabbits and monkeys at the lab. I simply refused, you know, to let him or anyone else talk about it when I was around. And with the time machine, too, they sent so many to God knows where before they'd got it working properly. When can I stop this charade, Doctor...?'

Volospion raised a finger to his lips. Bloom was some distance away but had turned, detecting the voice, no doubt, of his loved one.

'Rags and bones,' said Doctor Volospion, as if he had been reiterating his opinions to Miss Ming.

'No,' called Bloom from where he stood beside a case containing many slightly differently shaped strips of metal, 'these were merely the instruments used to focus faith. Witness their variety. Anything would do as a lens to harness the soul's fire. A bit of wood. A stone. A cup. A custard pie. Nothing here means anything without the presence of the beings who believed in their validity. Whether that piece of worm-eaten wood really did come from Christ's cross or not is immaterial. As a symbol...'

'You question the authenticity of my prizes?'

'It is not important...'

Doctor Volospion betrayed agitation. It was genuine. 'It is to me, Mr Bloom. I will have nothing in my museum that is not authentic!'

'So you have a faith of your own, after all.' Bloom's painted lips formed a smile.

He leaned, a tiny jester, a cockerel, against a force-dome.

Doctor Volospion lost none of his composure. 'If you mean that I pride myself on my ability to sniff out any fakes, any piece of doubtful origin, then you speak rightly. I have faith in my own taste and judgement. But come, let us move on. It is not the museum that I wish you to inspect, but the menagerie, which is of greater interest, for there...'

'Show me this cup you have. This Holy Grail. I was looking for it.'

'Well, if you feel you have the leisure. Certainly. There it is. In the cabinet with Jissard's space-helmet and Panjit's belt.'

Emmanuel Bloom trotted rapidly in the direction indicated by Doctor Volospion, weaving his way among the various displays, until he came to the far wall where, behind a slightly quivering energy-screen, between the helmet and the belt, stood a pulsing, golden cup, semi-transparent, in which a red liquid swirled.

Bloom's glance at the cup was casual. He made no serious attempt to inspect it. He turned back to Doctor Volospion, who had followed behind.

'Well?' said Volospion.

Bloom laughed. 'Your taste and judgement fail you, Doctor Volospion. It is a fake, that Grail.'

'How could you know?'

'I assure you that I am right.'

Bloom began to leave the case, but Doctor Volospion tugged at his arm. 'You would argue that it is merely mythical, wouldn't you? That it never existed. Yet there is proof that it did.'

'Oh, I need no proof of the Grail's existence. But if it were the true Grail how could you, of all people, keep it?'

Doctor Volospion frowned. 'You are vaguer than usual, Mr Bloom. I keep the cup because it is mine.'

'Yours?'

'I had it from a time-traveller who had spent his entire life searching for it and who, as it happens, found it in one of our own cities. Unfortunately, the traveller destroyed himself soon after coming to stay with me. They are all mad, such people. But the thing itself is authentic. He had found many fakes before he found the true Grail. He vouched for this one. And he should have known, a man who had dedicated himself to his quest and who was willing to kill himself once that quest was over.'

'He probably thought it would bring him back to life,' mused the Fireclown. 'That is part of the legend, you know. One of the real Grail's minor properties.'

'Real? This man's opinion was irrefutable.'

'Well, I am glad that he is dead,' said Bloom, and then he laughed a strange, deep-throated laugh which had no business coming from that puny frame, 'for I should not have liked to have disappointed him.'

'Disappointed?' Volospion flushed. 'Now –'

'That cup is not even a very good copy of the original, Doctor Volospion.'

Doctor Volospion drew himself up and arranged the folds of his robe carefully in front of him. His voice was calm when he next spoke. 'How would you know such a thing, Mr Bloom? You claim great knowledge, yet you exhibit no signs of it in your rather foolish behaviour, your pointless pursuits. You dress a fool and you are a fool, say I.'

'Possibly. Nonetheless, that Grail is a fake.'

'Why do you know?' Doctor Volospion's gaze was not quite as steady as it might have been.

'Because,' explained Bloom amicably, 'I am, among many other things, the Guardian of the Grail. That is to say, specifically, that I am graced by the presence of the Holy Grail.'

'What!' Doctor Volospion was openly contemptuous.

'You probably do not know,' Mr Bloom went on, 'that only those who are absolutely pure in spirit, who never commit the sin of accidie (moral torpor, if you prefer) may ever see the Grail and only one such as myself may ever receive the sacred trust of Joseph of Arimathaea, the Good Soldier, who carried the Grail to Glastonbury. I have had this trust for several centuries, at least. I am probably the only mortal being left alive who deserves the honour (though, of course, I am not so proud as to be certain of it). My ship is full of such things – relics to rival any of these here – collected in an eternity of wandering the many dimensions of the universe, tumbling through time, companion to chronons...'

Doctor Volospion's face wore an expression quite different from anything Miss Ming had ever seen. He was deeply serious. His voice contained an unusual vibrancy.

'Oh, don't be taken in by him, Doctor Volospion,' she said, giving up any idea of trying to placate the Fireclown. 'He's an obvious charlatan.'

Bloom bowed. Doctor Volospion did not even hear her.

'How can you prove that your Grail is the original, Mr Bloom?'

'I do not have to *prove* such a thing. The Grail chooses its own guardian. The Grail will only appear to one whose Faith is Absolute. My Faith is Absolute.'

Bloom began to stride towards Mavis Ming. Volospion followed thoughtfully in his wake.

'Oo!' squeaked Miss Ming, seeing her protector distracted and fearing a sudden leap. 'Get off!'

'I am not, Miss Ming, on. I promise you no violence, not yet, not until you come to me.'

'Oh! You think that I'd –?' She struggled with her own revulsion and the remembrance of her promise to Doctor Volospion.

'You still make a pretence at resistance, I see.' Bloom beamed. 'Such is female pride. I came here to claim a world and now I willingly renounce that claim if it means that I can possess you, woman, body and soul. You are the most beautiful creature I have ever seen in all the aeons of my wandering. Mavis! Mavis! Music floods my being at the murmur of your exquisite name. Queen Mavis – Maeve, Sorceress Queen, Destroyer of Cuchulain, Beloved of the Sun – ah, you have the power to do it – but you shall not destroy me again, Beautiful Maeve. You shall find me in Fire and in Fire shall we be united!'

It was true that, for the first time, Miss Ming's expression began to soften, but Doctor Volospion came to her aid.

'I am sure Miss Ming is duly flattered,' he said. It was evident, with his next statement, that he merely resented the interruption to his line of thought. 'But as for the Holy Grail, you do not, I suppose, have it about you?'

'Of course not. It appears only at my prayer.'

'You can summon it to you?'

'No. It appears. During my meditations.'

'You would not care to meditate now? To prove that yours is the true one.'

'I have no urge to meditate.' Mr Bloom dismissed the Doctor from his attention and, hands outstretched in that stiff, awkward way of his, moved to embrace Miss Ming, only to pause as he felt Volospion's touch on his arm.

'It is in your ship, then?'

'It visits my ship, yes.'

'Visits?'

'Doctor Volospion. I have tried to explain to you clearly enough. The Grail you have is not a mystical artefact, no matter how miraculous it seems to be. The true Holy Grail *is* a mystical artefact and therefore it comes and goes, according to the spiritual ambience. That is why your so-called Grail is plainly a fake. It if were real, it would not be here!'

'This is mere obfuscation…'

'Doctor Volospion, you are a most obtuse creature.'

Miss Ming began to move slowly backwards.

'Mr Bloom, I ask only for illumination…'

'I try to bring it. But I have failed with you, as I have failed with everyone but Miss Ming. That is only to be expected of one who is not really alive at all. Can one hold an intelligent conversation with a corpse?'

'You are crudely insulting, Mr Bloom. There is no call…' Doctor Volospion had lost most of his usual self-control.

Mavis Ming, terrified of further conflict in which, somehow, she knew she would be the worst sufferer, if her experience were anything to go by, broke in with a nervous yelp:

'Show Mr Bloom your menagerie, Doctor Volospion! The menagerie! The menagerie!'

Doctor Volospion turned glazed and dreaming eyes upon her. 'What?'

'The menagerie. There are many entities there that Mr Bloom might wish to converse with.'

The Fireclown bent to straighten one of his long shoes and Mavis Ming seized the chance to wink broadly at Doctor Volospion.

'Ah, yes, the menagerie. Mr Bloom?'

'You wish to show me the menagerie?'

'Yes.'

'Then lead me to it,' said Bloom generously.

Doctor Volospion continued to brood as he advanced before them, through another series of gloomy passages whose gently sloping floors took them still deeper underground. Doctor Volospion had a tendency to favour the subterranean in almost everything.

By the time, however, that they had reached the series of chambers Doctor Volospion chose to call his 'crypts', their guide had resumed his normal manner of poised irony.

These halls were far larger than the museum. On either side were reproduced many different environments, in the manner of zoological gardens, in which were incarcerated his collection of creatures culled from countless cultures, some indigenous and others alien to Earth.

Enthusiasm returned to Volospion's voice as he pointed out his prizes while they progressed slowly down the central aisle.

'My Christians and my Hare Krishnans,' declaimed the Doctor, 'my Moslems and my Marxists, my Jews and my Joypushers, my Dervishes, Buddhists, Hindus, Nature-worshippers, Confucians, Leavisites, Sufis, Shintoists, New Shintoists, Reformed Shintoists, Shinto-Scientologists, Mansonite Water-sharers, Anthroposophists, Flumers, Haythornthwaitists, Fundamentalist Ouspenskyians, Sperm Worshippers, followers of the Five Larger Moon Devils, followers of the Stone that Cannot Be Weighed, followers of the Sword and the Stallion, Awaiters of the Epoch, Mensans, Doo-en Skin Slicers, Crab-bellied Milestriders, Poobem Wrigglers, Tribunites, Calligraphic Diviners, Betelgeusian Grass Sniffers, Aldebaranian Grass Sniffers, Terran Grass Sniffers and Frexian Anti-Grass Sniffers. There are the Racists (Various) – I mix them together in the one environment because it makes for greater interest. The River of Blood was my own idea. It blends very well, I think, into the general landscape.' Doctor Volospion was evidently extremely proud of his collection. 'They are all, of course, in their normal environments. Every care is taken to see that they are preserved in the best of health and happiness. You will note, Mr Bloom, that the majority are content, so long as they are allowed to speak or perform the occasional small miracle.'

The Fireclown's attention seemed elsewhere.

'The sound,' said Doctor Volospion, and he touched a power ring, whereupon the air was filled with a babble of voices as prophets prophesied, preachers preached, messiahs announced various millennia, saviours summoned disciples, archbishops proclaimed Armageddon, fakirs mourned materialism, priests prayed, imams intoned, rabbis railed and druids droned. 'Enough?'

The Fireclown raised a hand in assent and Doctor Volospion touched the ring again so that much of the noise died away.

'Well, Mr Bloom, do you find these pronouncements essentially distinguishable from your own?'

But the Fireclown was again studying Mavis Ming who was, in turn, looking extremely self-conscious. She was blushing through her rouge. She pretended to take an interest in the sermon being delivered by a snail-like being from some remote world near the galaxy's centre.

'What?'

Bloom cocked an ear in Volospion's direction. 'Distinguishable? Oh, of course. Of course. I respect all the views being expressed. They are, I would agree, a little familiar, some of them. But these poor creatures lack either my power or my experience. I would guess, too, that they lack my courage. Or my purity of purpose. Why do you keep them locked up here?'

Doctor Volospion ignored the final sentence. 'Many would differ with you, I think.'

'Quite so. But you cease to entertain me, Doctor Volospion. I have decided to take Miss Ming, my madonna, back to my ship now. The visit has been fairly interesting. More interesting than I believed it would be. Are you coming, Miss Ming?'

Miss Ming hesitated. She glanced at Doctor Volospion. 'Well, I –'

'Do not consult this corpse,' Mr Bloom told her. 'I shall be your mentor. It is my duty and destiny to remove you from this environment at once, to bring you to the knowledge of your own divinity!'

Mavis Ming breathed heavily, still flushed. Her eyes darted from Bloom to Volospion. 'I don't think you'll be removing either me or yourself from this castle, Mr Bloom.' She smiled openly now at Doctor Volospion and her eyes were full of hope and terror. They asked a hundred questions. She seemed close to panic and was poised to flee.

Emmanuel Bloom gave a snort of impatience. 'Miss Ming, my love, you are mine.' His high, fluting voice continued to trill, but it was plain that she no longer heard his words. His birdlike hands touched hers. She screamed.

'Doctor Volospion!'

Doctor Volospion was fully himself. 'It is hardly gentlemanly, as I have pointed out, to force your attentions upon a lady, Mr Bloom. I would remind you of your word.'

'I keep it. I use no violence.'

Doctor Volospion now appeared to be relishing the drama. The fingers of his left hand hovered over the fingers of his right, on which were most of his power rings.

The Fireclown's hands remained on Miss Ming's. 'He's really

strong!' she cried. 'I can't get free, Doctor Volospion. Oo…' It seemed that an almost euphoric weakness suffused her body now. She was panting, incapable of thought; her lips were dry, her tongue was dry, and the only word she could form was a whispered 'No'.

Doctor Volospion seemed ignorant of the degree of tension in the menagerie. Many of the prophets, both human and alien, had stopped their monologues and now pressed forward to watch the struggle.

Doctor Volospion said firmly: 'Mr Bloom, since you remain here as my guest, I would ask you to recall…'

The blue eyes became shrewd even as they stared into Mavis Ming's. 'Your guest? No longer. We leave. Do you come, Mavis mine?'

'I – I –' It was as if she wished to say yes to him, yet she continued to pull back as best she could.

'Mr Bloom, you have had your opportunity to leave this planet. You refused to take it. Well, now you have no choice. You shall stay for ever (which is not, we think, that long).'

Mr Bloom raised a knowing head. 'What?'

'You have told us, yourself, that you are unique, sir.' Doctor Volospion was triumphant. 'You prize yourself so highly, I must accept your valuation.'

'Eh?'

'Henceforth, sir prophet, you will grace my menagerie. Here you will stay my finest acquisition.'

'What? My power!' Did Mr Bloom show genuine surprise? His gestures became melodramatic to a degree.

Doctor Volospion was too full of victory to detect play-acting, if play-acting there was. 'Here you may preach to your heart's content. You will find the competition stimulating, I am certain.'

Bloom received this intelligence calmly. 'My power is greater than yours,' he said.

'I led you to think that it was, so that you would feel confident when I suggested a tour of my collection. Twelve force-screens of unimaginable strength now lie between you and your ship, cutting you off from the source of your energy. Do you think you could have shattered my first force-field if I had not allowed it?'

'It seemed singularly easy,' agreed the Fireclown. 'But you seem still unclear as to the nature of my own power. It does not derive from a physical source, as yours does, though you are right in assuming it comes from my ship. It is spiritual inspiration which allows me to work my miracles. The source of that inspiration lies in the ship.'

'This so-called Grail of yours?'

Bloom fell silent.

'Well, call on it, then,' said Doctor Volospion.

Every scrap of bombast had disappeared from Bloom. It was as if he discarded a useless weapon, or rather a piece of armour which had proved defective. 'There is no entity more free in all the teeming multiverse than the Fireclown.' His unblinking eyes stared into Miss Ming's again. 'You cannot imprison me, sir.'

'Imprison?' Doctor Volospion derided the idea with a gesture. 'You shall have everything you desire. Your favourite environment shall be re-created for you. If necessary, it is possible to supply the impression of distance, movement. Regard the state as well earned retirement, Mr Bloom.'

The avian head turned on the long neck, the paint around the mouth formed an expression of some gravity (albeit exaggerated). Mr Bloom did not relax his grip upon Miss Ming's hands.

'Your satire palls, Doctor Volospion. It is the sort that easily grows stale, for it lacks love; it is inspired by self-hatred. You are typical of those faithless priests of the 5th millennium who were once your comrades in vice.'

Doctor Volospion showed shock. 'How could you possibly know my origins? The secret…'

'There are no secrets from the Sun,' said the Fireclown. 'The Sun knows All. Old He may be, but His memory is clearer than those of your poor, senescent cities.'

'Do not seek to confound me, sir, with airy generalities of that sort. How do you know?'

'I have eyes,' said Bloom, 'which have seen all things. One gesture reveals a society to me – two words reveal an individual. A conversation betrays every origin.'

'This Grail of yours? It helps you?'

The Fireclown ignored him. 'The eagle floats on currents of

light, high above the world, and the light is recollection, the light is history. I know you, Doctor Volospion, and I know you for a villain, just as I know Mavis Ming as a goddess – chained and gagged, perverted and alone, but still a goddess.'

Doctor Volospion's laugh was cruel. 'All you do, Mr Bloom, is to reveal yourself as a buffoon! Not even your insane faith can make an angel of Miss Ming!'

Mavis Ming was not resentful. 'I've got my good points,' she said, 'but I'm no Gloria Gutzmann. And I try too hard, I guess, and people don't like that. I can be neurotic, probably. After all, that affair with Snuffles didn't do anyone any good in the end though I was trying to do Dafnish Armatuce a favour.'

She babbled on, scarcely conscious of her words, while the adversaries, pausing in their conflict, watched her.

'But then, maybe I *was* acting selfishly, after all. Well, it's all water under the bridge, isn't it? What's done is done. Who can blame anybody, at the end of the day?'

Mr Bloom's voice became a caressing murmur. He stroked her hands. 'Fear not, Miss Ming. I am the Flame of Life. I carry a torch that will resurrect the spirit, and I carry a source to drive out devils. I need no armour, save my faith, my knowledge, my understanding. I am the Sun's soldier, keeper of His mysteries. Give yourself to me and become fully yourself, alive and free.'

Mavis Ming began to cry. The Fireclown's vivid mask smiled in a grotesque of sympathy.

'Come with me now,' said Bloom.

'I would remind you that you are powerless to leave,' said Doctor Volospion.

The Fireclown dropped her hands and turned so that his back was to her. His little frame twitched and trembled, his red-gold mass of hair might have been the bristling crest of some exotic fowl, his little hands clenched and unclenched at his sides, like claws, as his beautiful musical voice filled that dreadful menagerie.

'Ah, Volospion, I should destroy you – but one cannot destroy the dead!'

Doctor Volospion was apparently unmoved. 'Possibly, Mr Bloom, but the dead can imprison the living, can they not? If that is so, I possess the advantage which men like myself have always possessed over men such as you.'

The Fireclown wheeled to grasp Miss Ming. She cried out:

'Stop him, Doctor Volospion, for Christ's sake!'

And at last Doctor Volospion's long hand touched a power ring and the Fireclown was surrounded by bars of blue, pulsing energy.

'Ha!' The clown capered this way and that, trying to free himself and then, as if reconciled, sat down on the floor, crossing his little legs, his blue eyes blinking up at them as if in sudden bewilderment.

Doctor Volospion smiled.

'Eagle, is it? Phoenix? I must admit that I see only a caged sparrow.'

Emmanuel Bloom paid him no heed. He addressed Mavis Ming.

'Free me,' he said. 'It will mean your own freedom.'

Mavis Ming giggled.

Chapter Thirteen
In Which Doctor Volospion Asks Mavis Ming to Make a Sacrifice

SHE AWOKE FROM another nightmare.

Mavis Ming was filled with a sense of desolation worse than she had experienced in the past.

'Oh dear,' she murmured through her night-mask.

An impression of her dream was all that was left to her, but she seemed to recall that it involved Mr Bloom.

'What a wicked little creature! He's frightened me more than anything's ever frightened me before. Even Donny's tantrums weren't as bad. He deserves to be locked up. He deserves it. In any other world it would be his just punishment for doing what he has done. If Doctor Volospion hadn't stopped him, he would have raped me, for sure. Oh, why can't I stop thinking about what he said to me? It's all nonsense. I wish I was braver. I can't believe he's safely out of the way. I wish I had the nerve to go and see for myself. It would make me feel so much better.'

She sank into her many pillows, pulling the sheets over her eyes. 'I know what those energy-cages are like. It's the same sort I was in when I first arrived. He'll never get out. And I can't go to see him. That ridiculous flattery. And Doctor Volospion doesn't help by telling me all the time that he thinks Bloom's love is "genuine", whatever *that* means. Oh, it's worse now. It is. Why couldn't Doctor Volospion have made him go away? Keeping him here is *torture*!'

Doctor Volospion had even suggested, earlier, that it would be charitable if she went to his cage to 'comfort' him.

'Repulsive little runt!' She pushed her pink silky sheets and turned up the lamp (already fairly bright) whose stand was in the shape of a flesh-coloured nymph rising naked from the powder-blue petals of an open rose. 'I do wish Doctor Volospion would let me have a power ring of my own. It would make everything much easier. Everyone else has them. Lots of time-travellers do.' She crossed the soft pale yellow carpet to her gilded Empire-style dressing table to look at her face in the mirror.

'Oh, I look *awful*! That dreadful creature.'

She sighed. She often had trouble sleeping, for she was very highly strung, but this was much worse. For all their extravagant entertainments, their parties where the world was moulded to their whims, what they really needed, thought Mavis, was a decent TV network. TV would be just the answer to her problems right now.

'Perhaps Doctor Volospion could find something for me in one of those old cities,' she mused. 'I'll ask him. Not that he seems to be doing me many favours, these days. How long's he had the Fireclown now? A couple of weeks? And spending all his time down there. Maybe he loves Bloom and that's what it's all about.' She laughed, but immediately became miserable again.

'Oh, Mavis. Why is it always you? The world just isn't on your side.' She gave one of her funny little crooked smiles, very similar to those she had seen Barbara Stanwyck giving in those beautiful old movies.

'If only I could have gone *back* in time, to the 20th century, even, where the sort of clothes and lifestyle they had were so *graceful*. They had simpler lives, then. Oh, I know they must have had their problems, but how I wish I could be there now! It's what I was looking forward to, when they elected me to be the first person to try out the time machine. Of course, it was proof of how popular I was with the other guys at the department. Everyone agreed unanimously that I should be the first to go. It was a great honour.'

Apparently, this thought did not succeed in lifting her spirits. She raised a hand to her head.

'Oh, oh – here comes the headache! Poor old Mavis!'

She began to pad back towards the big circular bed. But the thought of a continuance of those dreams, even though she had pushed them right out of her mind, stopped her. It had been Doctor Volospion's suggestion that she continue to lead the sort of life she had been used to – with regular periods of darkness and daylight and a corresponding need to sleep and eat, even though he could easily have changed all that for her.

To be fair to him, she thought, he tended to follow a similar routine himself, ever since he had heard that Lord Jagged of Canaria had adopted this ancient affectation. If she had had a power ring or an air car at her disposal (again she was completely reliant on Volospion's good graces) she would have left the palace and gone to find some fun, something to take her mind off things. She looked at her Winnie-the-Pooh clock – another three hours before the palace would be properly activated. Until then she would not even be able to get a snack with which to console herself.

'I'm not much better off than that little creep down there,' she said. 'Oh, Mavis, what sort of a state have they got you into?'

A tap, now, at the door.

Grateful for the interruption, Mavis pulled on her fluffy blue dressing robe. 'Come in!'

Doctor Volospion, a satanic Hamlet in black-and-white doublet and hose, entered her room. 'You are not sleeping, Miss Ming? I heard your voice as I passed...'

Hope revealed itself in her eyes. 'I've got a bit of a headache, Doctor.' He could normally cure her headaches. Her mood improved. She became eager, anxious to win his approval. 'Silly little Mavis is having nightmares again.'

'You are unhappy?'

'Oh, no! In this lovely room? In your lovely palace? It's everything a little girl dreams about. It's just that awful Mr Bloom. Ever since...'

'I see.' The saturnine features showed enlightenment. 'You are still afraid. He can never escape, Miss Ming. He has tried, but I assure you my powers are far greater than his. He becomes tiresome, but he is no threat.'

'You'll let him go, then?'

'If I could be sure that he would leave the planet, for he fails to be as entertaining as I had hoped. And if he would give me that Grail of his, from which his power, I am now certain, derives. But he refuses.'

'You could take it now, couldn't you?'

'Not from him. Not from his ship. The screen is still impenetrable. No, you are our only hope.'

'Me?'

'He would not have allowed himself to be trapped at all, if it had not been for you.' Doctor Volospion sighed deeply. 'Well, I have just returned from visiting him again. I have offered him his liberty in return for that one piece of property, but he fobs me off with arguments that are typically specious, with vague talk of faith and trust – you have heard his babble.'

Mavis murmured sympathetically. 'I've never seen you so cast down, Doctor Volospion. You never know with some people, do you? He's best locked up for his own good. He's a sort of cripple, isn't he? You know what some cripples are like. You can't blame them. It's the frustration. It's all bottled up in them. It turns them into sex maniacs.'

'To do him justice, Miss Ming, his interest seems only in you. I have offered him many women, both real and artificial, from the menageries. Many of them are very beautiful, but he insists that none of them has your "soul", your – um – true beauty.'

'Really?' She was sceptical, still. 'He's insane. A lot of men are like that. That's one of the reasons I gave them up. At least with a lady you know where you are on that score. And Mr Bloom has got about as much sex-appeal as a seagull – less! Did you ever hear of a really sweet old book called *Jonathan*...'

'Your headache is better, Miss Ming?'

'Why, yes.' She touched her hair. 'It's almost gone. Did you...?'

Doctor Volospion drew his own brows together and traced beringed fingers across the creases. 'You do not give yourself enough credit, Miss Ming...'

She smiled. 'That's what Betty was always telling me when I used to feel low. But poor old Mavis...'

'He demands that you see him. He speaks of nothing else.'

'Oh!' She paused. She shook her head. 'No, I couldn't, really. As it is, I haven't had a good night's sleep since the day he arrived.'

'Of course, I understand.'

Miss Ming was touched by Doctor Volospion's uncharacteristic sadness. He seemed to have none of his usual confidence. She moved closer to him.

'Don't worry, Doctor Volospion. Maybe it would be best if you tried to forget about him.'

'I need the Grail. I am obsessed with it. And I cannot rid myself of the notion that, somehow, *he* is tricking *me*.'

'Impossible. You're far too clever. Why is this Grail so important to you?'

Doctor Volospion withdrew from her.

'I'm sorry,' she said. 'I didn't mean to pry.'

'Only you can help me, Miss Ming.'

The apparent pleading in his voice moved her to heights of sympathy. 'Oh...'

'You could convince him, I think, where I could not.'

She was relenting, against all her instincts. 'Well, if I saw him for a few moments... And it might help me, too – to lay the ghost, if you know what I mean.'

His voice was low. 'I should be very grateful to you, Miss Ming. Perhaps we should go immediately.'

She hesitated. Then she patted his arm. 'Oh, all right. Give me a few minutes to get dressed.'

With a deep bow, Doctor Volospion left the room.

Miss Ming began to consider her clothes. On the one hand, she thought, some sort of sexless boiler suit would be best, to dampen Mr Bloom's ardour as much as possible. Another impulse was to put on her very sexiest clothes, to feed her vanity. In the end she compromised, donning a flowery mou-mou which, she thought, disguised her plumpness. Courageously, she went to join Doctor Volospion, who awaited her in the corridor. Together they made their way to the menagerie.

As they descended flights of stone stairs she observed: 'Surprisingly, I'm feeling quite light-headed. Almost gay!'

They passed through the tiered rows of his many devotional trophies, past the bones and the sticks and the bits of cloth, the cauldrons, idols, masks and weapons, the crowns and the boxes, the scrolls, tablets and books, the prayer-wheels and crystals and jujus, until they reached the door of the first section of the menagerie, the Jewish House.

'I had thought of putting him in here,' Doctor Volospion told her as they passed by the inmates, who ranted, wailed, chanted, tore their clothing or merely turned aside as they passed, 'but finally I decided on the Non-Sectarian Prophet House.'

'I hadn't realised your collection was so big. I've never seen it all, as you know.' Miss Ming made conversation as best she could. Evidently, the place still disturbed her.

'It grows almost without one realising it,' said Doctor Volospion. 'I suppose, because so many people of a messianic disposition take an interest in the future, we are bound to get more than our fair share of prophets, anxious to discover if their particular version of the millennium has come about. Because they are frequently disappointed, many are glad of the refuge I offer.'

They went through another door.

'Martyrdom, it would seem, is the next best thing to affirmation,' he said.

They passed through a score of different Houses until, finally, they came to the Fireclown's habitat. It was designed to resemble a desert, scorched by a permanently blazing sun.

'He refused,' whispered Doctor Volospion, as they approached, 'to tell me what sort of environment he favoured, so I chose this one. It is the most popular with my prophets, as you'll have noted.'

Emmanuel Bloom, in his clown's costume, sat on a rock in the centre of his energy-cage. His greasepaint seemed to have run a little, as if he had been weeping, but he did not seem in particularly low spirits now. He had not, it appeared, noticed them. He was reciting poetry to himself.

'… Took shape and were unfolded like as flowers.
And I beheld the hours
As maidens, and the days as labouring men,
And the soft nights again
As wearied women to their own souls wed,
And ages as the dead.
And over these living, and them that died,
From one to the other side
A lordlier light than comes of earth or air
Made the world's future fair.
A woman like to love in face, but not
A thing of transient lot –

And like to hope, but having hold on truth –
And like to joy or youth,
Save that upon the rock her feet were set –
And like what men forget,
Faith, innocence, high thought, laborious peace –'

He had seen her. His great blue eyes blinked. His stiff little body began to rise. His birdlike, fluting voice took on a different tone.

'*And yet like none of these...*' He put an awkward finger to his small mouth. He put his painted head on one side.

Mavis Ming cleared her throat. Doctor Volospion's hand forced her further towards the cage.

The Fireclown spoke first. 'So Guinevere comes at last to her Lancelot – or is it Kundry, come to call me Parsifal? Sorceress, you have incarcerated me. Tell your servant to release me so that, in turn, I may free you from the evil that holds you with stronger bonds than any that chain me!'

Miss Ming's smile was insincere. 'Why don't you talk properly, Mr Bloom? This is childish. Anyway, you know he's not my servant.' She was very pale.

Mr Bloom crossed the stretch of sand until he was as close to her as the cage permitted. 'He is not your master, you may be sure of that, this imitation Klingsor!'

'I haven't the faintest idea what you're talking about.' Her voice was shaking.

He pressed his tiny body against the energy-screen. 'I must be free,' he said. 'There is no mission for me here, now, at the End of Time. I must continue my quest, perhaps into another universe where Faith may yet flourish.'

Doctor Volospion came forward. 'I have brought Miss Ming, as you have so constantly demanded. You have talked to her. Now, if you will give up the Grail to me...'

Mr Bloom's manner became agitated. 'I have explained to you, demi-demon, that you could not keep it, even if, by some means, I *could* transfer it to you. Only the pure in spirit are entitled to its trust. If I agreed to your bargain I should lose the Grail myself, for ever. Neither would gain!'

'I find your objections without foundation.' Doctor Volospion was unruffled by the Fireclown's anger. 'What you believe, Mr Bloom, is one thing. The truth, however, is quite another! Faith dies, but the objects of faith do not, as you saw in my museum.'

'Those things have no value without Faith!'

'They are valuable to me. That is why I collect them. I desire this Grail of yours so that I may, at least, compare it with my own.'

'You know yours to be false,' said the Fireclown. 'I can tell.'

'I shall decide which is false and which is not when I have both in my possession. I know it is on your ship, for all that you deny it.'

'It is not. It manifests itself at certain times.'

Doctor Volospion allowed his own ill-temper to show. 'Miss Ming...'

'Please let him have it, Mr Bloom,' said Mavis Ming in her best wheedling voice. 'He'll let you go if you do.'

The Fireclown was amused. 'I can leave whenever I please. But I gave my word on two matters. I said that I would not take you by force and that I would take you with me when I left.'

'Your boasts are shown to be empty, sir,' said Doctor Volospion. He laid the flat of his hand against the energy-screen. 'There.'

Mr Bloom ran his hand through his auburn mop, continuing to speak to Miss Ming. 'You demean yourself, woman, when you aid this wretch, when you adopt that idiotic tone of voice.'

'Well!' It was possible to observe that Miss Ming's legs were shaking. 'I'm not staying here, not even for you, Doctor Volospion! It's too much. I can stand a lot of things, but not this.'

'Be silent!' The Fireclown's voice was low and firm. 'Listen to your soul. It will tell you what I tell you.'

'Miss Ming!' Seeing that she prepared to flee, Doctor Volospion seized her arm. 'For my sake do not give up. If I have that Grail...'

'You may see the Grail, beautiful Mavis, when I have redeemed you,' murmured the Fireclown. 'But it shall always be denied to such as he! Come with me and I shall let you witness more than Mystery.'

She panicked. 'Oh, Christ!' She was unable to control herself as she sensed the terrible pressure coming from both sides. She tried to free herself from Doctor Volospion's restraining hand. 'I can't take any more. I can't!'

'Miss Ming!' fiercely croaked a desperate Volospion. 'You promised to help.'

'Come with me!' cried the Fireclown.

She still struggled, trying to prise his grip away from the sleeve of her mou-mou. 'You can both do what you like. I don't want any part of it.'

Hysteria ruled now. She scratched Doctor Volospion's hand so that at last he released her. She ran away from them. She ran crazily between the cages of roaring, screaming, moaning prophets. 'Leave me alone! Leave me alone!'

And then, just before a door shut her from their view:

'I'm sorry! I'm sorry!'

Chapter Fourteen

In Which Miss Mavis Ming Is Given an Opportunity to Win the Forgiveness of Her Protector

When Mavis Ming next awoke, finding herself in the soft pink security of her own bed, where she had fled in terror after scratching Doctor Volospion, she was surprised by how refreshed she felt, how confident. Even the threat of Doctor Volospion's anger, which she feared almost as much as the Fireclown's love, failed to thrill her.

'What can he do, after all?' she asked herself. She still wore the mou-mou. She looked at the ripped sleeve, and she inspected the bruise on her arm. She doubted if the scratch she had given Doctor Volospion was any worse than the bruise he had given her, but she also recalled that, in her experience, men had a different way of looking at these things.

'Why do I feel so good? Because of a fight?' She was almost buoyant. 'Maybe because it's over. I tried to please him. I really tried. But he's got a way of double-binding a girl like nobody else. I guess little Mavis will have to find a new berth.'

She removed the mou-mou and went to take a shower. 'Well, it was high time for a change. And I'm not much gone on sharing the same roof with that mad midget downstairs.'

The shower was refreshing.

'I'm going to go out. I'm going to visit a few people. Now,' elbow on palm of hand, fingertip to chin, 'who shall I visit first?'

She reviewed her acquaintances, wondering who would be most sympathetic. Who would welcome her.

And then, of a sudden, depression swept back. It caught her so unexpectedly that she had to sit down on the edge of the unmade bed, dropping her towel to the floor. 'Oh, Christ! Oh, Christ! What in hell's wrong with you, Mavis?'

A knock on her door interrupted the catharsis before it had properly got under way.

'Yes?'

'Miss Ming?' It was, of course, Doctor Volospion.

'This is it, Mavis.' She pulled herself together. She put on a robe. 'Time for the tongue-lashing. Well. I'll tell him I'm leaving. He'll be glad of that.' She raised her voice. 'Come in!'

But he was smiling when he entered.

She looked at him in nervous astonishment.

He was dressed in robes of scarlet and green. There was a tight-fitting dark green hood on his head, emphasising the sharpness of his features.

'You are well, Miss Ming?' As he spoke he drew on dark green gloves.

'Better than I thought. I wanted to...'

'I came to apologise,' he said.

She had glanced at his hand before the glove went on. There was, of course, no sign of her scratch.

'Oh,' she said. She was taken aback.

'If I had realised exactly how badly that Mr Bloom affected you, I would never have subjected you to the ordeal,' he said.

'Well, you weren't to know.' She bit her lip, as if she sensed her determination dissipating already.

'The fault was wholly mine.' He had all his old authority. It comforted her.

'I lost my cool, I guess.' Her voice shook. 'I'm sorry about your hand.'

'I deserved worse.'

His voice was warm and, as always, it caused her to purr. It would not have been surprising if she had arched her back and rubbed her body against him. 'That Mr Bloom, he just freaks me, Doctor Volospion. I don't know what it is. I suppose I've completely blown it for you, haven't I?'

'No, no,' he reassured her.

'You talked? After I'd gone?'

'Somewhat. He remains quite adamant.'

'He won't give you the Grail?'

'Unfortunately not...'

'It *was* my fault. I'm *really* sorry.' She responded almost without any sort of consciousness, mesmerised by him.

'It grieves me. I can think of no way of obtaining it without your help.'

'You know I'd like to.' The words emerged as if another spoke them for her. 'I mean, if there's anything I can do to make up for what happened last night...'

'I would not put you to further embarrassment.' He turned to leave.

'Oh, no!' She paused, making an effort of will. 'I mean, I couldn't face actually seeing him again, but if there's anything else...'

'I can think of nothing. Goodbye, Miss Ming.'

'There must be something?'

He paused by the door, frowning. 'Well, I suppose it is possible for you to get the Grail for me.'

'How?'

'He said that he would allow you to see it, you recall?'

'I can't really remember the details of what he said. I was too frightened.'

'Quite. You see, somehow he controls his ship's protective devices from where he is. After you had gone he told me again that he would let you see the Grail, but not me. I think he believes that if you see it you will realise that he is this spiritual saviour he sets himself up to be.'

'You mean I could get into the ship and find the Grail?'

'Exactly. Once I had it in my possession, I would let him go. You would be free of him.'

'But he'd suspect.'

'His infatuation blinds him.'

'I wouldn't have to see him again?' She spoke as firmly as she could. 'I won't do that, whatever else.'

'You will never be asked to go to the menagerie and, in a while, he will have left this planet.'

'It's stealing, of course,' she said.

'Call it recompense for all the damage he has done while here. Call it justice.'

'Yes. That's fair enough.'

'But no,' he looked kindly down on her. 'I ask too much of you.'

'You don't, really.' He had inspired in her a kind of eager courage. 'Let me help.'

'He has assured me that he will lower the barriers of his ship for you alone.'

'Then it's up to Mavis, isn't it?'

'If you feel you can do it, Miss Ming, I would show my gratitude to you in many ways when you returned with the cup.'

'It's enough to help out.' But she glanced at the power rings on his gloved fingers. 'When shall I go?' She paused. 'There won't be any danger, I suppose…?'

'None at all. He genuinely loves you, Miss Ming. Of course, if you consider this action a betrayal of Mr Bloom…'

'Betrayal? I didn't make any deals with him.'

His voice was rich with gratification. 'It would mean much to me, as you know. My collection is important to my happiness. If I thought that I possessed an artefact that was not authentic, well, I should never be content.'

'Rely on Mavis.' Her eyes began to shine.

'You are possessed of a great and admirable generosity,' he said.

His praise sent a pulse of well-being through her whole body.

Chapter Fifteen
In Which Mavis Sets Off in Search of the Holy Grail

Doctor Volospion had made no alterations to his force-screen since the Fireclown had passed beyond it. Mavis Ming moved through the eternal twilight of the castle's grounds, towards the dark and ragged hole in the wall of ice. On the other side of the hole she could see the brilliant scarlet of Emmanuel Bloom's ship.

Gingerly, she stepped through the gap, sensitive to the stillness and silence of her surroundings. She wished that Doctor Volospion had been able to accompany her, at least this far, but he was wary, he had told her, of the Fireclown suspecting treachery. If Bloom detected another presence, it was likely that he would immediately restore his ship's defences.

The teardrop-shaped ship was a red silhouette against a background of dark trees. Its airlock remained open, its ramp was down. She paused as she looked up at it.

It was impossible from where she stood to see anything of the ship's interior, but she could smell a warm mustiness coming from the entrance, together with a suggestion of pale smoke. If she had not known otherwise, she might have suspected the Fireclown to be still inside. The ship was redolent of his presence.

She spoke aloud, to dispel the silence. 'Here goes, Mavis.'

She was wearing her blue-and-orange kimono over her bikini, for Doctor Volospion had warned her that it might be uncomfortably warm within the Fireclown's ship. She struggled up the pebbled surface of the ramp and hesitated again outside the entrance, peering in. It seemed to her that points of fire still flickered on the other side of the airlock's open door.

'Coo-ee!' she said.

She wet her lips. 'What manner of creature is lord of this fair castle?' She reassured herself with the language of her favourite books. 'Shall I find my handsome prince within? Or an ugly ogre...?'

CAWTHORN 35

She shuddered. She looked back at the battlements and towers of gloomy Castle Volospion, hoping perhaps to see her protector, but the castle seemed entirely deserted. She drew a breath and entered the airlock. It was not quite as warm as she had been led to believe.

She moved from the airlock into the true interior of the ship. She found herself pleasantly surprised by its ordinariness. It was as if firelight illuminated the large chamber, although the source of that light was mysterious.

The rosy, flickering light cast her shadow, enlarged and distorted, upon the far wall. The chamber was in disorder, as if the shock of landing had dislodged everything from its place. Boxes, parchments, books and pictures were scattered everywhere; figurines lay dented or broken upon the carpeted floor; drapes, once used to cover portholes, hung lopsidedly upon the walls, which curved inwards.

'What a lot of junk!' Her voice held more confidence. Apparently, the place had been Mr Bloom's storeroom, for there was no sign of furniture.

She stumbled over crates and bales of cloth until she reached a companionway leading up to the next chamber. Doctor Volospion had told her that she would probably find the cup in the control room, which must be above. She climbed, pushed open a hatch, and found herself in a circular room which was lit very similarly to the storage chamber, but so realistically that she found herself searching for the open fireplace which seemed to be the source of the light.

Save for a faint smell of burning timber, there was no sign of a fire.

'Mavis,' she said determinedly, 'keep that imagination of yours well under control!'

This room, as she had suspected, was the Fireclown's living quarters. It contained a good-sized bed, shelves, storage lockers, a desk, a chair and a screen whereby the occupant could check the ship's functions.

She wiped sweat from her forehead, glancing around her.

Against one wall, at the end of the bed, was a large metal ziggurat which looked as if it had once been the base for something else. Would this be where the cup was normally kept? If so, Emmanuel Bloom had hidden it and her job was going to be harder. On the wall were various pictures: some were paintings, others photographs and holographs, primarily of men in the costumes of many periods. On the wall, too, was a narrow shelf, about two feet long, apparently empty. She reached to touch it and felt something there. It was thin, like a long pencil. Curiously, she rolled the object towards her until it fell into her hand. She was surprised.

It was a baton in black onyx which gave her a peculiar sensation of peace. Uncertain of her motives she put it back out of sight.

Wishing that the light were stronger, she began to search for the cup or goblet (Doctor Volospion's description had been vague). First, she looked under the bed, finding only a collection of books and manuscripts, many of them dusty.

'This whole ship could do with a good spring-clean!' She searched through the wardrobe and drawers, finding a collection of clothes to match those worn by the men whose pictures decorated the wall. This sudden intimacy with Mr Bloom's personal possessions had not only whetted her curiosity about him – his clothes, to her, were much more interesting than anything he had said – but had somehow given her a greater sympathy for him.

She began to feel unhappy about rummaging through his things; her search for the goblet seemed increasingly like simple thievery.

Her search became more rapid as she sought to find the Grail and leave as soon as she could. If she had not made a promise to Doctor Volospion, she would have left the ship there and then.

'You're a fool, Mavis. Everyone's told you. And do you ever listen?'

As she opened a mahogany trunk, inlaid with silver and mother-of-pearl, the lid squeaked and, at the same time, she thought she heard a faint noise from below. She paused and listened, but there was no further sound. She saw at once that the trunk contained only faded manuscripts.

Miss Ming decided to return to the storeroom. The curiosity which had at first directed her energy was now dissipating, to be replaced by a familiar sense of panic.

She felt her heart-rate increase and the ship seemed to give a series of little tremors, in sympathy. She returned to the companionway and lifted the hatch. She was halfway down when the whole ship shook itself like an animal, roared, as if sentient, and she was pressed back against the steps, clinging to the rail as, swaying from side to side, the ship took off.

Sweating, Miss Ming turned herself round with difficulty and began to climb back towards the living quarters where she felt she would be safer. If her throat had been less constricted, she would have screamed. The ship, she knew, was taking off under its own power. It was quite possible that she had activated it herself. Unless she could work out how to control it she would soon be adrift in the cosmos, floating through space until she died.

And she would be all alone.

It was this latter thought which terrified her most. She reached the cabin and crawled across the dusty carpet as the pressure increased, climbing onto the bed in the hope that it would cushion the acceleration effects.

The sensations she was experiencing were not dissimilar to those she had experienced on her trip through time and, as such, did not alarm her. It was the prospect of what would become of her when the ship was beyond Earth's gravity which she could not bear to consider.

It was not, she thought, as if there were many planets left in the universe. Earth might now be the only one.

The pressure began to lift, but she remained face down upon the bed (*these sheets could do with a wash*, she was thinking) even when it was obvious that the ship was travelling at last through free space.

'Oh, you've let yourself in for it this time, Mavis,' she told herself. 'You've been conned properly, my girl.'

She wondered if, for reasons of his own, Doctor Volospion had deliberately sent her into space. She knew his capacity for revenge. Had that silly tiff meant so much to him? He had beguiled her into suggesting her own trap, her own punishment, just because of a silly scratch on the hand!

'What a bastard! What bastards they all are!' And what an idiot she had made of herself! It taught you never to be sympathetic to a man. They always used it against you. 'That's Mavis all over,' she continued, 'trusting the world. And this is how the world repays you!' But there was little conviction in her tone; her self-pity was half-hearted. Actually, she realised, she was not feeling particularly bad now that there was a genuine threat to her life. All the little anxieties fled away.

Miss Ming began to roll over on the bed. At least the ship itself was comfortable enough.

'It's cosy, really.' She smiled. 'A sort of den. Just like when I was a little girl, with my own little room, and my books and dolls.' She laughed. 'I'm actually safer here than anywhere I've been since I grew up. It shouldn't be difficult to work out a way of getting back to Earth – *if* I want to go back. What's Earth got to offer, anyway, except deceit, hypocrisy and treachery?'

She swung her legs over the edge of the bed. She looked at her new home, all her new toys.

'I think it's really what I've always wanted,' she declared.

'Now you realise that I spoke the truth!' said the triumphant voice of Emmanuel Bloom from the shadows overhead.

'My God!' said Miss Ming as she realised the full extent of Doctor Volospion's deception.

Chapter Sixteen

In Which Doctor Volospion Receives the Congratulations of His Peers and Celebrates the Acquisition of His New Treasure

My Lady Charlotina rose from Doctor Volospion's bed and swiftly demolished her double (Doctor Volospion would only make love to pairs of women) before touching a power ring to adorn herself in white and cerise poppies. In the shadows of the four-poster Doctor Volospion lay relishing his several victories, a beautiful cup held in his hands. He turned the cup round and round, running his fingers over an inscription which he could not read, for it was in ancient English.

'You doubt none of my powers now, I hope, My Lady Charlotina,' he said.

Her smile was slow. She knew he would have her speak of Jagged, perhaps make a comparison, but she did not have it in her to satisfy Volospion's curiosity. Lord Jagged was Lord Jagged, she thought.

'I was privileged,' she said, 'to know your plan from the start and to see it work so smoothly. I am most impressed. First, you incarcerated Miss Ming, then you lured Mr Bloom to your castle, then you pretended that his power was great enough to destroy your force-field, then you captured him, knowing that he would give anything to escape. You originally meant to hold him, of course, as one of your collection, but then you learned of the Grail...'

'So I offered Miss Ming in exchange for the Grail. Thus he thought he took her from me without force and that she went willingly to him – for I did not, of course, explain to Mr Bloom that I had deceived Miss Ming.'

'So much deception! It is quite hard for me to follow!' She laughed. 'What a match! The greatest cynic of our world (with the exception of Lord Shark who does not really count) pitted against the greatest idealist in the universe!'

'And the cynic won,' said Doctor Volospion. 'As they always do.'

'Well, a cynic *would* draw that conclusion,' she pointed out. 'I had a liking for Mr Bloom, though he was a bore.'

'As was Miss Ming.'

'Great bores, both.'

'And by one stroke I rid the world of its two most awful bores,' said Doctor Volospion, in case she had not considered this achievement with the rest.

'Exactly.'

Yawning, My Lady Charlotina drifted towards a dark window. 'You have your cup. He has his queen.'

'Exactly.'

My Lady Charlotina looked up at the featureless heavens. No stars gleamed here. Perhaps they were all extinguished. She sighed.

'My only regret,' said Doctor Volospion as he carefully laid the cup upon his pillow and straightened his body, 'is that I was not able to ask Mr Bloom the meaning of this inscription.'

'Doubtless a warning to the curious,' she said 'or an offer of eternal salvation. You know more about these things, Doctor Volospion.'

A cap appeared on his head. Robes formed. Black velvet and mink. 'Oh, yes, they are always very similar. And often disappointingly ordinary.'

'It does seem a very ordinary cup.'

'The faithful would see that as a sign of its true holiness,' he told her knowledgeably.

From outside they detected a halloo.

'It is Abu Thaleb,' she said in some animation. 'And Argonheart Po and others. Li Pao, I think, is with them. Shall you admit them?'

'Of course. They will want to see my cup.'

My Lady Charlotina and Doctor Volospion left his bedroom and went down to the hall to greet their guests.

Doctor Volospion placed the cup upon the table. The ill-functioning neon played across its bright silver.

'Beautiful!' said Abu Thaleb, without as much enthusiasm as

perhaps Doctor Volospion would have wished. The Commissar of Bengal brushed feathers from his eyes. 'A fitting reward for your services to us all, Doctor Volospion.'

Argonheart Po bore a tray in his great hands. He set this, now, beside the cup. 'I am always thorough in my research,' he said, 'and hope you find this small offering appropriate.' He removed the cloth to reveal his savouries. 'That is a pemmican spear. This cross is primarily the flavour of sole *à la crème*. The taste of the wafers and the blood is rather more difficult to describe.'

'What an elegant notion!' Doctor Volospion took one of the savouries between finger and thumb and nibbled politely.

Li Pao asked: 'May I inspect the cup?'

'Of course.' Doctor Volospion waved a generous hand. 'You do not, by any chance, read, do you, Li Pao? Specifically, Dawn Age English.'

'Once,' said Li Pao. He studied the inscription. He shook his head. 'I am baffled.'

'A great shame.'

'Does it *do* anything,' wondered Sweet Orb Mace, moving from the shadows where he had been studying Doctor Volospion's portrait.

'I think not,' said My Lady Charlotina. 'It has done nothing yet, at any rate.'

Doctor Volospion stared at his cup somewhat wistfully. 'Ah, well,' he said, 'I fear I shall grow tired of it soon enough.'

My Lady Charlotina came to stand beside him. 'Perhaps it will fill the room with light or something,' she said encouragingly.

'We can always hope,' he said.

Chapter Seventeen

In Which Miss Mavis Ming at Last Attains a State of Grace

EMMANUEL BLOOM SWUNG himself from the ceiling, an awkward macaw. He no longer wore his paint and motley but was again dressed in his black velvet suit.

Mavis Ming saw that he had entered by means of a hatch. Doubtless, the control cabin of the ship was above.

'My Goddess,' said the Fireclown.

She still sat on the edge of the bed. Her voice was without emotion. 'You traded me for the cup. That's what it was all about. What a fool I am!'

'No, not you. Doctor Volospion proposed the bargain and so enabled me to keep my word to him. He demanded the cup which I kept in my ship. I gave it to him.' He strutted across the cabin and manipulated a dial. Red-gold light began to fill his living quarters. Now everything glowed and each piece of fabric, wood or metal seemed to have a life of its own.

Mavis Ming stood up, and edged away from the bed. She drew her kimono about her, over her pendulous breasts, her fat stomach, her wide thighs.

'Listen,' she began. She was breathing rapidly once more. 'You can't really want me, Mr Bloom. I'm fat old Mavis. I'm ugly. I'm stupid. I'm selfish. I should be left on my own. I'm better off on my own. I know I'm always looking for company, but really it's just because I never realised...'

He raised a stiff right arm in a gesture of impatience. 'What has any of that to do with my love for you? What does it matter if foolish Volospion thought he was killing two birds with one stone when he was actually freeing two eagles?'

'Look,' she said, 'if...'

'I am the Fireclown! I am Bloom, the Fireclown! I have lived the span of Man's existence. I have made Time and Space my toys. I have juggled with chronons and made the multiverse laugh. I have mocked Reality and Reality has shrivelled to be reborn. My eyes have stared unblinking into the hearts of stars, and I have stood at the very core of the Sun and feasted on freshly created photons. I am Bloom, Eternally Blooming Bloom. Bloom the Phoenix. Bloom, the Destroyer of Darkness. These eyes, these large bulging eyes of mine, do you think they cannot see into souls as easily as they see into suns? Can they not detect an aura of pain that disguises the true centre of a being as smoke hides fire? That is why I choose to make you wise, to enslave you so that you may know true freedom.'

Miss Ming forced herself to speak. 'This is kidnapping and kidnapping is kidnapping whatever you prefer to call it…'

He ignored her.

'Of all the beings on that wasteland planet, you were one of the few who still lived. Oh, you lived as a frightened rodent lives, your spirit perverted, your mind enshelled with cynicism, refusing for a moment to look upon Reality for fear that it would detect you and devour you, like a wakened lion. Yet when Reality occasionally impinged and could not be escaped, how did you respond?'

'Look,' she said, 'you've got no right…'

'Right? I have every right! I am Bloom! You are my Bride, my Consort, my Queen, my Goddess. There is no woman deserves the honour more!'

'Oh, Christ!' she said. 'Please let me go. Please. I can't give you anything. I can't understand you. I can't love you.' She began to cry. 'I've never loved anyone! No-one but myself.'

His voice was gentle. He took a few jerky steps closer to her. 'You lie, Mavis Ming. You do not love yourself.'

'Donny said I did. They all said I did, sooner or later.'

'If you loved yourself,' he told her, 'you would love me.'

Her voice shook. 'That's good…'

To Mavis Ming's own ears her words were without resonance of any kind. The collection of platitudes with which she had always responded to pain; the borrowed ironies, the barren tropes with which, instinctively, she had encumbered herself in order to placate a world she had seen as essentially malevolent, all were at once revealed as the meaningless things they were, with the result that an appalling self-consciousness, worse than anything she had suffered in the past, swept over her and every phrase she had ever uttered seemed to ring in her ears for what it had been: a mew of pain, a whimper of frustration, a cry for attention, a groan of hunger.

'Oh…'

She became incapable of speech. She could only stare at him, backing around the wall as he came, half-strutting, half-hopping, towards her, his head on one side, an appalling amusement in his unwinking, protuberant eyes, until her escape was blocked by a heavy wardrobe.

She became incapable of movement. She watched as he reached a twitching hand towards her face; the hand was firm and gentle as it touched her and its warmth made her realise how cold, how clammy, her own skin felt. She was close to collapse, only supported by the wall of the ship.

'The Earth is far behind us now,' he said. 'We shall never return. It does not deserve us.' He pointed to the bed. 'Go there. Remove your clothes.'

She gasped at him, trying to make him understand that she could not walk. She did not care, now, what his intentions were, but she was too exhausted to obey him.

'Tired…' she said at last.

He shook his head. 'No. You shall not escape by that route, madam.' He spoke kindly. 'Come.'

The high-pitched, ridiculous voice carried greater authority than any she had heard before. She began to walk towards the bed. She stood looking down at the sheets; the light made these, too, seem vibrant with life of their own. She felt his little clawlike hands pull the kimono from her shoulders, undo the tie, removing the garment entirely.

She felt him break the fastening on her bikini top so that her breasts hung even lower on her body. She felt no revulsion, nothing sexual at all, as his fingers pushed the bikini bottom over her hips and down her legs. And yet she was more aware of her nakedness than she had ever been, seeing the fatness, the pale flesh, without any emotion at all, remarking its poor condition as if it did not belong to her.

'Fat...' she murmured.

His voice was distant. 'It is of no importance, this body. Besides, it shall not be fat for very long.

She began to anticipate his rape of her, wondering if, when he began, she would feel anything. He ordered her to lie face down upon the bed. She obeyed. She heard him move away, then. Perhaps he was undressing. She turned to look, but he was still in his tattered velvet suit, taking something from a shelf. From a little bottle, he poured sweet-smelling liquid into his palms.

She tried to feel afraid, because she knew that she should feel fear, but fear would not come. She continued to look up at him, over her shoulder, as he returned. Still her body made no response. This was quite unlike her sexual fantasies. What happened now neither excited her imagination nor her body. She wished that she could feel something, even terror. Instead she was possessed by a calmness, a sense of inevitability, unlike anything she had known.

'Now,' she heard him say, 'I shall bring your blood into the light. And with it shall come the devils that inhabit it, to be withered as weeds in the sun. And when I have finished you will know Rebirth, Freedom, Dominion over the Multiverse, and more. For I am the Fireclown and my very touch is fire.'

Was it a mark of her own insanity that she could detect no insanity in his words?

His touch fell upon her flesh. He stroked her buttocks and the pain stole her breath. She did not scream, but she gasped.

He stroked again, just below the first place, and she thought his flames lashed her. Her whole body jerked, trying to escape, but a firm hand held her down again, and again he touched her.

She did not scream, but she groaned as she drew in her breath. Next he stroked her thighs; next behind her knees, and his hands were firm now as she struggled. He held her by the back of the neck; he gripped her by the shoulder, by the loose flesh of her waist, and each time he gripped her she knew fresh pain.

Mavis Ming believed at last that it was Emmanuel Bloom's

intention to sear every piece of skin from her body. He held her lips, her ears, her breasts, her vagina, the tender parts of her inner thighs, and every touch was fire.

She screamed, she blubbered for him to stop, she could not believe that he, any more than she, was any longer in control of what was happening. And yet he stroked her with a regularity which denied her even this consolation, until, at length, her whole body burned and she lay still, consumed.

Slowly, the fire faded from this peak of intensity and it seemed to her that, again, her body and mind were united; this unity was new.

Emmanuel Bloom said nothing. She heard him cross the chamber to replace the bottle. She began to breathe with deep regularity, as if she slept. Her consciousness of her body produced an indefinable emotion in her. She moved her head to look at him and the movement was painful.

'I feel…' Her voice was soft.

He stood with his arms stiffly at his sides. His head was cocked, his expression was tender and expectant.

She could find no word.

'It is your pride,' he said.

He reached to caress her face.

'I love you,' he said.

'I love you.' She began to weep.

He made her rise and look at her body in the oval mirror he revealed. It seemed that her skin was a lattice of long, red bruises; she could see where he had gripped her shoulders and her breasts. The pain was hard to tolerate without making at least a whisper of sound, but she controlled herself.

'Will you do this again?' she asked.

He shook his little head.

She walked back to the bed. Her back, though lacerated, was straight. She had never walked in that way before, with dignity. She sat down. 'Why did you do it?'

'In this manner? Perhaps because I lack patience. It is one of my characteristics. It was quick.' He laughed. 'Why do it to you, at all? Because I love you. Because I wished to reveal to you the woman that you are, the individual that you are. I had to destroy the shell.'

'It won't fade, this feeling?'

'Only the marks will go. It is within you to retain the rest. Will you be my wife?'

She smiled. 'Yes.'

'Well, then, this has been a satisfactory expedition, after all. Better, really, than I expected. Oh, what leaping delights we shall share, what wonders I can show you! No woman could desire more than to be the consort of Bloom, the Good Soldier, the Champion Eternal, the Master of the Multiverse! As you are my mistress, Mavis Ming.' He fell with a peculiar, spastic jerk, on his knees beside her. 'For Eternity. Will you stay? I can return you within an hour or two.'

'I will stay,' she said. 'Yet you gave up so much for me. That cup. It was your honour?'

He looked shamefaced. 'He asked for the cup I kept in my ship. I could not give him the Holy Grail, for it is not mine to give. I gave him something almost as dear to me, however. If Doctor Volospion ever deciphers the inscription on the cup, he will discover that it was awarded, in 1980, to Leonard Bloom, by the union of Master Bakers, for the best chollah of the Annual Bakery Show, Whitechapel, London. He was a very good baker, my father. I loved him. I had kept his cup in all my journeys back and forth through the time streams and it was the most valuable thing I possessed.'

'So you do not have the Grail.' She smiled. 'It was all part of your plan – pretending to own it, pretending to be powerless – you tricked Doctor Volospion completely.'

'And he tricked me. Both are satisfied, for it is unlikely he shall ever know the extent of my trickery and doubtless considers himself a fine fellow! All are satisfied!'

'And now…?' she began.

'And now,' he said, 'I'll leave you. I must set my controls. You shall see all that is left of this universe and then, through the centre of the brightest star, into the greater vastness of the multiverse beyond! There we shall find others to inspire and if we find no life at all, upon our wanderings, it is within our power to create it, for I am the Fireclown. I am the Voice of the Sun! Aha! Look! It has come to you, too. This, my love, is Grace. This is our reward!'

The cabin was filled suddenly by brilliant golden light, apparently having as its source a beam which entered through the very shell of the spaceship, falling directly upon the ziggurat at the end of the bed.

A smell, like sweet spring flowers after the rain, filled the cabin, and then a crystal cup, brimming with scarlet liquid, appeared at the top of the ziggurat.

Scarlet rays spread from a hundred points in the crystal, almost blinding her, and, although Mavis Ming could hear nothing, she received an impression of sonorous, delicate music. She could not help herself as she lifted her aching body from the bed to the floor and knelt, staring into the goblet in awe.

From behind her the Fireclown chuckled and he knelt beside her, taking her hand.

'We are married now,' he said, 'before the Holy Grail. Married individually and together. And this is our Trust which shall be taken from us should we ever commit the sin of accidie. Here is proof of all my claims. Here is Hope. And should we ever cease to forget our purpose, should we ever fall into that sin of inertia, should we lose, for more than a moment, our Faith in our high resolve, the Grail will leave us and shall vanish forever from the sight of Man, for I am Bloom, the Last Pure Knight, and you are the Pure Lady, chastised and chaste, who shall share these Mysteries with me.'

She began: 'It is too much. I am not capable…' But then she lifted her head and she smiled, staring into the very heart of the goblet. 'Very well.'

'Look,' he said, as the vision began to fade, 'your wounds have vanished.'

The [illegible] [illegible] [illegible] suddenly [illegible] [illegible] [illegible] after having [illegible] [illegible] [illegible] through the very [illegible] of the [illegible] [illegible] upon the [illegible] at the end of the bed.

[illegible] [illegible] [illegible] [illegible] [illegible] the [illegible] and [illegible] [illegible] [illegible] [illegible] [illegible] appeared [illegible] of the [illegible].

[illegible] [illegible] [illegible] [illegible] [illegible] could [illegible] [illegible] [illegible] [illegible] [illegible] she could not [illegible] [illegible] [illegible] [illegible] [illegible] and [illegible] [illegible] the [illegible].

[illegible] [illegible] [illegible] [illegible] [illegible] beside her hand.

[illegible] [illegible] [illegible] [illegible] [illegible] shall be taken [illegible] [illegible] [illegible] [illegible] [illegible] should we [illegible] [illegible] [illegible] [illegible] [illegible] with us [illegible] [illegible] [illegible] and of [illegible] who shall share [illegible] with me.

She [illegible] [illegible] I am not [illegible] [illegible] then she [illegible] her head [illegible] [illegible] into the very [illegible] of the [illegible].

[illegible] he said [illegible] [illegible] [illegible] [illegible] [illegible] [illegible] vanished.

Elric at the End of Time

For Terry Pratchett

LEGEND THE FIFTH

Chapter One
In Which Mrs Persson Detects an Above Average Degree of Chaos in the Megaflow

ETURNING FROM CHINA to London and the Spring of 1936, Una Persson found an unfamiliar quality of pathos in most of the friends she had last seen, as far as she recalled, during the Blitz on her way back from 1970. Then they had been desperately hearty: it was a comfort to understand that the condition was not permanent. Here, at present, Pierrot ruled and she felt she possessed a better grip on her power. This was, she admitted with shame, her favourite moral climate for it encouraged in her an enormously gratifying sense of spiritual superiority: the advantage of having been born, originally, into a later and probably more sophisticated age. The 1960s. Some women, she reflected, were forced to have children in order to enjoy this pleasure.

But she was uneasy, so she reported to the local Time Centre and the bearded, sullen features of Sergeant Alvarez who welcomed her in white, apologising for the fact that he had himself only just that morning left the Lower Devonian and had not had time to change.

'It's the megaflow, as you guessed,' he told her, operating toggles to reveal his crazy display systems. 'We've lost control.'

'We never really had it.' She lit a Sherman's and shook her long hair back over the headrest of the swivel chair, opening her military overcoat and loosening her webbing. 'Is it worse than usual?'

'Much.' He sipped cold coffee from his battered silver mug. 'It cuts through every plane we can pick up – a rogue current swerving through the dimensions. Something of a twister.'

'Jerry?'

'He's dormant. We checked. But it's like him, certainly. Most probably another aspect.'

'Oh, sod.' Una straightened her shoulders.

'That's what I thought,' said Alvarez. 'Someone's going to have to do a spot of rubato.' He studied a screen. It was Greek to Una. For a moment a pattern formed. Alvarez made a note. 'Yes. It can either be fixed at the nadir or the zenith. It's too late to try anywhere in between. I think it's up to you, Mrs P.'

She got to her feet. 'Where's the zenith?'

'The End of Time.'

'Well,' she said, 'that's something.'

She opened her bag and made sure of her jar of instant coffee. It was the one thing she couldn't get at the End of Time.

'Sorry,' said Alvarez, glad that the expert had been there and that he could remain behind.

'It's just as well,' she said. 'This period's no good for my moral well-being. I'll be off, then.'

'Someone's got to.' Alvarez failed to seem sympathetic.

'It's Chaos out there.'

'You don't have to tell me.'

She entered the makeshift chamber and was on her way to the End of Time.

Chapter Two

In Which the Eternal Champion Finds Himself at the End of Time

Elric of Melniboné shook a bone-white fist at the greedy, glaring stars – the eyes of all those men whose souls he had stolen to sustain his own enfeebled body. He looked down. Though it seemed he stood on something solid, there was only more blackness falling away below him. It was as if he hung at the centre of the universe. And here, too, were staring points of yellow light. Was he to be judged?

His half-sentient runesword, Stormbringer, in its scabbard on his left hip, murmured like a nervous dog.

He had been on his way to Imrryr, to his home, to reclaim his kingdom from his cousin Yyrkoon; sailing from the Isle of the Purple Towns where he had guested with Count Smiorgan Baldhead. Magic winds had caught the Filkharian trader as she crossed the unnamed water between the Vilmirian peninsula and the Isle of Melniboné. She had been borne into the Dragon Sea and thence to Sorcerers' Isle, so called because that barren place had been the home of Cran Liret, the Thief of Spells, a wizard infamous for his borrowings, who had, at length, been dispatched by those he sought to rival. But much residual magic had been left behind. Certain spells had come into the keeping of the Krettii, a tribe of near-brutes who had migrated to the island from the region of The Silent Land less than fifty years before. Their shaman, one Grrodd Ybene Eenr, had made unthinking use of devices buried by the dying sorcerer as the spells of his peers sucked life and sanity from them. Elric had dealt with more than one clever wizard, but never with so mindless a power. His battle had been long and exhausting and had required the sacrifice of most of the Filkharians as well as the entire tribe of Krettii. His sorcery had become increasingly desperate. Sprite fought sprite, devil fell upon devil, in both physical and astral, all around the region of Sorcerers' Isle. Eventually Elric had mounted a massive Summoning against the allies of Grrodd Ybene Eenr with the result that the shaman had been at last overwhelmed and his remains scattered in limbo. But Elric, captured by his own monstrous magickings, had followed his enemy and now he stood in the Void, crying out into appalling silence, hearing his words only in his skull:

'Arioch! Arioch! Aid me!'

But his patron Duke of Hell was absent. He could not exist here. He could not, for once, even hear his favourite protégé.

'Arioch! Repay my loyalty! I have given you blood and souls!'

He did not breathe. His heart had stopped. All his movements were sluggish.

The eyes looked down at him. They looked up at him. Were they glad? Did they rejoice in his terror?

'Arioch!'

He yearned for a reply. He would have wept, but no tears would come. His body was cold; less than dead, yet not alive. A fear was in him greater than any fear he had known before.

'Oh, Arioch! Aid me!'

He forced his right hand towards the pulsing pommel of Stormbringer which, alone, still possessed energy. The hilt of the sword was warm to his touch and, as slowly he folded his fingers around it, it seemed to swell in his fist and propel his arm upwards so that he did not draw the sword. Rather the sword forced his limbs into motion.

And now it challenged the Void, glowing with black fire, singing its high, gleeful battle-song.

'Our destinies are intertwined, Stormbringer,' said Elric. 'Bring us from this place, or those destinies shall never be fulfilled.'

Stormbringer swung like the needle of a compass and Elric's unfeeling arm was wrenched round to go with it. In eight directions the sword swung, as if to the eight points of Chaos. It was questing – like a hound sniffing a trail. Then a yell sounded from within the strange metal of the blade; a distant cry of delight, it seemed to Elric. The sound one would hear if one stood above a valley listening to children playing far below.

Elric knew that Stormbringer had sensed a plane they might reach. Not necessarily their own, but one which would accept them. And, as a drowning mariner must yearn for the most inhospitable rock rather than no rock at all, Elric yearned for that plane.

'*Stormbringer. Take us there!*'

The sword hesitated. It moaned. It was suspicious.

'*Take us there!*' whispered the albino to his runesword.

The sword struck back and forth, up and down, as if it battled invisible enemies. Elric scarcely kept his grip on it. It seemed that Stormbringer was frightened of the world it had detected and sought to drive it back but the act of seeking had in itself set them both in motion. Already Elric could feel himself being drawn through the darkness, towards something he could see very dimly beyond the myriad eyes, as dawn reveals clouds undetected in the night sky.

Elric thought he saw the shapes of crags, pointed and crazy. He thought he saw water, flat and ice-blue. The stars faded and there was snow beneath his feet, mountains all around him, a huge, blazing sun overhead – and above that another landscape, a desert, as a magic mirror might reflect the contrasting character of he who peered into it – a desert, quite as real as the snowy peaks in which he crouched, sword in hand, waiting for one of these landscapes to fade so that he might establish, to a degree, his bearings. Evidently the two planes had intersected.

But the landscape overhead did not fade. He could look up and see sand, mountains, vegetation, a sky which met his own sky at a point halfway along the curve of the huge sun – and blended with it. He looked about him. Snowy peaks in all directions. Above – desert everywhere. He felt dizzy, found that he was staring downwards, reaching to cup some of the snow in his hand. It was ordinary snow, though it seemed reluctant to melt in contact with his flesh.

'This is a world of Chaos,' he muttered. 'It obeys no natural laws.' His voice seemed loud, amplified by the peaks, perhaps. 'That is why you did not want to come here. This is the world of powerful rivals.'

Stormbringer was silent, as if all its energy were spent. But Elric did not sheathe the blade. He began to trudge through the snow towards what seemed to be an abyss. Every so often he glanced upward, but the desert overhead had not faded; sun and sky remained the same. He wondered if he walked around the surface of a miniature world, that if he continued to go forward he might eventually reach the point where the two landscapes met. He wondered if this were not some punishment wished upon him by his untrustworthy allies of Chaos. Perhaps he must choose between death in the snow or death in the desert. He reached the edge of the abyss and looked down.

The walls of the abyss fell for all of five feet before reaching a floor of gold and silver squares which stretched for perhaps another seven feet before they reached the far wall, where the landscape continued – snow and crags – uninterrupted.

'This is undoubtedly where Chaos rules,' said the Prince of Melniboné. He studied the smooth, chequered floor. It reflected parts of the snowy terrain and the desert world above it. It reflected the crimson-eyed albino who peered down at it, his features drawn in bewilderment and tiredness.

'I am at their mercy,' said Elric. 'They play with me. But I shall resist them, even as they destroy me.' And some of his wild, careless spirit came back to him as he prepared to lower himself onto the chequered floor and cross to the opposite bank.

He was halfway over when he heard a grunting sound in the distance and a beast appeared, its paws slithering uncertainly on the smooth surface, its seven savage eyes glaring in all directions as if it sought the instigator of its terrible indignity.

And, at last, all seven eyes focused on Elric and the beast opened a mouth in which row upon row of thin, vicious teeth were arranged, and uttered a growl of unmistakeable resentment.

Elric raised his sword. 'Back, creature of Chaos. You threaten the Prince of Melniboné!'

The beast was already propelling itself towards him. Elric flung his body to one side, aiming a blow with the sword as he did so, succeeding only in making a thin incision in the monster's heavily muscled hind leg. It shrieked and began to turn.

'Back!'

Elric's voice was the brave, thin squeak of a lemming attacked by a hawk. He drove at the thing's snout with Stormbringer. The sword was heavy. It had spent all its energy and there was no more to give. Elric wondered why he, himself, did not weaken. Possibly the Laws of Nature were entirely abolished in the Realm of Chaos. He struck and drew blood. The beast paused, more in astonishment than fear.

Then it opened its jaws, pushed its back legs against the snowy bank, and shot towards the albino who tried to dodge it, lost his footing, and fell, sprawling backwards, on the gold and silver surface.

Chapter Three

In Which Una Persson Discovers an Unexpected Snag

THE GIGANTIC BEETLE, rainbow carapace glittering, turned as if into the wind, which blew from the distant mountains, its thick, flashing wings beating rapidly as it bore its single passenger over the queer landscape.

On its back Mrs Persson checked the instruments on her wrist. Ever since Man had begun to travel in time it had become necessary for the Guild to develop techniques to compensate for the fluctuations and disruptions in the space-time continua; perpetually monitoring the chronoflow and megaflow. She pursed her lips. She had picked up the signal. She made the semi-sentient beetle swing a degree or two SSE and head directly for the mountains. She was in some sort of enclosed (but vast) environment. These mountains, as well as everything surrounding them, lay in the territory most utilised by the gloomy, natural-born Werther de Goethe, poet and romantic, solitary seeker after truth in a world no longer differentiating between the degrees of reality. He would not remember her, she knew, because, as far as Werther was concerned, they had not met yet. Had Werther even experienced his adventure with Mistress Christia, the Everlasting Concubine? A story on which she had dined out more than once, in duller eras.

The mountains drew closer. From here it was possible to see the entire arrangement (a creation of Werther's very much in character): a desert landscape, a central sun, and, inverted above it, winter mountains. Werther strove to make statements, like so many naïve artists before him, by presenting simple contrasts: The World is Bleak / The World is Cold / Barren am I As I Grow Old / Tomorrow I Die, Entombed in Cold / For Silver My Poor Soul Was Sold – she remembered he was perhaps the worst poet she had encountered in an eternity of meetings with bad poets. He had taught himself to read and write in old, old English so that he might carve those words on one of his many abandoned tombs (half his time was spent in composing obituaries for himself). Like so many others he seemed to equate self-pity with artistic inspiration. In an earlier age he might have discovered his public and become quite rich (self-pity passing for passion in the popular understanding). Sometimes she regretted the passing of Wheldrake, so long ago, so far away, in a universe bearing scarcely any resemblances to those in which she normally operated.

She brought her wavering mind back to the problem. The beetle dipped and circled over the desert, but there was no sight of her quarry.

She was about to abandon the search when she heard a faint roaring overhead and she looked up to see another characteristic motif of Werther's – a gold and silver chessboard on which, upside down, a monstrous doglike creature was bearing down on a tiny white-haired man dressed in the most abominable taste Una had seen for some time.

She directed the air car upwards and then, reversing the machine as she entered the opposing gravity, downwards to where the barbarically costumed swordsman was about to be eaten by the beast.

'Shoo!' cried Una commandingly.

The beast raised a befuddled head.

'Shoo.'

It licked its lips and returned its seven-eyed gaze to the albino, who was now on his knees, using his large sword to steady himself as he climbed to his feet.

The jaws opened wider and wider. The pale man prepared, shakily, to defend himself.

Una directed the air car at the beast's unkempt head. The great beetle connected with a loud crack. The monster's eyes widened in dismay. It yelped. It sat on its haunches and began to slide away, its claws making an unpleasant noise on the gold and silver tiles.

Una landed the air car and gestured for the stranger to enter. She noticed with distaste that he was a somewhat unhealthy-looking albino with gaunt features, exaggeratedly large and slanting eyes, ears that were virtually pointed, and glaring, half-mad red pupils.

And yet, undoubtedly, it was her quarry and there was nothing for it but to be polite.

'Do, please, get in,' she said. 'I am here to rescue you.'

'*Shaarmraaam torjistoo quellahm vyeearrr,*' said the stranger in an accent that seemed to Una to be vaguely Scottish.

'Damn,' she said, 'that's all we need.' She had been anxious to approach the albino in private, before one of the denizens of the End of Time could arrive and select him for a menagerie, but now she regretted that Werther or perhaps Lord Jagged were not here, for she realised that she needed one of their translation pills, those tiny tablets which could 'engineer' the brain to understand a new language. By a fluke – or perhaps because of her presence here so often – the people at the End of Time currently spoke formal early-20th-century English.

The albino – who wore a kind of tartan divided kilt, knee-length boots, a blue-and-white jerkin, a green cloak and a silver breast-plate, with a variety of leather belts and metal buckles here and there upon his person – was vehemently refusing her offer of a lift. He raised the sword before him as he backed away, slipped once, reached the bank, scrambled through snow and disappeared behind a rock.

Mrs Persson sighed and put the car into motion again.

Chapter Four

In Which the Prince of Melniboné Encounters Further Terrors

XIOMBARG HERSELF, THOUGHT Elric as he slid beneath the snows into the cave. Well, he would have no dealings with the Queen of Chaos; not until he was forced to do so.

The cave was large. In the thin light from the gap above his head he could not see far. He wondered whether to return to the surface or risk going deeper into the cave. There was always the hope that he would find another way out. He was attempting to recall some rune that would aid him, but all he knew depended either upon the aid of elementals who did not exist on this plane, or upon the Lords of Chaos themselves – and they were unlikely to come to his assistance in their own realm. He was marooned here: the single mouse in a world of cats.

Almost unconsciously, he found himself moving downwards, realising that the cave had become a tunnel. He was feeling hungry but, apart from the monster and the woman in the magical carriage, had seen no sign of life. Even the cavern did not seem entirely natural.

It widened; there was phosphorescent light. He realised that the walls were of transparent crystal, and behind the walls were all manner of artefacts. He saw crowns, sceptres and chains of precious jewels; cabinets of complicated carving; weapons of strangely turned metal; armour, clothing, things whose use he could not guess – and food. There were sweetmeats, fruits, flans and pies, all out of reach.

Elric groaned. This was torment. Perhaps deliberately planned torment. A thousand voices whispered to him in a beautiful, alien language.

'Bie-meee... Bie-meee...' the voices murmured. *'Baa-gen, baa-gen...'*

They seemed to be promising every delight, if only he could

pass through the walls; but they were of transparent quartz, lit from within. He raised Stormbringer, half-tempted to try to break down the barrier, but he knew that even his sword was, at its most powerful, incapable of destroying the magic of Chaos.

He paused, gasping with astonishment at a group of small dogs which looked at him with large brown eyes, tongues lolling, and jumped up at him.

'*O, Nee Tubbens!*' intoned one of the voices.

'Gods!' screamed Elric. 'This torture is too much!' He swung his body this way and that, threatening with his sword, but the voices continued to murmur and promise, displaying their riches but never allowing him to touch.

The albino panted. His crimson eyes glared about him. 'You would drive me insane, eh? Well, Elric of Melniboné has witnessed more frightful threats than this. You will need to do more if you would destroy his mind!'

And he ran through the whispering passages, looking to neither his right nor his left, until, quite suddenly, he had run into blazing daylight and stood staring down into pale infinity – a blue and endless void.

He looked up. And he screamed.

Overhead were the gentle hills and dales of a rural landscape, with rivers, grazing cattle, woods and cottages. He expected to fall, headlong, but he did not. He was on the brink of the abyss. The cliff face of red sandstone fell immediately below and then was the tranquil void. He looked back:

'*Baa-gen... O, Nee Tubbens...*'

A bitter smile played about the albino's bloodless lips as, decisively, he sheathed his sword.

'Well, then,' he said. 'Let them do their worst!'

And, laughing, he launched himself over the brink of the cliff.

Chapter Five
In Which Werther de Goethe Makes a Wonderful Discovery

WITH A GESTURE of quiet pride, Werther de Goethe indicated his gigantic skull.

'It is very large, Werther,' said Mistress Christia, the Everlasting Concubine, turning a power ring to adjust the shade of her eyes so that they perfectly matched the day.

'It is monstrous,' said Werther modestly. 'It reminds us all of the Inevitable Night.'

'Who was that?' enquired golden-haired Gaf the Horse in Tears, at present studying ancient legendry. 'Sir Lew Grady?'

'I mean Death,' Werther told him, 'which overwhelms us all.'

'Well, not us,' pointed out the Duke of Queens, as usual a trifle literal-minded. 'Because we're immortal, as you know.'

Werther offered him a sad, pitying look and sighed briefly. 'Retain your delusions, if you will.'

Mistress Christia stroked the gloomy Werther's long, dark locks. 'There, there,' she said. 'We have compensations, Werther.'

'Without Death,' intoned the Last Romantic, 'there is no point to Life.'

As usual, they could not follow him, but they nodded gravely and politely.

'The skull,' continued Werther, stroking the side of his air car (which was in the shape of a large flying reptile) to make it circle and head for the left eye-socket, 'is a Symbol not only of our Mortality, but also of our Fruitless Ambitions.'

'Fruit?' Bishop Castle, drowsing at the rear of the vehicle, became interested. His hobby was currently orchards. 'Less? My pine trees, you know, are proving a problem. The apples are much smaller than I was led to believe.'

'The skull is lovely,' said Mistress Christia with valiant enthusiasm. 'Well, now that we have seen it…'

'The outward shell,' Werther told her. 'It is what it hides which is more important. Man's Foolish Yearnings are all encompassed therein. His Greed, his Need for the Impossible, the Heat of his Passions, the Coldness which must Finally Overtake him. Through this eye-socket you will encounter a little invention of my own called The Bargain Basement of the Mind…'

He broke off in astonishment.

On the top edge of the eye-socket a tiny figure had emerged.

'What's that?' enquired the Duke of Queens, craning his head back. 'A random thought?'

'It is not mine at all!'

The figure launched itself into the sky and seemed to fly, with flailing limbs, towards the sun.

Werther frowned, watching the tiny man disappear. 'The gravity field is reversed there,' he said absently, 'in order to make the most of the paradox, you understand. There is a snowscape, a desert…' But he was much more interested in the newcomer. 'How do you think he got into my skull?'

'At least he's enjoying himself. He seems to be laughing.' Mistress Christia bent an ear towards the thin sound, which grew fainter and fainter at first, but became louder again. 'He's coming back.'

Werther nodded. 'Yes. The field's no longer reversed.' He touched a power ring.

The laughter stopped and became a yell of rage. The figure hurtled down on them. It had a sword in one white hand and its red eyes blazed.

Hastily, Werther stroked another ring. The stranger tumbled into the bottom of the air car and lay there panting, cursing and groaning.

'How wonderful!' cried Werther. 'Oh, this is a traveller from some rich, romantic past. Look at him! What else could he be? What a prize!'

The stranger rose to his feet and raised the sword high above his head, defying the amazed and delighted passengers as he screamed at the top of his voice:

'*Heeshigrowinaaz!*'

'Good afternoon,' said Mistress Christia. She reached in her purse for a translation pill and found one. 'I wonder if you would care to swallow this – it's quite harmless…'

'*Yakoom, oom glallio,*' said the albino contemptuously.

'Aha,' said Mistress Christia. 'Well, just as you please.'

The Duke of Queens pointed towards the other socket. A huge, whirring beetle came sailing from it. In its back was someone he recognised with pleasure. 'Mrs Persson!'

Una brought her air car alongside.

'Is he in your charge?' asked Werther with undisguised disappointment. 'If so, I could offer you…'

'I'm afraid he means a lot to me,' she said.

'From your own age?' Mistress Christia also recognised Una. She still offered the translation pill in the palm of her hand. 'He seems a mite suspicious of us.'

'I'd noticed,' said Una. 'It would be useful if he would accept the pill. However, if he will not, one of us…'

'I would be happy,' offered the generous Duke of Queens. He tugged at his green-and-gold beard. 'Werther de Goethe, Mrs Persson.'

'Perhaps I had better,' said Una nodding to Werther. The only problem with translation pills was that they did their job so thoroughly. You could speak the language perfectly, but you could speak no other.

Werther was, for once, positive. 'Let's all take a pill,' he suggested.

Everyone at the End of Time carried translation pills, in case of meeting a visitor from Space or the Past.

Mistress Christia handed hers to Una and found another. They swallowed.

'Creatures of Chaos,' said the newcomer with cool dignity, 'I demand that you release me. You cannot hold a mortal in this way, not unless he has struck a bargain with you. And no bargain was struck which would bring me to the Realm of Chaos.'

'It's actually more orderly than you'd think,' said Werther apologetically. 'Your first experience, you see, was the world of my skull, which was deliberately muddled. I meant to show what Confusion was the Mind of Man…'

'May I introduce Mistress Christia, the Everlasting Concubine,' said the Duke of Queens, on his best manners. 'This is Mrs Persson, Bishop Castle, Gaf the Horse in Tears. Werther de Goethe – your unwitting host – and I am the Duke of Queens. We welcome you to our world. Your name, sir…?'

'You must know me, my lord Duke,' said Elric. 'For I am Elric of Melniboné, Emperor by Right of Birth, Inheritor of the Ruby Throne, Bearer of the Actorios, Wielder of the Black Sword…'

'Indeed!' said Werther de Goethe. In a whispered aside to Mrs Persson: 'What a marvellous scowl! What a noble sneer!'

'You are an important personage in your world, then?' said Mistress Christia, fluttering the eyelashes she had just extended by half an inch. 'Perhaps you would allow me…'

'I think he wishes to be returned to his home,' said Mrs Persson hastily.

'Returned?' Werther was astonished. 'But the Morphail Effect! It is impossible.'

'Not in this case, I think,' she said. 'For if he is not returned there is no telling the fluctuations which will take place throughout the dimensions…'

They could not follow her, but they accepted her tone.

'Aye,' said Elric darkly, 'return me to my realm, so that I may fulfil my own doom-laden destiny…'

Werther looked upon the albino with affectionate delight. 'Aha! A fellow spirit! I, too, have a doom-laden destiny.'

'I doubt it is as doom-laden as mine.' Elric peered moodily back at the skull as the two air cars fled away towards a gentle horizon where exotic trees bloomed.

'Well,' said Werther with an effort, 'perhaps it is not, though I assure you…'

'I have looked upon hellborn horror,' said Elric, 'and communicated with the very Gods of the Uttermost Darkness. I have seen things which would turn other men's minds to useless jelly…'

'Jelly?' interrupted Bishop Castle. 'Do you, in your turn, have any expertise with, for instance, blackbird trees?'

'Your words are meaningless,' Elric told him, glowering. 'Why do you torment me so, my lords? I did not ask to visit your world. I belong in the world of men, in the Young Kingdoms, where I seek my weird. Why, I have but lately experienced adventures…'

'I do think we have one of those bores,' murmured Bishop Castle to the Duke of Queens, 'so common amongst time-travellers. They all believe themselves unique.'

But the Duke of Queens refused to be drawn. He had developed a liking for the frowning albino. Gaf the Horse in Tears was also plainly impressed, for he had fashioned his own features into a rough likeness of Elric's. The Prince of Melniboné pretended insouciance, but it was evident to Una that he was frightened. She tried to calm him.

'People here at the End of Time…' she began.

'No soft words, my lady.' A cynical smile played about the albino's lips. 'I know you for that great unholy temptress, Queen of the Swords, Xiombarg herself.'

'I assure you, I am as human as you, sir…'

'Human? I, human? I am not human, madam – though I be a mortal, 'tis true. I am of older blood, the blood of the Bright Empire itself, the Blood of R'lin K'ren A'a which Cran Liret mocked, not understanding what it was he laughed at. Aye, though forced to summon aid from Chaos, I made no bargain to become a slave in your realm…'

'I assure you – um – your majesty,' said Una, 'that we had not meant to insult you and your presence here was no doing of ours. I am, as it happens, a stranger here myself. I came especially to see you, to help you escape…'

'Ha!' said the albino. 'I have heard such words before. You would lure me into some worse trap than this. Tell me, where is Duke Arioch? He, at least, I owe some allegiance to.'

'We have no-one of that name,' apologised Mistress Christia. She enquired of Gaf, who knew everyone. 'No time-traveller?'

'None,' Gaf studied Elric's eyes and made a small adjustment to his own. He sat back, satisfied.

Elric shuddered and turned away mumbling.

'You are very welcome here,' said Werther. 'I cannot tell you how glad I am to meet one as essentially morbid and self-pitying as myself!'

Elric did not seem flattered.

'What can we do to make you feel at home?' asked Mistress Christia. She had changed her hair to a rather glossy blue in the hope, perhaps, that Elric would find it more attractive. 'Is there anything you need?'

'Need? Aye. Peace of mind. Knowledge of my true destiny. A quiet place where I can be with Cymoril, whom I love.'

'What does this Cymoril look like?' Mistress Christia became just a trifle overeager.

'She is the most beautiful creature in the universe,' said Elric.

'It isn't very much to go on,' said Mistress Christia. 'If you could imagine a picture, perhaps? There are devices in the old cities which could visualise your thoughts. We could go there. I should be happy to fill in for her, as it were…'

'What? You offer me a simulacrum? Do you not think I should detect such witchery at once? Ah, this is loathsome! Slay me, if you will, or continue the torment. I'll listen no longer!'

They were floating now, between high cliffs. On a ledge far below a group of time-travellers pointed up at them. One waved desperately.

'You've offended him, Mistress Christia,' said Werther pettishly. 'You don't understand how sensitive he is.'

'Yes I do.' She was aggrieved. 'I was only being sympathetic.'

'Sympathy!' Elric rubbed at his long, somewhat pointed jaw. 'Ha! What do I want with sympathy?'

'I never heard anyone who wanted it more.' Mistress Christia was kind. 'You're like a little boy, really, aren't you?'

'Compared to the ancient Lords of Chaos, I am a child, aye. But my blood is old and cold, the blood of decaying Melniboné, as well you know.' And with a huge sigh the albino seated himself at the far end of the car and rested his head on his fist. 'Well? What is your pleasure, my Lords and Ladies of Hell?'

'It is your pleasure we are anxious to achieve,' Werther told him. 'Is there anything at all we can do? Some environment we can manufacture? What are you used to?'

'Used to? I am used to the crack of leathery dragon wings in the sweet, sharp air of the early dawn. I am used to the sound of red battle, the drumming of hoofs on bloody earth, the screams of the dying, the yells of the victorious. I am used to warring against demons and monsters, sorcerers and ghouls. I have sailed on magic ships and fought hand to hand with reptilian savages. I have encountered the Jade Man himself. I have fought side by side with the elementals, who are my allies. I have battled black evil…'

'Well,' said Werther, 'that's something to go on, at any rate. I'm sure we can…'

'Lord Elric won't be staying,' began Una Persson politely. 'You see – these fluctuations in the megaflow – not to mention his own destiny… He should not be here, at all, Werther.'

'Nonsense!' Werther flung a black velvet arm about the stiff shoulders of his new friend. 'It is evident that our destinies are one. Lord Elric is as grief-haunted as myself!'

'How can you know what it is to be haunted by grief?' murmured the albino. His face was half-buried in Werther's generous sleeve.

Mrs Persson controlled herself. She rose from Werther's air car and made for her own. 'Well,' she said, 'I must be off. I hope to see you later, everybody.'

They sang out their farewells.

Una Persson turned her beetle westward, towards Castle Canaria, the home of her old friend Lord Jagged.

She needed help and advice.

Chapter Six

In Which Elric of Melniboné Resists the Temptations of the Chaos Lords

ELRIC REFLECTED ON the subtle way in which laughing Lords of Chaos had captured him. Apparently, he was merely a guest and quite free to wander where he would in their realm. Actually, he was in their power as much as if they had chained him, for he could not flee this flying dragon and they had already demonstrated their enormous magical gifts in subtle ways, primarily with their shape-changing. Only the one who called himself Werther de Goethe (plainly a leader in the hierarchy of Chaos) still had the face and clothing he had worn when first encountered.

It was evident that this realm obeyed no natural laws, that it was mutable according to the whims of its powerful inhabitants. They could destroy him with a breath and had, subtly enough, given him evidence of that fact. How could he possibly escape such danger? By calling upon the Lords of Law for aid? But he owed them no loyalty and they, doubtless, regarded him as their enemy. But if he were to transfer his allegiance to Law…

These thoughts and more continued to engage him, while his captors chatted easily in the ancient High Speech of Melniboné, itself a version of the very language of Chaos. It was one of the other ways in which they revealed themselves for what they were. He fingered his runesword, wondering if it would be possible to slay such a lord and steal his energy, giving himself enough power for a little while to hurl himself back to his own sphere…

The one called Lord Werther was leaning over the side of the beast-vessel. 'Oh, come and see, Elric. Look!'

Reluctantly, the albino moved to where Werther peered and pointed.

The entire landscape was filled with a monstrous battle. Creatures of all kinds and all combinations tore at one another with huge teeth and claws. Shapeless things slithered and hopped; giants, naked but for helmets and greaves, slashed at these beasts with great broadswords and axes, but were borne down. Flame and black smoke drifted everywhere. There was a smell. The stink of blood?

'What do you miss most?' asked the female. She pressed a soft body against him. He pretended not to be aware of it. He knew what magic flesh could hide on a she-witch.

'I miss peace,' said Elric almost to himself, 'and I miss war. For in battle I find a kind of peace…'

'Very good!' Bishop Castle applauded. 'You are beginning to learn our ways. You will soon become one of our best conversationalists.'

Elric touched the hilt of Stormbringer, hoping to feel it grow warm and vibrant under his hand, but it was still, impotent in the Realm of Chaos. He uttered a heavy sigh.

'You are an adventurer, then, in your own world?' said the Duke of Queens. He was bluff. He had changed his beard to an ordinary sort of black and was wearing a scarlet costume; quilted doublet and tight-fitting hose, with a blue-and-white ruff, an elaborately feathered hat on his head. 'I, too, am something of a vagabond. As far, of course, as it is possible to be here. A buccaneer, of sorts. That is, my actions are in the main bolder than those of my fellows. More spectacular. Vulgar. Like yourself, sir. I admire your costume.'

Elric knew that this Duke of Hell was referring to the fact that he affected the costume of the southern barbarian, that he did not wear the more restrained colours and more cleverly wrought silks and metals of his own folk. He gave tit for tat at this time. He bowed.

'Thank you, sir. Your own clothes rival mine.'

'Do you think so?' The hell-lord pretended pleasure. If Elric had not known better, the creature would seem to be swelling with pride.

'Look!' cried Werther again. 'Look, Lord Elric – we are attacked.'

Elric whirled.

From below were rising oddly wrought vessels – something like ships, but with huge round wheels at their sides, like the wheels of water-clocks he had seen once in Pikarayd. Coloured smoke issued from chimneys mounted on their decks which swarmed with huge birds dressed in human clothing. The birds had multicoloured plumage, curved beaks, and they held swords in their claws, while on their heads were strangely shaped black hats on which were blazed skulls with crossed bones beneath.

'Heave to!' squawked the birds. 'Or we'll put a shot across your bowels!'

'What can they be?' cried Bishop Castle.

'Parrots,' said Werther de Goethe soberly. 'Otherwise known as the hawks of the sea. And they mean us no good.'

Mistress Christia blinked.

'Don't you mean pirates, dear?'

Elric took a firm grip on his sword. Some of the words the Chaos Lords used were absolutely meaningless to him. But whether the attacking creatures were of their own conception, or whether they were true enemies of his captors, Elric prepared to do bloody battle. His spirits improved. At least here was something substantial to fight.

Chapter Seven

In Which Mrs Persson Becomes Anxious About the Future of the Universe

Lord Jagged of Canaria was nowhere to be found. His huge castle, of gold and yellow spires, an embellished replica of Kings Cross station, was populated entirely by his quaint robots, whom Jagged found at once more mysterious and more trustworthy than android or human servants, for they could answer only according to a limited programme.

Una suspected that Jagged was, himself, upon some mission, for he, too, was a member of the Guild of Temporal Adventurers. But she needed aid. Somehow she had to return Elric to his own dimension without creating further disruptions in the fabric of time and space. The Conjunction was not due yet and, if things got any worse, might never come. So many plans depended on the Conjunction of the Million Spheres that she could not risk its failure. But she could not reveal too much either to Elric or his hosts. As a Guild member she was sworn to the utmost and indeed necessary secrecy. Even here at the End of Time there were certain laws which could be disobeyed only at enormous risk. Words alone were dangerous when they described ideas concerning the nature of time.

She racked her brains. She considered seeking out Jherek Carnelian, but then remembered that he had scarcely begun to understand his own destiny. Besides, there were certain similarities between Jherek and Elric which she could only sense at present. It would be best to go cautiously there.

She decided that she had no choice. She must return to the Time Centre and see if they could detect Lord Jagged for her.

She brought the necessary co-ordinates together in her mind and concentrated. For a moment all memories, all sense of identity left her.

Sergeant Alvarez was beside himself. His screens were no longer completely without form. Instead, peculiar shapes could be seen in the arrangements of lines. Una thought she saw faces, beasts, landscapes. That had never occurred before. The instruments, at least, had remained sane, even as they recorded insanity.

'It's getting worse,' said Alvarez. 'You've hardly any Time left. What there is, I've managed to borrow for you. Did you contact the rogue?'

She nodded. 'Yes. But getting him to return… I want you to find Jagged.'

'Jagged? Are you sure?'

'It's our only chance, I think.'

Alvarez sighed and bent a tense back over his controls.

Chapter Eight

In Which Elric and Werther Fight Side by Side Against Almost Overwhelming Odds

SOMEWHERE, IT SEEMED to Elric, as he parried and thrust at the attacking bird-monsters, rich and rousing music played. It must be a delusion, brought on by battle madness. Blood and feathers covered the carriage. He saw the one called Christia carried off screaming. Bishop Castle had disappeared. Gaf had gone. Only the three of them, shoulder to shoulder, continued to fight. What was disconcerting to Elric was that Werther and the Duke of Queens bore swords absolutely identical to Stormbringer. Perhaps they were the legendary Brothers of the Black Sword, said to reside in Chaos?

He was forced to admit to himself that he experienced a sense of comradeship with these two, who were braver than most in defending themselves against such dreadful, unlikely monsters – perhaps some creation of their own which had turned against them.

Having captured the Lady Christia, the birds began to return to their own craft.

'We must rescue her!' cried Werther as the flying ships began to retreat. 'Quickly! In pursuit!'

'Should we not seek reinforcements?' asked Elric, further impressed by the courage of this Chaos Lord.

'No time!' cried the Duke of Queens. 'After them!'

Werther shouted to his vessel. 'Follow those ships!'

The vessel did not move.

'It has an enchantment on it,' said Werther. 'We are stranded! Ah, and I loved her so much!'

Elric became suspicious again. Werther had shown no signs, previously, of any affection for the female.

'You loved her?'

'From a distance,' Werther explained. 'Duke of Queens, what

can we do? Those parrots will ransom her savagely and mishandle her objects of virtue!'

'Dastardly poltroons!' roared the huge duke.

Elric could make little sense of this exchange. It dawned on him, then, that he could still hear the rousing music. He looked below. On some sort of dais in the middle of the bizarre landscape a large group of musicians was assembled. They played on, apparently oblivious of what happened above. This was truly a world dominated by Chaos.

Their ship began slowly to fall towards the band. It lurched. Elric gasped and clung to the side as they struck yielding ground and bumped to a halt.

The Duke of Queens, apparently elated, was already scrambling overboard. 'There! We can follow on those mounts.'

Tethered near the dais was a herd of creatures bearing some slight resemblance to horses but in a variety of dazzling, metallic colours, with horns and bony ridges on their backs. Saddles and bridles of alien workmanship showed that they were domestic beasts, doubtless belonging to the musicians.

'They will want some payment from us, surely,' said Elric, as they hurried towards the horses.

'Ah, true!' Werther reached into a purse at his belt and drew forth a handful of jewels. Casually he flung them towards the musicians and climbed into the saddle of the nearest beast. Elric and the Duke of Queens followed his example. Then Werther, with a whoop, was off in the direction in which the bird-monsters had gone.

The landscape of this world of Chaos changed rapidly as they rode. They galloped through forests of crystalline trees, over fields of glowing flowers, leapt rivers the colour of blood and the consistency of mercury, and their tireless mounts maintained a headlong pace which never faltered. Through clouds of boiling gas which wept, through rain, through snow, through intolerable heat, through shallow lakes in which oddly fashioned fish wriggled and gasped, until at last a range of mountains came in sight.

'There!' panted Werther, pointing with his own runesword. 'Their lair. Oh, the fiends! How can we climb such smooth cliffs?'

It was true that the base of the cliffs rose some hundred feet before they became suddenly ragged, like the rotting teeth of the beggars of Nadsokor. They were of dusky, purple obsidian and so smooth as to reflect the faces of the three adventurers who stared at them in despair.

It was Elric who saw the steps put into the side of the cliff.

'These will take us up some of the way, at least.'

'It could be a trap,' said the Duke of Queens. He, too, seemed to be relishing the opportunity to take action. Although a Lord of Chaos there was something about him that made Elric respond to a fellow spirit.

'Let them trap us,' said Elric laconically. 'We have our swords.'

With a wild laugh, Werther de Goethe was the first to swing himself from his saddle and run towards the steps, leaping up them almost as if he had the power of flight. Elric and the Duke of Queens followed more slowly.

Their feet slipping in the narrow spaces not meant for mortals to climb, ever aware of the dizzying drop on their left, the three came at last to the top of the cliff and stood clinging to sharp crags, staring across a plain at a crazy castle rising into the clouds before them.

'Their stronghold,' said Werther.

'What are these creatures?' Elric asked. 'Why do they attack you? Why do they capture the Lady Christia?'

'They nurse an abiding hatred for us,' explained the Duke of Queens, and looked expectantly at Werther, who added:

'This was their world before it became ours.'

'And before it became theirs,' said the Duke of Queens, 'it was the world of the Yargtroon.'

'The Yargtroon?' Elric frowned.

'They dispossessed the bodiless vampire goat-folk of Kia,' explained Werther. 'Who, in turn, destroyed – or thought they destroyed – the Grash-Tu-Xem, a race of Old Ones older than any Old Ones except the Elder Old Ones of Ancient Thriss.'

'Older even than Chaos?' asked Elric.

'Oh, far older,' said Werther.

'It's almost completely collapsed, it's so old,' added the Duke of Queens.

Elric was baffled. 'Thriss?'

'Chaos,' said the Duke.

Elric let a thin smile play about his lips. 'You still mock me, my lord. The power of Chaos is the greatest there is, only equalled by the power of Law.'

'Oh, certainly,' agreed the Duke of Queens.

Elric became suspicious again. 'Do you play with me, my lord?'

'Well, naturally, we try to please our guests…'

Werther interrupted. 'Yonder doomy edifice holds the one I love. Somewhere within its walls she is incarcerated, while ghouls taunt at her and devils threaten.'

'The bird-monsters…?' began Elric.

'Chimerae,' said the Duke of Queens. 'You saw only one of the shapes they assume.'

Elric understood this. 'Aha!'

'But how can we enter it?' Werther spoke almost to himself.

'We must wait until nightfall,' said Elric, 'and enter under the cover of darkness.'

'Nightfall?' Werther brightened.

Suddenly they were in utter darkness.

Somewhere the Duke of Queens lost his footing and fell with a muffled curse.

Chapter Nine

In Which Mrs Persson at Last Makes Contact with Her Old Friend

THEY STOOD TOGETHER beneath the striped awning of the tent while a short distance away armoured men, mounted on armoured horses, jousted, were injured or died. The two members wore appropriate costumes for the period. Lord Jagged looked handsome in his surcoat and mail, but Una Persson merely looked uncomfortable in her wimple and kirtle.

'I can't leave just now,' he was saying. 'I am laying the foundations for a very important development.'

'Which will come to nothing unless Elric is returned,' she said.

A knight with a broken lance thundered past, covering them in dust.

'Well played, Sir Holger!' called Lord Jagged. 'An ancestor of mine, you know,' he told her.

'You will not be able to recognise the world of the End of Time when you return, if this is allowed to continue,' she said.

'It's always difficult, isn't it?' But he was listening to her now.

'These disruptions could as easily affect us and leave us stranded,' she added. 'We would lose any freedom we have gained.'

He bit into a pomegranate and offered it to her. 'You can only get these in this area. Did you know? Impossible to find in England. In the 13th century, at any rate. The idea of freedom is such a nebulous one, isn't it? Most of the time when angry people are speaking of "freedom" what they are actually asking for is much simpler – respect. Do those in authority or those with power ever really respect those who do not have power?' He paused. 'Or do they mean "power" and not "freedom". Or are they the same...?'

'Really, Jagged, this is no time for self-indulgence.'

He looked about him. 'There's little else to do in the Middle East in the 13th century, I assure you, except eat pomegranates and philosophise...'

'You must come back to the End of Time.'

He wiped his handsome chin. 'Your urgency,' he said, 'worries me, Una. These matters should be handled with delicacy – slowly…'

'The entire fabric will collapse unless he is returned to his own dimension. He is an important factor in the whole plan.'

'Well, yes, I understand that.'

'He is, in one sense at least, your protégé.'

'I know. But not my responsibility.'

'You must help,' she said.

There was a loud bang and a crash.

A splinter flew into Mrs Persson's eye.

'Oh, zounds!' she said.

Chapter Ten
In Which the Castle is Assaulted and the Plot Thickened

A MOON HAD appeared above the spires of the castle which seemed to Elric to have changed its shape since he had first seen it. He meant to ask his companions for an explanation, but at present they were all sworn to silence as they crept nearer. From within the castle burst light, emanating from guttering brands stuck into brackets on the walls. There was laughter, noise of feasting. Hidden behind a rock they peered through one large window and inspected the scene within.

The entire hall was full of men wearing identical costumes. They had black skull-caps, loose white blouses and trousers, black shoes. Their eyebrows were black in dead white faces, even paler than Elric's and they had bright red lips.

'Aha,' whispered Werther, 'the parrots are celebrating their victory. Soon they will be too drunk to know what is happening to them.'

'Parrots?' said Elric. 'What is that word?'

'Pierrots, he means,' said the Duke of Queens. 'Don't you, Werther?' There were evidently certain words which did not translate easily into the High Speech of Melniboné.

'Shh,' said the Last Romantic, 'they will capture us and torture us to death if they detect our presence.'

They worked their way around the castle. It was guarded at intervals by gigantic warriors whom Elric at first mistook for statues, save that, when he looked closely, he could see them breathing very slowly. They were unarmed, but their fists and feet were disproportionately large and could crush any intruder they detected.

'They are sluggish, by the look of them,' said Elric. 'If we are quick, we can run beneath them and enter the castle before they realise it. Let me try first. If I succeed, you follow.'

Werther clapped his new comrade on the back. 'Very well.'

Elric waited until the nearest guard halted and spread his huge feet apart, then he dashed forward, scuttling like an insect between the giant's legs and flinging himself through a dimly lit window. He found himself in some sort of storeroom. He had not been seen, though the guard cocked his ear for half a moment before resuming his pace.

Elric looked cautiously out and signalled to his companions. The Duke of Queens waited for the guard to stop again, then he, too, made for the window and joined Elric. He was panting and grinning. 'This is wonderful,' he said.

Elric admired his spirit. There was no doubt that the guard could crush any of them to a pulp, even if (as still nagged at his brain) this was all some sort of complicated illusion.

Another dash, and Werther was with them.

Cautiously, Elric opened the door of the storeroom. They looked onto a deserted landing. They crossed the landing and looked over a balustrade. They had expected to see another hall, but instead there was a miniature lake on which floated the most beautiful miniature ship, all mother-of-pearl, brass and ebony, with golden sails and silver masts. Surrounding this ship were mermaids and mermen bearing trays of exotic food (reminding Elric how hungry he still was) which they fed to the ship's only passenger, Mistress Christia.

'She is under an enchantment,' said Elric. 'They beguile her with illusions so that she will not wish to come with us even if we do rescue her. Do you know no counter-spells?'

Werther thought for a moment. Then he shook his head.

'You must be very minor Lords of Chaos,' said Elric, biting his lower lip.

From the lake, Mistress Christia giggled and drew one of the mermaids towards her. 'Come here, my pretty piscine!'

'Mistress Christia!' hissed Werther de Goethe.

'Oh!' The captive widened her eyes (which were now both large and blue). 'At last!'

'You wish to be rescued?' said Elric.

'Rescued? Only by you, most alluring of albinos!'

Elric hardened his features. 'I am not the one who loves you, madam.'

'What? I am loved? By whom? By you, Duke of Queens?'

'Sshh,' said Elric. 'The demons will hear us.'

'Oh, of course,' said Mistress Christia gravely, and fell silent for a second. 'I'll get rid of all this, shall I?'

And she touched one of her rings.

Ship, lake and merfolk were gone. She lay on silken cushions, attended by monkeys.

'Sorcery!' said Elric. 'If she has such power, then why –?'

'It is limited,' explained Werther. 'Merely to such tricks.'

'Quite,' said Mistress Christia.

Elric glared at them. 'You surround me with illusions. You make me think I am aiding you, when really...'

'No, no!' cried Werther. 'I assure you, Lord Elric, you have our greatest respect – well, mine at least – we are only attempting to –'

There was a roar from the gallery above. Rank upon rank of grinning demons looked down upon them. They were armed to the teeth.

'Hurry!' The Duke of Queens leapt to the cushions and seized Mistress Christia, flinging her over his shoulder. 'We can never defeat so many!'

The demons were already rushing down the circular staircase. Elric, still not certain whether his new friends deceived him or not, made a decision. He called to the Duke of Queens. 'Get her from the castle. We'll keep them from you for a few moments, at least.' He could not help himself. He behaved impulsively.

The Duke of Queens, sword in hand, Mistress Christia over the other shoulder, ran into a narrow passage. Elric and Werther stood together as the demons rushed down on them. Blade met blade. There was an unbearable shrilling of steel mingled with the cacklings and shrieks of the demons as they gnashed their teeth and rolled their eyes and slashed at the pair with swords, knives and axes. But worst of all was the smell. The dreadful smell of burning flesh which filled the air and threatened to choke Elric. It came from the demons. The smell of hell. He did his best to cover his nostrils as he fought, certain that the smell must overwhelm him before the swords. Above him was a set of metal rungs fixed into the stones, leading high into a kind of chimney. As a pause came he pointed upward to Werther, who understood him. For a moment they managed to drive the demons back. Werther jumped onto Elric's shoulders (again displaying a strange lightness) and reached down to haul the albino after him.

While the demons wailed and cackled below, they began to climb the chimney.

They climbed for nearly fifty feet before they found themselves in a small, round room whose windows looked out over the purple crags and, beyond them, to a scene of bleak rocky pavements pitted with holes, like some vast, unlikely cheese.

And there, rolling over this relatively flat landscape, in full daylight (for the sun had risen) was the Duke of Queens in a carriage of brass and wood, studded with jewels, and drawn by two bovine creatures which looked to Elric as if they might be the fabulous oxen of mythology who had drawn the war chariot of his ancestors to do battle with the emerging nations of mankind.

Mistress Christia was beside the Duke of Queens. They seemed to be waiting for Elric and Werther.

'It's impossible,' said the albino. 'We could not get out of this tower, let alone across those crags. I wonder how they managed to move so quickly and so far. And where did the chariot itself come from?'

'Stolen, no doubt, from the demons,' said Werther. 'See, there are wings here.' He indicated a heap of feathers in the corner of the room. 'We can use those.'

'What wizardry is this?' said Elric. 'Man cannot fly on bird wings.'

'With the appropriate spell he can,' said Werther. 'I am not that well versed in the magic arts, of course, but let me see...' He picked up one set of wings. They were soft and glinted with subtle, rainbow colours. He placed them on Elric's back, murmuring his spell:

'Oh, for the wings, for the wings of a dove,
To carry me to the one I love...

'There!' He was very pleased with himself. Elric moved his shoulders and his wings began to flap. 'Excellent! Off you go, Elric. I'll join you in a moment.'

Elric hesitated, then saw the head of the first demon emerging from the hole in the floor. He jumped to the window ledge and leapt into space. The wings sustained him. Against all logic he flew smoothly towards the waiting chariot and behind him came Werther de Goethe. At the windows of the tower the demons crowded, shaking fists and weapons as their prey escaped them.

Elric landed rather awkwardly beside the chariot and was helped aboard by the Duke of Queens. Werther joined them, dropping expertly amongst them. He removed the wings from the albino's back and nodded to the Duke of Queens who yelled at the oxen, cracking his whip as they began to move.

Mistress Christia flung her arms about Elric's neck. 'What courage! What resourcefulness!' she breathed. 'Without you, I should now be ruined!'

Elric sheathed Stormbringer. 'We all three worked together for your rescue, madam.' Gently he removed her arms. Courteously he bowed and leaned against the far side of the chariot as it bumped and hurtled over the peculiar rocky surface.

'Swifter! Swifter!' called the Duke of Queens, casting urgent looks backwards. 'We are followed!'

From the disappearing tower there now poured a host of flying, gibbering things. Once again the creatures had changed shape and had assumed the form of striped, winged cats, all glaring eyes, fangs and extended claws.

The rock became viscous, clogging the wheels of the chariot, as they reached what appeared to be a silvery road, flowing between the high trees of an alien forest already touched by a weird twilight.

The first of the flying cats caught up with them, slashing.

Elric drew Stormbringer and cut back. The beast roared in pain, blood streaming from its severed leg, its wings flapping in Elric's face as it hovered and attempted to snap at the sword.

The chariot rolled faster, through the forest to green fields touched by the moon. The days were short, it seemed, in this part of Chaos. A path stretched skyward. The Duke of Queens drove the chariot straight up it, heading for the moon itself.

The moon grew larger and larger and still the demons pursued them, but they could not fly as fast as the chariot which went so swiftly that sorcery must surely speed it. Now they could only be heard in the darkness behind and the silver moon was huge.

'There!' called Werther. 'There is safety!'

On they raced until the moon was reached, the oxen leaping in their traces, galloping over the gleaming surface to where a white palace awaited them.

'Sanctuary,' said the Duke of Queens. And he laughed a wild, full laugh of sheer joy.

The palace was like ivory, carved and wrought by a million hands, every inch covered with delicate designs.

Elric wondered. 'Where is this place?' he asked. 'Does it lie outside the Realm of Chaos?'

Werther seemed nonplussed. 'You mean our world?'

'Aye.'

'It is still part of our world,' said the Duke of Queens.

'Is the palace to your liking?' asked Werther.

'It is lovely.'

'A trifle pale for my own taste,' said the Last Romantic. 'It was Mistress Christia's idea.'

'You built this?' The albino turned to the woman. 'When?'

'Just now.' She seemed surprised.

Elric nodded. 'Aha. It is within the power of Chaos to create whatever whims it pleases.'

The chariot crossed a white drawbridge and entered a white courtyard. In it grew white flowers. They dismounted and entered a huge hall, white as bone, in which red lights glowed. Again Elric began to suspect mockery, but the faces of the Chaos Lords showed only pleasure. He realised that he was dizzy with hunger and weariness, as he had been ever since he had been flung into this terrible world where no shape was constant, no idea permanent.

'Are you hungry?' asked Mistress Christia.

He nodded. And suddenly the room was filled by a long table on which all kinds of food were heaped – and everything, meats and fruits and vegetables, was white.

Elric moved to take the seat she indicated and he put some of the food on a silver plate and he touched it to his lips and he tasted it. It was delicious. Forgetting suspicion, he began to eat heartily, trying not to consider the colourless quality of the meal. Werther and the Duke of Queens also took some food, but it seemed they ate only from politeness. Werther glanced up at the faraway roof. 'What a wonderful tomb this would make,' he said. 'Your imagination improves, Mistress Christia.'

'Is this your domain?' asked Elric. 'The moon?'

'Oh no,' she said. 'It was all made for the occasion.'

'Occasion?'

'For your adventure,' she said. Then she fell silent.

Elric became grave. 'Those demons? They were not your enemies. They belong to you!'

'Belong?' said Mistress Christia. She shook her head.

Elric frowned and pushed back his plate. 'I am, however, most certainly your captive.' He stood up and paced the white floor. 'Will you not return me to my own plane?'

'You would come back almost immediately,' said Werther de Goethe. 'It is called the Morphail Effect. And if you did not come here, you would yet remain in your own future. It is in the nature of time.'

'This is nonsense,' said Elric. 'I have left my own realm before and returned – though admittedly memory becomes weak, as with dreams poorly recalled.'

'No man can go back in time,' said the Duke of Queens. 'Ask Brannart Morphail.'

'He, too, is a Lord of Chaos?'

'If you like. He is a colleague.'

'Could he not return me to my realm? He sounds a clever being.'

'He could not and he would not,' said Mistress Christia. 'Haven't you enjoyed your experiences here so far?'

'Enjoyed?' Elric was astonished. 'Madam, I think... Well, what has happened this day is not what we mortals would call "enjoyment"!'

'But you *seemed* to be enjoying yourself,' said the Duke of Queens in some disappointment. 'Didn't he, Werther?'

'You were much more cheerful through the whole episode,' agreed the Last Romantic. 'Particularly when you were fighting the demons.'

'As with many time-travellers who suffer from anxieties,' said

Mistress Christia, 'you appeared to relax when you had something immediate to capture your attention...'

Elric refused to listen. This was clever Chaos talk, meant to deceive him and take his mind from his chief concern.

'If I was any help to you,' he began, 'I am, of course...'

'He isn't very grateful,' Mistress Christia pouted.

Elric felt madness creeping nearer again. He calmed himself.

'I thank you for the food, madam. Now, I would sleep.'

'Sleep?' she was disconcerted. 'Oh! Of course. Yes. A bedroom?'

'If you have such a thing.'

'As many as you like.' She moved a stone on one of her rings. The walls seemed to draw back to show bedchamber after bedchamber, in all manner of styles, with beds of every shape and fashion. Elric controlled his temper. He bowed, thanked her, said good night to the two lords and made for the nearest bed.

As he closed the door behind him, he thought he heard Werther de Goethe say: 'We must try to think of a better entertainment for him when he wakes up.'

Chapter Eleven

In Which Mrs Persson Witnesses the First Sign of the Megaflow's Disintegration

In Castle Canaria Lord Jagged unrolled his antique charts. He had had them drawn for him by a baffled astrologer in 1950. They were one of his many affectations. At the moment, however, they were of considerably greater use than Alvarez's electronics.

While he used a wrist computer to check his figures, Una Persson looked out of the window of Castle Canaria and wondered who had invented this particular landscape. A green-and-orange sun cast sickening light over the herds of grazing beasts who resembled, from this distance at any rate, nothing so much as gigantic human hands. In the middle of the scene was raised some kind of building in the shape of a vast helmet, vaguely Greek in conception. Beyond that was a low, grey moon. She turned away.

'I must admit,' said Lord Jagged, 'that I had not understood the extent...'

'Exactly,' she said.

'You must forgive me. A certain amount of amnesia – euphoria, perhaps? – always comes over one in these very remote periods.'

'Quite.'

He looked up from the charts. 'We've a few hours at most.'

Her smile was thin, her nod barely perceptible.

While she made the most of having told him so, Lord Jagged frowned, turned a power ring and produced an already lit pipe which he placed thoughtfully in his mouth, taking it out again almost immediately. 'That wasn't Dunhill Standard Medium.' He laid the pipe aside.

There came a loud buzzing noise from the window. The scene

outside was disintegrating as if melting on glass. An eery golden light spread everywhere, flooding from an apex of deeper gold, as if forming a funnel.

'That's a rupture,' said Lord Jagged. His voice was tense. He put his arm about her shoulders. 'I've never seen anything of the size before.'

Rushing towards them along the funnel of light there came an entire city of turrets and towers and minarets in a wide variety of pastel colours. It was set into a saucer-shaped base which was almost certainly several miles in circumference.

For a moment the city seemed to retreat. The golden light faded. The city remained, some distance away, swaying a little as if on a gentle tide, a couple of thousand feet above the ground, the grey moon below it.

'That's what I call megaflow distortion,' said Una Persson in that inappropriately facetious tone adopted by those who are deeply frightened.

'I recognise the period.' Jagged drew a telescope from his robes. 'Second Candlemaker's Empire, mainly based in Arcturus. This is a village by their standards. After all, Earth was merely a rural park during that time.' He retreated into academe, his own response to fear.

Una craned her head. 'Isn't that some sort of vehicle heading towards the city. From the moon – good heavens, they've spotted it already. Are they going to try to put the whole thing into a menagerie?'

Jagged had the advantage of the telescope. 'I think not.' He handed her the instrument.

Through it she saw a scarlet-and-black chariot borne by what seemed to be some form of flying fairground horses. In the chariot, armed to the teeth with lances, bows, spears, swords, axes, morningstars, maces and almost every other barbaric hand-weapon, clad in quasi-mythological armour, were Werther de Goethe, the Duke of Queens and Elric of Melniboné.

'They're attacking it!' she said faintly. 'What will happen when the two groups intersect?'

'Three groups,' he pointed out. 'Untangling that in a few hours is going to be even harder.'

'And if we fail?'

He shrugged. 'We might just as well give ourselves up to the biggest chronoquake the universe has ever experienced.'

'You're exaggerating,' she said.

'Why not? Everyone else is.'

Chapter Twelve
The Attack on the Citadel of the Skies

'MELNIBONÉ! MELNIBONÉ!' CRIED the albino as the chariot circled over the spires and turrets of the city. They saw startled faces below. Strange engines were being dragged through the narrow streets.

'Surrender!' Elric demanded.

'I do not think they can understand us,' said the Duke of Queens. 'What a find, eh? A whole city from the past!'

Werther had been reluctant to embark on an adventure not of his own creation, but Elric, realising that here at last was a chance of escape, had been anxious to begin. The Duke of Queens had, in an instant, aided the albino by producing costumes, weapons, transport. Within minutes of the city's appearance, they had been on their way.

Exactly why Elric wished to attack the city, Werther could not make out, unless it was some test of the Melnibonéan's to see if his companions were true allies or merely pretending to have befriended him. Werther was learning a great deal from Elric, much more than he had ever learned from Mongrove, whose ideas of angst were only marginally less notional than Werther's own.

A broad, flat blue ray beamed from the city. It singed one wheel of the chariot.

'Ha! They make sorcerous weapons,' said Elric. 'Well, my friends. Let us see you counter with your own power.'

Werther obediently imitated the blue ray and sent it back from his fingers, slicing the tops off several towers. The Duke of Queens typically let loose a different coloured ray from each of his extended ten fingers and bored a hole all the way through the bottom of the city so that fields could be seen below. He was pleased with the effect.

'This is the power of the Gods of Chaos!' cried Elric, a familiar elation filling him as the blood of old Melniboné was fired. 'Surrender!'

'Why do you want them to surrender?' asked the Duke of Queens in some disappointment.

'Their city evidently has the power to fly through the dimensions. If I became its lord I could force it to return to my own plane,' said Elric reasonably.

'The Morphail Effect...' began Werther, but realised he was spoiling the spirit of the game. 'Sorry.'

The blue ray came again, but puttered out and faded before it reached them.

'Their power is gone!' cried Elric. 'Your sorcery defeats them, my lords. Let us land and demand they honour us as their new rulers.'

With a sigh, Werther ordered the chariot to set down in the largest square. Here they waited until a few of the citizens began to arrive, cautious and angry, but evidently in no mood to give any further resistance.

Elric addressed them. 'It was necessary to attack and conquer you, for I must return to my own realm, there to fulfil my great destiny. If you will take me to Melniboné, I will demand nothing further from you.'

'One of us really ought to take a translation pill,' said Werther. 'These people probably have no idea where they are.'

A meaningless babble came from the citizens. Elric frowned. 'They understand not the High Speech,' he said. 'I will try the common tongue.' He spoke in a language neither Werther, the Duke of Queens nor the citizens of this settlement could understand.

He began to show signs of frustration. He drew his sword Stormbringer. 'By the Black Sword, know that I am Elric, last of the royal line of Melniboné! You must obey me. Is there none here who understands the High Speech?'

Then, from the crowd, stepped a being far taller than the others. He was dressed in robes of dark blue and deepest scarlet and his face was haughty, beautiful and full of evil.

'I speak the High Tongue,' he said.

Werther and the Duke of Queens were nonplussed. This was no-one they recognised.

Elric gestured. 'You are the ruler of the city?'

'Call me that, if you will.'

'Your name?'

'I am known by many names. And you know me, Elric of Melniboné, for I am your lord and your friend.'

'Ah,' said Elric lowering his sword, 'this is the greatest deception of them all. I am a fool.'

'Merely a mortal,' said the newcomer, his voice soft, amused and full of a subtle arrogance. 'Are these the renegades who helped you?'

'Renegades?' said Werther. 'Who are you, sir?'

'You should know me, rogue lords. You aid a mortal and defy your brothers of Chaos.'

'Eh?' said the Duke of Queens. 'I haven't got a brother.'

The stranger ignored him. 'Demigods who thought that by helping this mortal they could threaten the power of the Greater Ones.'

'So you did aid me against your own,' said Elric. 'Oh, my friends!'

'And they shall be punished!'

Werther began: 'We regret any damage to your city. After all, you were not invited…'

The Duke of Queens was laughing. 'Who are you? What disguise is this?'

'Know me for your master.' The eyes of the stranger glowed with myriad fires. 'Know me for Arioch, Duke of Hell!'

'Arioch!' Elric became filled with a strange joy. 'Arioch! I called upon thee and was not answered!'

'I was not in this realm,' said the Duke of Hell. 'I was forced to be absent. And while I was gone, fools thought to displace me.'

'I really cannot follow all this,' said the Duke of Queens. He set aside his mace. 'I must confess I become a trifle bored, sir. If you will excuse me.'

'You will not escape me.' Arioch lifted a languid hand and the Duke of Queens was frozen to the ground, unable to move anything save his eyes.

'You are interfering, sir, with a perfectly –' Werther too was struck dumb and paralysed.

But Elric refused to quail. 'Lord Arioch, I have given you blood and souls. You owe me…'

'I owe you nothing, Elric of Melniboné. Nothing I do not choose to owe. You are my slave…'

'No,' said Elric. 'I serve you. There are old bonds. But you cannot control me, Lord Arioch, for I have a power within me which you fear. It is the power of my very mortality.'

The Duke of Hell shrugged. 'You will remain in the Realm of Chaos for ever. Your mortality will avail you little here.'

'You need me in my own realm, to be your agent. That, too, I know, Lord Arioch.'

The handsome head lowered a fraction as if Arioch considered this. The beautiful lips smiled. 'Aye, Elric. It is true that I need you to do my work. For the moment it is impossible for the Lords of Chaos to interfere directly in the world of mortals, for we should threaten our own existence. The rate of entropy would increase beyond even our control. The day has not yet come when Law and Chaos must decide the issue once and for all. But it will come soon enough for you, Elric.'

'And my sword will be at your service, Lord Arioch.'

'Will it, Elric?'

Elric was surprised by this doubting tone. He had always served Chaos, as his ancestors had. 'Why should I turn against you? Law has no attractions for one such as Elric of Melniboné.'

The Duke of Hell was silent.

'And there is the bargain,' added Elric. 'Return me to my own realm, Lord Arioch, so that I might keep it.'

Arioch sighed. 'I am reluctant.'

'I demand it,' bravely said the albino.

'Oho!' Arioch was amused. 'Well, mortal, I'll reward your courage and I'll punish your insolence. The reward will be that you are returned whence you came, before you called on Chaos in your battle with that pathetic wizard. The punishment is that you will recall every incident that occurred since then – but only in your dreams. You will be haunted by the puzzle for the rest of your life – and you will never for a moment be able to express what mystifies you.'

Elric smiled. 'I am already haunted by a curse of that kind, my lord.'

'Be that as it may, I have made my decision.

'I accept it,' said the albino, and he sheathed his sword, Stormbringer.

'Then come with me,' said Arioch, Duke of Hell. And he drifted forward, took Elric by the arm, and lifted them both high into the sky, floating over distorted scenes, half-formed dreamworlds, the whims of the Lords of Chaos, until they came to a gigantic rock shaped like a skull. And through one of the eye-sockets Lord Arioch bore Elric of Melniboné. And down strange corridors that whispered and displayed all manner of treasures. And up into a landscape, a desert in which grew many strange plants, while overhead could be seen a land of snow and mountains, equally alien. And from his robes Arioch, Duke of Hell, produced a wand and he bade Elric to take hold of the wand, which was hot to the touch and glittered, and he placed his own slender hand at the other end, and he murmured words which Elric could not understand and together they began to fade from the landscape, into the darkness of limbo where many eyes accused them, to an island in a grey and storm-tossed sea; an island littered with destruction and with the dead.

Then Arioch, Duke of Hell, laughed a little and vanished, leaving the Prince of Melniboné sprawled amongst corpses and ruins while heavy rain beat down upon him.

And in the scabbard at Elric's side, Stormbringer stirred and murmured once more.'

Chapter Thirteen
In Which There is a Small Celebration at the End of Time

WERTHER DE GOETHE and the Duke of Queens blinked their eyes and found that they could move their heads. They stood in a large, pleasant room full of charts and ancient instruments. Mistress Christia was there, too.

Una Persson was smiling as she watched golden light fade from the sky. The city had disappeared, hardly any the worse for its existence. She had managed to save the two friends without a great deal of fuss, for the citizens had still been bewildered by what had happened to them. Because of the megaflow distortion, the Morphail Effect would not manifest itself. They would never understand where they had been or what had actually happened.

'Who on earth was that fellow who turned up?' asked the Duke of Queens. 'Some friend of yours, Mrs Persson? He's certainly no sportsman.'

'Oh, I wouldn't agree. You could call him the ultimate sportsman,' she said. 'I am acquainted with him, as a matter of fact.'

'It's not Jagged in disguise, is it?' said Mistress Christia who did not really know what had gone on. 'This is Jagged's castle – but where is Jagged?'

'You are aware how mysterious he is,' Una answered. 'I happened to be here when I saw that Werther and the Duke were in trouble in the city and was able to be of help.'

Werther scowled (a very good copy of Elric's own scowl). 'Well, it isn't good enough.'

'It was a jolly adventure while it lasted, you must admit,' said the Duke of Queens.

'It wasn't meant to be jolly,' said Werther. 'It was meant to be significant.'

Lord Jagged entered the room. He wore his familiar yellow robes. 'How pleasant,' he said. 'When did all of you arrive?'

'I have been here for some time,' Mrs Persson explained, 'but Werther and the Duke of Queens…'

'Just got here,' explained the Duke. 'I hope we're not intruding. Only we had a slight mishap and Mrs Persson was good enough…'

'Always delighted,' said the insincere lord. 'Would you care to see my new –'

'I'm on my way home,' said the Duke of Queens. 'I just stopped by. Mrs Persson will explain.'

'I, too,' said Werther suspiciously, 'am on my way back.'

'Very well. Goodbye.'

Werther summoned an air car, a restrained figure of death, in rags with a sickle, who picked the three up in his hand and bore them towards a bleak horizon.

It was only days later, when he went to visit Mongrove to tell him of his adventures and solicit his friend's advice, that Werther realised he was still speaking High Melnibonéan. Some nagging thought remained with him for a long while after that. It concerned Lord Jagged, but he could not quite work out what was involved.

After this incident there were no further disruptions at the End of Time until the conclusion of the story concerning Jherek Carnelian and Mrs Amelia Underwood.

Chapter Fourteen

In Which Elric of Melniboné Recovers from a Variety of Enchantments and Becomes Determined to Return to the Dreaming City

ELRIC WAS AWAKENED by the rain on his face. Wearily he peered around him. To left and right there were only the dismembered corpses of the dead, the Krettii and the Filkharian sailors destroyed during his battle with the half-brute who had somehow gained so much sorcerous power. He shook his milk-white hair and he raised crimson eyes to the grey, boiling sky.

It seemed that Arioch had aided him, after all. The sorcerer was destroyed and he, Elric, remained alive. He recalled the sweet, bantering tones of his patron demon. Familiar tones, yet he could not remember what the words had been.

He dragged himself over the dead and waded through the shallows towards the Filkharian ship which still had some of its crew. They were, by now, anxious to head out into open sea again rather than face any more terrors on Sorcerers' Isle.

He determined to see Cymoril, whom he loved, to regain his throne from Yyrkoon, his cousin…

Chapter Fifteen

In Which a Brief Reunion Takes Place at the Time Centre

WITH THE MANUSCRIPT of Colonel Pyat's rather dangerous volume of memoirs safely back in her briefcase, Una Persson decided it was the right moment to check into the Time Centre. Alvarez should be on duty again and his instruments should be registering any minor imbalances resulting from the episode concerning the gloomy albino.

Alvarez was not alone. Lord Jagged was there, in a disreputable Norfolk jacket and smoking a battered briar. He had evidently been holidaying in Victorian England. He was pleased to see her.

Alvarez ran his gear through all functions. 'Sweet and neat,' he said. 'It hasn't been as good since I don't know when. We've you to thank for that, Mrs P.'

She was modest.

'Certainly not. Jagged was the one. Your disguise was wonderful, Jagged. How did you manage to imitate that character so thoroughly? It convinced Elric. He really thought you were whatever it was – a Chaos Duke?'

Jagged waved a modest hand.

'I mean,' said Una, 'it's almost as if you *were* this fellow "Arioch"...'

But Lord Jagged only puffed on his pipe and smiled a secret and superior smile.

Sumptuous Dress

A Question of Size at the End of Time

LEGEND THE SIXTH

Then like a python's sumptuous dress
The frame of things is cast away,
And out of Time's obscure distress,
The thundering scherzo crashes Day.

– John Davidson,
A Ballad of Heaven

Prologue

I HAVE ALREADY informed the reader how, at the instigation of HM Government, a decision was made to send a third expedition to Mars, on suspicion that the Franco-Arabian alliance (the 'AFA') had mounted a secret flight of its own. Christened His Majesty's Interplanetary Ship *Queen Elizabeth the Navigator*, our aerial frigate was the first to carry arms. Our orders were to look for signs of our earlier expeditions, which had both disappeared; we should seek evidence of the AFA ship *Leo Africanus*, take photographs, map the planet in so far that were possible, and continue to do the work originally assigned to HMIS *Golden Hinde* in 2001 and HMIS *Erasmus Darling* in 2019.

The *Queen Elizabeth the Navigator* was a superb ship of the very latest type. An up-to-date aerial vessel, she was, thanks to new methods of stabilising Edisonite, as capable of exploring the vast seas of interplanetary space as she was of negotiating the clouds of her native world. Driven by the very latest steam turbines, her fully rotating propeller nacelles made her capable of considerable manoeuvrability and enormous speeds through the atmosphere, while the Edisonite powered her across the void. A solid brass-bound oaken hull enclosed gasbags filled with super-distilled safety-helium capable of unprecedented lift. The hull also enclosed the large gondola. We planned to establish an anchorage in the Mare Pius X and assemble a great semaphore mirror, to signal immediately back to Earth. Powerful telescopes were trained to detect our message and elsewhere massive radio apparatus stood by to begin communication between Earth and Mars when conditions were favourable.

Our expedition was headed by Air-General Sir Ralph de Courcy, AVC, already the hero of several earlier adventures and the first man on the Moon. Captain of the ship was Mustapha Khan and I was his first officer. My name is ALt Jack Chance. My father was Captain John Chance of the *Golden Hinde*. I had promised my mother, still harassed by cruel creditors, grasping relatives and malicious gossip concerning my father's honour, to find him and, if he lived, return him to her side. To myself, I swore to clear his name or die in the attempt.

Leaving the Earth's atmosphere, we set off through space at an impressive rate, narrowly avoiding a vast meteor swarm which almost destroyed us. After several other hair-raising adventures, we approached the Red Planet's surface. All went relatively uneventfully until we were sailing towards our agreed destination, testing the atmosphere to discover when we could switch to our turbines. Slowly in descending orbit to the planet's surface, our instruments at first suggested we were safe to switch, but suddenly registered opposite readings, warning us urgently to maintain our Edisonite engine. The gauges became hopelessly erratic. Then, as we drifted helplessly over the planet's South Pole, our steering mechanisms refused to respond, yet the ship began to move very rapidly downwards until it seemed we must crash into the strangely smoking ice-field (proof that Mars had once, at least, supported carbon-based life).

Suddenly, to our astonishment, the erratically veering ship was dragged deep through the ice and our turbines came to life again just as we were about to crash into what appeared to be a bright blue ocean below. This ocean teemed with life! But it was life resembling that of our own Age of Dinosaurs. Then our instruments became erratic again. Even our compass became incoherent. As we were carried helplessly onward, our V-screens intermittently revealed nightmarish flying reptiles in the sky and, to our further astonishment, lush jungle below! The most unusual quality of this bizarre flora was its colour. Everything was a shade of blue!

As we were debating this fresh phenomenon, our ship was drawn downwards to what must surely be collision with dense jungle. It became clear to all of us what had befallen previous expeditions. Soon, it would surely be our fate to be similarly trapped, doomed never to leave the bowels of this alien world. As soon as we could land and tether our ship, we mounted an expedition, discovering to our astonishment that the 'prehistoric monsters' were less than two thirds of the size they had been on Earth and that the local Tyrannosaurus Rex, for instance, barely reached to the shoulder of a man of average height. This still made them terrifying adversaries, but possible to bring down with a good-sized hunting gun. When we eventually found the survivors of earlier expeditions, they were dressed like old-time frontiersmen in the skins of local beasts, a kind of rough-and-ready uniform, and my heart surged with pride when they announced themselves as 'Chance's Martian Foresters'. They were disciplined explorers and hunters and, of course, had been formed by my father when it became clear that they had no chance of escaping the blue innards of the red planet. They had seen the *Leo Africanus*, somewhere near the Martian equator, and had been in contact with both previous expeditions, though the *Darling* had experienced serious injury in an attempt to find the South Pole and break out through the thin covering of ice there. The remains of her crew, together with what could be saved of the ship, all occupied 'Fort Chance', named for my father, who was still alive, the hero and leader of the British settlement. They still sought ways of escaping the blue world and at least getting a message home. In this, they were somewhat hampered by the local humanoids, blue people whose menfolk were about the size of an eight-year-old boy and whose women were a little smaller. It was originally to deal with these that the Martian Foresters had been formed. There was also some talk of a theoretical means of travelling through 'the dimensions' and possibly getting back to Earth in that way. Scientists, who had travelled aboard both of our earlier ships, believed they knew a way of creating what they called a Martian Scaling Station, but most of us were sceptical. Our main efforts were spent on working out a way to reach the surface and use our existing communication tools to contact the Earth.

Now read on:

Chapter One
A Social Contretemps Possibly in the First Ether

THE BRONZE DAHLIA was not herself. Of late, she had very rarely been herself, but today she was unusually at odds with the kind of persona she generally favoured. She stared pensively into the bottomless depths of Faustus von Austus's 'Grand Campion Sweet', a vast red-and-white hard pimpernel at present being licked almost to transparency by some exceptionally large water bison which, Faustus had assured everyone, were native to the original region. How he had managed to keep the water suspended in those shapes was his own secret. But even this mystery failed to engage her keen intellect. She pondered the wisdom of arriving as the infamous Spinning Jenny. The rapid revolutions were making her a little ill and it was hard to concentrate.

'*Kroofrudi.*'

The Bronze Dahlia was surprised to discover she was not alone. However, it was a relief to stop spinning. She adjusted her appearance. Now none would fail to recognise her. Looking down, she raised a perfect eyebrow to quiz the little alien who leered back up at her. He was short, ugly and his turnip-shaped head revealed three pupils in a single socket.

She raised a second eyebrow. 'Are you part of Faustus's installation?' she wanted to know. 'Because, if so, I fail to see…'

'Mibix?' enquired the alien. There was something lascivious about this question.

If she had not been so tired from twirling, the Bronze Dahlia might have found it in herself to raise a third eyebrow. As it was, she had to rely on raising the two she habitually wore.

'How do you do?' She wondered from whose menagerie this dwarfish space-lecher had escaped.

'Ferkit?' he opined suggestively. In their socket his three orbs focused on her admittedly elegant elbows.

With a certain reluctance the Bronze Dahlia manipulated a translation ring.

'Can I help you?'

'Any time you like, you delicious little slut,' panted the pint-sized interplanetary Punch. 'Flash those elbows at me again and I don't need telling twice when the traffic lights are ultramarine.' He placed a happy hand on her bewildered bottom.

At that moment, arriving to cast his melancholy eye on his monstrous confection, Faustus von Austus stepped with a gusty sigh from his black coffin-shaped air car.

'Ah, fabulous Faustus! How pleasant to view your vivid vanities! I was admiring the magnificence of your comely comestibles, your craggy candy.' She looked about her. 'But your prospectus promised a setting sun.'

His second sigh was of exceptional enormity. 'I gather it has refused to set, most ironic of non-ferrous flowers. I fear it retains an unsolvable wobble. I am considering terminating myself and my monstrous creation in one quintessential conflagration.'

The alien coughed discreetly. 'What flavour is it?' he enquired roughly.

'*Eh?*'

'This jelly you're on about. I don't want to be boring and all scientific, but I – that is, I was once – I happened to be talking to a fellow who was cook aboard the old *Crossed Ankles*, yeah?' The alien clearly expected them to know the name, but swiftly absorbed their blank expressions. 'Anyway, he'd been here once in the old days, looking for recipes. That's how our scientists discovered that pineapple and jelly won't mix. Won't set. Something to do with the chemical make-up of the fruit and the gelatine. Gone a bit quiet. Am I butting in on something?' He shared a significant leer between the two of them.

The Bronze Dahlia responded icily. 'Where is your base? We must get you there as soon as possible. You are probably already missed.'

'Let's hope not. I came off the *Wrong Way Home* a couple of gurks ago, the captive of trans-dimensional kidnappers or slavers or something, and thought while I had the chance that I'd seek political asylum. I'm from Lat. Heard of it?'

'I fear –'

'Wouldn't expect you to have. But, believe me, you'd grant me instant asylum if you had. It's not just the scummiest planet in our system, it's also the ugliest. I'm one of the most beautiful things on it. Or, I should say, from it!'

Faustus scratched his huge head. 'You're not a time-traveller, then?'

'Possibly.'

'You're not sure?'

'Well, see, when it comes to trans-dimensional travel…'

The Bronze Dahlia interposed. 'It strikes me, sir, that you would know if you were from the distant past.' She frowned prettily. 'Perhaps, if we were to be introduced, some clue might come to us…? I,' she cleared her throat, then frowned again. 'I am the Brass – no Bronze – Dahlia. And this is –?' Again she had a moment's pause. 'This is Faustus von Austus, our Great and Glorious Dictator of Doom. And you are –?'

'Oh, you can call me Captain Kippers. Although…' His speech petered out. 'Well, I'm from space, see…?'

'How did you come to this world? There are so few people left out there, these days. This being, as you doubtless know, the End of Time.'

'This world –' He paused. 'Well, it's all wrong, see? By rights it should have crumbled to cinders aeons ago. Like that planet next to you.'

'The one we turned to caramel and chocolate?' Faustus brightened.

The Lat shook his hideous head. 'I think it's turned back again. We landed on it first. It's mostly red dust now. As artificially maintained as this one in its way. Our instruments went nuts. We were looking for a way into the Second Ether, see…?'

'The what?' asked Faustus, engaged at last. Like most inhabitants of the End of Time, he was forever seeking novelty. 'Do what?'

'The Second Ether. We're now in what the old guys called the First. The Archetype. Judging by its age –' He became embarrassed.

'Well, this comes as a shock if you're not prepared. Theoretically, there's a Third, Fourth and so on Ethers. Nobody has any idea how many and it's hard enough moving between ours – this one – and the other – the Second. It's all to do with the multiverse. And cats, of course. Then there's the Martian Scaling Station. Our cap – that is, we – we were looking for a way through to something – I don't know, more familiar… Then we bumped into this band of loonies – ever heard of the Chaos Engineers?'

But he had lost them. They were fiddling with their translator rings, convinced there was something wrong.

Chapter Two
Crisis in the Second Ether

CAPTAIN BILLY-BOB BEGG curled a coruscating quasi-tentacle around her omniphone and stepped desperately on the General Call pedal. 'Prof? Any luck?' There was little chance of the wire being intercepted anywhere outside the Second Ether, still controlled by the famous Chaos Engineers. 'Prof? We're running out of all the time there is! We're parked off Ketchup Cove and absorbing more scarlet than is good for us. We're expecting the Straight Arrows to break through at any minute. Apart from our emergency magazine, all we have left in the tubes are three Kid Ory records, some early Billy Joel, a few flashy Nigel Kennedy Elgar sides and some '80s sixties covers. Hardly enough to stop them. They're massing at the Martian Scaling Station and it's pi to a hotpot they'll be through come Candlemass and gobbling up our resources like Eccles cakes – as they've gobbled their own! Prof, do you hear me? What's happened to that back-up you thought Captain Otherly had found?'

'Gone, both of 'em.' The voice of the hirsute genius was a distant, baffled crackle. 'The storm threw Otherly off course the moment he found the Scaling Station and there's no telling where they've gone.'

'Can't you track 'em, Prof?'

'What? Into the First Ether? I couldn't do it without some coordinates and there's not a whisper, not a brack. The only thing I could do is to bust through into the First Ether myself and look for them somehow...'

Silence from Professor Pop.

'He claimed he carried our only chance of survival!'

'True.'

The faintest hum and whistle sounded through the receptors and Captain Begg switched her amplifiers to max, for she had recognised the signal as her old lover's. 'Is that you, Buggerly?'

'Can you hear me?' came the captain's faraway tones. 'Is anyone out there?'

'It's Buggerly! Beloved!' She gasped and recovered herself. 'And lost, by the sound of it. Buggerly, my beauty! Did you get the ordnance we mentioned? State your position and name your course, if you can. Don't worry. Old Reg can't pick us up this far out.'

'I won't say that's still true.' The Yorkshireman's vibrant brogue broke over the 'phone. For I'm somewhere in t' First Ether with half a score of super-tempered Straight Arrow ships on me tail. Not much longer before they make a breakthrough – and then we're all plucked, gutted and oven-ready, if you catch my drift. Well, any road, I snared the answer to our predicament. Or thought I had. I ran across some of those brigand-musicians we'd heard about, right? Rather than tons of heavy records, I reckoned all we needed was a few of these Lat blokes.'

'They were still in the First Ether, then?'

'Trying to find a way through to t' Second. "I'm t' very lad to help thee", I told 'em. Stupidest bloody decision I ever made. All they'd let me have was one bloke. And I had to pay through t' nose for him. They didn't trust me. Once I'd told them how Old Reg had enclosed the First Ether within a massive buckyball, they reckoned they could follow me through, via t' Scaling Station. Turned out nobody could find a way. So I'm buzzing around like a pricked balloon. What's more, I've lost the musician, all the shells I was going to buy records with, *and* I'm hanging off a husk of a planet that looks bleak as a Dent weaver's dinner. That is to say,' at her puzzled silence, 'not a scrap of meat nor vegetation to be seen. Or so me instruments tell me. Yet the weird thing is I'm being informed by me own senses that it's lush and rich and crammed to t' core with life. Ever come across that, B-B, me dear?'

She took a ten-fingered appendage to her glorious skull and drummed on it in surprise. 'Only legendary Earth, the so-called Syren Planet. Well, you must do your best, sweet Buggerly. You are our hope of salvation. Not for the first time, I should add. Though in the past there has been a little more leeway. Now it's a matter of minutes before we're sucked into their filthy vacuum and become manure for their massive egos. For fear of repeating myself, we're in a spot tighter than a stockbroker's rectum. Can you hear the sound of those soupy strings?'

'That's Old Reg and his ships warming us up for a blast of Sullivan *sans* Gilbert. "Lost Chord" by t'opening bars and that means no quarter.'

'Greed personified,' confirmed Billy-Bob. 'You can't mistake those fiddles.' She shuddered. 'What's your plan?'

'Hardly a plan,' responded the bluff skipper of the skies, 'more like a desperate tic. I picked up some sort of virus coming through t' Martian Scaling Station and caught me Lat sooner than I thought. Then, when I tried to come out t' same way, I couldn't do it. Lost me Lat, too. Now we're all trapped in t' First Ether with no collateral and no bloody musician. He gave us the slip over this waste-heap. I shall have to make planetfall and hope I can find our nasty little Last Chance down there somewhere. All logic is against it, but I'm going to take *The Mandelbrot Anomaly* onto her surface and do an old-fashioned visual scan. Don't laugh, pards. I know you're all listening in. If anyone has a better idea, let me know!'

In response there came only the whispering of a quasi-infinite multiverse.

Then Billy-Bob Begg sighed her assent.

Buggerly Otherly twisted a knot on his keyboard. 'Right we are, Our Gretchen,' he addressed his loyal first mate, 'get her ready for physical flat-landing. We're going to do one.'

With astonished terror in her lovely eyes, Our Gretchen flipped a thousand toggles and steadied the old girl for the slow go down.

'And here we are.'

Chapter Three
A Bit of a Scuffle at the End of Time

'SEE, WE WERE looking for the mysterious second universe and this Captain Otherly he was actually *from* the second universe. So at last we were on our way. And in time to help save our new host. That's when we realised he needed us more than we needed him and Captain Rubbers decided to ask for cash on top of the booking.' The Lat's translation pill, slipped to him by Faustus von Austus, was working if anything too well. He took a breath and almost continued:

'Cash?' The Bronze Dahlia drew her beautiful brows together. 'The name's familiar, but...'

'Dosh. Mazoolah. He told them nothing was doing under fifty billion.'

'Fifty billion singers?' Recalling where she had heard the name.

'Smackers.'

'*Really*?' Faustus von Austus showed renewed interest. 'And this Otherly was one of the smackers. What did he say?'

Now the Lat looked puzzled. 'Um, well, he said we'd have to wait till the banks opened.'

'So you waited?'

'For a while. By the fifth day we suspected the whole thing was a scam. We were on the point of leaving when Otherly throws some sort of hallucinogenic grenade. When I came out of that bit of gaga gas, there was only me. I was in a sack, and no shipmates evident. Shanghaied!'

'You were in this second universe?' The Bronze Dahlia wondered vaguely what he tasted like.

'I thought I was. When I realised I'd been drugged and that nobody else was with me, I got out of the sack while he was concentrating on his controls. Funny sort of ship. I found some sort of safety raft. It took nothing to work out the controls and I was out of that gibbering weird ship in an instant.'

'When did you realise you were still in the First Ether?' This was a fresh voice at their conference. The Lat turned and saw two more of the tall humans. One was male, with a long, rather amused face while the other was female and pinkly sexy almost in direct contrast to her companion's aloof allure. 'Forgive me. I noted we had a visitor and couldn't resist… I am Lord Jagged of Canaria and this is my friend Tootie Frootie Fun-Fun.' She simpered beneath her strawberry blonde do and rustled her pleated silks. She had broken off a piece of unlicked Grand Canyon and sucked it prettily. 'So pleased to meet you.' She checked out the Lat. 'Aren't you cute?'

'Hold that thought,' declared the little monster, rubbing his elbow significantly. 'Pretty much immediately,' he told Jagged. 'When I hit the roof!'

'The roof?' Lord Jagged frowned.

'Yeah, the buckyball they put around this universe. You can't get out without knowing more than I do. That's when I wished I'd stayed with the kidnapper. I took the only course possible. I went to sleep. And woke up surrounded by –' He waved a stubby hand. 'Tasty. I always knew places like this existed.'

'Like what?' suavely enquired Jagged.

'A candy planet. It's in our scriptures. We thought it a myth. I wish the rest of the lads were here.'

'So do I,' confirmed Tootie Frootie Fun-Fun eagerly. 'Where do you suppose they've got to?'

'Possibly over there.' Lord Jagged waved a handsome hand. They all turned to look. Some distance off, shimmering blue, they saw a rather lush stretch of jungle.

'Who on Earth made that?' enquired Faustus von Austus a little jealously. 'Can't they see how it clashes with my candy?'

'Blimey!' exclaimed the brigand-musician. 'We're back in Mars! Whoopee. The others have got to be here somewhere!

'Mars! Mars!' And with another joyous yelp, Captain Kippers dashed into the bright blue jungle and disappeared.

'After 'im, thou daft buggers!' came a voice from behind.

Standing beside a rather strange artefact which seemed constantly to be changing shape, hue and size, a large, red-faced man with aggressive muttonchops pointed in the direction of the fleeing Lat. 'That were supposed to attract his curiosity, not offer him a bloody hiding place.'

'You must be Captain Otherly.' Extending a hospitable hand, Lord Jagged stepped forward to greet the newcomer. 'Still adrift in the wrong Ether, I see.'

Chapter Four
Getting a Bit Desperate in the Second Ether

'BILLY-BOB TO POP. Billy-Bob to Pop. Are you out there, Prof? Things are getting sticky at this end of the Original Insect. We've lost our beloved Otherly. He's not responding to any omniphone signals. Meanwhile, that wicked Old Reg, Mrs Old Reg and General Freddy Force are packing the space-waves with every kind of poison. We barely resisted some synthetic Salieri by breaking out virtually every emergency Stevie Ray Vaughan we had. But if they bring up anything like that again, we're pretty surely done for. We can hit them with that Decembrist file, but it's probably corrupted. They'll be in through one of their fissures and gobbling up what's left of our energy before we can say "We'll always have Paris". Is it goodbye to all that? Answer me, Pop, darling, or fold into yourself for ever. We've run out of time at last.'

'Come in, Billy-Bob, pet. The prof's here, but nothing's looking too good from where I'm sitting at my omniview. The buckyball's likely to be torn apart by some frightening activity. A massing of buck-folded supercarbon hulls growling with the most vicious kinds of linear logic. If they come through, we're decidedly done for. You can kiss the First Ether goodbye once they're out. They'll leave nothing behind except a massive hole – and we'll be the ones to fill it!'

'Anything we can do, Prof?' There was controlled fear in her voice. She had always known this was the threat. Having consumed most of one universe, Old Reg and his people now cast their greedy gaze on a second.

'We need something funky to stop them.' Professor Pop combed his white whiskers with a lively pink hand. 'And we thought Buggerly had found that. Now all I can hope to do is use my Speedshell to slip down some fissure of their own creation and hope to get into the First Ether and out with whatever sounds might save us.'

'A chancy one,' murmured Little Rupoldo, not without a tinge of terror. 'Those cracks are hard to track and harder to negotiate, even in a Speedshell. It's like firing a Winchester into soft toffee. But if it has to be done, we have the experience to do it.'

'No telling whether we'll find Otherly or his catch, assuming he's recaptured it.'

'Ouch,' announced the chief Chaos Engineer. 'Hear that, Prof? They've found another battery of '80s Broadway bombs. Every corrupted chord sequence known to musical wisdom is packed into those folded carbon calliopes and not a note without our names on it. Are we completely out of Sondheim? By the time they spring an entire score of *Jesus Christ Superstar* and another of *Joseph and the Amazing Technicolor Dreamcoat* on us, we might as well be eating ether. We're scuppered. Find Buggery Otherly, Prof, or this will be the last time we ever whistle "Dixie".'

'Going in, boss,' gritted the grizzled veteran of a thousand psychic wars. 'Give me whatever Kingsize Taylor you can spare for cover.'

And with a murmured word to his own Little Rupoldo to strip every control to basic mode, the intrepid Sage of the Second Ether drew on his orchestral gauntlets and stepped coolly into the cockpit of the throbbing Speedshell.

Chapter Five
Blues for the End of Time

As Buggerly Otherly and the inhabitants of the End of Time raced in pursuit of the escaping Lat into the garish blue jungle, only Lord Jagged hung back. Captain Otherly had paused for scarcely a second after he had leapt from his ship and gone after the Lat. Thoughtfully, Jagged fingered his remarkable features and gave his attention to the general situation. Then he strolled over to *The Mandelbrot Anomaly* and knocked politely on what he assumed to be the hatch.

Meanwhile, the others had reached the jungle. Captain Otherly paused in the first clearing while they caught him up. 'I suspect it's in our common interest to fan out and try to get him in a sweep,' he suggested. 'It's only a relatively small spinney, after all.'

'Where did it come from?' Faustus von Austus wanted to know. 'It's awfully well thought out.'

Otherly rubbed a grizzled chin. 'I had a few seeds,' he said, 'I'd planned to plant outside my little place in Blueberry Bay. But I can't see how anyone got hold of *them*. It is authentic, isn't it? Could be the original.'

'Original what, darling?' asked Tootie Frootie Fun-Fun, wide-eyed.

'Martian Forest,' said the captain. 'We all know the tale of how they were forced to exist in the bowels of Mars until their scientists at last discovered the nature of Chaos Engineering. A means of shifting up and down the multiversal plates. It's they who first discovered that space is a dimension of time. It's where they hid the first Scaling Station. Who knows? Maybe it's still there and our little Lat's instinctively heading for it. Who could have brought it here? I don't think it was me.'

'There!' cried the Bronze Dahlia. 'That's him, isn't it?' A glimpse of a turnip head with one eye-socket and three pupils. They all saw it through the undergrowth. 'Is he lost, too?'

'Let's hope not. He could lead us to salvation. Of sorts,' added Buggerly Otherly, again running after his escaped prey. 'Hey, sir! There's a big bag of clam shells over here for you!' he called. But there was no response. Then:

'Uurk! Ferkit! Mibix hawkquards!'

Panting, Faustus von Austus emerged from a clump of indigo bushes. He held a wriggling Lat snug in his arms. 'Here's our poor little fellow! Ouch!' Delighted, he dropped the snarling dwarf and inspected his hand. 'I think he bit me! Is that a bite, dear Dahlia?'

But the Bronze Dahlia was helping Buggerly Otherly, who almost had the sack over the Lat's head before he had wriggled free and was off through the jungle again.

'Buggerly! Buggerly!' came a desperate voice, apparently from Captain Otherly's head. 'We're as good as done for. We need that Lat or anything else you can send us. The Straight Arrows are massed to invade and all we have between us and doom is some late Chet Baker! Where are you, Buggerly, dear?'

Otherly paused. 'Not t' first time a's been saved by a bloody junkie.' He frowned in thought.

Another pounce, this time from Tootie Frootie Fun-Fun. A squeal of delight. A complaint and then a grunt of satisfaction.

'I think I've got him, everyone!' she called. 'I caught him in the folds and pleats of my ra-ra skirt. At least, I think it's a ra-ra skirt.'

From somewhere deeper in the jungle, Buggerly Otherly gave a cry of satisfaction. 'Hold on to him! I've found t' Scaling Station!'

'Sod it,' came the Lat's muffled tones. 'Have you really?'

'You can't fake t'old original S.S.,' proclaimed Otherly. 'Look at those waves. Those Edisonian structures.' He emerged, grinning. A radiating ring of purple pulsed from behind him. 'Now, you little bastard, get playing, or you'll never see t' Second Ether again. Or ever. Phew. That were a narrow squeak. Just in time!'

'Er, um, ah,' said the Lat. 'There could be a bit of a hitch here.'

'Hitch?' enquired Otherly in a smaller than usual voice. He pointed. 'Get blowing, or plucking. Or squeezing, or whatever else it is gets your instrument into attack mode.' He hesitated, alerted by an expression in the Lat's rolling pupils. 'That is an instrument, isn't it?'

'After a fashion.'

'It makes music, right?'

'Some would say so.' The Lat wriggled experimentally. 'Of sorts…'

'What sorts?' Buggerly wanted to know.

'Well, cookery music, I suppose.'

'Do what? You *are* a brigand-musician, aren't you?'

'I'm a brigand, definitely. And I work with a lot of musicians. They sometimes appreciate what I do.'

'What do you do, Captain Kippers?' sweetly enquired Tootie Frootie Fun-Fun. 'Darling?'

He blushed and looked shifty. 'Well, I'm not a captain, for a start…'

'Fair enough.' Buggerly Otherly displayed a cheerful equanimity. 'But you can play that thing, can't you?'

'In my way. Actually, I'm the ship's cook…'

'And that is?' Indicating the bulbous instrument from which curved a long handle.

'I'd call it a pressure cooker, I suppose.' The Lat blinked with a certain embarrassment.

'A what?'

'It cooks. Under pressure.'

'So you don't play?' The Chaos Engineer spoke as one who sees the Four Horsemen of the Apocalypse getting ready to make a stables out of his living room. 'Even under pressure. In other words, this was all for nothing? I got hold of t'one bloody Lat in t' whole bloody universe who can't actually blow our antagonists out of the water?'

'There's my brother Hardstop,' offered the false captain. 'He's tone deaf. He was a stoker before he failed to hear the warning klaxon on his last ship. Now he's just deaf.'

With a groan which impressed Faustus von Austus, Captain Buggerly Otherly buried his mighty head in his equally mighty hands. 'I've let 'em all down now. It's t'end for t' Chaos Engineers!'

'Oh, dear,' said the Bronze Dahlia in sweet disappointment. 'Does that mean you're trapped here?'

'Possibly.' He sighed. 'But what it does mean is that Chaos is defeated. Law has us all where t' hair grows shortest and curliest. It spells something like t'end for t' glories of t' Second Ether and t' famous Chaos Engineers!'

'You can always come and live with us, dear boy,' promised Faustus von Austus. 'A little temporal cul-de-sac where Law and Chaos are always in balance. Or nearly always.'

Moodily, Buggerly Otherly transferred a humbled space-cook from Tootie Frootie Fun-Fun's skirts to his sack. The Lat went without a whimper and scarcely complained as the bluff Chaos Engineer swung the sack over his shoulder and began to tramp back towards the edge of the forest.

They were surprised to find, instead of *The Mandelbrot Anomaly*, a steaming metallic canister of some kind, with a tapered end and some very small observation windows let into its length.

'Where's *your* ship, captain?' asked the Bronze Dahlia. 'And what would this newcomer be?'

'Pop!' exclaimed Otherly. 'Pop! Pop! It's Pop, as I live and breathe! But where's my ship? And where's Our Gretchen?'

At that moment, that wondrously bearded face partly obscured by his omniphone, a beaming Professor Pop, accompanied by the bean-bald Little Rupoldo, burst from the Speedshell and, running across the rather sticky red-and-white landscape, embraced his fellow Chaos Engineer. 'You did it, Buggerly, my boy. What a plan! What an orchestration. What a wheeze!'

'What wheeze?' the puzzled Chaos captain wished to know.

'Why, your wheeze, of course,' pronounced the delighted Pop. 'Only a genius would have thought of it.'

Captain Otherly sat down on his sack. There was little protest from its demoralised contents. 'Do what?'

Professor Pop reached a hand to his omniphone and cranked up the volume. 'It's working, Buggers, me old pal. It's driven 'em back and drained their tanks dry of audio-syrup. They used up every unreleased track in the *Princess Di Songbook*. They won't be trying to conquer the Second Ether for an aeon or two! Listen, it's still coming over!'

And now they all heard it. A powerful, easily recognised voice pounded from the omniphone. 'I was born in a black widow morn, before the devil broke the dawn…' It could have been the Stones themselves, down to the five-string guitar. And then, maybe for a moment, it was Robert Johnson. And it could have been The Who in their prime. Hendrix. It could have been, in fact, all the combined greatest blues and rock-and-roll in the world pounding out across the candied landscape, the pulsing jungle. And it was all of these and something else…

'Good heavens!' murmured the Bronze Dahlia. 'I know who that is. I remember. It's – surely – it's –'

'It's Jagged!' cried Tootie Frootie Fun-Fun, and then giggled. 'Or my name's not My Lady Charlotina. What do you think, Werther?'

Faustus von Austus brightened and then sank into a long, delicious scowl of the deepest self-recognition. 'Werther de Goethe! I remember! I remember! I have found myself and must prepare my lifeplan. Ah, how sad to be *moi*!'

And the Bronze Dahlia's perfect brow was clearing as she murmured to herself. 'The Iron Orchid! Oh, I know the villain behind this plot. Where is he? Where is that playful Jagged?'

It was clear to most of them that they had been hoaxed again. Meanwhile Lord Jagged sang on, his powerful voice single-handedly driving back the invaders of the Second Ether.

An atmosphere of celebration spread across the End of Time.

'But where's Our Gretchen?' Captain Otherly wanted to know. 'And what's happened to my ship?'

Chapter Six
Finale at the End of Time

'REALLY, JAGGED, MY eternal love, how could you have played such a trick on us?' demanded the Iron Orchid after the great master of deception had stepped from his borrowed *The Mandelbrot Anomaly* to their considerable applause.

There was little doubt that Jagged was pleased with himself, being praised by his peers of both Ethers. He had received their fullest possible congratulations on his performance. Not only had he provided his admirers with an outstanding concert, he had saved the day for Chaos (and possibly, for there are subtleties involved, Law, too). Meanwhile, with his encouragement, the Martian Foresters had found the Lat hiding near the equator of Inner Mars.

Everyone was enjoying the celebration. The Iron Orchid had re-created Inner Mars for the occasion, with the Scaling Station rebuilt to twice its old size in all its gleaming metals and precious stones, pulsing rather shyly in the shadows. Werther de Goethe had brought boiling masses of thunderclouds to the party which flashed and rumbled to the tunes of a thousand favourite tracks. My Lady Charlotina had created a great tent in which she, most of the Lat and some of the Martian Foresters now sported to delighted cries of 'Mibix' and 'Kroofrudi'. Lord Jagged enjoyed the admiration of Billy-Bob Begg, Professor Pop, Our Gretchen, Little Rupoldo and others. He pretended to a humility which he clearly did not feel. 'Nobody here ever asked me to give them a concert,' he told Billy-Bob, whose tentacles were curled girlishly around his waist. 'So I was only too pleased to help out…'

'A prophet in his own planet and all that,' murmured Our Gretchen. 'Who knits your socks for you?'

Little Rupoldo, displaying just a touch of jealousy, enquired: 'More importantly, Grand Master Jack, what did you do with that cook you found?'

'Kippers?' Lord 'Jagger' beamed rather self-importantly. 'Oh, I have a friend at the Surrealist Sporting Club who needed a steady sparring partner. And they're short a night cook. I sorted that out.'

'But why, dear Jagged,' the Iron Orchid wanted to know, 'did you steal our memories and identities?'

'Steal, sweet, sweet blossom?' He demurred. 'It was not my idea, but yours. You had complained how everything seemed so stale, that you were even tired of your name. You begged me to make our lives more interesting. Do you remember now?'

'Of course I do!' She blinked. 'And how cleverly you organised everything. Even the Lat are happy, since eventually they will settle in Mars or return with the Chaos Engineers to the very Ether they have been seeking for so long. The only tears shed today, I suspect, were by that stern old Old Reg and his nasty Mrs – who, you insist, now occupy a somewhat smaller universe than they initially hoped to conquer.' She fingered the rather ostentatious jewelled ball at her throat. 'And such a lovely present, too.'

'To you, most delicious of flowers,' declared Lord Jagged with a long and elegant bow, 'I could offer only a universe.'

Introduction to the White Wolf edition of *Legends from the End of time* (1998)

DEAR READER,

ALL but the last of these stories appeared in *New Worlds Quarterly*, which was what NEW WORLDS magazine became after it had been forced to cease monthly publication under pressure from British distributors and retailers, who persisted in believing it to be some kind of threat when it became the brief focus for a tabloid press who hated our attitude and were furious that public money (via the UK Arts Council) was being awarded to writers of 'filth'. A familiar enough debate. Flattering and frustrating at the same time. Especially since I wasn't sure about accepting that public money, either.

While never as timid as most American publishers, who speak constantly and self-importantly of free speech, but are always glad to suppress it to protect a status quo favouring the privileged, and encourage a level of self-censorship unheard of in most modern democracies, British magazine and book distributors are a cautious breed. Self-censorship – that which anticipates angering some element and cuts the offending words before publication – is probably the most despicable kind in the free world and it has reached epidemic proportions in the US. Those who would control us are always the very people we should never let control us. That to me seems a fundamental of real democracy. The general policies of our great civic lawmakers have reflected their attempts to keep direct representatives of the military-industrial complex out of civil life as much as possible. But while such great threatened public institutions as the BBC still speak largely on the public's behalf, the so-called 'public' broadcasting in the US is essentially a sham, only able to maintain itself with handouts from big business ('endorsements' and 'support' rather than direct advertising). Like so many current American institutions, it no longer is what it says it is. While trade and soldiering go hand in hand in imperial cultures such as ours, the *moral* voice of the nation should never be used in their promotion. On a practical level, business leaders and high-ranking soldiers always display an abysmal record when they try to take control of society. They are absolutely useless at it. Authoritarianism, however disguised, simply doesn't work very well. The healthier the democracy, the more powerful and effective its civil institutions, the healthier and more secure the society. Yet, in spite of all the evidence, nowadays, there seems an alarming tendency in the free countries of the world to invite the soldiers and tradesmen in to run things… Which always produces some version of Pinochet's Chile. Or Serbia.

Censorship is one of democracy's greatest enemies. It attacks the very basis of our system – which demands an informed, educated public if it is to function as it was intended to function. It corrupts debate. It never lets us discuss the whole problem. It is against the public interest. Our interest.

The fact that our distributors were scarcely literate, were baffled by the fiction and had difficulty distinguishing between 'libel' and 'obscenity' (we were publishing neither) always gave the whole NEW WORLDS affair a strong element of farce. But, like a lot of farces involving vast public power (including the botched military adventures the UK and US seem to be so good at) it put a brutal finish on that particular phase of our existence.

The fourth estate – a Press which reflects and represents the public interest – is a crucial arm of our democracies. It is understood to represent our interests and, when it does not, it becomes rapidly corrupt, as much of a fraud as any state-run newspaper or TV station, an affront to a free society. When it represents the interests of big business – or any other specific interest before the interests of the public, it becomes our enemy. When it pretends to represent our interest (characteristically the flavour of the Murdoch press) it becomes an abomination. Where public opinion is important for the survival of the powerful, control of the media is paramount.

When big business controls the media in its own interest, it no longer represents the public interest. In fact, it is fundamentally at odds with our interest.

I have actually experienced more direct censorship of my work in the United States than in any other country, including several former dictatorships. The first US editions of *The Final Programme* and *Byzantium Endures*, for instance, are massively censored.

Thanks to the untimely nervousness of our distributors, NEW WORLDS became a paperback. The paperback contained exactly the same kind of material and received excellent distribution from the same people who had effectively killed the magazine! The farcical aspect of the affair was further emphasised when the same distributors also gave wide distribution to the *Best of* anthologies taken from the magazine and to novels serialised in the magazine, all of which had been the source of their nervousness in the first place. As we see with the abuses of our constitutional institutions, we need to think about making some new and better laws where political freedom is involved. Most of us rocking the ship of state aren't trying to sink it. We're trying to make sure that it's seaworthy. That we're not actually on board the *Titanic*...

Perhaps because farce seemed to dominate those years so magnificently, I took readily to writing these stories for NEW WORLDS. Certainly the world of the End of Time seemed no stranger or more bizarre than my own at that point and most of the characters were a lot more attractive.

I took huge pleasure in writing them. They are my light-hearted homage to George Meredith, in particular, but also to Dowson, Beardsley, Symons, Swinburne and the Irish wits, to all those contributors to THE SAVOY and the YELLOW BOOK (many of whom knew censorship), who impressed me with their glorious insouciance and cleverness when I was a boy and wanting to have done nothing more than spend an evening at the Café Royal in their company.

Eventually I did get to spend quite a lot of time and money drinking champagne with the late Kyril Bonfiglioli, art-dealer extraordinary, ex-Balliol and the Olympic fencing team, comedy-thriller writer and editor of SCIENCE FANTASY magazine, with Brian

Aldiss, Diane Lambert, Barry Bayley, Tom Disch, Dave Britton, Mike Butterworth and a few others, in the last of the Grill Room's glory days.

Britton and Butterworth went on to found Savoy, that wonderful, independent, eccentric publishing house and record company based in Manchester, England, and began their own long battle with the authorities through the courts. It doesn't seem to be over yet. I would like to dedicate this volume jointly to Britton and Butterworth, for their determination to challenge our repressive Press laws (visit their Savoy website, if you can), to John Coulthart, Phil Meadley and the other Savoyards, to all those willing to risk their money and comfort in pursuit of equity and freedom, and to that great restaurant, which witnessed more good fighting talk for at least a quarter of a century than any other in England, the old Café Royal.

Yours,
Michael Moorcock
Lost Pines, Texas
December 1998

MICHAEL MOORCOCK (1939–) is one of the most important figures in British SF and Fantasy literature. The author of many literary novels and stories in practically every genre, he has won and been shortlisted for numerous awards including the Hugo, Nebula, World Fantasy, Whitbread and Guardian Fiction Prize. He is also a musician who performed in the seventies with his own band, the Deep Fix; and, as a member of the space-rock band, Hawkwind, won a platinum disc. His tenure as editor of NEW WORLDS magazine in the sixties and seventies is seen as the high watermark of SF editorship in the UK, and was crucial in the development of the SF New Wave. Michael Moorcock's literary creations include Hawkmoon, Corum, Von Bek, Jerry Cornelius and, of course, his most famous character, Elric. He has been compared to, among others, Balzac, Dumas, Dickens, James Joyce, Ian Fleming, J.R.R. Tolkien and Robert E. Howard. Although born in London, he now splits his time between homes in Texas and Paris.

For a more detailed biography, please see Michael Moorcock's entry in *The Encyclopedia of Science Fiction* at: http://www.sf-encyclopedia.com/

For further information about Michael Moorcock and his work, please visit www.multiverse.org, or send S.A.E. to The Nomads Of The Time Streams, Mo Dhachaidh, Loch Awe, Dalmally, Argyll, PA33 1AQ, Scotland, or P.O. Box 385716, Waikoloa, HI 96738, USA.

[illegible] including the Hugo, Nebula, World Fantasy, [illegible]

[illegible]

[illegible] Michael Moorcock [illegible]

[illegible]